*From the first touch,
he branded her as his...
forever.*

Praise for

JEANIENE FROST

"Frost's dazzling blend of urban fantasy action and passionate relationships makes her a true phenomenon."

RT BOOKreviews

"A stay-up-until-sunrise read . . . There are many Draculas out there, but only one Vlad, and you owe it to yourself to meet him."

Ilona Andrews on *Once Burned*

"Passionate and tantalizing . . . filled with dark sensuality and fast-paced action."

Kresley Cole on *First Drop of Crimson*

"Sexy-hot and a thrill-ride on every page. I'm officially addicted to the series."

Gena Showalter on *At Grave's End*

By Jeaniene Frost

Jeaniene Frost

Into the Fire

A NIGHT PRINCE NOVEL

AVONBOOKS

An Imprint of HarperCollinsPublishers

Excerpts from *Halfway to the Grave; One Foot in the Grave; At Grave's End; Destined for an Early Grave; This Side of the Grave; One Grave at a Time; Up From the Grave* copyright © 2007, 2008, 2009, 2011, 2014 by Jeaniene Frost

INTO THE FIRE. Copyright © 2017 by Jeaniene Frost. All rights reserved. Printed in the United States of America. No part of this book may be used or reproduced in any manner whatsoever without written permission except in the case of brief quotations embodied in critical articles and reviews. For information, address HarperCollins Publishers, 195 Broadway, New York, NY 10007.

First Avon Books mass market printing: March 2017
First Avon Books hardcover printing: February 2017

ISBN 978-0-06-207640-3

17 18 19 20 21   QGM   10 9 8 7 6 5 4 3 2 1

before shopping for a birthday present for my husband. True to form, my mother couldn't even go on a shopping excursion without whipping out one of my books (she carried them next to her oxygen tank in her wheelchair), showing it to the clerks, and going on and on about how her daughter was an author. She showed them my picture at the back of the book, too, which is how the clerks recognized me. I was embarrassed by all this, of course, and apologized for the scene my mother must have caused, but the clerks just laughed and said, "Honey, she's proud of you."

I am proud of her, too, for too many reasons to list, but I'll name a few. Three decades ago, when my father's company went out of business, my mom took a job scrubbing toilets at the same hospital where my parents had previously been affluent donors. She then worked her way up to becoming one of the few female directors at that hospital, even winning local, regional, and national director's awards. Yet more than being an example of not letting tough circumstances defeat you, she also personified the importance of family. This wasn't by giving speeches, although she gave a lot of speeches on that topic. Instead, I learned it by watching her stay in touch with relatives even if she hadn't seen them in decades, or by seeing her forgive family grievances that seemed unforgivable, or by arguing with her over her insistence on helping relatives despite her own stretched finances, or by seeing her open her door to any family member who needed a place to stay.

In short, I'm glad for every day I had with my mother, and I'm even happier that she married my father because he loved her in a way that not even death can diminish. I doubt I'll live up to her example (or my grandmother's example, or my great grandmother's, or my great-aunt's, and the list goes on), but when people ask me "Why do you write strong heroines?" the answer is easy: I grew up seeing them.

Thanks, Mom. Love you and miss you.

Chapter 1

 Flying at high speeds through a forest is less dangerous than it looks. At least, that's what I told myself the few times I opened my eyes. Mostly, I kept them shut. Not just because it was easier to maintain my psychic link with the man we were hunting, but I also didn't need to know how close we came to the countless trees Vlad maneuvered us around as we flew through the thickly wooded countryside.

You'll survive if he hits one, I reminded myself. We were both vampires, so we could heal almost any injury in seconds, but I hoped I wasn't about to find out how much it would hurt if we splatted into a tree at over a hundred miles an hour. I already knew more about pain than most people ever would, and I didn't want to add to that repertoire.

"Is Branson still in the manor?" Vlad said, raising his voice so the wind couldn't snatch away his words.

I ran my fingers over the belt buckle I'd been holding on to this entire time. It had once belonged to Branson, and Branson was in league with Vlad's nephew/stepson/new worst enemy, Mircea. We'd been looking for Mircea for months, yet had come up empty. Branson was our best lead on him, and soon we'd find out exactly what Branson knew about Mircea.

I concentrated on the essence trail that Branson had imprinted upon the belt buckle until it sharpened my inner focus. Once I had followed it back to its source, my surroundings changed, taking on the look of an odd double exposure. Part of me saw the forest we flew through while the rest of me saw a long, ornate room with high ceilings and tall, fancy paintings lining both sides of the walls.

"Yes. He's pacing now, and he keeps checking his cell phone."

I felt Vlad's chuckle as it vibrated against my forehead, and it had the distinct undercurrent of a predator's growl. "He won't be waiting long for my reply."

With that, we broke through the tree line. I dropped my link so I could see the imposing structure I'd only glimpsed before through my psychic connection. The large house was made entirely of gray stone, with the main building over two stories high and ancient lookout towers over the formal entryway. The tall trees hid the city beyond, and the vast grounds kept the other views of civilization away, making it look as if we'd been dropped back in time several hundred years.

Since Vlad had been born in the fourteen hundreds, he ought to feel right at home in this medieval setting. Since I was only twenty-six, I didn't.

Vlad slowed down, dropping us onto the manicured part of the lawn that surrounded the fortress. "Stay here," he said, striding toward the entrance.

I caught up to him instead. "What part of 'we do this together' did you translate as 'leave Leila behind'?" I hissed, keeping my voice down since we weren't the only ones with supernatural hearing.

His aura broke through his inner shields. Even though he'd released only a sliver of his power, it still felt as if I'd just gotten subconsciously scalded. If I were anyone else, I'd be terrified at pissing off the legendary Vlad Tepesh, meaning "Impaler," aka Dracula, aka don't-ever-call-him-Dracula-if-you-want-to-live, but I was Mrs. Vlad Dracul, thank you very much. Uncrowned prince of darkness or no, Vlad wasn't pulling this crap with me.

"We can fight about it until Branson hears us, or we can get him together quietly," I went on, narrowing my eyes. "Your choice."

The high-arched portico covering the fortress's main entrance suddenly exploded, jetting out fire and pieces of stone. I ducked from instinct, but Vlad walked right toward the burning chaos, the fire parting to let him pass.

"Does that answer your question?" he asked.

Before I could respond, a wall of fire sprang up, spreading until it encompassed the entire castle. Guess he'd changed his mind about being stealthy. Worse, now I couldn't follow him. Unlike Vlad, I wasn't fireproof.

"That's cheating!" I shouted. No need to talk softly now.

I thought I heard him laugh, but between the roar of the fire and the cracking of stone from the crumpling entryway, I couldn't be sure. Damn Vlad and his archaic ideas about women in combat. He'd rather I be under heavy guard back at his castle in Romania. I probably would be, if an enemy hadn't blown up his castle and kidnapped me from its rubble months ago. Otherwise, Vlad would never have agreed to go back on his no-wife-allowed-on-killing-missions rule.

Or, I thought, eyeing the wall of fire that only he could pass through, it seemed he'd only partially gone back on it. My teeth ground. I could stand here and seethe, or I could make myself useful. Besides, revenge was a dish best served cold, and I *would* get him back. I just had to wait until everything around me wasn't on fire.

I rubbed the belt buckle again, seeking the essence imprint. Once I had it, my surroundings changed into the richly furnished room that our quarry was still standing in. Branson wasn't looking at his phone anymore. He was staring out the window in horror at flames that leapt all the way up to the roof. Branson knew only one vampire in the world could control fire this way, and it was the same vampire that he'd been caught betraying.

Then Branson ran, which I expected, but he didn't head for the door. Instead, he pressed a panel near one of the room's many paintings. A hidden door swung open, and he darted inside a steel-lined room and closed the door before I could mentally switch channels.

Branson has a panic room! I sent to Vlad once I was tuned in to him.

Vlad paused on his way up a long, curved staircase, giving an amused glance toward the second floor.

"Then he's in for another surprise."

His words reached me through our link instead of the normal way, so the continual portico collapse must be drowning out everything else. Once I had hated my psychic abilities so much that I'd attempted suicide, but now they came in handy. I still loathed reliving people's worst sins the first time I touched them, but nothing important came without a cost.

A red Porsche bursting through the wall of fire surprised me into dropping my link to Vlad. The car's speed caused it to fishtail as soon as it hit grassy terrain. Glowing green eyes revealed that the driver was a vampire, but it couldn't be Branson. He'd locked himself in a panic room.

This had to be one of Branson's friends. Maybe he was in league with Mircea, too. Even if he wasn't, only someone who'd also betrayed Vlad would be in such a hurry to get out of here. With Vlad busy trying to bust in the panic room, I was the only person standing in the way of this treacherous driver and his freedom. I chased after the car. If it reached the driveway, I'd be screwed. Unlike Vlad, I couldn't fly, and the Porsche could go much faster than me once it was on flat, paved ground.

The car shot forward with a burst of speed. Damn, the driver must've spotted me. Now he was only a dozen feet away from the driveway. I put everything I had into a desperate lunge. If I reached the car's bumper, I could flip it—

I ducked when multiple cracks smashed through the back windshield. Two bullets whizzed over my head, and the third one struck me in the shoulder instead of the heart. From the burn, the bullets were silver. Of course. Any other ammunition was useless against vampires.

Pain caused my powers to flare. A long, sizzling whip shot from my right hand and I cracked it toward the car. The electricity it contained caused it to tear through the Porsche's frame as if it were butter. More gunshots had me spinning to avoid another volley of bullets, and I used my velocity to full advantage. When I swung back around, my electrical whip had lengthened, and I lashed the car with all the force I had in me.

It split in two, the front section still going several feet before the car's weight caused it to cave in. A fire broke out, and I couldn't tell if it was those flames that made the driver scream, or if I'd sliced through more than the car's frame. I stayed low as I circled around to the driver's door, my whip crackling as I readied it to strike again.

"Drop the gun and get out, or—"

I didn't get a chance to complete my threat. Flames shot over the car, too thick and numerous to be from the electrical fire. Then Vlad slammed down next to me, the ground shuddering from the force of his impact. He shoved me behind him and rounded on the burning car.

"You shot at *my* wife?" The flames intensified. High-pitched, panicked screams made me wince from more than their assault on my enhanced hearing.

I grabbed his arm. "Stop, we might need him alive."

Vlad glanced at me and saw the blood from the bullet wound in my shoulder. At once, his arm became so hot that my hand started to catch fire. I let him go, and he turned back to the car with a smile that made further argument useless.

I knew that smile. It meant someone was about to die.

I took a few steps backward as the screams from inside the car became even more frenzied. When Vlad's shields dropped and I felt the full force of his rage, it didn't surprise me to see the Porsche begin to glow as red as the car's paint job.

Then the car melted into itself as Vlad's incredible power turned metal into molten liquid. The screams

stopped. So did the sounds of breaking glass and twisting steel. Soon, all I heard was a hiss as the ground
caught fire.

I reached out to Vlad again, this time not dropping my hand even though his flesh still scorched me
through the thin material of his shirt. "You might
want to consider working on your anger management
issues," I said in a light tone.

A bark of laughter escaped him. "So say my many
enemies."

When he turned around and pulled me to him, his
body was no longer scorching, and the emotions in-
tertwining with mine now felt only marginally insane
with rage; a vast improvement. He kissed me, and I
didn't care that the stubble shadowing his chiseled jaw
rasped my face. All I focused on was his kiss and the
wave of love pouring through our connection, even
more powerful than the rage that had caused him to
melt a car as easily as a normal person could strike a
match.

When Vlad stopped kissing me, another emotion
poured through the bond that had formed the moment
Vlad had raised me as a vampire. Regret.

"I shouldn't have done that." He gave a frustrated
glance at the smoldering heap of melted metal. "I
know better than to kill an enemy before I interrogate
him, but I saw the bullet hole in your shirt and . . ."

"Blew your fuse," I finished, giving him a lopsided
smile. "Happens to the best of men, I'm told."

Another harsh laugh. "Perhaps, but never to me."
Until you, was left unsaid, but I didn't need to feel his
emotions to know he was thinking it.

"Cheer up," I said, striving to lighten his mood.
"Once you bust through that panic room door, you

can interrogate Branson for *days*, and no one will ever know you spilled your lighter fluid too soon with this guy."

This time, his laughter held hints of real amusement. "I look forward to such a redemption."

"Well, let me make sure Branson didn't try to run for it while you were out here," I said, grabbing the belt buckle again. In moments, I saw the inside of a small panic room. It had a single chair, a twin set of control panels, and several screens that showed live video feed from both the interior and the exterior of the manor.

Branson was staring at the screen that showed Vlad and me next to the smoking, misshapen remains of the Porsche. Then he looked at the steel walls of his panic room, and an expression of horror crossed his features.

"He's watching us, and I think he just realized you can melt your way into his hideout," I narrated.

Vlad's hands erupted into flames and he gave Branson a cheery wave while mouthing the words, *Here I come*.

Vampires were naturally pale, but Branson blanched a shade I'd only seen on someone *dead* dead. Vlad began striding toward the manor, and I watched as Branson reached into a drawer. He came up with a gun, and with shaking hands, he checked the clip to make sure that it was loaded. It was, and from the look of them, they were silver bullets.

"He's got a gun filled with silver," I told Vlad, who was now at the front of the manor.

He snorted. "Branson just saw me melt a car. Doesn't he realize I can melt a gun, too?"

"I'm sure you can," Branson said, and though Vlad couldn't hear him, I could through my psychic link.

Then, very calmly, Branson put the gun to his chest and pulled the trigger.

"Oh shit!" I shouted, seeing Branson continue to shoot himself although his movements were becoming stiff and uncoordinated. "Hurry, Vlad, he's killing himself!"

Vlad flew the rest of the way, blasting through walls to get to the second floor. Then, with an expulsion of power that knocked me to my knees even a hundred yards away, he tore a molten hole into the panic room. He was kneeling by Branson's prone form less than thirty seconds after my warning.

It was still too late. My link to Branson weakened as he began to wither, his body reverting to its original age as all vampires did when true death overtook them. When the link dropped completely and I felt nothing but emptiness on the other side of Branson's essence trail, I spat out a curse.

Branson had been our best chance to find Mircea. With him dead, we were now back to square one, which was having no idea where Mircea was.

Vlad had had powerful enemies before, but Mircea was unique. He was a powerful sorcerer, though *necromancer* was a more accurate term since Mircea could bespell the undead as well as humans. That and a spell linking us together meant that Mircea could find me any time he wanted to. I gave one more look at the smoking car and the still-burning mansion. Yeah, I had no doubt that I'd be hearing from Mircea soon. Very soon.

Chapter 2

Vlad and I didn't speak much on the flight back to Romania. He also had his emotions locked up, but I figured that was more to shut out the pilots than me. They were also vampires he'd sired and thus could feel him the same way I did. I'd spent several hours of the flight looking through the memories locked inside Branson's bones—another handy perk of my psychic abilities—but I hadn't found anything useful.

Memories in bones were more erratic and imprecise, like trying to understand a movie if you watched it backward at a high speed. All I'd been able to glean from his bones was that Branson had been in league with Mircea for at least a few months, which we already knew from Vlad's diligent spies. Yet those spies hadn't been able to discover where Mircea was, and if Branson knew, he'd taken that secret with him to the grave.

I'd spent the rest of the flight trying to diminish the grimness of our coming back empty-handed, but Vlad had brushed off my attempts at optimism. When we arrived at the magnificent castle that was an exact replica of the one that Vlad had destroyed several months ago, he announced that he had business to attend to and he'd see me later.

I knew him well enough not to argue. He needed some time to blow off steam, and I needed time to shower and feed, preferably in that order. I nodded to the few vampires I saw as I walked up the four flights of stairs that led to our bedroom. Even though they weren't on display like the various works of art in this house, Vlad had a lot of his people on guard here, and the ones I walked by bowed to me as I passed.

I'd never get used to that, but I'd tried asking them to stop, and it was the only request of mine they didn't obey. Many of them still considered Vlad their prince in addition to the master of their line. So, as his wife, I got bowed to the way they bowed to him, no matter my preference on the subject.

I entered the midnight-green room that Vlad and I shared. I went right into the bathroom, ignoring the marble tub in favor of the large glass shower. I spent the next several minutes enjoying the hot water and the clean, herbal smells of the specially formulated shampoo, conditioner, and body wash I used.

I was out of the shower and dressed in one of my favorite caftans when a metaphysical knife suddenly slashed me across the shoulder. *Magic sucks!* I thought, scowling at the crimson stain that instantly appeared on my dress. Figures I'd be wearing white when my batshit nephew-in-law decided to carve into me.

Hello, Leila, said an all-too-familiar voice, his words slithering across my mind as if they were a snake.

Hello, Mircea, I thought in reply, allowing my hatred of him to invade my mental voice. *What an unpleasant surprise.*

I heard his laughter as if he were on the other end of a cell phone. In a way, he was, except this was a magical connection and I hadn't figured out how to hang up on him yet.

You didn't miss me? he mocked. *How strange. Most women do.*

Yes, Mircea was beautiful in a stop-and-stare way, complete with copper-colored eyes that had obviously run in the family. Mircea was Vlad's nephew by blood *and* his stepson by marriage, thanks to Vlad's second wife getting it on with Vlad's brother, Radu. But Mircea was also as vicious as he was pretty. I had this tie to him after the most powerful of his magical attempts to murder me had backfired, linking us together in a way that no one seemed to know how to break.

I heard about Branson, Mircea went on. *Poor Leila, are you still trying to find me? Don't you know that you won't succeed?*

One day we will, I sent back, fighting a swell of frustration and bitterness.

Vlad and I were forced to search for Mircea the normal way because he'd somehow managed to block me. I could link to anyone else if I had their essence imprint, but though Vlad had brought me artifact after artifact of Mircea's, I was unable to link to him. He was either magically or psychically preventing me. If it was the former, I was screwed, so I chose to believe it was the latter. That way, I still had a chance that my powers would grow, and I'd beat him at his own psychic game.

So naïve, Mircea said, ending his words with a tsking sound. *I wonder how my father stands you.*

Stepfather, I corrected immediately. *Or call him Uncle Drac if you must, but Vlad is not your father.*

Another mystical slash across my shoulders had me biting back a cry of pain. Wow, he's sensitive about that, I realized, filing the information away for later. Good thing Mircea couldn't hear my thoughts unless I deliberately directed them to him. Unfortunately, that meant I couldn't hear his thoughts, either, or I might have learned where he was.

Within moments, the pain faded and my skin knit itself back into smooth, unblemished flesh. That's one of the reasons why I didn't call out for help. Mircea could hurt me, yes, but there were limits on what he'd do. It wasn't because he had a conscience; every injury he inflicted on me had to be carved into his own flesh first.

That was the beauty—and the curse—of the spell that bound us together. It had forced Mircea to stop the suicide-inducing aspect of it so I no longer had the urge to chop off my own head. The flip side was, even if Vlad and I did find Mircea, we couldn't kill him. Not without killing me, too.

Seriously, what do you get out of our little talks? I went on, thanking God that Vlad lost his ability to read my mind as soon as I became a vampire. Otherwise, he'd overhear everything I was thinking, and know that Mircea was mentally messaging me as well as cutting into me.

Perhaps I do it to find out why you mean so much to Vlad, he snapped. *Thus far, it's a mystery. You're not as beautiful as his former lovers and you're a damn sight less intelligent.*

Must be my electric personality, then, I deadpanned, but inwardly, I was intrigued. Why *did* he keep logging on to my mind to talk to me? It couldn't be just to trade insults. Sure, Mircea had only been in his late teens when he was turned into a vampire, but that was over five hundred years ago. More than that, Mircea was usually smug when he used our link for his mental and physical assaults. Now, he sounded upset. Maybe enough to lose his cool and reveal something critical for me to use against him?

I pressed my advantage. *This is the sixth time you've contacted me in the past four months. I used to think it was because you were testing our connection to make sure that the spell still bound us flesh to flesh and blood to blood, but you don't need to talk me up to cut into me. Why do you keep doing it? Are you bored? Or are you just really, really lonely?*

I'll show you why, he said with a snarl.

I didn't like the sound of that. Before I could reply, he said, *What?* in a surprised way, then abruptly dropped our link.

"Damn you," I muttered. Not that he could hear me anymore. I didn't know how I could always tell when he was really gone, but it was as if a door closed in my mind.

Didn't matter, I decided. Mircea was probably bluffing on whatever he was about to "show" me. In any event, now I had to change clothes and destroy this bloody dress. If Vlad caught sight of it, it would enrage him, and he was wound up enough already.

If I were the vindictive type like Mircea, I could get his attention back by cutting into him the same way he'd carved into me. But, even though my dress was already trashed, I didn't do it. For one, I might be getting more vindictive by the day, but I wasn't masochistic. Yet.

I went into my bedroom closet. A few minutes later, I was deciding between a pale blue dress and a lavender one when a new pain erupted in my chest. Unlike before, this pain was so ferocious, I dropped to the floor. Once there, I found myself gasping for air I no longer needed. I recognized this kind of pain, and fear made me attempt to crawl to the door, but my limbs stopped working. All I could do was twitch in agony.

This wasn't Mircea hurting me for his usual cruel kicks. It was something far worse.

Hollywood had it wrong when it came to vampires. You didn't shove a wooden stake through their heart to kill one. That would only give those of my kind a nasty splinter and an even worse temper. Instead, you cut their head off, burned them into ashes, or destroyed their heart with silver. From what I was feeling, Mircea had just stabbed himself—and thus me—in the heart with a silver knife. The only reason we weren't already dead was because Mircea hadn't twisted the blade. Yet.

Chapter 3

I tried to call out to Vlad. He couldn't do anything to stop this, but some desperate part of me needed to see him one last time. Yet all I could manage was a gasping whisper. Vlad might have supernatural hearing, but he was three floors below me and there was endless banging, clanging, and other noise from the construction on the mansion's south wing.

All I had was my mind, and though it felt almost as frozen as my limbs, I summoned the last of my strength to establish a link to him, then let out a mental shout.

Vlad!

A wave of energy filled the room, followed by a slew of emotions slamming into mine. That was more effective than a reply to let me know that he'd heard me. Moments later, I saw a tall, dark form moving with blurring speed toward me.

"Leila." He lifted me up, leaning in so close that his hair formed a blackish-brown veil around us. "What—?"

He stopped when my arms fell away, revealing the bloody hole directly into my heart. A shockwave of emotion exploded from him, and the rebounding effects hit me with such force that I almost passed out.

"No," he said, anguish choking the word. "*No!*"

His scream echoed through every part of me. Vlad clutched me while grief, panic, and despair howled through our bond. In the midst of the awful, clawing pain in my chest, I felt burning spots on my face that I didn't understand until he drew away enough for me to see him.

Pink lines streaked his face. They had to be tears, but I hadn't known that Vlad was capable of crying. I also had never seen the tiny orange droplets that now beaded on his skin before burning my clothes and anything else they touched.

He's sweating fire, I realized, amazement threading through me even as death dragged me down farther into its grasp. *I love you*, I tried to say, but all that came out was a gasp.

So I stared at him, trying to concentrate on his face instead of the awful coldness overwhelming me. I loved the dark stubble on his jaw, the winged black brows framing his coppery-green eyes, and his masculine yet sensual mouth. I loved his long dark hair and the scars covering his hands, and most of all, I loved his fierce, beautiful soul. I wished I could tell him all of that, but speech was beyond me.

I love you, I thought again, trying to force the words into his mind. From the fresh wave of emotions that rolled over mine, he'd heard me. *I love you*, I repeated as my vision went black and everything else slipped away. *Forever . . .*

All of a sudden, that excruciating coldness vanished. My limbs began to flop as if belatedly following the frantic instructions I'd given them before. Vlad jerked back, his grief turning to incredulous relief as we both watched new, healing skin cover over the deep, blade-shaped hole in my chest.

Mircea must have pulled the knife out instead of twisting it. The knowledge that I *wasn't* about to die filled me with such joy that I let out a choked laugh. Vlad shouted something in Romanian, then he kissed me, bruising my lips while more feelings tore through our connection.

"I love you, too." His voice vibrated as he broke away to press searing kisses all over my face. "Forever." He kissed me again before stopping far too soon.

"Get out," he said in a very calm tone.

The sound of rapidly retreating footsteps made me aware that we hadn't been alone in the room. Right, Vlad's people would've felt his emotions the same way I had, and just moments ago, he'd been a maelstrom of grief and panic. Not surprisingly, that must've sent several of them running to see what was wrong.

Vlad's relief continued to strafe my subconscious, yet now it was mixed with ever-growing fury. I felt him struggle to get control of it until he drew his inner shields up and blocked everything off. He let out a slow breath, and the droplets of flaming sweat that had burned little holes all over my dress disappeared from his skin. Yet his hands remained scorching hot as he reached out to touch my face.

"That was close," I said in a shaky voice.

"Too close."

Even with the iron control he was exercising, he couldn't keep the fury from his voice. I'd be furious at Mircea later, too, but at the moment, I was too grateful to be alive to be mad at the viciousness of his last attack.

Vlad's shields were up, yet I didn't need our tie to know that he was still ping-ponging between relief and killing rage. Waves of energy kept spilling from him, and his scent changed from smoky cinnamon to something that smelled more like a forest fire. I was concerned that he was on the verge of spontaneously combusting. While that was normally a figure of speech, he was a centuries-old pyrokinetic vampire with staggering abilities and an equally impressive temper, so for Vlad, that was a real possibility.

"You need to power down," I said. "You leveled this house once, and you *just* finished putting in the new fourth floor."

His quick smile smoothed some of the harshness from his face, but I knew better than to believe the crisis was over.

"Vlad," I began again.

"I'm fine, but you're too weak to keep talking," he said.

I would've argued, but I felt almost as tired as I'd been when I was a brand-new vampire and the sunrise rendered me unconscious. That's why I didn't protest when he carried me to the bed, barking out an order in Romanian at the same time.

Somewhere down the hall, I heard footsteps scurry to obey. Vlad had ordered his people out of our room, but they obviously hadn't gone far. By the time he'd set me down on the bed and smoothed my hair away from my face, the captain of Vlad's guard, Samir, had already returned with three bags full of blood.

I flashed a limp smile of thanks at Samir. He and I had gotten to be friends over the past several months. When I bit into the first bag, that red liquid hit my veins like a jolt of pure caffeine, reviving my strength and making me feel merely half dead instead of circling the grave like I had before. The second bag was even better, chasing the lingering haziness from my mind. After the third, I felt almost normal again.

Vlad stared at me, green flaring around the rich copper shade of his irises. "Better?"

I nodded, leaning back against the pillows. Vlad turned to Samir. "Check all the perimeter sensors, then double the guards. This might have been used as a tactical distraction."

Samir bowed smartly and left, taking the rest of Vlad's people with them. I heard Samir order three to stay on this floor, however, and I looked at Vlad with fresh alarm.

"You think someone's about to attack?"

Vlad's mouth twisted in a humorless smile. "Probably not. If that was the goal, they would've struck when I was consumed with worry over you. Still, no need to neglect due diligence."

Then he touched the bloodstained smear over my chest. An electric current slid into him with the contact, and I marveled at how weak it felt. Being that close to death must have drained me more than the lightning rods I normally used to offload my excess kinetic energy. Vlad's gaze moved to the other bloody stains on my dress. His expression darkened, and when his eyes met mine, new fury burned in their depths.

I tried to head off the inevitable fight. "Vlad, I was just about to tell you about that—"

"How long was Mircea cutting into you before you called out to me?" he interrupted.

I was so busted, not only for hiding those initial slashes today, but also the other times. The glint in Vlad's eyes warned me that he'd figured that out, too.

"About six times that you don't know about, but Mircea never did anything this serious before, I swear."

"Six times," he repeated. His hand grew hotter,

until I was surprised that my dress didn't catch fire beneath it. "And you decided to hide this from me *why*?"

"I can't stop Mircea from using our link this way," I replied, frustration leaking into my tone. "Nor can I stop him from mentally taunting me when he does it, which is something else I hadn't told you about. But I *can* stop him from hurting you." My voice caught. "I told you before, I am sick of being the weapon your enemies use to bludgeon you. Every time I didn't tell you about Mircea's attacks, I was thwarting him from hurting you. I might not be able to stop him yet, but I can damn sure not play into his hands."

Vlad closed his eyes. For nearly six hundred years, he'd built up his power, abilities, and brutal reputation to ensure that neither he nor his people would be at an enemy's mercy again, and he'd been successful . . . until me.

Admitting that he loved me had done everything Vlad had warned me about. In his enemies' eyes, I was now the ultimate tool to use against him, and Mircea had hardly been the first to exploit that. As a result, I'd been through hell and back over the past year, yet every wound that others had inflicted on me had hurt Vlad worse because he blamed himself.

When he opened his eyes again, their color had changed from coppery green to bright, vampiric emerald. "I understand why you did it," he said through gritted teeth. "But promise me that you will never hide such a thing from me again."

If Mircea hadn't nearly killed me several minutes ago, I might have refused. But the stakes had just been substantially raised. "I promise," I said, holding his gaze. "Vlad, I—"

Razorlike pain hit me in multiple places, stopping me from saying anything more. I clutched my abdomen, which did nothing to protect me from blades that were magical instead of tangible.

Vlad let out a vicious curse as fresh blood leaked out between my hands. His shields dropped and his emotions once more smashed through mine. Amidst the blasts of rage, I caught barely controlled panic as he watched Mircea magically cut into me. Would he stab us both in the heart again, finishing the job this time? Had my reprieve been a cruel trick?

If so, there was nothing I could do, so I tried to calm both Vlad and myself in case the worst wasn't about to happen.

"It's not that bad," I said in a tight voice. Thank God our sire tie went only one way and Vlad couldn't feel that I was lying. "He's not going near my heart," I added.

The new cuts were all well below my chest, and I fought not to wince at each fresh slice. These weren't the long, deep slices Mircea normally went for. They were short, shallow, and connected. What was Mircea doing? Trying the famed death-of-a-thousand-cuts torture on me?

"I am going to break my brain thinking up ways to make him suffer," Vlad swore, his fists clenching. Then his gaze narrowed and he leaned closer, ripping my now-sodden dress off me.

"Stay still," Vlad ordered, surprising me by grabbing the vase of flowers from the nightstand and dumping the water it contained all over me. Then, he stretched a dry sheet over me.

When I saw the new bloodstains mar it, I thought, *First my dress, now the sheets. Mircea has been hell on the white fabrics today.* Then a loud voice in my mind broke through the pain. It was Mircea, and he sounded panicked.

Respond back through your flesh or they'll kill me!

Chapter 4

"What?" I said out loud. "Who are 'they'?"

Vlad looked around. "Who are you talking to?"

"Mircea," I said through gritted teeth, trying to focus, but I only heard silence in my mind now. *What do you mean?* I mentally shouted back, yet still heard nothing in response.

Vlad gripped my shoulders. "Mircea? What did he say?"

I shook my head, wincing at the continued slashes that I now realized were the words *Who is there?* carved over and over. "He said, 'Reply back through your flesh or they'll kill me.' I don't know who he means and I can't ask. He's gone now."

"They?" Vlad repeated, his mouth tightening into a steely line. "If this isn't Mircea's doing, who is it?"

With a glance at me that managed to be both ruthless and apologetic, he drew a scorching finger across my thigh. It left a thin trail of burned flesh that read as clear as ink. Even as I gritted my teeth against the pain, I noted with ironic appreciation that Vlad's handwriting was flawless.

I need Mircea alive. Name your price—Vlad Dracul

The other mystical cuts on my stomach ceased at once. Vlad dumped the rest of the water from the flower vase over me, washing away the old blood so that any new reply would be easily seen. We both waited in tense silence. If I'd still been human, I would have been holding my breath.

Minutes ticked by, and nothing happened. I never thought I'd be disappointed over *not* being sliced up, but I was almost twitching from agitation as my skin remained unbroken.

"Try sending them something else," I urged. I might not enjoy this, but I needed to know what was going on.

Vlad flashed me another cruelly tender glance, then started burning out his new message. It was much longer this time, so he needed my entire abdomen to write it out.

Bring me Mircea and be richly rewarded. Kill him, and I will destroy you and everyone you care about.

"Way to butter up whoever this is," I muttered.

This time, there wasn't a hint of softness in his gaze as he looked at me. "It's the truth."

I didn't need to feel his emotions to know he'd meant every word. Vlad's brutal side was my least favorite part of him, yet it was part of him nonetheless. When he'd been a human prince of Romania, he hadn't held off a far larger invading empire with flowery rhetoric. He'd done it with sheer ferocity, and his centuries as a vampire after that had only hardened him more.

"What if this is Mircea and he's toying with us?"

Vlad touched the spot over my heart. "One faulty flick of that blade, and both you and Mircea would have perished. I didn't think it through earlier, but it makes sense that it wasn't Mircea. He hates me, but he wouldn't risk his own life so recklessly. That means someone else did it, and Mircea must have told that person about his connection to you—and thus me—in order to save himself."

Made sense, especially considering the odd *What?* I'd caught from Mircea right before that happened. He had sounded as if someone had surprised him, and not in a good way. Still . . .

"Mircea is a vampire-turned-necromancer who can disappear into thin air," I pointed out. "How could someone even manage to hold him down long enough to stab him with silver, if Mircea can dematerialize at will?"

"Only one way," Vlad said, and his caressing tone reminded me of the sound knives made when they pierced flesh. "Mircea is being held by people even more powerful than he."

Magic sucks! I thought again, with far more vehemence this time. It wasn't enough that we'd finally defeated the vampire who'd allied with Mircea in a centuries-long attempt to kill Vlad. Now, we had to worry about a group of mysterious sorcerers, too. And how would we find them when we didn't even know who "they" were?

I closed my eyes. I hadn't been afraid of my tie to Mircea before because he couldn't kill me without taking himself out. Now, my life was in the hands of people I knew nothing about, except that they were powerful sorcerers and they appeared to want the person I was magically tethered to dead.

"We need to break the spell that's tying me to Mircea," I said, opening my eyes. "One way or another."

"Oh, we will. Never doubt that."

Vlad's gaze was so bright, it resembled burning emeralds as he stroked my face. Then his hand descended, flattening when it reached the spot where that invisible, magic-fueled knife had stabbed me.

"Mere moments from losing you."

His emotions remained locked down, but the muscle flexing in his jaw along with his elevated temperature was enough to let me know that inside, he was still incendiary. I reached out and twined my fingers through his, until our clasped hands rested over my heart.

"You didn't lose me."

And I hadn't lost him. Less than an hour ago, I thought I had. I stared at Vlad, remembering how I'd tried to memorize his face because I thought I wouldn't see it again. Now, I wanted something more tangible than a long stare to remind me that we *both* still had each other.

I pulled his head down and kissed him. It only took the brush of my lips on his for him to respond. He muttered something wordless, then pulled me out of the soaked, bloodstained bed to lay me in front of the fireplace. The fire rose higher as he stared at me, until those orange and blue flames looked as if they were trying to claw their way past the grate to reach us.

"No one is taking you away from me," Vlad growled, his shirt tearing away after a single swipe. His pants met the same fate, then his molten body covered mine and he kissed me.

I couldn't stop the currents that pulsed into him when I clutched his back, and from the low, darkly erotic sounds he made, he didn't want me to. His hands moved over me with the ruthless knowledge of a lover who wouldn't settle for anything less than my total, uninhibited surrender. Then his fingers taunted me with strokes that matched the sensual flicks of his tongue. After that, I was more than ready to give him everything he wanted . . . and to take everything I needed.

I reached down, grasping his cock while I arched beneath him. His groan vibrated against my lips as he rubbed that thick, hard length against me, sending a starburst of sensation into my loins. Instead of thrusting forward the way I desperately wanted him to, he grabbed both my hands and pinned them above my head.

"Not yet," he said in a throaty voice.

My sound of protest turned into an extended moan as he slid down, burying his mouth between my legs. His tongue was a sinuous, fiery brand that had me half sobbing from pleasure, and my right hand shot ever-increasing bolts of electricity into him as my passion reached the breaking point.

"Please," I found myself gasping.

His low laugh teased my aching flesh. "You know that word doesn't work on me."

I was too frenzied with desire to let him draw this out. I flipped over, crying out when my abrupt move slammed his mouth against me and he grabbed my hips to hold himself there. Then, even as I was shuddering from the beginnings of an orgasm, I forced his head up and slid down at the same time, until our hips were lined up and I could stare into his now-emerald-colored eyes.

"Since you hate the word *please*," I said, voice ragged from passion. "What about *now*?"

His mouth claimed mine at the same time that he thrust deeply inside me.

Chapter 5

 Several hours later, we landed at a private airport in London, England. When Vlad's new, sleek Learjet rolled to a complete stop, I let out the breath I'd inadvertently sucked in.

He glanced at me, his lips curling. "With everything else going on, you're nervous about *flying*?"

"It's not the flying part I mind," I responded tartly. "It's the crashing part I have issues with."

This plane was new because Mircea had magically compelled Vlad's pilots to crash the old one. We'd only survived because Vlad had torn open the side door and flown us away moments before impact. Vampires could survive a lot, but no one could live through a plane hitting the ground at maximum velocity.

"We tested everyone to make sure they're not bound by one of Mircea's spells," Vlad reminded me. "Plus, he would never attempt to crash our plane while you're still linked to him."

"Hopefully, that won't be for much longer," I muttered.

There had been no new "messages" during the time it had taken us to fly to London from Romania. Not knowing what Mircea's captors intended was sawing at my nerves. On the plus side, I wasn't dead, so the mysterious sorcerers had to be taking Vlad's threat against them seriously. On the negative side, we hadn't been contacted to say that Mircea was being delivered with a big red bow, so whoever "they" were, they didn't seem in a hurry to give Mircea up, either.

"Where are we meeting Mencheres?" I asked when Vlad opened the interior door that converted into stairs.

"Here," an accented voice replied from beyond that doorway. Before I had time to recover from my surprise, a Middle Eastern man with waist-length black hair vaulted up the staircase.

Vlad embraced Mencheres, a show of affection he reserved for only a few people in the world. But Vlad had often referred to Mencheres as his "honorary sire," so I wasn't surprised when he also accepted a kiss on each cheek from Mencheres.

Then Mencheres turned his charcoal-colored gaze my way, and I wondered why he'd bothered to tamp down his aura to undetectable levels. Mencheres looked like an attractive man in his early twenties, but looking into his eyes was like staring through a time portal into the ancient past. He was so old; one of the famed pyramids in the Giza plateau had been his.

"Leila," he said, extending his hand. I shook it because I was wearing my current-repelling gloves and thus couldn't shock him from the simple contact.

"Thanks for coming," I said, not adding, *but I don't know why you're here*. Mencheres hadn't been able to break Mircea's spell before, although he'd given it his best shot. Unless Mencheres had had a breakthrough since then, I didn't know why Vlad wanted to meet with him.

"I was in New York, so it was a short flight,"

Mencheres said, dismissing how he'd dropped everything to meet us here.

"Where's Kira?" I asked when Vlad hit the button that caused the staircase to fold back into a door.

"Still there," he replied, waving a casual hand. "I saw no need to interrupt her time with her sister."

At the word *sister*, a pang shot through me. I'd promised my own sister, Gretchen, that once Vlad's enemy Szilagyi was dead, she and my dad could return to a normal life. Then I'd had to go back on that promise as soon as Vlad had killed Szilagyi. Gretchen had not been pleased about having to stay in hiding indefinitely, and neither had my father.

I was distracted from thoughts of my family when Vlad ordered his pilots to take off. "Where are we going?" I asked, grabbing a chair as the engines roared back to life.

"Nowhere," Vlad replied. "Just far enough off the ground that no one can overhear us."

Mencheres settled into one of the plush seats. I sat down, too. This plane could hustle when Vlad wanted it to, and his pilots could obviously guess that Vlad was in a hurry.

"Want a drink?" I asked Mencheres, gesturing to the mini bar protected by a clear glass panel. Just because vampires needed blood to survive didn't mean we skipped other libations.

He inclined his head. "Whisky, if you have it."

Vlad gave him a sardonic smile. "From that provincial choice, I can tell you've been spending time with Bones."

A smile ghosted across Mencheres's lips. "If you two weren't so similar, you'd likely be friends."

I stifled a snort as I handed Mencheres a glass of

whisky. I didn't know why Vlad disliked Mencheres's co-ruler so much, but I didn't see him getting over it anytime soon.

"Enough about that," Vlad said, dismissing Bones with a swipe of his hand. "Magic is one of the few things forbidden under vampire law, but like Mircea, there are those who still practice it in secret. I need a guide into that world, at once."

Mencheres leaned forward, his expression turning very serious. "You are too well-known to slip in and out unnoticed, and vampires who practice magic will kill to keep their identities from reaching the Law Guardians."

I agreed, and felt guilty over telling Vlad we had to break Mircea's spell at all costs. "There has to be another way—"

"There isn't," he interrupted. Despite his hard tone, the hand he laid on my arm was gentle. "If the sorcerers holding Mircea had any intention of returning him, they would have accepted my offer. Their silence means that they're either still intending to kill him, or they're thinking of the best way to use him against me."

I wasn't a fan of either option, but I didn't want Vlad to throw himself into even more dangerous circumstances. His abilities would protect him from almost anyone in the vampire world, but in a secret underworld where magic reigned? Not even his feared pyrokinesis was a match for that.

"We'll see the voodoo queen again," I said. "Maybe there's something she didn't think of before."

"Her previous leads came to naught, and if she'd thought of anything new, she would have told me." His tone became flat. "Marie Laveau would love to have me owe her such a stunning debt. She amasses favors the way the greedy amass fortunes."

"Who are these sorcerers, and how do they have Mircea?" Mencheres asked quietly.

Vlad let out a frustrated sound. "If I knew either, I would be on my way to kill them instead of sitting here with you."

I filled in the blanks that Vlad's frustration had left out. "Whoever they are, they were going to kill Mircea until he proved his connection to me. Vlad offered them a bounty if they returned Mircea to him alive. That was several hours ago, and we haven't heard anything since."

Mencheres closed his eyes. After an extended silence, he opened them and looked at Vlad. "I left that world more than three millennia ago when magic became outlawed, but I know one person with recent ties to it, and I trust him to act as your guide. First, however, I need your promise that you will not kill him."

I felt Vlad's surprise as his shields dropped and he considered this. "I can't promise that of anyone who betrays me or Leila," he finally said. "Aside from that, you have my word."

"No matter how badly you will want to," Mencheres stressed. "Despite his many flaws, he is dear to me, and it would pain me to lose him."

My curiosity was piqued. If this person wasn't a threat to us, why was Mencheres so sure that Vlad would want to kill him?

"Aside from my conditions, yes," Vlad said, the annoyance in his tone emphasizing that he didn't appreciate repeating himself. "Now, who is he?"

Mencheres gave Vlad a look of grim amusement. "Oh, you know him. And you dislike him even more than Bones."

Chapter 6

 We landed in Cheshire, England, which thankfully was only a short flight from London. A chauffeur was already waiting for us, and the unfamiliar driver whisked us away to a manor that looked right out of the show *Downton Abbey*. The driver dropped us off and then sped away, leaving us in front of the manor's large double doors.

They opened before Mencheres could knock, revealing a startlingly handsome vampire with vivid turquoise eyes and shoulder-length, auburn hair. I had time to notice particulars about his face and hair because after one glance, I kept my gaze firmly directed upward. Vlad muttered a curse even as the naked vampire let out an aggravated huff.

"You said it was urgent, Mencheres, so do come in."

"Ian," Mencheres said in a chiding tone. "You should have at least gotten dressed."

Ian glanced down, as if just now realizing that the only thing he wore was a very intimately placed silver piercing.

"Do you see a seven-foot-tall woman on my face?" he asked in a conversational tone. "No, because I stopped what I was doing and emptied out my house as you requested, so the least you could do is not scold me for failing to put on a tux."

I was so startled by the graphic description, I didn't know how to react. *Nice to meet you* didn't seem applicable. *Sorry to interrupt your cunnilingus!* was probably more appropriate, yet I wasn't about to say that, either.

"Ah, but who's this?" Ian went on, angling his head around Vlad to get a better look at me. "Mmmm, isn't she stunning? If she's my consolation prize, then I accept—"

"She's my wife," Vlad growled before I could correct the misassumption. "And if your cock twitches *one* more time while you look at her, I'll burn it off."

"Vlad, you swore," Mencheres said low.

"Castration won't kill him," Vlad responded at once. "His life was all I promised, and his extremities can grow back."

Instead of being concerned, Ian laughed. "Here I thought today was going to be boring. Now, I simply *must* know what's brought the infamous Impaler to my door, especially if it's so important, my sire made you swear an oath not to kill me."

His sire. I cast a surprised look at Mencheres. Ian didn't seem like the type that the reserved vampire would choose for a member of his line. And what had Ian been thinking, putting silver *there*? He might not even notice if Vlad burned his cock off. It had to be burning like hell right now.

"Are you quite sure you don't know anyone else?" Vlad said to Mencheres, not moving to enter the house.

"Few vampires are foolish enough to risk the Law Guardians' wrath by practicing magic, and fewer still are alive after such reckless disobedience," Mencheres replied. Ian shrugged, not disputing either charge. "Out of those, Ian is the only one I trust . . . after I secure *his* word, that is."

"Mencheres, you wound me," Ian said, sounding hurt.

"Do not trifle with me." Mencheres's new tone startled me. I had never heard him raise his voice before. "Just as I know Vlad, I know you. You would misdirect Vlad for your own amusement, let alone if someone offered you financial incentive. That is why you will promise to show Vlad and his wife the same loyalty you would show to me, and you will swear it on the love you have for me."

Ian's mouth curled in what could only be called a pout. "That's not fair."

"Swear it," Mencheres insisted. "And before you argue any further, when was the last time I asked you for a favor? Would you truly deny me now?"

"No," Ian said, sounding as if the word soured in his throat. "You are one of only four people that I would never deny. Very well, I swear on my love for you that I will show Tepesh and his wife the same loyalty I'd show you during the duration of whatever task you're about to talk me into."

A vow with conditions, but then Vlad had had conditions, too. Besides, if we were successful, we wouldn't need Ian's loyalty after we broke the spell that bound me to Mircea.

Mencheres turned to Vlad. "See?" he said in his usual calm manner. "Now that that's been settled, we can proceed."

Vlad eyed Mencheres in a way that made me wonder if he was about to take my arm, turn around, and leave. Yet finally he shrugged, as if to say, *So be it.*

"My vow is void if you betray me or Leila," Vlad said to Ian, flashing him his most charming smile. "And in that case, death will be a kindness compared to what I'll do to you."

Ian rolled his eyes. "Save your threats. Thanks to the promise Mencheres forced from me, you don't need them. Now, what sort of magical trouble are you intending to get into? It must be more than casting a simple spell or Mencheres would've done it himself. Before magic became outlawed, he was one of the best practitioners around."

"It does involve a spell, but we don't want to cast one," Vlad said. "We need to break one. To do that, we'll need access to master sorcerers of even greater skill than Mencheres."

Ian cast an annoyed look at his sire. "If you wanted to kill me, you could've picked a nicer way to do it."

"This is important, Ian," Mencheres said quietly.

"Why?" Ian asked, turning to Vlad now. "Getting tired of offing your enemies the fiery way?"

I answered before Vlad could. "I'm spellbound to a necromancer who's being held hostage by people who want him dead. If he dies, our link means that I die, too, so finding someone more powerful to break that link is our only option."

Ian looked at me. Not the perverted way he had the first time, but coldly, as if he could care less whether I dropped dead at his feet right that second. Then he looked at Mencheres. In quick succession, affection, resignation, and irritation skipped over his features. I didn't know what to make of that mishmash, or of Ian's admitted tendency to backstab for profit or amusement, but Mencheres must trust that he'd hold to his word or we wouldn't be here. Because of that, we had no choice except to trust Ian, too. For now.

Finally, Ian's expression settled into cheerful cockiness. When he flashed a smile that turned up the volume on his already dazzling looks, I actually felt an instinctive feminine flutter that I instantly squashed.

"Who wants to live forever anyway?" Ian said. "Right, then, we'll start with a magic speakeasy in the heart of London. And I do hope that you're as tough as Tepesh is, my lovely raven-haired poppet, because this *will* get dicey."

Chapter 7

 By "heart of London" Ian meant the seedy section, judging from the derelict alleys we walked through. If we didn't have the vampiric ability to hypnotize anyone who approached us with nefarious intentions, we would have been mugged twice by now. As it was, the would-be muggers were the ones who lost something. I still wasn't skilled at biting someone's neck without causing harm, but I could handle a wrist. Vlad had been hungry, too. Ian wasn't, saying he'd eaten earlier.

Considering Ian's description of what we'd interrupted, I wasn't about to ask him to elaborate. At least Ian had finally put on some clothes, although his shirt was all the way open and his jeans were so tight, the black denim looked painted on.

Mencheres hadn't joined us, so it was just the three of us striding through the smelly, graffiti-ridden alleys. I would have liked Mencheres to come along, but he'd said it was best that he stay away since he had many enemies in the magical world due to his former wife. Vlad and Ian had nodded as if they knew the story behind that statement. I didn't and I was curious, but it would have to wait until later. First, we had to find the speakeasy, and after half an hour of walking, I was beginning to wonder if Ian was too cocky to admit that he was lost.

Finally, Ian sauntered up to what I assumed was a bar only since I couldn't imagine any other industry surviving in this area. I didn't catch the name because only one letter in the neon sign remained. From the repeated crunching under our feet as we crossed the bar's threshold, I wondered if the broken glass from those other letters had ever been swept up.

The interior wasn't any nicer. Empty tables with rickety chairs took up half the space, and a bar that had the distinct scent of urine emanating from it occupied the other half. The bartender looked up from his conversation with the business's only two customers, and from the baleful looks the three of them gave us, they weren't happy to have new company.

Then the barkeep's face really darkened as Ian vaulted over the bar. He went over to a large, ancient-looking freezer that was shoved against the bar's far corner. Ian opened the freezer door, and as expected, it was empty except for layers of dust.

Ian pulled on something I couldn't see, and the back of the industrial-sized freezer fell away, revealing a small, spotless room. Ian ducked into that room, ignoring the bartender's continued protestations, then poked his head out.

"Are you coming or not?" he asked us.

Vlad jumped over the counter, one single glare causing the bartender to shut up and back away. I followed suit, and soon the three of us were all jostling for space in the small room. When Ian pressed a button and we abruptly began to descend, I realized it wasn't a room at all. It was an elevator.

After going down about thirty feet, it came to a halt. The elevator had no doors, so our new accommodations were immediately revealed to us, and I looked around in amazement.

Cigar smoke and incense caused a faint haze over an area that was as luxurious as the bar had been derelict. Velvet couches and chairs were arranged around gaming tables, a tuxedoed band played jazz, and from what I could see behind its many occupants, the sprawling bar looked to be made entirely of huge, different-colored prisms of crystal.

But that wasn't what made me stare. The voluptuous blackjack dealer with the deck of cards floating well over her head had been the first thing to catch my eyes, quickly eclipsed by the bottles behind the crystal bar. There was no bartender, and bottles came off the shelves by themselves, either pouring their contents directly into patrons' glasses or blending them with juices, sodas, and other mixers first.

As I watched, a champagne bottle uncorked itself, expertly avoiding the usual bubbly runoff. Then it poured its gold-colored contents into a floating glass that, once full, whisked itself over to a gorgeous woman who took it without once glancing up from her companion.

"Welcome to Selenites," Ian said, with a cynical smirk. "London's premier location for magically inclined elites."

"Is all that magic, or is some of it telekinesis?" I whispered. Mencheres could do everything I was witnessing. Maybe Selenites had another vampire with telekinesis here.

Ian grunted. "Magic. Doubtless we're the only vampires here. Most would rather not be executed by the Law Guardians, and they would be, if word got out they were dabbling in magic."

"But you used to come here," I said. "Why?" Vlad and I certainly wouldn't be here if we didn't have to. Why would Ian willingly risk a death sentence just to hang out in this place?

Ian clucked his tongue at me. "None of that, poppet. Sharing my secrets isn't part of our agreement."

Vlad didn't seem to care why Ian had been a regular here, nor did he share my appreciation for the magical displays around us. His gaze swept the room in a calculated manner.

"Enough talk. We're here to speak with a true sorcerer, not waste time with pretenders playing tricks with floating cards and bottles."

He hadn't lowered his voice, so this caused more than a few heads to turn in our direction. Ian elbowed Vlad, hissing, "You can't bully your way into results here. Follow my lead, and for pity's sake, *don't* kill anyone."

Vlad stared at the elbow that was still prodding him in the ribs. Then he flashed a grin at Ian that alarmed me into throwing my arms around Vlad.

"Priorities, remember?" I whispered close to his ear.

I could feel it when his sudden spike of power drew down to nondangerous levels, and when Vlad pressed a kiss to my cheek, I knew that Ian was out of the woods. For now.

"Yes, priorities," Vlad agreed in a light tone. Then to Ian, he said, "Touch me again, and I'll feed your limbs to a pack of wolves."

Ian shook his head. "Can't even pretend to be marginally sane, can you? Fine, have it your way. Gents and gentlewomen," he said in a louder tone. "My friends and I seek the finest, most skilled entertainment tonight. If you're interested and can meet our expectations, we promise you an evening that you and your bank account will never forget."

If we'd piqued some people's interest before, we had all of theirs now. Years of performing on the carnival circuit had me smiling as if I was completely comfortable at suddenly being the center of attention. To be honest, it felt more unsettling not to have people instinctively wince when they first looked at me. Most days, I forgot that I no longer had a jagged scar running from my temple all the way to my right hand.

After several moments, a couple stepped out from the onlookers. The woman appeared to be in her forties, and her air of jaded sensuality hinted that she'd done it all twice and was looking for someone to tempt her into round three. Add that to striking features, curly brown hair, a dancer's build, and you had a woman who was used to being admired.

She was also human, so I didn't understand why Ian tensed when she approached. Then I wondered if I'd imagined that when he strode over and gave her a lingering, openmouthed kiss.

"Elena," Ian said once he'd let her up for air. "I hoped you'd be here tonight. And Klaus, mate, it's been too long."

Ian then kissed him with the same amount of tongue. When he was finished, Klaus gave him a light smack on the cheek.

"You know you're not supposed to come back here."

"Didn't the two of you miss me?" Ian asked, sounding hurt.

Elena let out a ladylike snort. "Parts of me did, but

the rest of me was too busy smarting over how you swindled me."

"You said not to come back until I was ready to pay you back triple, and I am," Ian countered. "Let me introduce you to my friends. Among other things, they're the money."

"Are they?" she drew out, coming over and extending her hand to Vlad. "Charmed, I'm sure."

Despite Vlad's hatred of being touched, he took Elena's hand with a smile she wouldn't have understood. I did, and almost pitied her. Vlad could burn objects without tactile contact first, but to burn people, he had to touch them first. Now, Elena was as good as kindling to him.

So was Klaus, after Vlad shook her handsome, dark-haired companion's hand next. I was wearing my current-repelling gloves, so I shook hands with them as well.

Elena barely glanced at me. Instead, she looked Vlad up and down while moistening her lips. I bristled in instinctive possessiveness, though to be fair, I couldn't blame her. Vlad's elegant outer coat was charcoal and his tailored pants were a lighter ash color, but his silk shirt was a subtly gleaming shade of silver. Instead of coming across as bland, Vlad looked as if he'd summoned every color of smoke, formed it into the richest material, then layered it over his muscular body. When you paired that with those piercing, coppery-green eyes, no wonder Elena seemed unable to look away.

Klaus also eyed Vlad with interest, although unlike Elena, he exuded more than a hint of wariness as well. "You look familiar. What did you say your name was?"

"I didn't," Vlad replied, his tone icily pleasant.

Elena stiffened and Klaus blanched. Ian rolled his eyes, stepping in front of Vlad. "Don't mind him, he's always cranky before he gets his knob rubbed. Now, while I know that both of you are magically delectable, my friends will need a demonstration before they commit themselves for the evening."

My brows shot into my hairline. Finding someone skilled in magic was important, but we hadn't agreed to *this*!

Vlad must have felt the same way. He shoved Ian aside with a muttered, "Enough of this." Then his gaze changed to glowing green as he glared at Elena and Klaus, then the rest of the room.

"All I see are cheap tricks, but if any of you social-ites or sycophants are true practitioners, I have a job for you."

Elena's face flushed an angry shade of red. "How dare you insult me and my establishment! Your arro-gance is why your kind is rarely welcomed here, *vam-pire*."

"Vampire?" Klaus repeated. Then his gaze wid-ened and he stared at Vlad with horrified recognition. "*Now* I know where I've seen you! You're Vl—!"

That's all he got out before his head exploded right off his shoulders, coating Elena in flaming spatters of goo.

"And here we go," Ian said resignedly.

Chapter 8

 Elena screamed and lunged at Vlad, who threw her aside hard enough to snap several bones. A collective gasp rose from the crowd, then all of them charged us en masse.

For a second, I just watched in amazement. Ian had said they were human, and from the heartbeats I heard, he was right. They might be magically inclined humans, but none of them seemed to have true powers, so what did they think they were going to do? Stun us into unconsciousness with their card tricks?

That's why I didn't take off my current-repelling gloves when several of them jumped me. The voltage from my right hand could kill them. As it was, all I had to do was wait until the electricity zapped into them as they came into close contact with my body. Then my attackers thinned when Vlad started flinging them away, some hitting the ceiling.

"Go easy, they can't hurt me," I said, grimacing when I watched a guy go limp after a hard fall to the floor.

Ian was also trying for the nonviolent approach. "This is a regrettable misunderstanding!" he shouted, ducking a series of wine bottles that began to torpedo into him. "Elena, we can—"

"He killed Klaus!" she roared, waving at the crowd, who had paused in their gang rush after Vlad's ruthless response. "What are you waiting for?" Elena continued. "Get them!"

"Imbeciles," Vlad muttered. "Still, this is the quickest way to find out if any of them has real ability."

I would've argued, but Klaus had ruined doing this the peaceful way. Yet if he'd succeeded in shouting out Vlad's name, we may as well have carved out a message in my skin to let Mircea's captors know that we were after them. Plus it probably wouldn't have taken long for the Law Guardians to hear of it, too, and we didn't need more people trying to kill us.

"Don't hurt them too badly," I said. "And let's split up, it'll be quicker that way." When Vlad didn't move from his position in front of me, I gave him a firm shove. "If I see any hint of dangerous magic, I'll yell for you, okay?"

"You'd better," he growled, his eyes glittering.

I smiled wide enough to show that my fangs were out. "Go."

He did, albeit after kicking aside the first group of people who charged us again. Then I was the one ducking as bottles from the bar came flying my way. Glass shattered as my quick maneuvers caused some to hit the wall behind me. My victory was short-lived as the velvet couches I'd admired were the next salvos. One briefly knocked me flat, although others knocked over the people trying to tackle me, so they helped me more than harmed me.

My blithe attitude changed when the next items magically hurled my way were knives. They came at me as fast as I could bob, weave, or knock them away, and the ones I avoided turned around in midair before zooming toward me again. Even with my speed, two sank into my back, and when I still felt searing pain after I'd yanked them out, I looked more closely at the blades.

Ragged bits of another metal coated them, and that lingering pain in my back meant only one thing.

"Silver!" I shouted, spinning around to put my back to the wall before any more of those deadly blades struck me from behind. That left my front vulnerable, but I grabbed a thick crystal ashtray and shoved it inside my bra. Now, I had a knife-proof patch over my heart. Vlad didn't, though, and more silver-edged knives were coming from seemingly out of nowhere.

Something sparkly caught my eye. A large grouping of rings, necklaces, bracelets, and other jewelry floated about twenty feet above the bar. As I watched, a necklace flew off the throat of one of my attackers, joining that mass. Then slivers from the jewelry bundle split off and stuck to the kitchen knives that were hovering in the air next to the jewelry bundle.

If our lives weren't in danger, I would've admired the spell caster's cleverness. Talk about making the most out of what was available. Yet that same someone had taken this fight to a whole new level. Who was it?

Not one of my attackers, I decided, since they were putting all their efforts into a physical assault. I shoved them aside more viciously than I'd done before and looked around for the spell caster.

Elena was on the floor about twenty feet away, her legs still bent at odd angles. She wasn't crawling away from the chaos or doing anything else a normal person

would. Instead, her hands were up as if in supplica-
tion, and beneath the various sounds from the fight
around us, I caught a hint of her muttering in a strange
language.

I couldn't translate what she was saying, but I recognized what she was doing. I started toward her, then
stopped when a cloud of silver-edged knives suddenly
formed a protective barrier around her. I might not be
able to reach her, but I knew someone who could.

"Elena's the spell caster!" I shouted.

Just as quickly, Ian yelled, "Whatever you do, *don't*
kill her!"

Vlad spun around, not even looking at the person
who smashed a chair into him as soon as his back was
turned. "Stop," he ordered Elena, holding up a flaming
hand in warning.

She spat out an unfamiliar word and raised her
hands higher. Vlad clenched his fist, and Elena's whole
body exploded as if she'd swallowed a bag of grenades.
I winced, but he'd warned her, and that was more than
he normally did.

The people attacking us cast a horrified look at
Elena's flaming, scattered remains. Then everyone
stopped fighting and began to run for the elevator. I
thought it was fear over what Vlad had done, but then
I felt the ground start to shift. The entire room began
to plummet downward as if it had morphed into an
elevator whose cables had been cut.

"What's going on?" I screamed.

Ian reached me first, grabbing my arm and ignoring
the electricity that shot into him. "Elena's death triggered a spell that opened a thousand-foot sinkhole beneath us, so if you value your arse, we need to leave!"

Vlad reached us right as a shower of concrete began

to rain down from the ceiling. The walls cracked and folded, too, until it looked as if the room was also squeezed by a giant fist during its mad free fall. Vlad crushed me to him, huge bursts of fire shooting from his other hand. Ian flung his arms around my waist the instant before Vlad vaulted us upward.

The force of the fire blasted through the chunks of debris that threatened to throw us into the destruction below. I had to shut my eyes from all the rocks and ash that blinded me as Vlad continued to blast a path to the surface. I couldn't count all the impacts I felt along the way. One briefly knocked me unconscious, and more than once, fire came so close that I felt it melt off parts of my clothes.

Then the pain ceased and the awful sounds of destruction dimmed. I blinked hard, and through clouds of smoke saw that we were now clear of the underground club. In fact, we were now over the entire city block. Well, what was left of it. The sinkhole had claimed far more than the decoy bar. Now, instead of a row of tightly clustered buildings, there was only a smoking hole the size of a football field several stories deep.

"I told you not to kill Elena," Ian muttered, his tight grip on me causing new bruises to appear faster than the old ones could heal. "She might have been only a mediocre shag for me, but she fucked *you* right and proper, Tepesh."

Chapter 9

 We had barely cleared the sound of police sirens before Vlad dropped us into the middle of a section of deserted buildings. Then he backed Ian against the nearest wall and hauled him off of his feet with a single hand to the throat.

"You lied," Vlad said, biting the words out. "First you brought us to a place where you knew we wouldn't find the caliber of sorcerer we needed, then you failed to warn us that Elena's death would trigger a massive sinkhole. I should kill you right now for such betrayal."

". . . not . . . 'etrayal . . ." Ian got out, the words garbled.

Vlad's grip on his throat didn't loosen. I touched his arm. "At least let him explain." Then I gave Ian a warning look. "And it had better be good."

After a moment, Vlad let go of Ian's neck. "Talk."

Ian rubbed his throat where a blistered handprint now faded as his skin healed with vampiric swiftness. "For starters, I didn't tell you because you gave me no other choice."

I braced for Vlad to blow Ian to kingdom come, but all he did was say, "These may be your last words, so choose them well."

"You're used to being the most powerful person in the room, but in this world, you're not," Ian said, sound highly irritated. "Not that you'd take my word for it. That's why I took you to a place with more posers than practitioners. Knew you'd storm in with your 'I'm Vlad the Impaler, bow before me' approach, and you didn't disappoint. You also didn't listen when I told you not to kill Elena, and you wouldn't have listened if I'd warned you about her fail-safe. Besides all that"—a shrug—"if we couldn't survive a mid-level practitioner's booby trap, we bloody well couldn't survive real sorcerers. Now that we *have*, perhaps you'll heed my advice instead of continuing to assume that you know more about this world than I do."

Vlad stared at Ian. Ian stared back, oozing a mixture of aggravation and defiance. On one hand, I wanted to kill Ian myself for his show-don't-tell approach that had almost ended all our lives tonight. On the other hand . . .

"He's right," I said, shooting Vlad an apologetic glance. "You probably wouldn't have listened if Ian had warned you in advance. For that matter, I wouldn't have, either. How would I know a mid-level witch could cause the ground to swallow half a city block? We're both learning as we go, so for now, we need to trust that Ian knows better than we do."

Vlad didn't say anything. At last, he smiled at Ian. Not his charming, you're-about-to-die grin, but a flash of teeth that struck me as one predator acknowledging another.

"You are correct," he said. "I would've assumed cowardice made you exaggerate Elena's abilities since Mencheres had to force you into accompanying us. But since he did trust you for this task, I suppose I should've known there was more to you than the insipid whore you present yourself to be."

Instead of being insulted, Ian smiled almost flirtatiously. "Oh, I am all the whore you can imagine and more, but I do have other talents. Few people see them, although you and your lovely wife are about to."

"Then for now, we'll follow your lead, and you'll take us to where the true sorcerers gather," Vlad replied, his tone silky with challenge. "Once there, we will see if any of your supposed other talents can actually impress me."

If there was any good news about our disastrous visit to Selenites, it was that we were probably the only people to make it out alive. In addition to decimating the underground bar, Elena's spell had also claimed most of the city block above it, so the human bartender and the customers at the decoy bar had died, too. Thus, it was doubtful that anyone knew Ian had shown up at Selenites with one vampire who could manifest fire and another who could electrocute people. Our secret partnership with Ian was safe.

Then again, even if word had filtered out, no one would believe we were the same people in The Pirate's House parking lot in Savannah, Georgia, with Ian the next night. For starters, Vlad now looked like a short-haired redhead with a square face, a crooked nose, and light blue eyes. His lean, muscular frame had also expanded to a stocky build, and he'd lost over an inch in height. I, too, had a new face complete with shoulder-length blond hair, brown eyes, pouty lips, and a body with even more curves than Marilyn Monroe.

Ian had brushed off my admiration over his

appearance-altering spell, saying that "glamour" was only mid-level magic and the effects would wear off by dawn. Since glamour wasn't rare magic, he had reminded us that we needed something else to disguise ourselves. Something no one would question.

"Unless you want the sorcerers you seek to know that you're swimming in their waters, we need to hide your identities, agreed?" Ian had asked the night before.

"Of course," Vlad had said impatiently. "But I'm known to many people, as Klaus proved, and since vampires can spot theater makeup or a mask, I assume real sorcerers can spot those, too."

"Oh, easily," Ian had agreed.

Vlad's gaze had narrowed. "I am *not* staying behind, if that's what you're hinting at."

"Wouldn't dream of it," Ian had replied with a smirk.

That smirk had raised my suspicions. "You know a way around this, don't you?" I asked.

"First, let's establish that you'd do anything to find a sorcerer strong enough to break the spell on your wife, yes?" Ian said, not answering my question.

"Yes," Vlad replied without hesitation.

"Depends," I amended. When Ian's smirk widened into a full-fledged grin, I knew that my suspicions were well founded.

So here I was, about to play my role as part of a happy, horny threesome. As Ian reminded us, *no one* would believe that the homicidally possessive Vlad the Impaler would be into such a thing. Hell, Vlad had blown a guy's head off for merely grabbing my ass, and I'm sure word of that had made the undead rounds because he'd done it in front of hundreds of people.

I tried not to focus on what came next, so I allowed myself to enjoy the unusual perks of my new body. So *this* was what it felt like to have boobs and a bubble butt! Never before had I felt things bounce while I walked. I even put an extra sway in my step just to feel it all bounce a little more.

Vlad caught what I was doing, and a sideways grin curled his new, wider mouth. "Do I need to memorize this spell so we can use it for our private enjoyment later?"

Before I could answer, Ian spoke. "If you think this is impressive, I know a fellow whose wife can shape-shift into an actual dragon. I ache with envy at the thought of shagging one of those."

My jaw dropped. "You'd seriously bang a dragon?"

"Oh, for days," he responded at once. "Can you imagine the Internet videos? I'd be a bloody *legend*."

There was something very wrong with him, but to-night, we'd find out if Ian's ties to the magical world were everything he'd promised.

"Remember your roles," Ian said as we approached the entrance to The Pirate's House. He pushed himself between the two of us, linking an arm around each of our waists. "And whatever you do, *don't* kill anyone, Tepesh," he added.

Vlad's response was a low growl of "I said I wouldn't, didn't I?"

Yeah, but now our real disguise was about to begin. I took a deep breath to center myself. Show-time. I'd been a carnival performer for years, so I was no stranger to acting. This might be a different sort of role, but whatever, I could handle it.

When Ian's arm slipped lower around Vlad's waist, however, Vlad's anger pierced his shields enough to singe my emotions. Saying that Vlad was prickly about being touched was like saying that God was mildly annoyed by the Devil. I stopped even though we'd only made it a couple feet away from the car.

"Are you sure about this?" I said, holding Vlad's gaze.

It felt like molten steel coated my emotions with the resolve behind his reply. "Yes."

Ian glanced at Vlad, assessing the situation. Then, moving so fast that he startled me, he grabbed Vlad and kissed him.

Vlad's rage flash-fried my emotions with the intensity of a dozen wildfires. But he didn't shove Ian away or burn him with the flames I could practically see beneath his skin. Instead, he bent Ian backward with the force of his answering kiss. When Vlad released him, Ian gave him a crooked grin.

"Guess I was wrong to fret about your past experiences being stronger than your willpower."

I was so aghast at Ian's casual reference to Vlad's childhood imprisonment and rape that I slapped him as hard as I could. If I hadn't been wearing thick rubber gloves, my whip might have spontaneously shot out and taken his head off, too. Ian rocked back a few feet, and a group of people entering the parking lot let out shocked sounds as they gaped at us.

Ian straightened and gave me a single glare before he turned to the crowd and waved at them. "She loves to play rough," he told them. "That's why it takes two of us to handle her, the fierce little vixen."

One of girls let out an admiring giggle while the rest of the group averted their gaze as they walked by. Ian gave them another saluting wave, then he turned back to me.

"Seems Tepesh isn't the only one with a temper," he said in an exasperated tone. "Do I have to make you promise not to kill anyone, too, poppet?"

I stiffened even as part of me acknowledged that I'd gone too far. Vlad was more than able to defend himself, if he'd felt the need. At least our cover was still intact, even if it now looked like I was a sadist as well as a sex groupie.

"Sorry," I muttered.

"Don't be," Vlad said. His fingers traced up my arm and he dropped his shields long enough for me to feel satisfaction rising in him, mixed with the remains of his anger. He liked that I'd overreacted on his behalf, even if there had been no need. Then he fixed Ian with a laserlike glare.

"Don't ever bring that up again," he said, his pleasant tone belying the scent of smoke starting to emanate from him.

The smile wiped from Ian's face, replaced by an expression I hadn't seen before. On anyone else, I'd call it sincerity. "I wasn't making light. Men handle such things differently. Some heal and go on to live completely normal lives. Some abhor contact with others afterward, and some"—a shrug—"seek out all the contact they can get to prove that it's their choice now. I simply needed to know if your history, combined with your well-documented dislike of personal contact, would be a stumbling block to our goals tonight."

Ian continued to hold Vlad's gaze, and the tension in the air changed. Anger gave way to an unspoken acknowledgment that made me glance away, suddenly feeling like I'd walked in on a very personal conversation. I wanted to tell Ian that I was sorry for what had happened to him, which was how I interpreted the subtext of his statements. But if I was right, Ian wouldn't want my pity. No, if he was anything like Vlad, he'd scorn pity because he'd turned the pain from his former rape into steel that now made him unbreakable.

Then, abrupt as a thunderclap, Ian's expression transformed into his usual mocking smirk.

"But, since we've established that you're a *very* convincing actor—blimey, I'll fantasize all night about that blazingly hot tongue!—let's go find some sorcerers, shall we?"

"At The Pirate's House restaurant," I added, fighting a stab of ridiculous jealousy that made me want to inform Ian that Vlad's tongue and every other scorching part of him was *mine*.

"Not The Pirate's House, poppet," Ian said, his grin turning knowing, as if he'd guessed at my surge of possessiveness. "Next to it."

I followed his gaze, but saw nothing except an expanse of grass between the parking lot and the road. Or did he mean one of those smaller buildings to the right of the grassy expanse?

"Which one is it?" I said.

Ian pulled something grainy out of his pocket, then blew the glittering dust it contained right into my face. The sparkling cloud went right into my nose and mouth, burning as it made its way inside me.

Vlad grabbed Ian, snapping, "What was that?" at the same time that I sputtered out, "What the hell?"

"That's me pretending to be a gentleman," Ian said, winking at me. "Ladies first, isn't that the way it's done?"

"First for what?" I began, then stopped. "Oh," I breathed.

Chapter 10

 Right in the middle of the grassy expanse, a building seemed to form out of mists that hadn't been there a moment ago. It had to be at least seven stories high and the exterior looked black and shiny, as if covered by layers of the finest obsidian. The top came together like an obelisk, and an infinity waterfall spilled from the roof down to its mist-covered base. Through that thick, misty haze at the bottom, I glimpsed what appeared to be irregularly shaped, smoked-glass doors, and I couldn't be sure, but I thought I saw a bellman dressed in Merlin-esque robes waiting by the entrance.

"What are you staring at?" Vlad asked, sounding impatient.

"That," I said, gesturing to the mystical building.

He looked right at it, and annoyance brushed over my emotions. "The shacks next to the empty lot? What of them?"

"He still can't see it?" I asked Ian. "Or it's not real and I only *think* I see it because you just dosed me with a magical version of an acid trip?"

"The former," Ian said with a laugh. "Although the latter does exist, and I highly recommend it."

"Well, dose him so he can see it, too," I said, feeling Vlad's increasing annoyance brush over my emotions.

Ian held out his hand. Some sparkly, grainy bits were still in his palm. I nodded at Vlad, and he didn't move as Ian blew the magical sand into his face.

"Incredible," Vlad said moments later, staring at the mist-draped black building. "I sensed nothing there before."

Ian grunted. "That's why it's called magic, mate."

I'd thought I had some experience with magic, what with being killed by it twice and currently being infected by an unbreakable spell. Still, staring at the magnificent tall structure, I was stunned as I absorbed the fact that something this big could be right out in the open, yet because it had been cloaked, no one— even a vampire as old and powerful as Vlad—had known that it was there.

Of course, that begged an obvious question. "What's to keep people from accidentally bumping into this?"

"The same spell that prevents most people from seeing it," Ian replied. "It compels everyone else to stay away from the area. Without that dust I blew into your face, you could run right toward that building, yet you'd stop yourself every time before you got close enough to touch it."

It sounded impossible, but I was redefining my definition of that by the minute. "What's in the dust you dosed us with?"

Ian shrugged. "The magical version of performance-enhancing drugs. It mimics abilities you don't have, fooling the spell around the building into believing that you're at least a mid-level practitioner."

"Did you know any of this was possible?" I asked Vlad.

He shook his head. "I'd heard stories, but I dismissed them as nonsense."

Ian let out a derisive snort. "Denial is half the reason our race remains ignorant of magic."

"What's the other half?" I muttered, still grappling with everything I'd learned in the past five minutes.

"Fear," Ian said, his tone implying that it was obvious. "Same reason most humans refuse to acknowledge that vampires, ghouls, ghosts, and demons exist, even though we've done a poor job covering our tracks at times. Yet if humans pretend they're at the top of the food chain, they feel safer. And if vampires pretend that magic is mere smoke, mirrors, and the occasional minor spell, then we can pretend there's nothing greater than us, even if that's not true."

From Vlad's emotions, he was wrestling with this explanation. "Some believed otherwise," he said at last. "Or magic wouldn't have been outlawed thousands of years ago."

Another oblique shrug from Ian. "Population control. Vampires couldn't be subjugated by powerful sorcerers, wizards, mages, or witches if magic were illegal and any vampire caught practicing it was sentenced to death."

It sounded barbaric, but it certainly wouldn't be the first time a society had criminalized something it was afraid of. "Why only vampires?" I asked. "If the Law Guardians were so concerned about magic, why not go after human practitioners, too?"

"They did," Ian said, arching a brow. "But they recruited others to do their work for them."

Vlad let out a jaded grunt. "All the witch trials over the ages. That was our people manipulating the Church and fanatics?"

"So claim the survivors," Ian replied lightly. "And many of them still hold a grudge."

I cast another look at the mist-shrouded, gleaming black building. With that brutal history, we wouldn't only have to worry about the Law Guardians or the sorcerers holding Mircea finding out about our intrusion into the magical underworld. We'd also have to watch out for the understandable prejudice our lack of heartbeats would elicit. No wonder Elena had said that they normally didn't allow "our kind" in her place. Vampires were to witches what Cortés had been to the Aztecs.

"Second thoughts?" Ian asked, still in that light tone.

"Not from me," Vlad said at once. Then his voice softened. "Though perhaps you should remain here, Leila—"

"Are you serious?" I interrupted. "No way, Vlad. Bad things happen when we try to go it alone, remember?" Then I moved closer, putting my arms around him. "For better or for worse, it's you and me together, just like in our vows."

He caressed my back as he drew me nearer. His hands felt different due to the appearance-altering aspect of Ian's spell, but the warmth they radiated was singularly Vlad. So was the look in his eyes. I'd recognize the unyielding determination and relentless love no matter what gaze it stared out at me from.

"Reminds me," Ian muttered, shattering the moment. "One of you will slip and call the other by their real name, I just know it. Luckily, I have a spell for that, too."

I glanced at the mystical hotel. It was only about twenty yards away, and patrons were still coming and going from the nearby Pirate's House restaurant. "You want to do it here?"

Ian waved at the hotel. "They can't see us until we cross the warding line, and no one on this side of the line will understand what they see. Besides, this will be quick. Now, stick out your tongue."

I did, feeling a bit foolish at the strange looks a couple walking to their car gave us. Ian touched my tongue with his finger, said a few strange-sounding words, and then nodded.

"Try saying Vlad's name now."

"Angel," I said, then frowned, trying again. "Angel. Angel. ANGEL." It made no sense. My mind was saying *Vlad*, but my mouth wasn't listening to my commands.

Ian nodded, satisfied. "Until I lift this spell, that's the only word that will come out of your mouth when you attempt to say 'Vlad.'"

Vlad gave Ian a sardonic look. "An endearment? How unexpectedly sentimental of you."

Ian's smile slid into a grin. "Angel was a TV vampire whose endless angst was only outweighed by his devotion to his one true love." As Vlad's expression grew murderous, Ian added, "He did have a magnificently violent dark side, if that helps."

Vlad's hands erupted into flames, and I was afraid that he was about to show off his own magnificently violent dark side right now. Good thing Ian's spell hadn't resulted in me calling Vlad "Dracula." I don't think Ian would have survived that.

Then Vlad doused his flames and flashed Ian a decidedly tight smile. "I don't have to break my promise to repay you for that."

"True, but life's not worth living if it's dull," Ian replied, wagging his brows as if to say, *Bring it, Impaler!*

I rolled my eyes. Ian either had a death wish or he was the most reckless person I'd ever met. Vlad *would* pay him back, guaranteed. Ian had to know that. Why did he keep baiting him?

"Let's get my part of this over with," Vlad said shortly. "And if the name 'Buffy' comes out of my mouth, it *will* be the last word you ever hear."

Ian sighed as if disappointed, but touched Vlad's tongue and said those same strange words. When Vlad tried to say my name afterward, all that came out was "Mia."

"Shall we?" Ian said, extending both his arms.

I took one of his arms and Vlad, after a loaded glance at Ian, took the other. As we started toward the mist-laden perimeter, I fought the urge to chirp, "We're off to see the Wizard!" But this was no yellow brick road, and our destination wouldn't end with a fake wizard behind a mechanical mask. No, the wizards we were about to meet were all frighteningly real.

"Bibbidi-bobbidi-boo," Ian said in a singsong voice as we walked into the thick mist.

I could feel a thrum of power when we crossed the barrier that separated the magical territory from the normal world. When I looked back, I could no longer see the parking lot, the restaurant, or the highway. All I could see was mist behind us, and the gleaming black building in front of us.

Now that we were closer, I noticed flashes of color appearing and disappearing within the waterfall. It was as if someone was periodically squirting huge gobs of food coloring into the roaring falls. I looked up toward the roof, but couldn't figure out where the waterfall's source was. Then I frowned. Either the stars had disappeared, or the mists rose high enough to cover the sky with their thick, dark haze.

I looked down when the mists around us parted, revealing the entranceway of the building. I stared, realizing I had been wrong about the bellman dressed in stereotypical wizard garb. There was no bellman. Just a bunch of skeletons tightly grouped together, their rotting clothes billowing in the wind.

That wasn't the only thing I'd been mistaken about. The oddly shaped "doors" weren't doors at all. They were row upon row of crystalline teeth, and as we approached the building, they drew back to reveal a huge, obsidian-lined open mouth.

"We're supposed to go into *that*?" I asked, aghast.

Ian glanced at us and grinned. "Puts a whole new spin on entering freely and of your own free will, doesn't it?"

Chapter 11

 I barely registered that Ian had just quoted a line from Bram Stoker's most famous novel. Instead, I continued to stare at the huge mouth at the bottom of the building.

Go on, walk into the maw from Hell, my inner voice mocked, breaking its weeks-long silence. *What could possibly go wrong?*

For once, I had to agree with my hated internal voice. Facing a bunch of sorcerers was one thing, but doing so in a structure that was designed to literally *eat* us was another. I found myself digging my heels in when Ian attempted to propel me into the macabre entrance.

Vlad either felt my resistance or saw the look on my face because he stopped, too. "What is this building made of, Mia?" he asked, somehow managing to sound unconcerned.

"Teeth," I responded promptly. Okay, not the entire building, but the entrance was, and those teeth were almost twice as long as I was tall!

"Glass," Vlad countered, and his smooth tone deepened. "What can I do to glass, Mia?"

It was so strange to hear him call me by another

name; it took a moment for his meaning to penetrate. Right, Vlad could burn glass into a molten puddle. Failing that, he could blow a hole right through the center of the building. Granted, either would out him as Vlad the Impaler, but he was right. As frightening as this toothy entrance was, it was nothing he couldn't handle.

For that matter, it was nothing *I* couldn't handle, either, even if some childish fear of monsters had come roaring to the surface at the sight of that cavernous magical mouth. I pushed that fear back and gave the shiny black exterior a more calculated look. *What happens when thousands of volts of electricity shoot into glass?* I reminded myself. *It shatters.*

"Let's do this," I said in a far more confident tone.

Ian, Vlad, and I walked into that fanged, gaping maw. I even managed not to flinch when I heard it snap shut behind us. For a moment, the tunnel—or *throat?*—was bathed in the kind of darkness I hadn't seen since before I became a vampire. Vlad's emotions were locked behind the same impenetrable shields that tamped his aura down to barely detectable levels, but his hand snaked around Ian's back to brush mine. Then that disorienting darkness was broken when orbs of light began to appear at the end of the tunnel, their glow beckoning us forward.

We crossed another invisible barrier before we reached the end of the tunnel. The magic we passed through was a sharp crackle that thrummed along my nerves before dissipating, leaving only a faint tingle behind. It reminded me of electricity, and I found myself fighting a sudden urge to empty the nearest light socket of all its voltage. That would amp up the power in my right hand to its maximum level; a benefit if we needed to fight our way out of here, but plunging the entire structure into darkness wasn't any way to blend in.

We took a right at the end of the tunnel, then stepped into a . . . well, I didn't know what to call it. *Room* was too paltry a word. *Wonderland* was closer, but still didn't seem sufficient.

Water shot out from the base perimeter of the room with such force, it covered all the walls and the ceiling. Walking inside felt like being in the underbelly of an enormous tidal wave. Due to the flow's incredible power, we weren't getting wet. Instead, only a faint mist came down from the whirring canopy. In the center of the ceiling, the geyserlike flow disappeared into a large hole as if being sucked up by a vortex.

If the amazing aquatic walls weren't enough, lots of people lounged in pools that dotted the expansive space. For those who wanted to stay dry, there were also chairs and couches that looked to be made out of flowering trees. A long, curved bar drew my attention when what I thought were butterfly decorations suddenly flew away. The butterflies circled in the air a few times, resembling a cloud of brightly colored petals, before they returned to the bar and covered it with the living tapestry of their bodies again.

"This section of the hotel is called Atlantis," Ian said. "Too whimsical for my taste, though newcomers seem to love it."

I stared at the people frolicking in one of pools that towered at least thirty feet above us. The bottom was clear glass, revealing the unusual-looking swimmers inside.

"Are those real mermaids?" I asked, trying to sound casual.

Ian snorted. "No. That's merely glamour, but now you know how rumors of those creatures got started."

"Let's get to what we came for," Vlad said, his brusque tone reminding Ian that he wasn't a fan of sightseeing.

Ian sighed. "Always straight to business. How you stand it, poppet, I'll never know, but I suspect that fiery tongue has something to do with it. Ah, he's giving me that I'll-kill-you glare again. How many times must I tell you *not* to kill anyone tonight? It's like a sickness with you, isn't it? Have you ever gone a whole day without committing murder?"

"Has anyone who's spent their whole day with you?" I muttered.

Ian clucked his tongue. "You'll come to love me before this is over, promise. Now, let's get our drinks and start the search, before your adoring husband combusts on the spot."

We went over to the butterfly bar, and I tried not to notice how dozens of wings tickled my legs as we sat down. Ian ordered a round of drinks from the bartender, who was wearing nothing except glitter and her own strategically placed waist-length blond hair. She placed empty glasses in front of us, and I wasn't surprised when they filled all on their own.

Ian took our glasses and brought them over to one of the tree-styled chaise longues. I gladly followed him. One of those butterflies was going to fly up my dress, I just knew it.

"Cheers," Ian said, holding out our glasses to us.

Vlad eyed him warily. I also waited before taking mine. Ian waved his hand, spilling some of his drink with the gesture.

"These are harmless, though you're right to be cautious. In a place like this, never order an Orgasm, Mind Eraser, or Sex on the Beach unless you want exactly those things to happen."

"Good to know," I said under my breath. Then I took a cautious sip, surprised at the flavors that burst over my tongue. The golden liquid tasted like honey-covered sunshine mixed with spring rain.

"What is this?" I asked, finishing the rest in one swallow.

Ian gave me an amused look. "It's called Faery's Brew. Very potent despite its taste, so if you drink a few more that quickly, vampire or no, you'll soon be so drunk you'll believe that you can actually *see* faeries." Then Ian raised his own glass. "Ashael, this is Ian and I need to see you," he said before swallowing the contents in one gulp.

Vlad set his glass down without touching it. "That's either a very peculiar toast, or something else is going on."

"Something else," Ian affirmed, taking Vlad's glass from him. "Ashael, come as quickly as you can," he said before hoisting Vlad's glass and draining its contents, too.

"Who is Ashael?" Vlad said in a deceptively mild tone.

Ian signaled the bartender. "Another round!" he called out. Our glasses refilled on their own in the next few moments. Ian hoisted one, said "Ashael!" and downed it.

"You're trying to summon him," I said, figuring it out. "I didn't know we were looking for a particular person."

"Why didn't we know before?" Vlad said, the edge in his voice making it clear that he didn't appreciate being kept in the dark.

Ian blinked. "I didn't tell you?" When both of us glared at him, he gave up the pretense. "Right, well, it would have been very boring explaining that I know a bloke who knows a lot of mystical blokes, but no one who looks for Ashael can find him. Saying he spelled himself to be elusive is putting it mildly."

"We're looking for someone who's spelled so that he can't be found?" I repeated, incredulous.

"Yes and no," Ian replied. "No one can find Ashael by looking, but if you go to one of the few magically sealed places he frequents, then speak his name into a toast several times, he can hear you, and thus he finds *you*."

Chapter 12

 Vlad continued to stare at Ian, and from the look in his eye, he was mentally peeling Ian's skin off one layer at a time. "This person finds us?"

A nod. "If he's interested."

"And if he's not?" Vlad asked, his smooth voice belying the dangerous currents I felt pushing against his shields.

"Then he swipes left and we remain a trio instead of a quartet," Ian replied, his tone adding, *Isn't that obvious?*

Vlad leaned back in the chair, which creaked under his new, stockier body. "Then there was no need for Mia and me to be here." His words hung in the air like poison swirling inside the finest of wines. "Yet you insisted that we come. Why?"

Ian stiffened as if affronted, but I was starting to realize that very few things offended him. "You wouldn't want to be here if Ashael shows up?"

"If he did, you could have told him to meet us elsewhere," Vlad said. "No, that's not why you brought us, and since you're pathologically selfish, it must be because it benefits you."

"Backup."

The word left my mouth before I had time to think it over, but when I caught the faintest widening of Ian's eyes, I knew I'd guessed right. I let out a short laugh.

"You have enemies in this world. That's why Mencheres had to guilt trip you into helping us, so now that you're forced to be here, you're making sure that you're not coming alone."

Ian's silence was confirmation. "Seems you need us as much as we need you," Vlad noted in a darkly satisfied tone.

Ian's mouth tightened, that hard spark breaking through his devil-may-care façade. "For the moment, so I reckon that backing me up is the least you can do."

"You could have just asked us," I noted.

The look Ian gave me was disbelieving to the point of being thunderstruck. "Trust you?" he said, as if I'd suggested that he set himself on fire and jump into a gasoline-filled lake. "Why?"

"Not now," Vlad said, his gaze flicking around the room. "Too many ears, even if most of them are human."

Human, maybe, but the magic that pulsed through this place was tangible. Even if I'd been blind, I would've known I was somewhere special. Being able to see only meant that I was continually dazzled, if I allowed myself to keep looking around. But we weren't here as tourists, even if this was the kind of place that millions of people would pay through the nose to vacation at.

"How long do we have to wait to see if Ashael intends to respond to your summons?" I asked in a lower voice.

Ian settled himself back into the couch. "A few hours. If he doesn't show, we'll try again tomorrow, but before we leave, we have to pay our respects to the architect of this level. You don't snub a hydra mage unless you want to repeatedly drown for the next five days, as I discovered the hard way."

"So, you *are* trainable," Vlad drawled, while I glanced around with new understanding.

"Hydra mage. That's someone who can control water, right?"

Ian gave Vlad an evil look before responding. "Yes, elemental magic is the theme of this hotel. This level is water. There's also a level created by an earth wizard, another by an air witch, and one ruled by a fire sorceress."

"Fire?" An interested gleam appeared in Vlad's eyes.

Ian gave him a shrewd look. "Under other circumstances, I'd love nothing more than to pit you against her to see who would win, but I promised not to endanger you for my own amusement."

"Who is that?" Vlad said, nodding at an elegantly dressed, blond man who was staring at the back of Ian's head as if he could glare holes into it.

Ian turned and winced. "This might be a problem—"

The rest of what he said was cut off as he flew backward as if pulled by a giant string. Before Vlad or I could react, we were too swept up by that same unstoppable force. Quicker than a blink, the three of us hurtled toward the giant hole in middle of the ceiling, pushed along by invisible magic and the force of the countless gallons of water that were sucked up into the vortex along with us.

I now knew exactly what it felt like to be flushed down a toilet. That's the only way I could describe being shunted through a huge, interior pipe with uncontrollable force. Water exploded up my nose, giving me the sensation of drowning even though I didn't need to breathe. From the sick way my stomach plummeted, we were going up very fast, and the water pressure was so great, I couldn't take my glove off to manifest my whip to break the pipe and free us. Likewise, Vlad wouldn't be able to use his fire. Not while he was under water.

When the pressure abruptly dissipated and I felt cold air instead of painful wet surges, I was relieved . . . until I saw nothing but mist between me and the ground below. The pipe must have spat me well over the roof of the hotel, and the velocity had thrown me clear of anything to grab.

Instinct had me flailing in a mad, cartoonish attempt to slow my descent, but then I was caught in midair and hauled back against a large, heated body. In the time it took for Vlad to lower us safely to the ground, I had figured out that the infinity waterfall fell from the roof into drains at the building's base that must lead to the Atlantis floor. There, it was sucked back up to the roof so it could fall and thus replenish itself in an endless, repeating loop.

I would've admired the design, except I was still coughing. Having my lungs suddenly flooded with gallons of water hurt. Vlad gave me a few pounds on the back that helped expel the last of it, then brushed a swath of wet hair back from my face.

"Are you all right now?"

"Yeah," I said, trying for a smile. "Guess that's the way magical people show unwanted guests to the door."

"Bloody rude is what it is," Ian muttered between coughs of his own. He was about a dozen feet away, and when he stood, his skintight leather pants squeaked from being waterlogged. "Still, I expected much worse."

The last word had barely left his mouth when we were suddenly falling again. I didn't know how solid earth could all of a sudden change into thin air, but that's what happened. We hit the bottom of the pit about fifty yards down. Vlad grabbed me and tried to fly us through the mist that covered the new hole, but when we reached it, the hazy vapor was somehow so hard and impenetrable, we bounced off it instead of going through it.

"This is more like it," Ian said darkly as he, too, tried and failed to fly through the misty ceiling.

The ground began to shift, and something that looked like shiny tree roots snaked up from the earth. When one of them curled around my ankle, the sharp, distinct burn it left wasn't caused by anything wooden or organic. Instead, it was metal.

Or, more specifically, silver.

"A silver-rooted inescapable pit of death?" Ian almost sounded admiring. "You've outdone yourself, Blackstone."

"I'm glad I didn't disappoint," a smooth voice said from above us.

I looked up, and through the mist that was somehow unbreakable, saw the suave blond man from the Atlantis room. He knelt at the edge of our pit, wearing a very satisfied half smile as he stared down at us. From the steady beats in his chest, he was human, but he was obviously more than just human. He was a sorcerer. And a powerful one, considering everything he'd just done.

Vlad snatched me up, keeping me out of reach of more seeking silver roots, then fixed his most dangerous glare onto the blond sorcerer. "Release us at once."

Blackstone let out an amused snort. "Mind tricks don't work on my kind, vampire, and I have no intention of releasing anyone. I made this trap for this exact purpose, and now I intend to sit back and watch all of you die."

"Come on, Blackstone," Ian said in wheedling tone, "even *you* must agree that this is a bit excessive."

Blond eyebrows rose. "You left me at the mercy of the most powerful demon I've ever encountered just to save your own skin. If I were being excessive, I'd let you live for the thousand or so years it would take for the earth to push your body through its depths until you burned to death when you reached its core."

I winced. Okay, so we were dealing with someone powerful *and* psychotically bent on revenge. Being married to Vlad, I had experience with both those things.

"Your issue is with Ian, but you don't even know me or my husband," I said, giving Blackstone a friendly smile. "Let us go, then do whatever you want to him."

"Thanks ever so, poppet," Ian snapped.

I waved a hand. "From what Blackstone said, you deserve it, so stop whining and take your punishment like a man."

"You heartless little harpy!" Ian said, slack-jawed.

I just waved at him again in a dismissive way, but what I was really doing was edging my glove down. No, I wasn't really intending to leave Ian to his doom, even if I did think the sorcerer had a valid grudge. If we could manage to get past this force field of a mist, I could make mincemeat of Blackstone with my whip.

With how far below we were now, though, my whip couldn't reach Blackstone even if it could penetrate the mist, and since Vlad hadn't touched him yet, he couldn't burn him.

"Aren't you forgetting something?" Ian added, futilely kicking as one of those silver roots curled up his leg and then drove into his calf. "You need me," he finished.

Vlad eyed the sorcerer controlling those deadly silver roots, then glanced at Ian. "Maybe all we need now is him."

Chapter 13

"Filthy ingrate!" Ian said with a snarl as that silver root plunged into his thigh next. Another one began to slide up his other leg, and a third reached perilously near Ian's groin. For the moment, though, they had stopped coming after me or Vlad, so the sorcerer was considering what we'd said.

"Come on, you don't even know who we are, so it's not smart to kill us, too," I said, looking away from Ian to fix a steady gaze on Blackstone. "It might be more trouble than it's worth."

"And who are you that it's in my best interest to spare your lives?" Blackstone asked, not sounding very worried.

"New members of Mencheres's line," Vlad responded at once. "Both of us less than a year undead."

I schooled my features so my surprise didn't show. Why would Vlad say that? His reputation was more fearsome than Mencheres's, and didn't Mencheres say he had enemies in the magical world, too? What if Blackstone was one of those enemies?

The blond sorcerer's mouth pursed as if he'd swallowed something sour. "Baby vampires," he said, sounding both contemptuous and resigned. "You shouldn't be near a place like this, let alone with Ian. Didn't your sire warn you about him?"

Vlad hunched, somehow managing to look guilty and sheepish. "He did, and we know we shouldn't have come, but Ian swore he'd show us the time of our lives."

Once again, I was glad for all my years performing on the carnival circuit or I would have gaped at Vlad. Even his voice had changed. Gone were his usual deep, commanding tones. Now, he actually managed to sound scared and conciliatory, and if he hunched his shoulders any more, he'd break his collarbones.

Blackstone let out an annoyed sigh. "Too many people saw me force you out here, and your sire considers you too young to be responsible for your actions. Very well, it's your lucky night."

With that, Blackstone said a few words and flicked his fingers in a way that hardly looked magical, yet at once, an opening appeared in the steellike mist above us. Ian tried to hop over, but even more roots entangled him. Blackstone shot an arch look at him, then bent down and held out his hand to us.

"Jump, like you did before. I'll grab you and pull you up."

Vlad's smile showed all his teeth as he grasped me firmly to him and jumped, his other hand extended. When Blackstone grasped it, Vlad let him pull us all the way out of the ditch, and then fire shot from his hands.

Blackstone's scream was cut off when his mouth filled with flames, and I winced when both the sorcerer's hands exploded, leaving only charred stumps at the end of his arms.

"Well done, you magnificent bastard!" Ian crowed.

"Now, finish him! His magic will stop when he's dead."

Vlad glanced behind us, making sure that no one was coming to Blackstone's aid. Then he shoved the sorcerer to his knees.

"You must be the earth mage Ian was telling us about, yes?" When Blackstone only glared at him, Vlad let the flames coating his hands flare higher. "I can heal you by giving you my blood, or I can burn you to death. Decide which you'd prefer."

After another glare, Blackstone nodded, his mouth too charred to reply any other way. If he'd been a normal human, he'd probably be dead, but his magic was strong.

"Still getting stabbed by silver while stuck in a pit," Ian called out, but Vlad ignored him.

"Do you know a sorcerer named Mircea? He's a vampire, very handsome, with curly black hair and coppery-colored eyes."

Blackstone shook his head. Vlad's grip tightened where the sorcerer's hand used to be until another smoldering bit broke off. "Don't lie to me," he said in a frightening whisper.

The sorcerer shook his head no more vehemently. Vlad sighed. "That would be too easy, wouldn't it? Don't suppose you know anything about blood-bound spells?"

A shrug that seemed to say, *Some.* Vlad leaned closer. "What about a spell that binds two people together flesh to flesh and blood to blood, so strongly that killing one person kills the other person, too?"

Blackstone's eyes widened in surprise. Vlad made another disappointed sound. "No, didn't expect you to. You just stick to the things you're best at, don't you?" At the sorcerer's nod, Vlad said, "So do I," in a conversational tone. Then his grip tightened and a red glow suffused Blackstone. The sorcerer screamed soundlessly and I expected an explosion, but surprisingly, Vlad let him go.

"Wait, I can't kill him," he said, as if remembering something. "Ian made me swear not to kill anyone tonight."

"I release you from that vow!" Ian shouted.

"Oh, but I have a *real problem*," Vlad said with merciless mockery. "In fact, it's like a *sickness* for me, right?"

"I was wrong!" Ian yelled. "Not a sickness, it's a bloody marvelous gift. Now, practice that gift before I'm nothing more than a silver-pronged husk!"

Vlad shot a satisfied glance down at him. "Those roots still working their way through you, are they? That must be painful. What did you say you wanted me to do again?"

"Kill him! Kill him, for the love of God, kill him!" Ian roared. "Leila, poppet, don't just stand there, do something!"

I doubted Vlad would let the spell finish its lethal work, and after all Ian's taunts, incitements, and tricks, he deserved some payback. Hadn't I told Ian that if he kept pushing Vlad, he'd be sorry?

"Oh, I can't reason with him when he's like this," I said. "Like you said, sometimes he can't even *fake* being sane."

Vlad gave me an appreciative grin, but when Ian's new scream sounded a lot more agonized, he clenched his fist and Blackstone exploded. I wished there had been another way to stop the spell, yet it seemed I was the only one regretting Blackstone's necessary death.

"Finally," Ian said, sounding exhausted and relieved.

A wolfish smile curled Vlad's mouth. "It appears you're right—I simply *can't* go an entire day without murdering someone."

"Aren't you amusing?" Ian replied in a sullen tone. "And now that you and the Mrs. have had your fun, perhaps you can assist me. These nasty little roots have speared me in more places than even someone with my tastes can enjoy."

I leaned over the rim of the pit. In addition to the many roots that had worked their way through Ian, one looked to be very close to his heart. The roots had stopped moving, though, and the mist that had acted as an indestructible lid had started to dissipate. Ian was right; Blackstone's spell had died along with him, although it would be tricky getting Ian out with all that silver stuck in him.

Ian must have guessed what I was thinking because he said, "You'll need to melt the silver on both sides so I can pull the remaining pieces out."

I put my hand into the mist, testing to make sure that I could penetrate it. Yep, what was left wasn't that impenetrable shell anymore. Now it just felt sticky, like layers of cobwebs.

"Not so fast." Vlad's hard tone drew my attention back to him, and I paused instead of jumping into the pit. "We have some things to sort out first."

Ian let out a pained noise. "More games?"

"No games." Vlad walked around the edge of the pit like a predator circling its prey. "You've held our need for you over our heads ever since Mencheres forced you to help us, but tonight proves that you need us, too. So no more half truths, tests, or incessant taunts. If I get you out of that pit, you agree to swear to be our ally in full."

Ian glared up at us. "And if I don't? You'll break your vow to Mencheres by killing me?"

"He wouldn't have to," I said, also sick of seeing Ian dangle both of us from a metaphorical hook. "If we leave you, someone from that magical monstrosity of a building will find you, and since there's a very dead earth mage next to you, I don't think it will go over well."

Ian gave me a dirty look. "Very cruel, poppet. Aren't you the perfect mate for him?"

"She is," Vlad said at once. "And I intend for us to remain together for a very long time. Now, do we have a true partnership, or do we leave you here to rot?"

Ian was silent for so long, I started to worry about being caught by the same people I'd just taunted Ian about.

"There are some things I can't help," Ian finally said. "They're as much a part of me as your fire is to you, Tepesh."

Vlad gave an oblique shrug. "I can understand that. But swear to change what you do have control over, and swear it on your love for Mencheres."

Ian made a wistful noise. "I was so hoping you'd tell me to swear it on my honor."

Vlad let out a bark of laughter. "Not in this lifetime."

"Very well." Ian bowed as much as the silver roots pinning him would allow. "On my love for Mencheres, I swear that I will honor both you and Leila as my true partners, and I will keep my insolence, trickiness, filthiness, and general knavery to as much a minimum as I can manage."

"That was beautiful," an unfamiliar voice said while ironic applause started behind us.

I whirled, ripping my glove off. Vlad's hands were already lit with flames, and only Ian's yell of "Stop, it's Ashael!" kept us from flinging whips and streams of fire at the stranger who'd somehow managed to sneak up on us.

A tall, African-American man stared at us. His ebony suit and snow-white shirt were formal enough to wear to a ball, and he showed a marked lack of concern as he looked at Ian, pronged through with silver in a pit, then at the flames coating Vlad's hands, and finally at the electricity-infused whip that dangled from my right hand.

"Did I come at a bad time?" Ashael asked in a dry voice.

Chapter 14

"You came five minutes too late," Ian said, sounding very put out. "A little earlier, and these two wouldn't have wrangled an oath out of me that I know I'll regret."

Ashael smiled, crinkling almost invisible lines near his eyes. His hair was close-cropped and a hint of a beard shadowed his jaw. I would've pegged him in his mid-forties, except he had no heartbeat. Not human, obviously, but he didn't feel like a vampire. Ghoul, I decided, then changed that opinion when Ashael waved his hand and the silver roots piercing Ian began streaming out of his body as if they were snakes fleeing from a brushfire.

Okay, not a ghoul because telekinesis wasn't one of their powers. If he wasn't human, ghoul, or vampire, what was he?

"That's much better," Ian said, giving Ashael a salute. Then he flew out of the pit, wobbling for a minute when he landed. "Don't suppose you have any fresh blood on you?"

"Alas, no," Ashael said lightly.

Vlad's gaze was all for the stranger, who smiled back at him with a casual pleasantness that deepened my unease. Ashael had to know who Vlad was; the fire coating his hands was a dead giveaway. Yet our new companion looked as relaxed as if he was meeting up with friends at a bar, and Vlad hadn't even bothered to extinguish the flames on his hands.

"We should find somewhere private to speak," Ashael said, with a nod at the hotel. "We're bound to get interrupted here."

Vlad still stared at him. Then he inhaled deeply through his nostrils, and I was startled when he yanked me behind him faster than I had ever seen him move.

"Sulfur," he hissed, blasts of fire shooting from his hands now. "You summoned a *demon*, Ian?"

Ashael gave a dispassionate look at the flames. "You can put those out, Impaler. They're mother's milk to my kind."

I was stunned. After many years picking up psychic impressions, I'd suspected that demons existed, but I'd never thought to actually *see* one, let alone meet one.

Ian stepped between Vlad and Ashael, waving as if warding off any arguments. "Your reaction is why I didn't tell you. You never would've stood for it, and Ashael is your best chance to either find Mircea or break your wife's spell."

"You thought I would trust a demon?" Vlad's tone was more than dangerous. It was death made into air.

"Trust?" Ian snorted. "Of course not. But barter with, yes. Demons are always in the market for a profitable bargain, and you do have an embarrassment of riches, Tepesh."

Ashael glanced around. "Someone's coming," he said in a mild tone. "So I am leaving, with or without you."

"With," Ian said promptly. "No more tricks, as I

swore," he said, first holding Vlad's gaze, then mine. "This is truly your best chance, I promise you."

Vlad's reaction to finding out that Ashael was a demon mirrored my own thoughts on the subject. We could never trust the debonair creature who looked like a slightly more rugged version of Idris Elba. But, as Ian had said, what demons lacked in trustworthiness, they might make up for in greed, and Vlad did have lots of fancy stuff and *lots* of money.

"We've come this far," I said quietly, then smiled with grim humor. "And we don't have anything else to do tonight."

Vlad let out a short laugh. "I can think of many things I'd rather do, yet unique problems call for unique solutions."

Ian breathed a sigh of relief, then put his hand on Ashael's shoulder. Ashael placed one hand on mine and the other on Vlad's. At once, angry green spilled from Vlad's gaze.

"Don't," he began.

That's all he got out before a *whoosh* stole his words away. Everything blurred with incredible motion, reminding me of the wild, sickening ride when the magical building had flushed us. This time, there was no water. Just a rush of air, sound, and light that left hotspots in my vision when I was finally able to see again.

We were no longer near that looming, magical building. In fact, I was pretty sure we weren't in Georgia anymore since the sky was no longer midnight black. Instead, it was streaked with the last few rays of dusk. We had a great view of the sun disappearing behind the horizon, too, because we were on the roof of a high-rise hotel that overlooked the ocean.

And this was no normal hotel roof. It looked like a

fancy courtyard and a country club combined, complete with impeccably dressed staff that showed no surprise at our sudden appearance. Ashael nodded at them, and at once, they politely whisked away the other patrons who were seated around an elegant, crushed glass fire pit. Then they bowed to Ashael with the same deference that Vlad's staff showed to him.

"Where are we?" Vlad said.

"And what did you just do?" I added, still trying to process that I'd somehow dematerialized and rematerialized.

Ian gave an appreciative glance around. "We're in Los Angeles, if I recognize the skyline, and Ashael teleported us here." He shrugged as if both were no big deal. "That's how demons get around, and if one has a hold on you, they can take you with them, too."

Teleportation. No wonder we hadn't heard Ashael approach us before! With that trick, he could sneak up on anyone.

Ashael strolled over and sat in one of the contemporary-styled chairs that were arranged to face the ocean. "Who else wants a drink?" he asked. "I'll take my usual," he told the nearest attendant, who bowed and then hurried off.

"A bourbon for me," Ian sang out. "Tepesh? Leila?"

"Nothing," I said, not surprised when Vlad refused, too. Ian might be acting as if Ashael were an old buddy, but this was no social visit for the rest of us.

In moments, the attendant returned with two bottles and two glasses. She poured Ashael's drink first, and I couldn't stop myself from checking out the bottle. What was a demon's drink of choice? Triple malt Balvenie Scotch whisky, aged fifty years, according to the bottle.

"Please, sit," Ashael said, nodding at the chairs next to him.

His smile made it seem like a request, but a flash of red in his eyes caused fear to skitter up my spine. Without one threatening word, Ashael was more intimidating than anyone I'd ever encountered, and I had come up against some real monsters in my short twenty-six years.

Yet all of them could only hurt me in this lifetime. With that single flash of red, Ashael was reminding me that his kind could torment me well beyond death. I'd rather throw myself off the nearest ledge than sit next to him. Plunging headfirst from a high-rise building was probably safer.

Still, we needed him, so I was trying to formulate a polite way to refuse when a large, invisible blade suddenly sliced me from groin to sternum. I bent in instinctive need to stop my guts from spilling onto the ground, screaming as a sickening wetness rushed past my clutching hands.

Amidst the horrible pain, I was aware of two things: Vlad gripping me from behind, his fiery hands trying to cauterize the huge wound, and an answering wail in my mind that wasn't part of my own uncontrollable screams.

Make him do it, Leila! Oh please, you have to make him do it or they'll kill us!

Mircea. It had to be him, although I hadn't recognized his voice. All the previous times, he'd sounded like the cruel, smug man that he was. Now he was so terrified, his voice had raised several octaves, until he sounded like a young boy.

Then do something! I thought back, fighting to push past the pain and focus my thoughts so he'd hear me. *Tell me where you are and who "they" are, and we'll stop this!*

Mircea might have replied, but another brutal slash across my midsection emptied my mind of everything except the animalistic urge to get away from the pain or kill the person inflicting it on me. When I healed enough to overcome that mindless response, I heard Mircea over Vlad's hoarse directive telling an attendant to get me blood.

. . . can't! Mircea was saying. *Even if Vlad could best them, he'd do worse than this to me if given the chance!*

I gritted my teeth, shoving aside the wrist that some unknown person pressed to my mouth. Feeding now would be too distracting and I didn't know how long I had to reason with him.

No matter what Vlad might want *to do to you, as long as you're tied to me, he can't,* I mentally snapped. *He can't even backhand you without hurting me, so you'll fare a hell of a lot better under Vlad's care than you will staying with the people who just gutted us twice for fun!*

They didn't do it for fun, Mircea replied in an ominous way. *They did it because they want Vlad to know that they won't hesitate to torture and kill you.*

Couldn't they just text him? I thought back sarcastically, then a chill went through me that had nothing to do with my drastic blood loss. *Why would they want to torture or kill me? I don't even know them.*

No, but you're the rudder, Mircea said darkly. *And Vlad is the ship they want to steer.*

I shuddered more from that than the new, far smaller burning sensations that pricked my still-healing abdomen in several places. Compared to being gutted over and over in quick succession, these were nothing. *Make him do it, Leila!* Mircea had said when he first contacted me. *Oh please, you have to make him do it or they'll kill us!*

"Let me go," I said out loud, pushing at the ironlike grip that encircled me. When Vlad didn't budge, I said in a stronger voice, "Let me go! I think they're writing something on me."

Vlad's arms dropped at once. I ripped off my blood-sodden blouse and yanked my skirt down. As I'd guessed, words were now forming across my abdomen. Whoever was doing this had taken a cue from Vlad because they were now burning them instead of cutting them into my skin. When a shiny gleam caught the last rays of the sun and they continued to hurt long after they should have healed, I let out a grunt of pained appreciation.

Mircea's captors were also rubbing liquid silver into the wounds. Now, their message wouldn't fade until we removed all the silver, giving Vlad plenty of time to read their demand, and they were obviously writing it to Vlad since it wasn't in English. In fact, I didn't recognize the language at all.

"Well?" I asked impatiently. "Can you read it?"

Shock flashed across Vlad's features, answering my question before he spoke. Then I tensed as wildest rage blasted into my emotions next, until I was driven to my knees because my body couldn't handle the sheer intensity of what Vlad was feeling.

"I can't see it, what does it say?" I heard Ian demand through the overwhelming assault on my subconscious.

When Vlad spoke, his voice was a stunned rasp. "It says . . . it says, 'Kill Samir and give us proof of his death or Leila dies.'"

Chapter 15

 "Samir?" I repeated, horror filling me. "Not Samir, the captain of your guards?"

"Who else?" Vlad replied, his voice now edged with an emotion I couldn't name.

I was shocked into stuttering. "B-but you can't. Samir's our friend. He's been with you for over five hundred years!"

Ashael whistled. The sound snapped my head up and I looked at him, but the demon wasn't looking at me. He was staring at Vlad.

Vlad's expression had been twisted with frustration and pain as he'd watched me being cut open over and over, but now it hardened into a blankness that actually frightened me. Never before had he looked so cold, as if he were dead inside. If his shields weren't cracking, sending out bursts of geyserlike emotions into mine, I would've sworn that he *was* dead inside.

But he wasn't. Another massacre-inducing rage roared through our connection, so strong it took several moments for me to feel the hopelessness beneath it, like spikes being hammered into Vlad's soul. Viciousness at its most primal followed, then the burn of bitterness, and finally, the agony of remembered loss.

That agony grew, until it covered over everything else. When it was done, Vlad felt like scorched earth inside, and when that charred darkness touched me, I recoiled from it. Then the link between us slammed shut. The abrupt loss was like having half of me suddenly ripped away, and in some ways, that's exactly what had just happened.

"Stay still," Vlad ordered, his hand splaying over my stomach. Their heat flared and I choked on a scream as I felt my flesh blacken and blister. His grip tightened, keeping me pinned to the ground, and in a few moments, the pain faded. When I looked down, the silver-embedded, murderous directive was gone.

"You can't do it," I said, my voice ragged. "Betraying and killing your friend will destroy you."

"And losing you won't?" he said, with a bleak little laugh.

"We'll find another way," I insisted.

He drew me to my feet, stripping off his jacket. It was soaked with the same blood that had my shirt wringing wet, and he pulled that off me, throwing it to the ground as if it were foul. My bra followed in a wet heap, leaving me topless for the few seconds it took for Vlad to take off his own shirt and settle it over me. It hung to my thighs, and I kicked off my scarlet-soaked skirt without being prompted.

"Thanks," I said, not even caring that I'd flashed a rooftop full of strangers during this exchange.

His hand settled beneath his former shirt to rest on my stomach. "Anything for you."

He began to stroke my abdomen. I leaned closer,

but then one of his fingers suddenly turned stovetop hot, leaving a burning path in its wake.

"What are you doing?" I gasped.

He didn't speak, but one look into his hard, flat stare and I figured it out. I tried to wrest away and his grip tightened, his other arm a cage I couldn't escape as he continued to scorch his reply to Mircea's captors into my flesh.

I couldn't tell what he said, but whatever it was, it was short. When he was done, he gripped me to him, not letting go until his reply had faded from my flesh.

"Dammit, Vlad." Tears clogged my throat, but they weren't from physical pain. That had vanished along with the words on my stomach. "You *can't* do this!"

With my face pressed into his neck, I both heard and felt his scoff. "I've done far worse, and for less reason. You keep forgetting that about me, Leila."

I opened my mouth to argue, then shut it. We had an audience, and an untrustworthy one at that. In fact, we'd already revealed too much to this group. I wasn't about to give them any more ammunition.

We'll fight about this later, my look promised Vlad. There had to be a way to avoid killing Samir without signing my death warrant, too.

Vlad drew back until we were standing shoulder to shoulder, yet he kept one arm folded around me. The demon sat exactly where he had been, his hand around his glass as if he were about to take a drink. Ian had risen at some point, and he actually looked a little pale as his gaze flicked between me and Vlad.

"You didn't tell me that the spell she was bound with could do *that* to her," Ian said quietly.

"Why would I?" Vlad replied, green flashing in his eyes.

That's when an important fact belatedly hit me. Yes, I was slow on the draw, but in my defense, a lot had happened in the short time since we'd been teleported by the demon.

"You look like you again," I said, running my fingers over Vlad's dark hair, then touching the stubble that shaded his jaw. "And I've been saying your name instead of Angel, plus, I must look like me again, too," I added, feeling that my hair was long again instead of short. How had I not noticed that before? Guess trying to keep *more* of my guts from splashing onto my feet had been a real attention-getter.

Vlad frowned, looking at Ian. "I didn't notice you doing anything to break those spells."

"He didn't. I did when I brought you here," Ashael said, only now getting up from his chair. "I wanted to know exactly who I was dealing with, and undoing a bit of glamour as well as that other little spell is a small matter for my kind."

"Demons do magic?" This day kept getting worse and worse.

Ashael's little smile turned into a full-fledged grin. "Of course. Who do you think invented it in the first place?"

Chapter 16

 "So . . . demons invented magic." Why was I repeating what he'd said, as if doing so could change anything?

Ashael continued to smile. "Who else? Humans couldn't have conceived of it, and vampires and ghouls came afterward when Cain was cursed."

A scoff escaped me. "You buy into the story that vampires were created when God cursed Cain to forever drink blood after killing his brother, Abel? I don't. If that were true, how come no vampire on earth has ever met Cain?"

"Perhaps because long ago, someone killed Cain and all those loyal to him," Ashael nearly purred.

"We're not here to debate the vampire creation story," Vlad said shortly. "If your kind invented magic, then breaking any spell should be well within your purview, yes?"

The demon gave a careless shrug. "Perhaps."

I narrowed my gaze. Ian had said that demons were always in the market for a profitable bargain. Did Ashael truly not know the answer? Or was he only acting unsure in order to increase our desperation and thus increase his fee? I'd seen that negotiation tactic before from my old carnie pawnbroker pal.

Vlad had seen it before, too. He smiled at Ashael as if this situation didn't have life-or-death stakes. "Leila has a spell on her, as you have clearly seen. I want it broken. Can you do it, or do I take my embarrassment of riches, as Ian called them, elsewhere?"

Ashael rose, coming over to me. Vlad didn't stop him when the demon reached for me, but his aura crackled with anger. Maybe that's why the demon didn't touch me. Instead, he ran his hand over the space right in front of me.

"This spell isn't bound by an inanimate object like most are," Ashael said. He sounded surprised, and a furrow appeared between his brows. "It's bound to another person. I see both vampire and sorcerer traces here . . . no, wait. More than a sorcerer. The vampire you're bound to is a necromancer."

I stifled my gasp. We hadn't told Ashael that. We hadn't even told Ian that. How had the demon figured it out?

"Yes," Vlad said, displaying none of the surprise I felt. "And as I said, I want the spell broken."

Ashael dropped his hand and his eyes glittered red. He also lost his cool, debonair demeanor and suddenly seemed annoyed. "The only sure way to break this type of spell is to kill the necromancer who cast it."

"We can't," Vlad replied tightly. "It would kill her, too."

"That would also work," the demon muttered.

Flames flashed all around Vlad, so sudden and quick, it was as if his aura had caught fire. Just as fast, those flames disappeared. "Are you mocking me?"

"Are you threatening me?" Ashael shot back.

The temperature on the roof spiked about thirty degrees, and the new heat wasn't coming from Vlad. I tensed. The demon had said that fire was mother's milk to his kind. What if Vlad wasn't the only one on this roof who was pyrokinetic?

Ian stepped between them. "Come now," he said in a cajoling way. "This situation could still make one of you very happy and the other very rich, so let's save the violence for later, hmm?"

Vlad's gaze never left the demon's face. Ashael didn't move, either, but the temperature began to drop back down to normal levels.

"You see how much this means to me," Vlad finally said. "Is there truly no other way to break this spell?"

Ashael's gaze gleamed. "There is *one* way . . ."

"No," Ian interrupted. "Not that—"

Vlad's hand shot out, crushing Ian's throat to cut him off. "You were saying, Ashael?"

"A simple sale," the demon replied in a much lighter tone. "Your soul in exchange for Leila's freedom from the spell."

"Fuck no," I burst out, grabbing Vlad's arm. "Don't even think of it! I swear I will silver myself in the heart if you do. I mean it! You make that deal and I *will* take myself out, so you wouldn't be saving me. You'd be guaranteeing my death!"

Fear had me sucking in breaths to get the words out before Vlad could agree to something so awful, and my grip on his arm was so fierce, I'd dug my fingers an inch into his flesh. "I mean it," I said again.

Vlad let go of Ian, who garbled out, "'razy ungrateful 'astard . . ." as soon as he could speak. Then Vlad finally broke his staring contest with the demon, but

I couldn't read the look he gave me. Was that anger? Frustration? Amusement? All three?

"I wasn't going to say yes, Leila. We're not there yet." When I opened my mouth at the ominous "yet," he pressed a finger to my lips. "I heard your warning, and I believe you. Ashael," he said, turning back to the demon. "If that's all you have to offer, then I decline."

"Are you certain?" Ashael said, his smooth tone deepening with promise. "You don't know the power that such oaths unleash. I could have Leila freed before the next tick of the clock."

"No means no," I snapped, furious at his continued attempts to damn Vlad. "Go soul-scrounge somewhere else!"

The demon's eyes flashed red again. "Scrounge?"

"That *was* rude," Ian said, shooting an accusing look at me. "Not right for her to insult you simply because of your species. Would she criticize a lion because it eats gazelles? No, because it's a bloody lion and eating gazelles is what they do, just like making soul contracts are what demons do."

"The bigotry does get wearisome," Ashael agreed. "And demons don't scrounge, we negotiate. There's a vast difference."

I had so much to say to that, but I clamped my mouth shut. "If we're done here?" Vlad said, trailing off with meaning.

Ian elbowed Ashael in a companionable way. "I doubt it. Since you can't get the real prize you're after, you're going to drive up the monetary price on your services, aren't you?" When the demon hesitated, Ian chortled. "Crafty bugger, I knew it! It's why I so admire your kind. I'd tack on an insult surcharge, too. Teach her to mind her mouth."

I stared at Ian in disbelief. "Whose side are you on?"

"Mine, always," he replied, and the demon chuckled. "Ah, Ian, if you didn't have fangs, I'd swear you were one of ours."

Ian bowed as if that were the highest compliment. Ashael chuckled again, then he regarded Vlad and me with a lot less humor. "As I said, without a soul contract, I don't have the power to break her spell, and no other demon will, either."

I could hear a grinding noise as Vlad's jaw clenched. "Then we're finished here," he said, striding us toward the edge of the roof. "Ian, stay or leave, I don't care."

"Wait."

The single word stopped Vlad from vaulting us over the roof's edge, but it didn't come from Ian. It came from Ashael.

Vlad turned, arching a brow. The demon's smile was sharklike. "There might be *one* other way."

"And that is?" Vlad prodded when Ashael didn't go on.

The demon lifted his shoulder in a half shrug. "Her magic."

"Her who?" I asked, barely concealing my dismay at the thought of going on another magical wild-goose chase.

Ashael looked at me as if I were slow. "You."

Chapter 17

"Me?" I said.

At the same time, Vlad ground out, "I am not amused," in a tone that sounded like sharp-edged gravel.

Ashael let out an elegant snort. "Don't play coy. When I drew forth your aura, I could see the magic in you, and it has nothing to do with that spell."

Ian cast an interested look at me. "Hiding a big secret, were you, poppet? Naughty lass, and here I thought we had agreed to honesty all the way 'round."

"I'm not hiding anything!" My arm flung out in Ashael's direction. "He's lying. I don't have any magic."

Another snort from the demon. "No, you just vibrate all over from electricity because you're excited to see me."

Oh, so he'd misunderstood. "That's not magic; it's a crazy side effect from touching a downed power line when I was thirteen." That power line accident had given me my psychic abilities, too. Before it, I had been completely normal.

Ashael cocked his head, staring at me. "You didn't know," he finally said. "How curious. Did you, Impaler?"

I expected Vlad to say, *Know what?* in his usual annoyed, imperious manner. But he didn't. Instead, Vlad looked at me in a way that made me take several steps backward.

"No," I whispered. "You don't believe this, do you?"

"I suspected," he replied, shattering me. "No human ever came close to harnessing your level of abilities. It either had to be magic, or you had vampire blood somewhere in your lineage."

Ashael grunted. "Not just magic; she's a trueborn witch with an added benefit of legacy power. That's as rare a combination for witches as Cain's legacy is for vampires."

I still couldn't believe what I was hearing. "But I'm not a witch. And even if way up in my family tree someone else might have been, how would *you* know?"

"The same way you know which color is yellow and which is red," Ashael replied in a mild tone. "You were born with the ability to see and differentiate colors. I was born with the ability to see and differentiate magic from a person's aura, whether that magic is infused by a spell, inherited, or other."

It shouldn't sound too incredible to be true. After all, I saw people's worst sins if I touched them with my bare right hand. But I still couldn't believe that the demon could just *look* at me and know more about me or my family than I did.

"How could Leila's magic be used to break the spell?" Vlad asked, moving right along while I still grappled with disbelief.

Ashael came closer. Then he did that weird, feel-the-air-around-me thing again.

"Those with trueborn magic are rare. They didn't

used to be, but most trueborns were killed centuries ago in the great witch purges. Yet a trueborn with *legacy* magic is even rarer. I've only come across one other person with both. If memory serves, she was one of the Ani-kutani."

I flinched, and Vlad noticed. "You're familiar with what that means?" he asked me.

"I'm one quarter Cherokee," I replied. Vlad's look became pointed. Right, he knew a lot of history, but obviously not much Native American lore. "The Ani-kutani used to be a powerful Cherokee ruling priesthood. No one knows how long they reigned, but they were rumored to have been the ancient Appalachian mound builders. Legend says the Ani-kutani eventually became so corrupt and hated that their entire line was massacred by the Cherokee around the thirteenth century. To this day, most Cherokees still despise their memory."

Ashael's gaze gleamed. "Yet you are most likely a direct descendant from the Ani-kutani. That's what you get when you leave annihilation to humans. Someone usually weakens and spares a baby." He punctuated his criticism of humanity's mercy with a contemptuous snort. "With all that incredible magic in your bloodline, you never noticed anything special about your family?"

I didn't like the disdain in his tone, as if I wouldn't have noticed if Mom was fond of pointy hats or rode around on brooms. "Unless you count the fact that Mom had a real talent for gardening, no, there was nothing unusual about her."

"How did she die?" Ashael asked bluntly. "I'll bet there was something unusual about *that*."

My hand tingled as grief and self-blame caused electricity to surge into it. "Yeah. She tried to pull me off the power line I accidentally touched and it killed her."

Satisfaction spread over the demon's features. "Both you and your mother experienced the same deadly voltage, yet you lived and she died. Did you never wonder why?"

"Of course I did!" I snapped. "What's your point?"

A thick brow arched. "Those with trueborn magic can use their inherited powers to enhance their abilities, but they still have to learn those abilities first. Yet legacy magic allows for an instant transfer of fully functional power."

"What does any of this have to do with my mother's death?" I asked impatiently.

Ashael passed his hand in front of me again. Now I knew what he was doing. He was drawing upon my aura to see the different types of magic hidden beneath it.

"It's called legacy magic because it's passed from one relative to another. It also changes according to the needs of the person who receives it. You're a trueborn witch, but that wouldn't have saved you when you touched that power line. Only a sudden, incredible infusion of magic would. Your mother must have willed her legacy magic into you that day. When she did, it not only saved your life—it also transformed all the deadly voltage you'd absorbed into a functioning part of you."

I stared at him. As fast as I could reject what he was saying, it also made sense. Doctors had never been able to explain why I'd lived and my mother had died when we'd both been exposed to the same lethal currents. In fact, I'd been exposed to them longer than her. I had been stuck to that power line for a couple minutes before all the sparks shooting from me alerted my mom to something horrible going on in the backyard. Yet not only had I survived, I'd also kept all my brain functions and eventually regained full mobility, two things all my doctors had said were impossible at the beginning.

Since then, I couldn't count the times I'd wondered why, *why* had I lived but Mom had died? I'd also endlessly wondered why I had woken up from that horrible accident with freakish new voltage running through me and even more frightening visions of other people's sins. Now, at last, it looked like I had those answers, and only years of hardening myself from various pains kept me from breaking into sobs.

I'd always felt responsible for my mother's death because we wouldn't have been in that storm-prone state if I hadn't told her about my dad cheating on her. I'd also blamed myself because Mom wouldn't have died if I'd stayed inside the house after that storm instead of trying to rescue a dog from what I assumed was only downed tree branches. Now, I knew it went much deeper.

Mom hadn't grabbed me out of mindless panic when she saw me stuck to that power line, as everyone had always believed. If the demon was correct, then she'd put her hands on me in order to transfer her legacy magic into me. If she was thinking that clearly, she would have known that touching me while I was stuck to the power line would kill her, but she made a deliberate choice to give her life for mine.

I wanted to fall onto her grave weeping in awe at her courage and self-sacrifice while also yelling at her for doing it. I wanted to ask why she had never told me about trueborn magic or legacies or anything else I'd just learned from this smug demon, and why she hadn't told my father, either. He sure as hell hadn't known, not with how he'd freaked over the discovery of vampires, and Gretchen hadn't known. If my aunt had, then she'd taken her secrets to the grave a few years ago.

I was startled away from those thoughts when Vlad's aura flared. It didn't feel like its usual blast of energy. Instead, it curled around me like a warm, tingling cloud, enveloping me from the top of my head to the bottom of my feet. It was as personal as a loving embrace without him moving a muscle, and I knew why he did it when he spoke.

"Get to the point, Ashael. While interesting, none of what you've told us gives any indication how Leila's magic might be used to break the spell on her."

The brusque words would have stung if I wasn't still wrapped inside the cocoon of his aura. How like Vlad to sound like an uncaring prick even while secretly comforting me.

Ashael smiled. "I told you those other things for free but *that*, Impaler, is going to cost you."

"How much?" Vlad asked flatly.

Ashael tilted his head, his smile turning knowing. "I'm not negotiating with you today. You're not nearly motivated enough. Besides, you only half believe what I've already said. Go, verify the rest of it, and we'll talk price after that."

Now Vlad's aura flared with such anger that the former comforting embrace changed into the sting of a thousand tiny, invisible whips. The demon waved a dismissive hand, making it worse, but before Vlad could even speak, Ashael disappeared.

I was still blinking at the empty space in front of me when Vlad began to storm around the roof. "Don't bother searching for him," Ian said. "Demons love their vanishing acts, and remember; no one can find Ashael by looking."

"Then I'll summon him," Vlad all but snarled.

Ian grunted. "You can summon him all night and all day, but if he doesn't want to talk to you, you'll be wasting your time."

Vlad continued to pace in long, angry strides. My head felt like it was about to explode from everything I'd learned, which was why I was mildly surprised to hear myself say, "So let's do it," in a very calm tone.

Vlad stopped pacing. "Do what?"

"Find out if Ashael is right about me." I let out a short laugh. "I can't be the only one who doesn't want to take a demon at his word. With some digging, we can find out if any of my mother's family is still alive. If they are, maybe we'll be lucky and one of them will know about this magic legacy thing."

"And if you're very, *very* lucky," Ian chimed in, "that same person might also know the possible spell-breaking information that Ashael intends to charge you so handsomely for."

Vlad gave Ian a level look. "You don't truly believe that."

"I don't," Ian agreed with a laugh. "But I've been wrong before. Think it was on a Tuesday."

Chapter 18

 My mother hadn't spoken much about her Cherokee heritage. Neither had my aunt Brenda. I knew that Mom and Aunt Brenda had spent their childhood on the Cherokee Indian land trust in North Carolina, but that was about it. Not that I'd shown much interest in finding out more. As a child, all I'd been interested in was gymnastics. I'd trained obsessively, winning competition after competition until I finally had a chance at making the U.S. Olympic team.

Then, after the power line accident, all I could focus on was how my life had been blasted apart. Mom was dead, Dad was emotionally distant, and in addition to terrifying new psychic visions, I had also become a walking live wire. Fast forward six hellish years to my becoming a carnie with my now-best-friend and father figure, Marty, and I'd spent exactly zero time dwelling on my Native American heritage.

Now, yes, I needed to verify if I was a magic-born descendant of the ancient Ani-kutani, but I also felt ashamed that I had never explored my Cherokee roots before. My pale blue eyes and light skin caused most people to peg me as all Caucasian, but I wasn't, and I had more than my poker-straight, thick black hair to show for it. A lot more, if the demon was right and all my incredible abilities were the direct result of my Cherokee heritage, too.

That's why, although Vlad grumbled because it cost us the entire afternoon while we waited for her to fly in, I wasn't going to be the only Dalton who went to the Eastern Band of Cherokees looking for answers. My sister's heritage was here, too, and not just the possible trueborn-witch, descendant-of-the-Ani-kutani one.

"What is it with you and meeting in casinos?" were Gretchen's first words when she walked into our room. Despite her long flight and the very early morning hour, my sister's makeup was flawless and her hair still held artificial waves that made it look even fuller.

"This was the safest option," I told her. "There's so many people going in and out, we're just more faces in a crowd."

Gretchen looked around our pretty, two-room suite with mild disdain. "For the record, I like the villas at Caesar's Palace in Vegas much more than this place."

I rolled my eyes as I hugged her. "You hate being in Vlad's version of protective custody, but you've obviously become accustomed to his fancy standards of living, huh?"

"Since I'm an inmate, at least the prisons should be nice," she replied tartly. But she held on a few seconds longer than she usually did, even with getting zapped by my electricity. Her snarkiness was just for show, as usual. She'd missed me. She just didn't know how to tell me that.

So I went first. "I'm so glad to see you," I said when we finally let go. "I missed you."

"You did?" she said with such surprise that it hurt. Had I really been that bad of a sister?

Yes, my inner voice suddenly roared. *You're an awful sister! You let Gretchen find you half dead in a tub full of blood from a suicide attempt when you were sixteen, and that's just for starters!*

I clenched my jaw hard enough to hear cartilage snap. I'd had that vocal, evil inner critic ever since I'd woken up from my accident. Lately, it had been a lot more silent, but it wasn't totally gone. Maybe it never would be.

I can't have more than one voice in my head at a time, I snapped back at it. *Since I need to hear Mircea if he ever shows up again, YOU need to shut it!* Then, mild version of schizophrenia back under control, I returned to Gretchen.

"Of course I missed you. If things weren't still so crazy dangerous, we'd be seeing a lot more of each other."

Her pretty features scrunched into a scowl, making her look younger than her twenty-three years. "Right, you're still at war. Guess I should've known that your husband wouldn't pick this place over his castle for a victory celebration. Can't you hurry things along? I'd like to live my *own* life again sometime this century." Then, with only slightly less of a scowl, Gretchen turned to Vlad. "Speaking of that, hiya, Drac-in-law."

"Don't call him that!" I said with a gasp.

"What?" she said in exasperation. "It's not like 'Drac' is the *other* word. It's just a nickname."

"One you will never use again," Vlad said in a deceptively smooth voice.

A snicker came from the suite next to ours. It was quiet at this predawn hour, with most of the hotel's guests finally asleep in their rooms. That made it easier for a vampire to eavesdrop, if one wasn't polite enough to mind his own business.

"Love it!" Ian called out. "Now I must meet the little chippie who called you Drac to your face."

"Don't," I said loudly, but I wasn't surprised when Ian appeared in our suite moments later.

"Hallo," he said in a purr, looking Gretchen up and down in a way that raised my hackles. "What's your name, sweeting?"

"Her name is No," I said at once.

Gretchen stared at Ian, her mouth opening and closing while her blue eyes widened into almost comical proportions. Oh right. Ian's looks were dazzling. Funny how easy it was for me to forget that with his annoying personality.

"Hiiiiii," Gretchen finally breathed. "Don't listen to my sister. For you, my name is Hell *Yes*."

"Gretchen!" I snapped. "This guy is probably a petri dish for as-yet-to-be-discovered STDs."

"Am not," Ian replied, taking Gretchen's hand and kissing it, which made her giggle uncontrollably. "I'm a vampire, so diseases can't survive in me."

"Ian." Vlad sent out his aura in a concentrated burst that made Ian recoil as if he'd been struck. "*No*," Vlad finished.

Gretchen turned around and glared at Vlad. He glared back, and he had over six centuries of battle-tested, don't-even-think-about-it in his gaze. Very quickly, she dropped hers.

With a moue of disappointment, Ian released Gretchen's hand. "Just as well, poppet. I eat sweet little mortals like you for breakfast, and I do mean that literally."

Gretchen's eyes widened again. Ian flashed a wicked smile at her, then the bedroom door opened once more and Marty bustled in, carrying so many suitcases piled on top of each other that they almost concealed his four-foot frame.

"Could you have packed any *more* clothes, Gretchen?" Marty grumbled, giving me an apologetic look as he dropped them onto the floor. "These bags are why she beat me to your hotel room."

I bent at once to give Marty a hug, grinning as he squeezed me back hard enough to force an *ooof* from me. "Missed you, kid," he murmured when he let me go.

I'd barely finished telling Marty I had missed him, too, when Ian said, "And who is *this* handsome lad?" in the same purring tone he'd used with Gretchen.

"Also someone you're not getting lucky with," I replied tartly. "Marty is my best friend, and he's straight."

Ian gave me an aggravated look. "Can't shag your sister, can't shag your friend, can't shag you, can't shag Vlad. If I wanted to be this sexless and miserable, I'd get married."

"You're not here for your own entertainment," Vlad said in a curt tone.

Ian's mouth curled down. "And well I know it. Damn Mencheres, forcing a promise from me that I can't renege on."

"Yeah, it's truly tragic to have to honor your word," I said, fighting another eye roll. "Cheer up, Ian," I continued. "All we have on the agenda this afternoon is a trip to the Qualla Boundary. We shouldn't need your magical expertise there, so you can stay here and find some poor soul to get nasty with."

"If only," Ian said with feeling. "But I have to—"

"That's enough."

The warning in Vlad's voice startled me. "What's going on?" I asked in a sharp tone.

"You dragged me out here for a field trip into our Cherokee past," Gretchen said, sounding impatient. "I know it's almost dawn and you're still dealing with new vampire sunrise disease, but you can't have forgotten *that*."

I ignored her because I hadn't been talking to Gretchen. Everyone else here knew that, especially the man I'd married.

"Vlad," I said, drawing his name out for emphasis.

All at once, the air vibrated with barely contained energy. Those invisible pulses whipped against my skin like the sting of sand during a storm at the beach.

"I'm going away for a short time." Vlad's cool tone was so at odds with what I was feeling from his aura. Where was he going, and why wasn't I going with him?

Then the answer hit me with the impact of a gunshot wound.

"No," I whispered. Then louder, "*No*. You can't. Samir is your *friend*. You can't kill him, we'll find another way!"

"Leila." Vlad's voice was utterly dispassionate. "Don't bother arguing. It's as good as done."

Chapter 19

 Before Vlad had finished speaking, Marty and Ian rushed me. I was locked inside the grips of the two strong vampires before I could even get my gloves off.

"What did you say?" Gretchen demanded shrilly. "You're going to kill Samir? Why?"

Vlad's eyes lit up with green as he turned to Gretchen. "Be quiet. Sit down."

Gretchen sat right on the floor without another word. I continued to struggle, but Marty had my legs trapped in a bear hug and Ian had my upper body mostly immobilized. Other emotions began to pour into my fury at being blindsided this way. The PTSD I'd been battling for months returned, and each new, futile struggle only fueled my irrational panic. Still, I struggled harder when Vlad walked to the door.

"Don't do this, Vlad, please!"

He paused and looked at me. His eyes had bled back to their normal burnished color, and for a moment, I glimpsed profound sadness in them. Then they hardened like ice-encrusted copper. "I must."

He left without another word. Ian slapped a hand

over my mouth when I yelled after him, and I bit down until blood ran.

"Wrong strategy," Ian muttered. "I enjoy pain, so between biting me and the deliciously agonizing bolts of electricity your whole body is giving off, you're making my entire morning."

I stopped biting him. From the disappointed noise he made, he hadn't been kidding. He also removed his hand from my mouth slowly, as if giving me the chance to bite him again. Great, I hadn't stopped Vlad from leaving, so all my struggles had succeeding in doing was panicking me, making Ian happy, and hurting Marty. I was furious with them for the surprise ambush, but I didn't want to truly hurt them.

Plus, if my voltage got too out of control, I might inadvertently kill one of them.

"Let me go," I said, trying to power myself down so I no longer shot dangerous electricity out of every pore.

"Not yet," Ian answered grimly. "Need a little help in here holding her," he called out in a louder voice.

Moments later, I heard another metallic key card being used on our hotel room door. Good, Vlad had come back. He might think the matter was settled and Samir was as good as dead, but I hadn't begun to give up this fight—

It wasn't Vlad. Instead, a very tall, very blond vampire filled the doorframe. For a moment, all I did was stare, my emotions swinging like a pendulum.

I hadn't seen Maximus since we killed Szilagyi and met Mircea in that underground, ancient Turkish prison. Maximus had saved our lives that day from a deadly self-destruct sequence that Szilagyi had set off, just like he'd saved my life before that from Szilagyi's horrible napalm attack on Vlad's castle. Those and many other brave deeds had more than made up for Maximus's brief disloyalty to Vlad over me, and I considered him to be a very dear friend.

But . . .

I looked at Maximus, and a cold, creeping fear swept over me that was as irrational as it was unfair. It wasn't Maximus's fault that Szilagyi had treated me so brutally when I'd been his captive. Maximus had saved me from even worse torture while pretending to be Szilagyi's ally, and I wouldn't have been able to psychically transmit my location to Vlad if not for Maximus. Yet just looking at him made me feel a double onset of the same post-traumatic stress disorder I'd fought so hard to overcome, and when he came over to help hold me as Ian had requested, a flood of memories came back, trapping me in the same anxiety I'd felt last time I had been forcibly restrained.

The circle of men around me suddenly changed into the gray rock of an underground cell. Then their hands changed into metal clamps that bit into my wrists, arms, legs, and ankles. That wasn't the worst part. Once again, I saw a cruel, platinum-haired vampire holding a curved knife with a partial loop on the handle. Szilagyi's hired torturer smiled as he came nearer. I twisted until blood ran from every clamp restraining me, but I couldn't get away . . .

Random snatches of dialog broke into the nightmare that held me in its merciless grip. They were faint compared to the echo of my own screams and the horrible memory of my flesh being sliced and ripped from my body, but I still heard them.

"Something's wrong."

"There goes the power."

"Leila? Kid, you gotta stop that!"

"Where's a bloody fire master when you need one?"

"Try letting her go, see if that helps."

"No, it's only getting worse."

"She's drawing in too much electricity!"

"Stand back, I'll handle this. I said, stand back!"

Color suddenly exploded in my mind, shattering the memory and hurtling me into the present. I fell forward only to pull away with a gasp of pain. What had I just burned myself on?

The carpet, I realized. It was still smoldering despite the sprinklers in the hotel room shooting water in every direction. I shook my head, feeling as if I were waking up from a particularly bad hangover, then looked around in shock.

The power in the room was off, smoke and sprinkler water clogged the air, the carpet was burned in multiple places, and the ceiling looked as if a kid had set off fireworks that scorched their way half through it to the floor above us. Ian, Maximus, and Marty were all sopping wet, and their clothes had dozens of tiny burn holes in them.

And I didn't know how any of this has happened.

"Where's Gretchen?" I said, filled with a different kind of panic when I didn't see her anywhere.

"She's on the first floor waiting by the front desk," Marty replied, tapping the side of his eye for emphasis. "I used these, so she won't go anywhere else."

I gestured at the destruction around us. "And, um . . . I'm guessing I'm somehow responsible for this?" I didn't remember doing it, but what other explanation was there?

"Too bloody right," Ian said instantly. "You started

shooting electricity from your body as if you'd transformed into a living lightning bolt. Burned the shite out of us, the carpet, and the ceiling, and then you got *truly* destructive—"

"That's enough," Marty said curtly.

"Hardly," Ian countered. "If she doesn't know what she's capable of, she can't begin to control it. As I was saying, then you upped your electricity by siphoning more voltage from the power outlets. You didn't even need to touch them—the currents streamed out and fed into you as if summoned. You kept doing that until you'd short-circuited the whole bloody hotel. After that, you were so amped up, no one could touch you without catching fire. Thought you were about to self-detonate and blow us all to hell, so I threw a reality spell at you. Thankfully, it snapped you out of whatever crazy trance you were in."

I couldn't begin to process what I was hearing. Yes, I'd siphoned electricity before, but only when I was *touching* a power outlet. Plus, it had only amped up my right hand, not my entire body. Had my abilities grown to where my hand wasn't my only deadly weapon anymore? To hear Ian tell it, yes.

I wasn't ready to deal with the ramifications of that, so I started with the last bit. "A reality spell? That's an actual thing?"

Ian huffed. "Yes, and it's something they should regularly cast in schools, but the vampire world isn't the only place where magic is forbidden."

Sprinkler water continued to soak the three of us. I ran a hand through my sopping hair to push it out of my face.

"Kid?" Marty said in a hesitant way. "You okay?"

I couldn't stop my disbelieving laugh. "You mean

aside from my husband running off to murder his good friend in order to save me? Or are you talking about my newfound ability to go nuclear on an electrical level if a bad case of PTSD sets in?"

"Both," Marty said cautiously.

The sun had just come up; I could feel it in the sudden exhaustion that swept over me. But I sank to my knees from more than new-vampire-at-dawn weariness. Despite having enough power to short-circuit an entire hotel, I was helpless when it came to saving Vlad from doing something he would forever regret.

"I'm not nearly okay," I mumbled.

"You need to be." Maximus's deep voice jerked my attention back to him. He stared at me, dark gray gaze penetrating. "I'm sorry my presence and this situation triggered such an episode, but you have to rise above the worst of your memories because we don't have much time."

"For what?" I asked, unable to stop the bitterness that crept into my tone. Vlad was probably on his private jet already, flying toward an innocent man who had no idea that the prince he'd served for almost five hundred years was coming to kill him. If this was tearing me up inside, it had to be killing Vlad. But he'd still do it because of me.

Maximus had once warned me that everything Vlad loved, he destroyed. If you asked me, Maximus had had it wrong. Before this was over, I might end up destroying Vlad.

"To stop whatever it is that Mircea's captors are truly after," Maximus said, his soft voice managing to land with the weight of a thousand bricks. "In blackmail, your first demand is usually a test. Once you know you can get the person to comply, you move forward with what you really want. If something as brutal as killing Samir is Vlad's compliance test, you don't want to find out what they'll demand once they know they have Vlad the Impaler as their willing instrument."

"Not willing," I said instantly. "Forced."

More guilt mixed with the stress, anger, and awful old memories that still simmered inside me. If not for me, Vlad could tell whoever this was to fuck off. Instead, he was about to betray not only a dear friend, but also his entire way of life. Vlad might be brutal to others, but he did whatever was necessary to keep his people safe. Everyone knew that. His line and his reputation had been built on it.

"I understand why you had a meltdown," Maximus said in that same soft tone. "Becoming a vampire doesn't mean you have superhuman *emotional* strength. Only superhuman physical strength, and sometimes, that isn't the real power. But you are strong, Leila. And you're right, Vlad *is* being forced. That's why we need to find out everything we can about this supposed magic heritage of yours so we can get one step closer to freeing both of you."

Several months ago, I'd promised Vlad that I would never again let myself be crippled by guilt, fear, or hesitation, yet here I was, beating myself up for circumstances that were beyond my control. All of this might be because of me but it wasn't my *fault*, no matter if it felt that way. I had to stop punishing myself for the consequences of Mircea's spell. He'd cast it, not me. Against all odds, I'd survived it, and I would survive this, too. So would Vlad. I'd make sure of that.

I rose, pushing off my tiredness with all the willpower I had left in me. I'd start with trying to save

Samir. Vlad might have left me here, but that didn't mean I was helpless.

"Who's got a cell phone?"

Ian disappeared into the room next door before returning with a cell. "Here," he said, and I grabbed one of my gloves and put it on before accepting it.

Maximus shot a censuring look at Ian. "Vlad won't like you doing that."

Ian snorted. "If her calling him will make him stop, then Vlad didn't truly want to kill this bloke to begin with."

From the flash of power I'd caught from Vlad's aura, I didn't question his determination. Him having my friends physically stop me from coming after him also didn't smack of any indecisiveness. Extreme dickishness, yes, and we'd have words over that when I saw him again, but first things first.

"I'm not calling Vlad," I said, dialing.

Marty cocked his head. "Who are you calling?"

"It won't matter who," Maximus said, his gaze almost pitying. "Vlad has nearly six hundred years' experience in these matters. Whatever you're planning, Leila, he has a contingency."

I gave Maximus a level look. "We'll see about that."

Chapter 20

 Three hours later, I was seething with frustration. I'd called and texted Samir repeatedly, yet he hadn't answered. That could have been coincidence, so I then called and texted every single person in Vlad's line whose number I remembered. None of them answered. For all of Vlad's people to suddenly ignore dozens of my calls and texts was no coincidence. He must have ordered them not to respond to me.

Undeterred, I called the airline next and tried to book a flight to Romania. That's when I found out that all of my credit cards had been canceled. When the guys refused to let me use one of their cards, I went into the lobby, grabbed the first well-dressed person I saw, and green-eyed him into letting me use his credit card instead.

That's when I also found out that my name was now on the no-fly list. No airline in the country would book a flight for me, and I couldn't green-eye my way past a national computer system. Finally, in desperation, I called Vlad. No surprise, he didn't answer.

"I told you," Maximus said without any smugness. "Vlad has made up his mind. When he does that, he doesn't let anyone stand in his way, even someone he loves. It's not your fault, Leila. You can't save Samir, but you might be able to prevent Vlad from ever having to do this again."

It didn't seem nearly enough, yet I had run out of ideas, and the clock was ticking. Maybe the only way I could stop this was by finding out something useful from my mother's people. I certainly hadn't been able to do anything here at the casino.

"Fine," I said shortly. "Let's do this."

We checked out of the hotel—not even vampire hypnosis could hide the fact that the fire in our suite had been responsible for shorting the electricity in the entire hotel. Only mesmerizing the hotel manager kept us from going to jail. Hypnosis had also cleared Gretchen's memory of where Vlad had gone and why, once we met back up with her.

Marty did that last part. I hated altering her memory, but I agreed with the reason behind it. Gretchen would have a fit if she remembered Vlad's grisly task, not that I could blame her. No, I had to focus on other ways to save Samir, and to stop whatever Mircea's captors had planned for Vlad next.

We drove past the "Welcome, Cherokee Indian Reservation" sign that must've annoyed my mother a lot because it was one of the few things she'd mentioned about growing up here. Technically, the Eastern Band of Cherokees didn't live on a reservation. The government hadn't given them part of their own land back—it had been purchased by the tribe as a trust back in the nineteenth century. The trust still gave the Cherokees the same tribal sovereignty that true reservations had, so when we crossed over the Qualla Boundary, we were now under the authority of the tribe instead of the state.

I expected that the part of the land trust where people actually lived would look different from the rest of it, and I was right. The hotel, casino, museum, and other attractions were glitzy, tourist-ready versions of the Eastern Band of Cherokees, complete with more than a few people dressed in old-fashioned Native American garb. The residential area didn't have any of those things.

The economic downturn once we left the tourist areas was also readily apparent, and that hurt to see. I wondered how my life would have changed if I'd grown up here instead of on different military bases because of my father's frequent change of duty stations. Gretchen looked around with wide eyes, too. When she saw two little black-haired girls playing in a yard, I knew she was flashing back to our childhood like I was.

Despite my longing to know more about our roots, we needed to find out things that couldn't be discovered by researching tribal records. However, I couldn't just knock on doors and ask if anyone knew whether my mother had been a descendant of the Ani-kutani. Maybe no one here even remembered my mother. She and my aunt Brenda had left over thirty years ago.

We were stopped by a tribal officer before we had gotten halfway through the first section of the residential area. "I'll do the talking," I said, rolling down my window.

"You lost?" the grizzled, white-haired officer asked.

"*Osiyo*," I said, which was exactly one third of all the Cherokee words I knew. "No, I'm not lost. My mother used to live here. I'm, ah, trying to see if anyone here knew her."

The officer gave me a jaded look. Clearly, greeting him in Cherokee had done nothing to endear me to him. "There are over ten thousand residents here. Do you even know what street your mother used to live on?"

"No," I said, embarrassed. Why had I never asked her that?

His expression said he'd expected that. "How about which of the seven clans she was from?"

I paused. Mom had always said we were from the Blue clan, but if the demon was right, we weren't. Still, at some point, Mom's ancestors must have been adopted by the Blue clan in order to help them hide, so would talking to those members help?

I took another look at the officer. Multiple wrinkles gave his skin the appearance of worn leather, and his white hair had only a few sprinkles of black left in it. He might be old enough to remember my mom. Even if he hadn't known her, maybe he'd been around long enough to know something else useful. Sure, it would sound crazy to come right out and say why I was really here, but I had a way of getting around sounding crazy, didn't I?

"I just found out that my mom might have descended from the Ani-kutani clan," I said, putting the full force of vampire power into my gaze. "I need to know if that's true. Can you take me to someone who would know about Ani-kutani survivors and if their descendants had inherited any special magic legacies?"

"Holy shit," Gretchen breathed. Right, I hadn't filled her in on that yet. Well, no time like the present.

The officer nodded, his expression becoming glazed. "I can. Follow me," he said, and got back into his vehicle.

"Isn't it refreshing to cut through the shite and get what you want?" Ian said as we began to follow the officer.

This *did* save more time and we were running against a merciless clock, but still. "I actually don't like mind-manipulating people."

Ian grunted. "Give it time. You'll grow to love it."

"Are you forgetting something, Leila?" Gretchen said, leaning forward to pinch my arm. "Like *Mom* being an Ani-kutani?"

I filled her in on what had happened when we met the demon while we followed the officer. Well, most of it. I left out the part where I'd been gutted in front of everyone in order to deliver a murderous directive to Vlad that Gretchen now forgot.

I expected a flurry of questions when I was finished. Instead, Gretchen said nothing, which concerned me enough to look back at her several times in my rear-view mirror. Then I really grew worried when I caught her scent. Beneath her normal lemon-and-sea-spray scent, she smelled very, very upset. What had caused this sort of reaction? Discovering the real reason Mom had died? Finding out that we both might be witches? The magic legacy thing? All the above?

"Tell me what's wrong," I urged her.

She looked at me with cornflower-blue eyes shiny from unshed tears. "Don't worry about it. Look, the officer's stopping. Brake or you'll hit him, Leila."

I hit the brakes in time to avoid rear-ending the other car. Marty muttered something about my being a terrible driver. Okay, maybe, but I'd learned how to drive just last year, and the only way to get better was with practice.

"We're talking about this later," I told Gretchen as I parked and we got out. She muttered "Whatever" under her breath.

"Here," the officer said, pointing to the house he'd stopped in front of. It was a small structure with wooden siding that needed repainting and a broken section in the wraparound porch. But its position near a precipice gave it a magnificent view of the mountains, and intricate dream catchers swayed gently from their perches over the porch.

"Who lives here?" I asked the officer.

"Leotie Shayne," he said, gesturing to the door. "Go. Knock. She is home."

I did hear a heartbeat inside, slow, steady, and coming closer to the door. Leotie Shayne must have heard us pull up.

The officer got back in his car. I debated telling him to stay, then decided not to. I might not like mind manipulation, but it did ensure that I'd get the truth out of Leotie Shayne.

I blinked in surprise when the door opened and a girl who looked years younger than Gretchen stared back at us. "Yeah?" she said with a teenager's unmistakable attitude.

"Leotie Shayne?" I asked.

"Grandma!" she yelled in reply, turning around. "Some people are here to see you!"

Scraping sounds preceded the appearance of a stooped Native American woman. Like the officer, her hair was almost completely white and her skin was crisscrossed with wrinkles. She also leaned heavily on her walker as she limped toward the door.

Nothing about her appeared threatening, but I stiffened. So did Maximus, Ian, and Marty, and Maximus pushed Gretchen behind him with one swipe of his hand.

"What's your problem?" she hissed, not catching the reason for our new, heightened tension.

I'd heard only one heartbeat, yet two people had been inside the house. Sharp, intelligent black eyes met mine as the wizened old woman stared at me. Then laughter that sounded decades younger than her appearance spilled out of her.

"Lisa, go to Toby's," she said in perfect English.

The teenager let out an annoyed huff. "Why?"

A torrent of Cherokee followed. Whatever the old woman said lit a fire under the teenager's ass. She was out the door and running toward what I assumed was Toby's house in less than a minute flat.

"So," Leotie Shayne said, shoving her walker aside and straightening into a posture that had looked impossible moments before. "What brings a group of vampires and witches to my house?"

Chapter 21

"What makes you say witches?" I said, masking my surprise. How she'd known we were vampires was obvious. That no-heartbeat thing was a dead giveaway, pun intended.

The old woman laughed again, a light, tinkling sound that reminded me of champagne flutes clinking together. "Dear, I know exactly what you and your sister are, and *who* you are."

I exchanged a quick, measured glance with Ian. "Did Ashael tell you we'd be coming?" I asked in a casual tone that belied me starting to pull off my right glove.

Leotie Shayne cast a pointed look at my hands. "Don't. I've heard very impressive things about your whip, but I don't need a demonstration."

"You didn't answer her question, luv," Ian said, flashing her one of his brilliant smiles.

She smiled back wide enough to reveal that she was missing several teeth. "Don't try to charm *my* panties off, boy. Your gender doesn't tempt me."

Ian puffed up in outrage. "Uppity crone, you should be so lucky! You'd never enjoy getting your hips broken more!"

Now Leotie's laughter held a snort. "Who is this one?" she asked me. "He's not your husband and neither are the other two."

Frustration made my fists clench. How quickly Ian had proven correct when he said I'd grow to love mesmerizing people. I'd give a lot to just glare the answers I needed out of this old woman, but since it was impossible to mesmerize another vampire, I'd have to do this the slow way.

"Let's try this again," I said, giving her what I hoped was a friendly smile. "I'm Leila, as you already seem to know. This is my sister, Gretchen; the very tall vampire is Maximus; the very short one is Marty; and the very offended one is Ian. Now, who are you, and how do you know so much about us?"

Leotie eyed me shrewdly. "You and your sister can come in and I will answer your questions, but the rest of them must leave."

"No," Marty and Maximus said in unison before I could get a word out. Gretchen stomped forward, glaring at me when I grabbed her arm to snatch her back.

"If this old woman has answers, then we're hearing her out. They can stay out here and guard the perimeter or something."

"No," Maximus said. "Vlad sent me to protect you. I cannot do that if I can't even see you."

Gretchen waved at Leotie. "She's only one old vampire! Leila's taken on much more than that and walked away, so I'd be the only one in danger. Since I'm no one's priority, just stay outside and let us get this over with."

"Your safety is *my* priority," I said at once. "And I'm not risking you without more information." To Leotie, I said, "You're masking your aura. That's why we couldn't feel you when we first got here. Drop your shields, or we get what we came here for the unpleasant way."

The old woman looked at me with the strangest expression. Was that approval? I didn't know why she'd like being threatened. Then I forgot that as she freed her aura.

Power enveloped me like an inescapable avalanche. Endless, sharp tinges had me looking at my arms as if expecting to see thousands of tiny needles sticking out of them. That power continued to swell until birds abandoned their perches in trees and coyotes howled as if startled awake.

That wasn't the only thing that startled me. A shimmer appeared over the old woman, then fast as a blink, it dropped and someone completely different stood before us. Blue-black hair hung in lustrous swaths around a face that was strikingly beautiful—and young. Gone were the wrinkles and missing teeth. Creamy, sepia skin set off red lips and a mouth full of pearly whites. Her body filled out into strong, curvy dimensions that had Ian moving toward her with his most charming smile. Only her gaze remained the same, and she stared at me in open challenge.

"No more shields or deceptive appearances. I have met your terms, Leila. Will you now honor mine?"

Leotie's powerful aura marked her as either a Master vampire or one several centuries old. Either way, she'd make a formidable opponent. She also must be versed in magic to have glamoured her appearance into the old woman mirage she'd first shown us, so who knew how much more magic she was capable of? Maybe enough to make my electrical whip useless against her?

Yet if I refused to meet her terms, I'd get nothing out of her. I saw that in her steely black gaze as surely as I saw the danger. If it was only me, I'd already be inside her house, but I had Gretchen to worry about. Part of me wanted to shove her at Maximus and tell him to run. But if I did that, I wouldn't only be ruining *my* chances at finding out what Leotie knew. These were Gretchen's answers, too. If I ruined that without even giving Gretchen the choice, I'd be driving another wedge between me and my sister, and I already had plenty of those as it was.

I took in a slow breath to steady myself. "Gretchen," I said in a very calm tone, "this woman is very dangerous. If we send the guys away and go inside with her, I can't guarantee your safety. Do you still want to do this?"

"Yes." Gretchen's answer was immediate.

I looked back at Leotie. "Then we accept your invitation."

"Kid," Marty began.

"We came for answers and she has some," I interrupted. "Not knowing could be even more dangerous." Then I flashed a quick, feral smile at Leotie that I must have learned from Vlad. "Don't worry. If she pulls anything, you'll know it because you'll hear her screaming from what I'll do to her."

She smiled back, and again, it seemed to contain a layer of approval I didn't understand. "Agreed," she said silkily.

"Wait."

I stiffened at Maximus's unyielding tone and turned around. "Look, you can tell Vlad that I made you—"

"I'm not talking to you," Maximus said. Then he went over to Gretchen, who gave him an irritated look.

"Don't bother. I'm not staying out here with you."

"You're not," Maximus agreed, smiling thinly. "But you're also not going inside until you do this."

I had forgotten how fast Maximus was. Granted, I had only seen him fight a couple of times, and during those times, I'd been preoccupied with keeping myself alive. Now I could only marvel at how he'd whipped out his knife, cut himself on the arm, and pressed Gretchen's mouth to the wound, all before I could get out a shocked "What the hell?"

It sounded like Gretchen was trying to say something, too, but her words were muffled by the brawny arm clamped across her mouth. I yanked at it, and it didn't move. All Maximus did was shove me back with his other hand.

"What was that?" Gretchen sputtered when he finally let her go. Then she touched her red-smeared mouth. "Did you just make me drink your *blood*?"

"Yes," Maximus said, meeting my gaze over Gretchen's head. "Now she can go inside with you."

"Why would you do that?" Gretchen demanded, punching the thick arm that had been pressed to her face. "Did you forget that I'm the only one here who *doesn't* like blood?"

"I didn't forget." Maximus bent down until they were eye level. His gaze wasn't lit up with vampire green, but Gretchen stared at him as if he'd mesmerized her. "But you're wrong. Leila's safety isn't my only priority. I also care about you."

The confusion in her expression said she didn't understand. I did, and I wished I'd thought of it myself. With vampire blood in her system, Gretchen would be stronger, faster, and heal more easily. She also now had a "Get Out of Dead Free" card. If a human died right after drinking vampire blood, they could be raised as a ghoul. That would be our very last resort, but I was relieved to have the option, if the worst happened.

"Thank you," I said to Maximus. When Gretchen swung an amazed look my way, I said, "I'll tell you later."

I waited until the guys backed away enough to merge with the woods. Then Gretchen and I followed Leotie inside the house. When the door closed behind us, it seemed to shut with a finality that silenced everything beyond it.

Chapter 22

 The inside was much nicer than the outside, as if I'd needed more confirmation that things weren't what they seemed with Leotie Shayne. The interior might be small but it was very clean, and the furniture had the faded look of age, yet it was also homey and welcoming.

"Tea?" Leotie asked, as if this was a social call.

I remembered Ian's warning about side effects of magical drinks. "No thank you."

"Love some," Gretchen said, her glare daring me to argue.

My lips compressed, stopping the words that tried to fly out. Why couldn't she follow my lead for once? Now, if I didn't let her drink it, I'd be causing a scene that would escalate the already strangling tension. Worse, Leotie smiled as if amused by this battle of sisterly wills.

"Which were you first, a witch or a vampire?" Gretchen went on, startling me with her blunt question.

"A witch," Leotie replied, thankfully unruffled. "From a long line of them, in fact."

"Which line?" I asked, making the question sound casual.

She gave me a look as she set a kettle on an old-fashioned stove. "Don't be coy. You know which or you wouldn't be here."

I wasn't about to give her information if she were just fishing. "I want to hear you say it," I replied, my glare telling Gretchen, *Don't you dare fill it in for her!*

Leotie lit the gas under the kettle and turned the flame up. Then she gestured to a faded blue couch adorned with brightly colored crocheted pillows. "Won't you sit?"

Gretchen did. I continued to stand. I'd have better range of motion that way if I had to manifest my whip, and if that happened, I didn't want Gretchen in my immediate vicinity.

"Well?" I asked, masking my impatience. "Which line?"

"You look more like your father than your mother" was what Leotie replied, casting an almost disparaging glance at Gretchen next. "You too. Blue-eyed pale faces, the both of you."

"It's what's inside that counts," I said at once. "And I've got more than a few interesting things from my Cherokee blood."

Leotie grunted. "Very true. Without it, there would be nothing exceptional about you, Leila Dalton."

If she thought to insult me, she failed. I used my powers because I had to, not because I wanted to get into what Vlad had once called a supernatural dick-measuring contest.

"Another one," Gretchen muttered.

Leotie's black gaze gleamed. "One what?"

"'Normal' basher," Gretchen stated. "Dealt with it my whole life. News flash: being normal isn't a cakewalk. *You* try slogging through this life with nothing special about you when you're surrounded by people who are exceptional."

Her words sidetracked me. "But you are special," I began.

She gave me a look. "Don't patronize me. I'm fine with what I am. I'm just sick of hearing other people say that 'normal' isn't good enough for them."

Yes, I had gotten a lot of attention as a kid because of my gymnastic abilities, and yes, the horrible power line accident and its aftermath had only increased the focus on me, but I hadn't wanted it to. I'd ached for the normal she described.

Until now, I hadn't looked past my own pain enough to realize that perhaps Gretchen had ached, too. The squeaky wheel got the grease; everyone knew that. Well, I hadn't just squeaked—I'd been laden with trophies and accolades until the power line accident had left me literally sparking. Where had that left Gretchen? Perhaps feeling as if she didn't matter as much, which wasn't true at all.

We needed to have a long, long talk, but now wasn't the time. The irony that her needs once again had to wait because mine took priority wasn't lost on me. *Soon*, I promised silently. We'd talk right after everyone's lives weren't in danger.

The kettle began to make a hissing sound. Leotie shut off the flame and poured the hot water into one of those teapot-leaf-strainer combo things. "The leaves need to steep," she told Gretchen, as if that was the most important topic of the day.

"What Cherokee clan are you from?" I said, not giving up. "And did Ashael warn you that we'd be coming? No more small talk, Leotie. You promised us answers if we met your terms."

She turned those sharp black eyes on me. "Answers. Is that what you're really here for?"

"Yes," I repeated, impatience making my voice hard.

"For what purpose?" she asked in an equally hard tone. Her gaze raked over me, as if measuring my worth and finding it lacking. "This is your first visit to your mother's people, yet you didn't truly come to learn. You only came to take. As I said, you are much more your father's child than your mother's."

Anger almost blinded me to it, but even as I bristled, I recognized the other flash of emotion in her eyes. Why would she look at me as if I'd somehow *personally* let her down . . . ?

The truth hit me. "What should I call you, Leotie? My ten-times great grandmother? Or my ten-times great-aunt?"

Gretchen gasped, but a small smile touched Leotie's mouth. "How did you figure it out?"

"Easy," I said with a short laugh. "Only family can be *that* disappointed in someone, let alone someone they've just met."

She let out a gravelly chuckle. "I suppose that's true."

Despite her being centuries up the line in my family tree, I found myself searching Leotie's face for traces of my mother's features. No surprise, I didn't find any. She didn't look like my aunt Brenda, either. Still, she was family. I could feel the truth of that in my bones.

Gretchen didn't settle for merely looking at Leotie. She got off the couch and went over to her, touching Leotie's face as if trying to see her with her hands. Leotie stood immobile, letting Gretchen pet her. Only her dark eyes moved as she stared at me.

I stared back and found that another of Vlad's traits had rubbed off on me: a near-paranoid suspicion of everyone. Leotie might say she was family and I might have an inner conviction that agreed with her, but none of those things was proof.

"You must have pictures," I said, smiling as if driven by curiosity rather than suspicion. "I'd love to see them. We have so few of Mom and Aunt Brenda when they were little."

Leotie snorted. "You're a terrible liar. I hope it means that you don't do it often. Yes, I have proof that we're family. Here."

She pulled out an old-looking box from beneath the room's only display case and flipped back the lid. At once, my school picture from the eighth grade stared back at me.

Gretchen grabbed the box and began digging through the photos. Her school pictures were there, too. All of ours were, going all the way back to kindergarten. Then Gretchen pulled out more photos that couldn't have been copied from yearbooks or school records. There were endless pictures of the two of us at birthdays, holidays, or family events, and ones of my mother beaming as she held her hands over her very pregnant belly.

Then there were photos of my mom's wedding to my dad, of my aunt Brenda at various stages of her life, and even photos of my mom and Aunt Brenda as teenagers and also as little girls playing in front of a newer version of this house.

There were other photos, too, including a duplicate of the only picture I'd seen of my grandparents along with other photos of them that I hadn't seen. Then there were older ones of people who might have been farther up in my family's line, but I didn't recognize them. The pictures continued, until looking at the backgrounds and clothing styles was like traveling back in time. Finally, at the very bottom of the box, Gretchen pulled out a faded daguerreotype photo of Leotie as she appeared now, standing with several Native American men and women. They were dressed in full tribal clothing, and their expressions were very grim.

Leotie glanced at it and a shadow crossed her face. "That was taken after most of my people were forced to go to the reservation out West. I was among those who stayed and hid. Many who stayed died, but so did many on the Trail."

I shuddered. The infamous Trail of Tears was where thousands of my Cherokee ancestors had died from starvation, exposure, and disease when they were forcibly removed from their lands. The history behind that photograph staggered me. I was torn between wanting to cry for those long-dead people and wanting to ask Leotie a thousand questions about them. Yet now wasn't the time. I had to stay focused. Those people were gone, but there were still other living people I could possibly save.

"All of our pictures stopped around the same time that Mom died," I noted instead. "Why didn't Aunt Brenda send more?"

"Because she didn't know I was still alive. Your mother didn't tell her what I was, or the truth about your real heritage." Leotie cast a meaningful glance between me and Gretchen. "Your mother believed that the less Brenda knew, the more she could protect her."

I looked away. Mom had been the oldest, too. Were my many omissions of truth with Gretchen just another case of history repeating itself?

"In any case, I'm the one who sent them away," Leotie went on. "It was too dangerous for them to stay, but your mother promised to send any children she would have back to me to learn about their true heritage, once they came of age."

My voice thickened from emotion. "She died before she had the chance to keep her promise."

"Why was it too dangerous?" Gretchen asked.

Leotie gestured toward her walker. "With props, assuming new identities, and altering my appearance, I've managed to hide my vampire nature for the past eight centuries. Very few among our tribe know what I am. Still, every so often, I run into another vampire from the outside world." She shrugged. "It usually amounts to nothing, but someone must have recognized me from the ancient days and talked. Thirty years ago, the female Law Guardian came to investigate these claims. I sent her away with lies, but afterward, I knew I had to get your mother and Brenda out of here. These lands are small, but the white world is so large, they could disappear into it. And they did. I didn't even know how to find you after your mother died and your father moved you away."

She had dropped big hints, but Leotie still hadn't confirmed what clan she was from, and I wasn't about to spill my secrets until she did. Leotie might be family, but that didn't make her trustworthy. Mircea was proof of that.

"Why would a visit from a Law Guardian frighten you enough to send Mom and Aunt Brenda away?" I asked her point-blank. "Being an old vampire is nothing interesting to them."

She gave me one of those half-approving, half-annoyed looks again. "No, but being a true-blood Ani-kutani witch *would* interest them, as the murder of my entire clan attests."

"And boom goes the dynamite," Gretchen said sardonically.

Chapter 23

I closed my eyes. The demon had been right; I *was* an Ani-kutani descendant and also a trueborn witch. What if he was also right and the possible key to breaking Mircea's spell lay in the legacy magic that had been passed along to me?

"What about the teenager who lives here, Lisa?" I asked abruptly. "She called you Grandma. If she's your family, too—"

"She isn't," Leotie said. "She calls me Grandma out of respect because I took her and her mother in when their house burned down a few years ago. But you and Gretchen are my only true descendants."

Then we didn't have any other living relatives. I'd thought not, but part of me had hoped. That brought up another question.

"You're our ancient ancestor and a trueborn Ani-kutani witch. But the legacy magic ended up being passed down to me. That means you would've had to give it up a long time ago. Why did you, if the power it contains is supposed to be legendary?"

She smiled a bit grimly. "For the same reason your mother did. Back when I was human, my child was dying from fear-of-water sickness, which you now call rabies. The only way I could save her was to transfer my legacy magic to her. That same night, my vampire lover changed me into a blood drinker."

"Why then?" Gretchen asked with her usual bluntness.

Leotie blinked. "To bring me back from death, of course."

The demon hadn't mentioned this part. "What do you mean?"

"You two truly know nothing," Leotie muttered. "When you receive legacy magic, it merges into every part of you and instantly transforms into whatever you need most. When I received it as a young human, I most needed the ability to hide from those slaughtering my entire clan. Therefore, the legacy magic gave me the ability to transform into whatever I wanted to look like. Magic that knows what you need and instantly adapts to be that very thing is the most potent magic there is."

Leotie paused as if letting that sink in. When her dark eyes seemed to become a richer shade of black, I knew we were getting to the catch. With great power, there was always a catch.

I wasn't wrong.

"Yet pulling that magic out to transfer it to someone else rips you apart in the same all-encompassing way that it first binds with you," she said. "It takes everything with it, even magic that you were born with. No one who has transferred it to another person has survived. That's the main reason it is called legacy magic. When you pass it on, you die."

I didn't say anything for several moments. My mind was too busy running through different scenarios.

Gretchen was silent, too. Then she said, "But *you're* still here."

Leotie lifted a shoulder. "My lover cheated the death price by bringing me back as a vampire after I died."

Just like I had cheated death by drinking vampire blood all those times before I became a vampire myself. Then, I'd nearly hacked my own head off in response to Mircea's spell. Wait . . .

"You said legacy magic instantly transforms into whatever you need the most. Yes, it saved me by transforming the power line voltage into a part of me back when I was thirteen, but I've almost been killed dozens of times since then and it didn't do shit to help."

Leotie's brow arched. "Power that *always* transforms into whatever you need isn't magic; that's mythology. Legacy magic morphs into what you most need at the time of your infusion. That's all you get, but that initial transformation contains more power than can be learned by centuries of studying spells."

Of course there had to be another catch. It would be too easy if legacy magic protected its host against every threat, every time. Then Mircea's suicide-inducing spell would've bounced right off me instead of merging and growing until he and I were bound together tighter than twins . . .

"Holy shit!" I burst out. Then I began to pace, feverishly trying to work out the details in my mind.

"Transferring legacy magic to another person strips all the magic out of you, even right down to any magic you were born with. So wouldn't transferring it to another person also strip any spell currently cast on you, too?"

"Yes," Leotie said, her puzzled voice drowned out from my instant whoop.

"Screw Ashael, we've got our solution right here!"

"Who is this Ashael you keep mentioning?" Leotie asked, then both of us ducked as her front door was suddenly kicked in with such force, it flew across the room.

Maximus stormed inside, shoving Gretchen and me behind him. At the same instant, Marty and Ian smashed through the windows. All three vampires were about to attack Leotie when my frantic cries of "Stand down!" finally registered to them.

"What are you doing?" I said, aghast.

"You screamed," Maximus replied, accompanied by a grunt of agreement from Marty.

"I made a *happy* noise," I said, embarrassed and yet also touched. "Leotie's information is a dream come true."

Leotie looked at the broken glass everywhere and her front door now lying next to her coffee table. "You owe me two new windows and a door," she said to the guys. Then she glanced at a crushed metal pile near Maximus's feet. "And a new walker."

"Wait, you shape-shifted into an old woman," Gretchen said, gesturing at the ruined walker. "How could you do that if giving away your legacy magic took all your other magic out of you?"

Leotie's mouth curled downward. "That wasn't my former shape-shifting ability; it was glamour. Such a painstaking process by comparison, but learning a spell doesn't take inborn magic. It only takes basic intelligence."

"See, guys, when Leotie transferred her legacy magic to her daughter, it stripped out all the other magic in her. *All of it*," I repeated, just in case they didn't get the implications.

Both of Ian's brows went up. "Seems Ashael made a very bad decision telling you to verify your heritage."

"Who is this Ashael?" Leotie asked again, more sharply this time.

I waved. "A demon that's going to be kicking himself for being too greedy, but forget him. He couldn't know that one of my ancient Ani-kutani ancestors was still alive. You said yourself that you carefully covered your tracks." Then, because this was too important to be left to assumption, I asked Leotie outright, "If I gave the legacy magic to someone else, would a hex that's on me transfer over to that other person, too?"

Gretchen gasped. Okay, I hadn't told her about that, but in my defense, today was the first time I'd seen her in months.

Leotie gave me one of her shrewd, probing looks. "How deeply is this spell bound to you?"

"Flesh to flesh and blood to blood," I replied. "If I get cut, the person on the other end of this spell has the same injury and vice versa, right down to if he dies, I die, too."

"What the fuck?" Gretchen breathed.

Leotie whistled through her teeth. "That's not a regular spell. Binding that magic to a vampire is necromancy."

"So I've been told," I said impatiently. "Well? If I give the legacy to someone else, would that spell transfer, too?"

"Without a doubt," Leotie said, and I almost cried from joy.

"I need to call Vlad," Maximus said, spinning around. "There's no signal here, but there is back at the hotel."

It was all I could do to keep from jumping up and down like a kid on Christmas morning. "Yes, call him and tell him not to touch Samir. All we need to get this spell off me is to find some nasty schmuck to transfer this legacy to!"

This world sadly didn't lack for murderers, child rapists, or other horrible people. Once I'd transferred the legacy magic, we would put that person out of their misery. It would mean the end of the magic legacy in my family, but oh well—

"You can't transfer it to just anyone," Leotie said, slashing through my happy inner narrative. "It can only be transferred to a close matrilineal blood relative."

I frowned. "What's that?"

"Matrilineal means a direct descendant of your mother's bloodline," Gretchen supplied.

My joy deflated like a popped balloon. "But Leotie just confirmed that we have no other living family on our mother's side." And at over eight hundred years old, Leotie was several centuries removed from being a "close" relation to my mother's direct bloodline.

Gretchen's expression changed. Suddenly, I had her attention in a way I'd never had it before. "Yeah, so the only person you can transfer the magic legacy to is me."

She wanted it, I realized in shock. "Did you miss the part about the deadly hex that came along with it?"

"I didn't miss it," Gretchen said, shrugging as if we weren't talking about life or death. "But I'll take the risk."

Of course she would, but as usual, Gretchen wasn't thinking things through. Well, I knew what she refused to admit: that she wouldn't live long enough to find out what cool magic ability the legacy would give her. I couldn't sign my sister's death warrant that way. Not even if it meant losing my best chance at freeing myself.

I drew in a deep breath. Then I looked at Maximus, Ian, and Marty. "You will not mention this to Vlad. I'll decide when and if and what he knows. If one of you goes behind my back and tells him, I will cut your heart out."

"Leila!" Gretchen snapped. "You *don't* get to make up their minds or mine about this!"

"This time I do," I said, and unleashed the light in my gaze. "You remember nothing of this conversation," I told Gretchen, my voice vibrating from vampire power. "You only know that Leotie is our distant relative and we are direct descendants of the Anikutani line. That is all."

A glazed look replaced Gretchen's angry expression, and I didn't miss how Leotie looked at me with a sort of pity. Yes, I might once again be following in my mother's footsteps by hiding things from my little sister for her own protection, but I didn't care. I also didn't care if this made me a total hypocrite for ever saying that I didn't like to mind-manipulate people. Gretchen wouldn't be able to keep her mouth shut otherwise, and transferring the legacy power to her would kill her as surely as if I shot her in the head. She was human; she wouldn't survive a gutting like Mircea's captors' had just given me, and Gretchen *really* wouldn't survive what would happen when those same captors realized that Vlad wouldn't do their bidding.

And he wouldn't. I loved Vlad, but I knew him. If only Gretchen's life hung in the balance, he wouldn't allow himself to be blackmailed by Mircea's captors.

Vlad would console me and he'd swear to avenge Gretchen, yet he would also let her die. And as much as I loved Vlad, I wouldn't sacrifice my sister's life for mine, even if my loss would be devastating to him.

Still, the ramifications of the enormous secret I'd be hiding from Vlad pierced me like silver in the heart. He'd take it as the most serious betrayal, and everyone knew that Vlad wasn't big on forgiving betrayal. With a muttered comment that I needed a few minutes alone, I ran out of the house. When I was far enough away that they couldn't hear me even with vampire senses, I screamed out my frustration at the gray December sky.

I now had more answers than I'd ever dreamed of, but part of me wished I'd never come here. Before, I had been tormented by my helplessness. Now, I was even more tormented by my choices. If I told Vlad this, he would do everything in his power to make me transfer the curse to Gretchen, yet if I did, it might end up killing her. But how could I *not* tell him?

It might not be today, but soon, I would have to pick between endless lies in order to protect my sister's life, or being a participant in Vlad's emotional torture. Yes, Vlad was strong, and he'd survived things that would have broken ninety-nine-point-nine percent of other people, but what if Mircea's captors demanded something that would scar him forever? How could I add a crushing weight to the awful burdens he already carried?

The brutal truth was, I didn't know if I could live with myself in either scenario.

Yet I couldn't stay here screaming at the sky. I'd promised never again to let any emotional turmoil defeat me, however horrible my circumstances. This had knocked me down worse than anything had before it, but I had to find a way to push past my feelings and go on. Maybe things weren't as bleak as they looked. Maybe I wouldn't have to choose between my sister's life and Vlad's soul. Another solution *had* to present itself, if I fought hard enough to find one.

Yeah, my inner voice sneered. *And maybe, you'll meet a leprechaun who'll lead you to a pot of gold, too!*

My fists clenched. Goddamn my hated internal voice, and goddamn Mircea. If not for him, none of this would be happening. In sudden, explosive rage, I spun around and punched the nearest tree. My bones shattered from the force of the blow, yet the instant, searing pain was oddly comforting. For those few brief seconds before I healed, it distracted me from the far worse pain inside.

I took both my gloves off and punched another tree. Then another one and another, until blood flowed freely from both my hands. How I wished these trees were Mircea. If he were here right now, I'd tear into him so much worse—

What are you doing, Leila? Stop it!

As if I'd summoned him, Mircea's roar echoed through my mind. Of course. He'd feel everything I was doing as if it were happening to him. Now I *really* enjoyed the pain.

Where are you, you miserable prick? I roared back at him. *This is all your fault!*

No, it's your *fault for not dying like you were supposed to!* was his instant reply. *Now, stop smashing your hands!*

What, like this? I snarled, and whacked the nearest tree hard enough to send my hand all the way through it.

Bitch! rang through my mind so loud, I almost

turned around to see if he was behind me. Our connection was somehow much clearer this time. And stronger, like if I concentrated really hard, I might be able to see him . . .

Stop it, Mircea said, the anger abruptly gone from his tone. *You can't find me this way, Leila.*

Then why do you suddenly sound concerned? I thought back, stunned to realize that Mircea no longer felt like an unwelcome, invisible shadow in my mind. Somehow, he now felt like a thread, and I grabbed at that thread with both hands and pulled.

Stop it or I'll leave! he thundered at me.

No, you won't, I said, a fierce exaltation filling me as I still felt him on the other end of our connection. In fact, he was now even closer, as if a few more hard tugs on that string could bring him into focus. Mircea cursed me and continued to threaten to leave, but I knew him. If he really could leave, he would. That meant that things weren't just a little different with our connection this time. Everything was different, and though it seemed impossible, there could only be one reason why.

Mircea hadn't been the one to contact me. Somehow, someway, I'd finally managed to link to *him*.

Chapter 24

I've got you, I've got you, I chanted in glee as I continued to pull on the thread connecting us. A haze began to fill my vision, slowly blocking out all the bare trees around me. I knew what that was, and excitement flared as that haze formed into the unmistakable look of another place.

The sky changed into a thick slab where no light penetrated while the trees around me were replaced by tall, jagged rocks. Faint illumination came from torches somewhere out of my line of sight, but it showed that most of the rocks looked like naturally formed pillars. Mircea was in the middle of a tight circle of those pillars, and the glow from his eyes cut through the darkness like twin emerald laser beams.

"I've got you!" I crowed out loud this time. I was so caught up in my triumph; it took several moments before I noticed that someone was hitting me on the leg. Hard.

"Leila, come on, it might already be too late!"

Marty. He sounded upset, but he didn't know I'd finally linked to Mircea after countless failed attempts. I wasn't dropping this connection. Who knew if I could get it back?

"Go away, Marty," I muttered.

Even splitting my attention for a few seconds caused those rocks to blur and form back into the trees of my actual surroundings. Dammit! I refocused my attention, cursing again as Marty pulled on me hard enough to knock me off balance.

"For fuck's sake, Leila, you gotta come with me *now!*"

Marty never used the F word, so something must be seriously wrong. Concern tore the thread linking me to Mircea, and I fell back into the present. Marty seemed nearly hysterical as he continued to try and drag me along with him.

I shook him off. "What's going on?"

"Maximus is killing Gretchen!" was his stunning reply.

I didn't ask any of the shocked questions that instantly sprang to mind. Instead, I ran as fast as I could back to Leotie's house, outpacing Marty with my much longer legs. I burst through the open doorway in time to see Maximus kneeling on the floor with Gretchen draped across his lap.

Her eyes were closed, her head was back, and blood trailed from both sides of her mouth. More blood splattered her shirt as well as Maximus's clothes, and from the smell of it, it wasn't just Gretchen's blood. It was Maximus's, too, and for some incomprehensible reason, Leotie and Ian stood like silent sentries behind them, doing nothing about the sight that almost knocked me to my knees from grief-filled rage.

"What. The. Fuck?" I screamed.

Electricity shot from my right hand to whip around like a snake. The only reason I didn't start lashing Maximus into pieces was because he was still holding my sister. A wrecking ball hit me when I strained my ears and still couldn't hear her heartbeat. Oh God, oh God, she *was* dead. More electricity began to shoot out of me, until I was vaguely aware that my entire body was starting to glow from an overload of voltage.

"Power down, Leila," Maximus said in a steady voice. "She's not dead."

I gestured at Gretchen, and without intending it to, my whip tore a five-foot trench in the floor.

"Then why isn't her *heart beating*, you murderer!"

"She's not dead," Maximus said again, shifting Gretchen in his arms. "She's just waiting to rise."

I looked at the blood around Gretchen's mouth with new understanding. Maximus hadn't killed her the permanent way; he had changed Gretchen into a vampire. Even amidst my relief that she wasn't lost to me forever, I was still so furious that crackling noises started to come from the nearby light sockets. Then thin lines of electricity began poking out of them.

"Leila," Ian said irritably, "if you start another electrical fire, you won't like the next spell I throw on you."

I found myself breathing in an effort to force my dangerous rage back. No matter what I was feeling—which amounted to *kill Maximus, kill him!*—I could not go all voltage-crazy again.

"I tried to stop him," Marty said, finally making it to the cabin. "He wouldn't listen, and neither would the rest of them."

Oh? My gaze landed on Leotie and Ian as I mentally added them to my hit list. Then I continued my inner struggle not to drain this place of all its voltage so I could give full vent to my wrath. Was this how Vlad felt when he was in a near-combustible rage? If so, then he showed a *lot* of self-control by not having a higher body count than he already did.

Maximus wiped the blood from Gretchen's mouth and set her down. She slumped onto the floor as if boneless. Seeing it once again struck me like a physical blow. Nothing looked as limp as a dead body, and right now, that's what Gretchen was.

My gaze landed on Maximus as if I could destroy him with a look. "What right did you have to do this?"

"The right Gretchen gave me," he replied. "As she said, you keep deciding what she wants for her, but Gretchen's old enough to do that for herself. So when you stormed out and Gretchen asked me to turn her into a vampire, I did."

I let out a noise that was more snarl than scoff. "She asks you one impulsive question, and you go ahead and change her very *species*? Bullshit. You didn't do this for her. You can barely stand Gretchen. You did it for Vlad. You changed her because you're *prepping* her for the hex you want me to transfer to her!"

Maximus stepped over Gretchen and moved within striking distance of my whip, which glowed a brighter shade of white.

"I did it for *both* of them," he snapped. "Yeah, Gretchen can be a pain in the ass, but that's mostly when she's around you. I realized that a couple months ago when Vlad assigned me to her as extra protection. You won't stop treating her like a child, so that's what she acts like with you. The rest of the time, she's a smart, funny, mostly levelheaded young woman. And Gretchen asked me to change her over many times before today. I kept refusing and warning her of the consequences, but she was undeterred. Humans are easy to kill compared to vampires, so Gretchen knew she would have better odds at surviving all of this if she was a vampire instead of a human. With what we're up against now, I finally agreed."

"Liar!" My whip snapped toward Maximus and Ian grabbed my wrist to yank it back. Then he let out a deafening yowl.

"Bloody fucking hell, that fried me right down to my frank and beans!"

I wasn't surprised. Touching me anywhere near my right hand when my power was up was very dangerous, as the burns breaking out all over Ian attested. Only Vlad could do that unscathed, yet Ian continued to grip my wrist despite his increasing burns.

"Let go, I'm not going to kill Maximus," I said shortly.

"Really?" Ian eyed my whip, which crackled and curled with sizzling energy. "Tell that to your sparking little friend."

"I'm not going to kill him," I repeated, and Ian finally let go. Yes, moments ago, I would've sliced Maximus's arm or leg off, but the surge of rage that had made me want to dismember him had drained away. Now I felt exhausted, as if losing that rabid anger caused all my other strength to abandon me, too.

My sister was in the in-between state of death and vampiric rebirth. Nothing I did to Maximus would change that, and now we had another problem on top of the cluster fuck that was today. In the next few to several hours, Gretchen would rise. In her newborn-vampire, blood-crazed state, she'd kill anyone with a pulse, be it man, woman, or child. We had to get her as far away from humans as possible, and we also had to have blood bags available to satiate her hunger. Lots and lots of blood bags.

Later, I'd give Maximus a more thorough piece of my mind over what he'd done and why, but first things first. "Do any of you know if there's a vampire safe house near here?"

"Vlad has a place in Raleigh," Maximus stated.

Ian glanced at Gretchen's prone form. "Cutting it close. Raleigh's five hours away in good traffic. I know a safe house that's less than three hours from here, and it's very remote."

"You know it, but it's not yours?" I liked the closer distance, but Ian hadn't gotten a warm welcome from anywhere he'd been and we couldn't risk getting kicked out or worse.

He flashed me a smile, guessing the reason behind my question. "It's empty. A mate of mine went through a dreadfully boring phase where he wanted to be all alone with his wife. Now they're overseas and I have a key to their mountain hideout."

That sounded perfect, but . . . "You're sure they're not there?"

He grunted with grim amusement. "Bet your life on it."

"I want to go with you," Leotie said, speaking for the first time since I'd come back.

I turned to her with the word *no* on my lips. I might be putting my feelings aside for the momentary greater good, but I was still very upset with all of them. Maximus had deliberately changed Gretchen when I wasn't there to stop him, and Leotie, like Ian, had done nothing to dissuade him. Only Marty had come after me in a vain attempt to stop it.

But if I were focusing on the greater good . . . "Sure," I said, glad that I didn't sound surly. "I want to talk more about our ancestors, anyway."

I was going to attempt linking to Mircea as soon as Gretchen was safely secured and I had some uninterrupted time, but if that didn't work, Leotie was almost a thousand years old and she knew more about magic than anyone I'd met before her.

Maybe, just maybe, she also knew where we could find some necromancers.

Chapter 25

Under other circumstances, I would have loved the cabin Ian brought us to. It was on top of a small mountain, and in addition to its sweeping, long-range views, it also had a helicopter pad and hangar. How convenient, if we had one of those. The log cabin blended in beautifully with its wooded surroundings, and the floor-to-ceiling windows showed off the majesty of the Blue Ridge Mountains beyond. It also had the exact number of bedrooms we needed so that no one had to double up. More importantly, it had a basement. A special one.

Vlad had taught me the advantage of building a home on top of a rock foundation. Nothing beat tons and tons of solid stone if you needed to vampire-proof a place. This house lacked the huge, underground dungeon that Vlad's castle had, but it did have a small, underground room surrounded by enough solid rock to secure even a bloodthirsty new vampire.

That's where Maximus and I put Gretchen. Maximus set her down on the single pallet the narrow room contained. I didn't speak as he then secured Gretchen's wrists and ankles to the shackles the room also came equipped with. I hated seeing Gretchen chained like an animal, yet it was the safest choice.

Ian had left to round up blood bags since he knew the area and we didn't. I fervently hoped that he got back before Gretchen rose. I remembered all too well the agonizing, all-consuming hunger I'd woken up with as a brand-new vampire, and I'd only had to wait seconds before my first liquid meal. If Gretchen had to wait hours before hers . . . well, we'd need to have her chained. Otherwise, she'd mindlessly try to bash her way out of this chamber no matter if she broke every bone in her body.

When Maximus was finished, he sat down on the floor and handed me the keys to both the underground room and Gretchen's shackles. "You need to lock me in here with her, Leila."

"I'm staying," I said at once.

He gave me a jaded look. "Gretchen will be worse than rabid when she wakes and these chains aren't as strong as I'd prefer."

"She's my sister," I said quietly. "I want to be here for her."

He grunted. "I get that, but you wouldn't be helping. When Gretchen goes into a feeding frenzy, I can't worry about restraining her *and* protecting you. Besides, you must be exhausted. You should catch a few hours of rest while you can."

I wanted to argue more, but Maximus was only reminding me of what I already knew. Still, I couldn't shake the feeling that I was abandoning my sister, even if Maximus was right. I would only be in the way when Gretchen went rabid, and she would. If she escaped her chains, Maximus had the brute strength to handle her without harming her or getting harmed himself. My methods of self-defense could kill her, and I'd had two near-blowups with my voltage today already. No point in tempting a third.

"Fine," was all I said. "Text me if you need anything, and let me know when she wakes up."

I leaned down and kissed my sister's forehead. Her flesh was now cooler than mine and she no longer gave off the low energy field all humans had. For all intents and purposes, she was dead, and Maximus had done this to her. All at once, I understood my father's anger at Vlad for changing me. It might be irrational because both Gretchen and I had asked for this, yet the urge to punish the person who'd killed—even temporarily—someone you loved was as strong as it was unreasonable.

Once back upstairs, I grabbed my suitcase and went looking for a bedroom that hadn't already been claimed. As it turned out, they'd left me the master suite on the top floor, and I eyed the comfy-looking bed almost lustfully.

I might have built up my fortitude so that dawn no longer knocked me unconscious, but I was still exhausted. Daylight made all of our kind tired. That's how the rumor that vampires couldn't go out in the sun got started. My being a mere half a year undead only made the weariness that much worse.

"I'm taking a nap," I called down to Marty and Leotie, then closed the bedroom door. But instead of crawling into the king-sized bed like I wanted to, I sat on the floor in front of it. I had a little time where

I wouldn't be interrupted, so I'd try reconnecting to Mircea.

I was about to close my eyes to increase my concentration when a photo on the nearby nightstand caught my eye. It showed a beautiful redhead with her arms around an equally attractive man. They both looked so happy and perfect, the picture could have come with the frame, but I recognized them. For starters, they were at my wedding. More importantly, the redhead had helped Vlad bust me out of Szilagyi's prison a few months ago.

Could Bones and Cat be the owners of this house? I looked around, spying another photo of them on the opposite nightstand. Must be. How ironic that they were the friends Ian had referred to. He truly ran in varied circles.

Then I pushed that out of my mind and refocused on Mircea. I didn't have anything of his to touch while I tried linking to him, but I hadn't needed his essence imprint when I'd reached him earlier. Maybe the spell that bound me to Mircea was enough of a link. It made sense; I didn't need Vlad's essence imprint to reach him psychically, either. My deepest tie to Vlad came from the blood he'd given me to raise me as a vampire.

If the same were true with the spell binding me to Mircea, all I had to do to reach him was concentrate on him personally. I cast my mind back to the brief moments I'd spent with Mircea, trying to summon up a picture of him in my mind.

He didn't look like the most dangerous sorcerer you'd ever meet. Mircea might even have been a couple years younger than Gretchen when he was changed. He also had a cockiness that probably came from lots and lots of women fawning over him. Mircea's biological father had been called Radu the Handsome, and according to Vlad, Mircea was the spitting image of him. Mircea's too-pretty face was set off by inky black curls and copper-colored eyes that would have been identical to Vlad's, if their irises also had emerald rings around them.

But they didn't, and that was the least of their dissimilarities. Sure, both Vlad and Mircea could be brutal and mercurial, but Vlad always had a good reason for his actions. Mircea was cruel for cruelty's sake. I'd spent less than an hour in his presence, yet it had been enough to show me that there was something permanently broken inside him. Despite centuries of war, death, power struggles, betrayals, and loss, Vlad had managed to keep both his heart and soul intact—

And I obviously missed him since I was now thinking more about him than Mircea. I gritted my teeth and tried again, forcing everyone else from my mind. *Come on, Mircea. I know you're out there. Let me find you.*

I sat that way until Ian came back with the blood bags over an hour later. Then I went downstairs and opened the stone cell to hand them off to Maximus. Gretchen still hadn't woken up, thank God, so after giving Maximus the bags, I sealed them back in. Ian left again, saying he had to go to another hospital farther away to get more blood. That was fine with me because I wanted to get back to my attempts to reach Mircea. It had taken me a long time to reach Vlad only using our inner tie, but I'd done it. I'd do it again with Mircea, now that I knew I could.

I was deep into my second attempt when my cell phone rang. My eyes snapped open, and I was surprised to see it was now completely dark outside. I'd been concentrating so hard that hours must have slipped by. This was probably Maximus calling to say that Gretchen had risen. But when I put my current-repelling glove back on my right hand to answer my cell, I didn't see Maximus's name over the number on the screen. It was Vlad's.

"Um, hi." The inane greeting was ridiculous, but what else could I say? I sure as hell couldn't ask how his day had gone.

"The hotel e-mailed," he said, his flat, impassive tone telling me nothing of what he was feeling. "All of you checked out this morning instead of tomorrow. Why?"

I didn't want to talk about our earlier-than-anticipated checkout, and I couldn't imagine that he really did, either. All I wanted to do was ask about Samir, but I didn't. If Vlad was finally returning my calls, then he'd already killed him. Period. My throat tightened and I fought to keep the evidence of that from showing in my voice. I was so angry at him for everything he'd done to thwart me from trying to save Samir, and yet I didn't want him to hear my burgeoning tears. He had to be in torment, too, even if he did sound rigidly cold.

"There was too much damage to the room to stay" was what I said, glad there were no cracks or wavers in my voice.

"Ah."

Neither of us said anything after that. Instead, the silence filled with everything we couldn't bring ourselves to say. Once, I heard him take in a breath as if about to speak, but then there was only more silence.

"I'm furious with you," I finally said when the building tension became unbearable. "When this is over, we're going to have a huge fight about your beyond unacceptable high-handedness, but even as I tear you a new one over killing Samir without exhausting all our other options, let alone having me physically restrained, cut off financially, and put on a no-fly list, for crying out loud . . ." I drew in a deep breath to get it all out, "I'm still no less in love with you, and we're going to get through this one way or the other. No matter what."

A short, harsh sound escaped him. I wished I could see him or be tied into his feelings to know what emotion had caused it.

"You madden me," he said, which was something I'd heard before and knew he didn't mean as a compliment. "Yet I will never love anyone as much as I love you, and you're right. We will get through this, no matter what it takes."

Now I was the one who let out a wordless noise as a sigh slipped from me. Our current problems still seemed insurmountable and we had more coming soon, yet the most important thing hadn't changed. No matter what our adversaries threw at us, they were helpless when it came to ruining what Vlad and I felt for each other. As for the rest, it could be fought over, cried over, decided on and/or faced down later. Right now, even across a thousand miles, we were together, and the silence between us was soothing instead of stifling this time. We'd already said what had mattered most.

"If you're not at the hotel, where are you?" he asked after several long moments.

"At Cat and Bones's cabin in the Blue Ridge Mountains. They're away somewhere and Ian had a key—"

"Is this the cabin in Valle Crucis?" he interrupted me, his tone turning brisk again.

"You know it?" I asked, taken aback.

"I've been there," was his even more surprising reply. "I'll see you in ten hours."

Then he hung up without saying good-bye, I love you, or anything else. I stared at the phone for a moment, feeling a hard little smile stretch my lips. Once again, Vlad had changed from loving husband back into medieval conqueror faster than I could blink. I'd add fixing that to my now very long to-do list.

Then I looked at the phone and debated calling him back. There were so many things I still had to tell him, like how Gretchen was now a vampire, or that Leotie, my long-lost ancestor, was here with us, or that I'd finally managed to connect to Mircea, or a thousand other things I'd discovered since I last saw him. Instead, I set the phone back on the nightstand.

Maybe Vlad needed all ten of those hours to help him recover from killing Samir. I probably needed them, too, for a lot of reasons, the biggest of those being the decision that had me feeling as if I were being torn right down the middle. How could I tell Vlad about the legacy transfer, knowing he'd try to make me give it to Gretchen to secure my own safety? Yet how could I continue to let Vlad kill people doing Mircea's captors' bidding because he believed that was his only option? It wasn't, yet at the same time, my sister's life wasn't *optional*.

My best way around this terrible dilemma was to link to Mircea and find where the hell he was, yet for some reason, I hadn't been able to after more hours of trying. Frustration had me clenching my fists. Since I hadn't put my left glove back on, my fingernails stabbed right through my palm from the force I used. Blood began dripping onto the carpet and I let out a yelp as I frantically dabbed it with my shirt. Great, now I was trashing another room. Guess I'd have to add a new carpet to the sky-high list of things Mircea had cost me, either directly through his actions or indirectly by making me so damn mad—

I fell forward into a cave as if a hole had opened up in front of me.

Chapter 26

 The bedroom disappeared and darkness surrounded me, broken only by faint glimmers of faraway torches. Mircea was here, still in that same tight circle of stones. It didn't look comfortable. Maybe he couldn't escape the cluster of rocks that surrounded him like tall obelisks.

Is this where they keep you locked up? I thought at Mircea, and his head jerked up as if I'd yanked it with a string.

Leila. My name was a sneer. *So, you finally figured out the real way to connect to me. Thought you'd never put the obvious together, although it made me laugh to imagine you chasing me through essence links that would only boomerang back to you.*

Is that why I couldn't reach him before? Because the link binding us together kept rerouting me back to my own location? If so, how had I done it this time? Not that I was about to ask.

I might be new at this, but I'm getting better every day, I replied, glad that my bluff sounded confident.

Mircea held up his left hand, where bloody half moons that mirrored the injury in my own palm were already starting to heal. *I'm surprised you were able to form a connection from such a weak conduit. Couldn't stand to harm yourself more, hmm?*

Conduit? What . . . ?

I would've smacked myself in the head if there wasn't a chance that Mircea would feel it, too. How many times had I told people that the spell linking me and Mircea was bound to both our flesh and blood? So *flesh and blood* were the links I needed. That's why I'd been able to reach him earlier when I smashed my hands to bleeding pulps while thinking about Mircea. Seems I'd done it again after accidentally stabbing myself with my nails.

Yeah, well, I didn't feel like doing one of your over-the-top slices, I replied, once again pretending that I'd known all this beforehand.

You take a big risk contacting me, Mircea said, scowling at me from the darkness. *Do you want them to kill us?*

Them. There was our confirmation that more than one sorcerer held Mircea captive. *Why would they care?* I asked, then answered my own question. *They don't know we can communicate telepathically this way, do they?*

Why would they? Mircea said. *No one has ever survived the initial effects of this spell before, and since you're logged into my mind, I have something to show you. You might be able to psychically relive memories through touch, but I can do so by will alone. Now, Leila, look upon who really brought us both to our current, sorry conditions.*

Mircea touched his temple, and I fell forward again, the cave around me dissolving into the black-and-white images of a past memory. I dissolved, too, and became someone else.

I danced ahead of my mother, ignoring her repeated urgings for me to slow down. Father was finally home! I couldn't wait to tell him I had learned to read and write in two languages, and I had also learned how to do courtly duties, but I hated those things. Father hated them, too, Mother had said. We were so alike. I danced again before sprinting ahead. There was Father now, climbing off his horse in the courtyard!

"Mircea," Mother yelled. "Return to me at once!"

I continued to race ahead. My older brothers were away, so this time, I would have all Father's attention for myself. Father's men gathered around him to welcome him home. They had missed him, too, but not as much as me. I burst through the crowd, tugging the back of his shirt and laughing when he turned around. "Father!" I said, throwing my arms around him.

He pushed me back. His hands were rough and scarred, but I didn't mind. One day, I would be a great warrior like he was and have rough, scarred hands, too.

"Mircea, what are you doing here?" he said. Then he straightened and looked past the crowd. "Ilona! Get your son."

"Father, wait," I said, fighting as one of Father's men began pulling me away. "I have to tell you—"

"Not now," Father said, turning away. "Ilona, take him."

"Father, wait!" I cried again.

He didn't turn around, and I was pulled backward until Mother caught up with us. She sighed as she bent down and wiped the tears from my cheeks that I hoped Father hadn't seen.

"Why won't he speak to me?" I asked, fighting a sob.

"Mircea," she said in a soft voice. "Your father is the prince, and he has many duties. He will see you later."

I turned away, ducking so my hair hid my face. "You said that last time, but then he left."

She sighed again. "There was a battle. You know this."

"There is always a battle," I cried. "He would rather be at war than spend any time with me!"

Mother tried to smooth back my hair, but I jerked away. What had I done to make him hate me so much?

I fell back into the cave with tears from Mircea's memory still streaming down my cheeks. The memory continued to cling to me, filling me with an ache that was as poignant as it was familiar. I knew how much it hurt to be rejected by your own father, and that's what Mircea had believed Vlad to be.

I can show you dozens more memories like that, Mircea said, a weary bitterness tingeing his tone. Would you like to see the one where I waited every day for a year in the hopes that Vlad would visit what he thought was my grave so I could tell him I was really alive? Yet he never came. He didn't care enough to.

Mircea wasn't trustworthy, but psychic memories didn't lie, and neither did the feelings they transmitted.

After he made me a vampire, Szilagyi told me I wasn't Vlad's real son, Mircea went on. But I spent my entire boyhood believing that I was, and I exhausted myself trying to excel at every task in the hope that Vlad would notice me. When he didn't, I blamed myself. He loved his firstborn son, so I believed his aversion to me had to be my fault.

It wasn't, and Vlad was a dick for treating you like that, I said, and meant it. But it doesn't give you an *excuse for everything you've done since then,* I continued. *For starters, you tried to murder me before we even met. You're quick to judge Vlad, but what kind of person does that make you?*

My father's son! he flung back at me. *I spent my first twenty years as Vlad Dracul's son, so I am a ruthless warmonger just as he is. Then Mihaly Szilagyi changed me and I became his son for the next five centuries, so I am on a never-ending quest for vengeance against Vlad just as he was. Finally, the blood of Radu Dracul runs through my veins, so I am insanely jealous of Vlad just as Radu was. Am I not all of my fathers' sons?* he finished, the bitterness in his voice turning to despair. *Did I ever have any hope of being anything different?*

I sighed. Yes, Mircea could have fought to be a better man since other people had been born into as much tragedy or worse. Still, the odds had indeed been against him, and while it didn't excuse what he'd done, I finally understood why he'd done it.

It was so much easier when I believed Vlad was incapable of love after he became a vampire, Mircea went on, sounding wistful now. *Szilagyi would prattle on about how he'd make Vlad pay, and I'd nod and play along, but I never helped him in any serious way. I'd mostly forgiven Vlad, you see, because how can you hate someone for not loving you when that person is too dead inside to love anyone?*

Briefly, I closed my eyes. *And then I came along,* I said.

Then you, Mircea agreed. *At first, I thought Vlad was simply fascinated by a human having your remarkable abilities. Then he went to war over you, turned you into a vampire, and married you. The*

*truth was obvious then. You know the real reason I
kept linking to you after that spell bound us together?*

To hurt me the way you were hurting? I asked
bluntly.

He let out a short laugh. *That was part of it, yes.
But even more, I wanted to find out what you had that
I didn't. Vlad loved you, a stranger, after a mere few
months, yet he never loved me despite my working
myself nearly to death for two decades.* He laughed
again, hard and humorless this time. *Nothing I did
back then made Vlad notice me, but he noticed me
when I came after you. Oh yes, he noticed me then.*

*So this whole thing is about you finally getting
Vlad's attention?* I asked in disbelief.

He shrugged. *That's an oversimplification. Still,
thoughts of me now consume Vlad in a way I'd only
dreamed of when I was a child, so even you must
agree that he had that coming.*

Why are you telling me all this? I asked, suddenly
suspicious.

We're both going to die, he said, as if it were obvious.

Out of instinct, I looked around for danger, yet saw
nothing except more rocks. *What makes you say that?*

He gave a jaded look in my general direction. *Vlad
won't carry out my jailers' demand no matter how
much he loves you. When he doesn't comply, they'll
kill me, and by extension, you.*

Mircea must know what the second demand was,
and it sounded as awful as Maximus had predicted.
What do they want him to do?

Another humorless laugh. *You don't know? Then
far be it from me to spoil the surprise.*

Look, you need to tell me where you are, I said,
my agitation growing as I thought about Vlad being

confronted with whatever this was. *Even if Vlad does do it, you and I are of no use to your captors after they get what they want.*

Oh, I agree, he said, voice as casual as if he were choosing between white wine or red. *But even if I told you where I was, you and Vlad aren't powerful enough to rescue me.*

Take a chance, I persisted, hitting him where I knew it would hurt. *You want to impress Vlad? Now's your chance. Show him you're not afraid to fight for your life despite the odds.*

His lips curled in a way that was all too familiar. *Under other circumstances, I might have liked you, Leila.*

Come on, Mircea, I said. *You're many things, but you're not a coward, so prove it. Fight to live instead of waiting to die.*

Fine, he said so suddenly that I was startled. *The good news is, all my captors know where I am. The bad news is, I don't. But I can tell you where to find some of them, and if you can keep one alive, I have every confidence that Vlad can torture the information out of him.*

Fine, I said just as quickly. I didn't trust Mircea in general, but I did trust that he didn't want to die, and we really were his best chance at surviving.

Now, I said, steeling myself for what was to come, *tell me where we can find these necromancers.*

Chapter 27

Several hours later, I was surprised to hear the unmistakable sound of a helicopter approaching the house. I exchanged a concerned glance with Marty, who'd stayed in the living room with me. Leotie and Ian had retired to their rooms a short while ago since dawn wasn't very far away, and of course, Maximus was still downstairs with Gretchen. He'd had a very busy night since she had risen in a bad, blood-crazed mood. Maximus had to be counting the seconds until dawn knocked her out.

"Does Vlad have a helicopter?" Marty asked me.

"No," I said, going to the window. Sure enough, someone's helicopter was landing on the pad near the house. "Maybe Ian was wrong and Cat and Bones aren't overseas anymore."

"They are, trust me," Ian called out from his room.

I ignored that, grabbing a coat and going outside. Marty followed me, now carrying two large silver knives.

"Put those away," I hissed. If Ian was wrong and this was Cat and Bones, they wouldn't be happy to find *armed* uninvited guests staying at their home.

"Not until I see who this is," Marty replied stubbornly.

The single pilot had a full-face helmet on, so I couldn't tell anything from that. Then the passenger door opened and Vlad jumped out. His hair blew wildly around his face from the still-churning rotors, and his long, dark trench coat flapped behind him like beating wings.

His features were so hard that they could have belonged on a statue, and he'd barricaded his emotions behind an impenetrable wall. Worse, when I met his gaze, there was none of the love he'd expressed earlier over the phone. Instead, his gaze passed over me as if I didn't merit further notice. It flicked over Marty with even more disregard, although his mouth curled when he saw the knives.

"Only two?" he asked.

Marty stiffened at the implication that he'd failed to adequately protect me. "Had I known that it was *you* touching down, I would've brought more."

I winced. The two of them had never been very fond of each other, but that hadn't been a problem before. Yet with Vlad's current mood as well as Marty's stretched nerves, a pissing contest between them now wouldn't result in anything good.

"I didn't realize you owned a helicopter," I said, trying to distract from their growing tension.

"I don't," Vlad replied, thankfully turning his attention back to me. "This is on loan from Mencheres."

I faked a laugh. "You said you'd been here before. Guess you remembered that this place had a helicopter pad. Glad you thought ahead and borrowed the chopper. Flying sure beats having to drive slow on these narrow, winding mountain roads. Come on, I'll show you our room," I said, taking Vlad's hand.

His demeanor might be icy, but it didn't surprise me that his flesh felt anything but cold. He could fool some people with this I-care-for-nothing! act, but not me. He only felt this hot when he was unleashing his incredible abilities, in the throes of passion, or really, really upset.

It also didn't surprise me when he immediately pulled away. "Later. I need to speak with Maximus first."

Oh no, he didn't. He might want to continue to wrap himself in bad attitude and fake apathy, but I wasn't going to let him. "Maximus is busy," I said. "He changed Gretchen into a vampire yesterday, and she woke up mad as hell on top of being ravenously hungry. You'll have to wait until dawn to talk to him."

Both his brows went up on hearing that Gretchen was now a vampire, then that sculpturelike hardness reclaimed his face as he looked over my shoulder. "And who is *that*?"

I turned, seeing Leotie outlined in the open door of the cabin. "My umpteenth-times-over great grand-mother. I have a lot to tell you, Vlad, so if you want to hear it in time to talk to Maximus at dawn, come with me. Besides, it's freezing out here."

It was, not that any of us were in danger of catching a cold. Still, I wanted to get him alone so we could talk about how he was really feeling. As if he knew what I intended, Vlad stared at me long enough for me to formulate several convincing arguments if he refused.

But at last, with an arrogant wave, he gestured to the helicopter behind him. "The pilot's leaving soon to return Mencheres's helicopter to him. Before he does, see to it that he has someone decent to eat, Martin."

Marty bristled at being ordered around like a servant, but I grabbed Vlad's hand and started walking toward the house. I'd apologize to Marty later for Vlad's rudeness. Right now, I had to seize my opportunity to break through his walls before he reinforced them—or built them any higher.

"Right this way, dear."

After the briefest possible introduction to Leotie, I had Vlad alone upstairs in the cabin's master suite. Granted, the walls weren't thick enough for this to be a truly private conversation, but sometimes the illusion of privacy was all that mattered. To boost that illusion, I locked the door behind us.

He gave me a sardonic look. "If I wanted to leave, a feeble lock couldn't stop me."

"No, nor can it keep anyone out who wants in, considering we're in a house full of vampires," I replied, shrugging. "Still, like a tie on the doorknob, this is a 'Do Not Disturb' sign for the rest of them."

His snort managed to be both elegant and contemptuous. "A tie on the doorknob? As if you brought me up here for sex."

I hadn't, but if that was the quickest way to break through his worrisome new walls . . . "What if I said I had?" I asked, holding his stare as I walked over to him.

His eyes were pure, burnished copper, the only green in them coming from the natural band around his irises. "Then I'd say you were a poor liar, as you always have been."

"Maybe I need to feel you that way to forget everything else for a little while," I said, challenging him by pushing his coat off his shoulders. "After all, I've had an awful day and I know yours was way worse."

"You know?" His gaze turned steely. "You think I've never killed a good man before? I've killed thousands of them."

Was he really going to act as if Samir was just another casualty in one of the countless wars he'd fought in? I wasn't buying that. I'd seen how Vlad acted when he lost someone he only cared about in general terms because that person had belonged to his line. It had looked nothing like this.

"When you thought I was in denial about Maximus raping me, you told me I couldn't keep lying to you or myself about it, or the pretense would destroy me." I held his face in my hands in much the same way he'd held mine all those months ago. "Now I'm telling that to you. Stop lying about what this is doing to you, Vlad. If you don't, that lie will grow until it poisons you."

He still said nothing, and his shields remained just as high and impenetrable. My jaw clenched. Why was it so hard for him to admit what we both already knew?

"Or are you blaming me for this?" I suddenly asked. Was that what he didn't want to tell me? "If you are, it's okay," I went on hastily. "I can handle whatever you're feeling, even if it's holding me responsible because this more than anything proves your point about your enemies using your love for me against you. I'd probably be mad, too, if I were you, so—"

"I don't blame you," he interrupted, brushing me away to pace the short distance that the length of the room provided. "I didn't have to publicly announce my love for you by marrying you, yet I did, so all the blame for this falls on me."

"Not all," I said softly, my heart breaking. "Samir died because of me. That makes it mine, too, and if it hurts me and I only knew him a few months, I *know* what it's doing to you."

"Oh, but you don't," he said, and my subconscious felt momentarily seared as a crack formed in his walls, allowing a sliver of his feelings to escape. All too quickly, it was gone, and despite not being able to decipher what he was feeling, that brief flash proved that he was nowhere near as detached as he was pretending to be.

"I know you're upset," I said, going over to him. "If you weren't, you wouldn't be trying so hard to keep yourself closed off. You need to stop. This is the 'for worse' part of our wedding vows, and I signed up for that, too. If we're going to get through this, we need to do it together."

"You think you want me to tell you what I'm feeling, but you don't." As he spoke, green rolled over his gaze. "Still, since you keep insisting, fine. More than anything else, I feel relieved."

I gasped in surprise at that, and his mouth twisted.

"I don't expect you to understand because you've never killed anyone except in self-defense. It's very different to take a life when you don't have your own survival as motivation. Take away anger or revenge as motivating factors, too, and it's not only different, it can be difficult. Add in truly caring for the person, and it's not only difficult; it takes a special degree of coldness that most people don't have. I have that coldness, Leila. I've had it for centuries, and time has taught me that when I have to do something necessary yet unpleasant, it's best to get it over with as soon as possible."

Then his voice roughened and he began to pace again.

"Yet that's not why I'm relieved that this part is over with. It's also not why I was in such a hurry both to leave and then to come back. It was because every hour that I was away from you, I knew you could be tortured or worse in order to incentivize me to do as Mircea's captors ordered. That is why what I feel most now is relief. I can see with my own eyes that you are unharmed, and my relief over that supersedes everything else, including any feelings I might have for a lost friend."

I was openmouthed as I processed all of this. My turbulent emotions must have shown on my face because he let out a derisive snort.

"As I said, you didn't really want to know what I was feeling. Perhaps next time, you'll simply take my word for it."

Chapter 28

"No," I whispered. "It's the truth, so no matter what, I want it."

"Oh?" He whirled, yanking me to him, his hands as hot as brands on my back. "What about this truth? I only care about keeping you safe, no matter who I have to kill. Yet that kind of selfishness makes me the very monster that my enemies have often accused me of being, so did you truly want to know this about me?"

Just as quickly, he shoved me away, his mouth curling with a cruelness that belied the flood of emotions that were starting to break down his walls. "Or instead, are you as horrified as I knew you would be when I tried to spare you this knowledge?"

I stared at him, trying and failing to articulate my thoughts through my own storm of emotions. No, I wasn't horrified by his brutally practical mindset when it came to killing Samir. I should have realized the same hardness that had allowed Vlad to overcome centuries of tragedy would also keep him from being crippled by grief now, even if he would mourn Samir later, as he'd implied.

But I *was* afraid of what this meant for Gretchen. Vlad had just confirmed my worst suspicions about what he'd do if he knew I could transfer the spell onto her. He'd see it as my life versus Gretchen's, and to him, the choice would be obvious.

But if we found Mircea, we could all win, and now we had a real chance of doing that. All I had to do was keep Vlad from finding out about the spell transfer option in the meantime. Once we had Mircea safely away from his captors, I'd tell Vlad, but until then . . .

I went over to him, moving with deliberate slowness so he could read the emotion in my eyes when I spoke.

"I told you before; I know you're the dragon instead of the knight. And I don't care. At your best or at your worst, I will always love you, Vlad." I slipped my arms around him and stood on tiptoe so my face was closer to his. "If you can't grieve for Samir until this is over, then I'll grieve him enough for both of us, but no matter what, I'll never stop loving you."

He bent down, bridging those last few inches between us. "Good," he growled against my lips. "Because I refuse to live without you."

He kissed me, hard, hungry, and demanding. At the same time, all his walls dropped and the instant crush of his full, unfiltered emotions would've made me stumble if his arms weren't around me. Relief and rage, lust and love, desperation and need, bitterness and vengeance; all of it flooded into me, until I felt like I was drowning beneath the deluge.

I kissed him back, suddenly clawing at his clothes with an urgency that might have been mine or his. I couldn't tell. All I knew was that I needed him, couldn't stand to wait a minute longer to feel his skin on mine, or to have our bodies be as fully entwined as our emotions now were.

Very soon, I was naked on the bed, the bare, scorching length of his body on top of mine. I was too consumed with desire to stand a delay, so I opened my legs with more demand than invitation. He moaned into my mouth as I rubbed against him, inciting him to lose the last of his control.

He did, gripping my hips while a deep thrust tore a cry from me. I held him tighter, arching against him for more despite the quicksilver flash of pain from his size and our lack of foreplay. Still, that was nothing compared to the rapturous burn of feeling him inside me, or the jolt that seared my most sensitive nerve endings when he erotically ground against my clitoris after fully sheathing himself within my depths.

My nails raked down his back as I arched harder against him. He made a low, guttural noise and lifted me, drawing all the way out before thrusting forward to penetrate even deeper. The sharp intensity of the pleasure made sparks spring up like beads of sweat on my skin, and he laughed with dark sensuality when he saw them.

"I love how passionate you are," he muttered as his mouth burned a path down to my neck. Then fangs pressed against the spot where my pulse used to be. He licked it before sinking those sharp points into my flesh and thrusting forward again, leaving me shuddering at the double impact of pleasure. He continued in that devastating rhythm, his hard strokes matched by deep, sensual suctions, until my mind was wiped of everything except the overwhelming pleasure and the urgent need for more.

My hands started to race around his body, alternatively gripping his head or his hips. I couldn't stop trying to get closer to him despite there being no air between us. Yet soon, even that wasn't enough. Lost in the primal sensations, I sank my fangs into his neck, wanting to fill myself with him that way, too. From the spike of pleasure that cascaded through our connection, he liked that, and I dug my fangs deeper into him in response, moaning as I swallowed his blood.

That rich liquid awakened a new hunger in me. His blood wasn't food, but it was still heady, intoxicating, and most of all, part of him. I drew deeper on the punctures, sliding my fangs in again when they closed as he healed with supernatural quickness, then felt his low, rasping laughter against my neck.

"Don't be gentle. Bite me harder."

I did, a gasp escaping me as he increased his pace and his teeth sank with rapturous roughness into my throat. Soon, my neck throbbed as much as my loins and I was rocking against him with a reckless disregard for anything except the ecstasy that straddled a knife's edge between too much pleasure and a dash of pain. It consumed me, until I didn't care that the sparks beading from me had the sheets smoking, or that the headboard banged hard enough against the wall to rattle the windowpanes.

Need more, yes, more, so good, please, yes, yes, yes!

My shout coincided with that incredible pleasure cresting within me. Then I shouted again at the additional, instant wave of ecstasy as Vlad shuddered against me, his grip turning to iron. My fangs slipped out of him as my head fell back, that sizzle replaced by a bone-deep languorousness that made my limbs feel heavy with satiation.

Moments later, Vlad's fangs left my neck and he pulled out of me. Then he shifted until I lay next to him instead of beneath him. His hands, only slightly less heated than before, began brushing back the wild tangle of hair from my face as he stared at me, the faintest smile curling his mouth.

"Seems you were right. We both needed that to forget for a little while."

I let out a breathy laugh. "You should listen without arguing next time."

He chuckled, continuing to tuck those errant black strands back from my face, but I mourned as I watched that former tenseness start to fill his features again. I didn't want to give up on our moment of peace this soon, yet neither of us could hide from reality. Ready or not, it was here, about to pounce.

Still, I wasn't without good news that I could share to help keep those dark thoughts at bay a little longer. "I figured out how to link to Mircea."

He sat up so abruptly that it startled me. "Do you know where he is?"

"No," I said with a small, frustrated sigh. "And he doesn't, either. His captors have him in an underground cave, so there are no landmarks or identifying structures. I could talk to him, though, like he's been able to talk to me, and he's willing to tell us how to find people who *do* know where he is."

Now Vlad's face was all stony again. Inwardly, I sighed. So much for our peaceful interlude. "Why should we believe a word he tells you?"

"He knows his captors will kill him anyway once they're done giving you grisly tasks to perform," I replied. "He also knows that with the spell linking us together, you can't kill him, so he realizes you're his best chance to survive."

"For now," Vlad muttered darkly. "He must know that I'll kill him the moment we find a way to break your spell."

I left that alone and chose my next words carefully, not wanting to blast him for sins he'd committed more than five hundred years ago, but also not wanting to leave him unaware of Mircea's other motivations.

"He also still longs for your respect, Vlad, even if he knows your approval is out of the question."

"My approval?" he repeated in disbelief. "Is he insane?"

"Maybe a bit," I replied, shrugging. "But he was a little boy who loved and idolized you once, and part of that little boy is still buried inside the hateful man he's become. He knows you despise cowardice more than anything else, so by giving you a chance to find him, he's showing you he's man enough to fight for his life even though the odds are very much against him."

He stared at me, an expression of disbelief overtaking his features. "You believe that ridiculous manipulation? Leila, he's lying in order to lure us into a trap."

How could I explain the awful, soul-scarring rejection Mircea had forced me to relive without slapping Vlad in the face with it? There was no way, and without my explaining it, Vlad wouldn't believe that Mircea's offer was real. I couldn't lose our best chance to find him by sparing Vlad's feelings, so I'd have to settle for the metaphoric face slap.

"You were a terrible father to him," I said bluntly. "Mircea didn't know he wasn't your son, so all he knew was that he loved you completely and you couldn't tolerate being near him. That broke something in him that's never healed, and I know he's not faking that because my father's continued rejections broke something in me, too. But just like a never-grown-up part of me still longs for my father's respect, Mircea still longs for yours, and this is his last chance to earn it."

He drew away even more. "You think I was a terrible father? *My* father sent me to live with his worst enemy in exchange for political security, resulting in my torture, rape, starvation, and abuse for over a decade. Even though they weren't my children, I never mistreated Mircea or Ilona's other child. Instead, the boys were protected, well-fed, and well-educated."

"Yes, of course you had it much worse."

And he had, by far. Yet that didn't negate what Mircea had gone through. How could I make him understand that? With his own horrendous childhood, no wonder he was having trouble relating. Add in Vlad being from a tyrannical medieval culture in general, and I could see why he found Mircea's genuine hurt nonsensical.

"But emotional damage can sometimes be just as scarring as physical abuse," I went on. "Back then, what you describe might have been considered stellar parenting, but Mircea was still really hurt. And if you think about it, you know a parent's rejection can be devastating to a person even long past their childhood. You even told my dad that he had no right to judge you so harshly because your firstborn son never had to plead for the love my dad kept withholding from me, remember?"

"That's not the same," Vlad muttered, but he looked away a little too quickly.

I moved closer, until he had to meet my gaze or turn his head to avoid it. "I'm sorry, but it is. Yes, things were incredibly difficult for you and all your focus was on saving your country, but you still left a boy who thought he was your son behind. Sometimes kids act out because negative attention is better than no attention. That's basically what Mircea has done, if you add in centuries of being warped by your revenge-obsessed enemy Szilagyi, while also learning lots of nasty magic from who-knows-who. I'm not saying it's okay, but I am saying that I one hundred percent believe he did all of it because he'd rather you hate him than continue to ignore him."

Vlad got off the bed, pausing to give a frustrated look at the small room before his strides began eating up the limited floor space. Maybe that's why his bedroom at the castle was so large. There, he had plenty of room to pace off his frustration.

"Mircea could have come to me," he finally said, daggers of his frustration starting to spike into my own emotions. "Had he done so beforehand, had he explained why he sided with Szilagyi and pretended to be dead . . . I might have forgiven him."

"Would you?" I asked with more brutal bluntness. "You're known for a lot of things, but forgiveness isn't one of them."

He threw me a jaded look. "True, but in the end, it doesn't matter. Mircea tried to kill you. Even if I were the most forgiving of souls, I wouldn't forgive that."

"I'm not asking you to," I said, getting out of bed, too. "But I *am* asking you to believe that Mircea wants your respect. Since you couldn't give it to him as your stepson, he's willing for you to respect him as your enemy. Take that, and the fact that he wants a chance to live versus the certainty of death by his captors, and I don't think he's lying with this lead."

I went over to Vlad, lightly running my hands over the back he'd turned to me. He'd closed his feelings off again. Maybe he was still consumed with anger, or maybe he was remembering back when he'd been the only father Mircea had ever known, and was rethinking his former treatment of him.

"What was the lead?" Vlad asked after a long silence.

I closed my eyes in relief. "To take down some necromancers in the group that's holding him captive. Apparently they're members of a cult that call themselves Acolytes of Imhotep, and all the members know where Mircea is. If we can keep one alive, we can get the location out of him."

Chapter 29

 As soon as dawn broke, Vlad and I went to the basement cell. Gretchen, as expected, was now passed out on the cot, her shirt so stained with red that I couldn't remember what its original color had been. Smelling the blood from her messy feedings reminded me that I hadn't eaten in over a day. I hadn't slept in over a day, either, and I'd have to do both if I was going to be fighting a group of powerful necromancers tonight.

But first . . . "I'll take her upstairs and get her cleaned up," I told Maximus, starting to unlock Gretchen's wrist and ankle cuffs. "She won't wake up until dusk, so it'll be safe. You should get some rest, too, while you can."

Maximus looked as tired as I felt, and he also was in bad need of a shower and new clothes. His shirt and pants were almost as stained as Gretchen's, and his hair was now the same russet color as Ian's from all the blood in it. But his gaze wasn't tired. It was flint-like as he looked past me to Vlad.

"What did you do with Samir?"

"I buried him on the ridge," Vlad replied.

Maximus gave a short nod. "I'm glad. When the

time comes, I want to spend my final rest with our other fallen brothers, too." Then he paused, and the laugh that came out of him sounded forced. "Unless that's no longer an option. I *have* been expelled from your line. I suppose that means you've changed your mind about burying me with the rest of your people after I'm gone."

Vlad didn't reply. He just looked at Maximus. The staggering amount of years between them, both good and bad, seemed to fill the space and the silence, adding a weight to the atmosphere that hadn't been there moments before.

"No," Vlad said at last, his voice rougher, almost hoarse. "I haven't changed my mind about that."

I had to look away, blinking back the tears that were welling in my eyes. This past year had pushed their friendship past the breaking point several times. Not too long ago, Maximus had been in Vlad's dungeons, and not long after that, Vlad's now-dead enemy Szilagyi had sent Vlad a video of what looked like Maximus raping me. None of us thought that Vlad could get past that even when he discovered that it wasn't real, but he had. He and Maximus still weren't back to where they'd been before, but maybe this was bringing them one step closer.

Then Maximus said, "Leila can transfer the spell on her to Gretchen," and my hopeful mood shattered.

Vlad spun to face me. "What?" he asked in a tone that could have split rock.

I stared at Maximus while my mind briefly went blank from rage. He stared back at me, unblinking.

"Go ahead, slice out my heart. I don't fear death, and to die for my prince is a great honor."

I was torn between that mind-numbing rage and

a frustrated sort of admiration. I hated Maximus for telling Vlad because of how it endangered Gretchen, and I respected him because his staunch loyalty meant he could do nothing else *except* tell Vlad.

"No one is dying for me today," Vlad said, his tone suddenly betraying a weariness that his sizzling aura gave no indication of. "But you *will* tell me what he means, Leila."

And so, far sooner than I intended, I found myself telling Vlad about the legacy magic in my Cherokee line, how Gretchen was the only matrilineal relative that it could be transferred to, and what it did to both the person giving it and receiving it. With each word, Vlad's gaze grew greener, brighter, until by the end, it felt as if I was staring into twin emerald suns.

"Do it" were his first words once I was finished.

I gave a seething glance at Maximus before refocusing my attention back on Vlad. Sometimes it sucked to be right.

"Look, I hate that you're being jerked around by Mircea's captors because of me. I hate it to my core, and I will carry the guilt of Samir's death for the rest of my life because you did it to save me. But I can't transfer this spell to Gretchen. For starters, I don't even know how, and—"

"Leotie!" Vlad thundered, spinning on his heel to face the open cell door. "I know you're listening, get down here!"

"And I can't condemn Gretchen to death that way," I went on as if he hadn't interrupted me. "Admit it, Vlad! Yesterday, if your choice would have been Gretchen's life or Samir's, you would have chosen Samir. I get why; he was your loyal friend for hundreds of years and you only met Gretchen a few months ago." I drew in a breath, forcing myself to go on. "The problem is, the reason why I understand is because I feel the same way. I liked Samir and I feel awful about his death, but I only knew him for a few months. Gretchen was born when I was three, so I don't have a single memory where she wasn't a part of my life. Hell, when we were little and had to cross a street, Mom would hold my hand and I would hold Gretchen's. I was her big sister, so of course I knew it was my job to watch out for her . . ."

I paused to dash away the tears that started to leak from my eyes. Dammit, I didn't have time for those any more than I had time for another electrical melt-down! My emotions would have to wait until things calmed down enough for them to take the wheel.

"She's my little sister and I love her," I summarized, fighting to sound brisk instead of broken, which was what I felt like over this next admission. "And I would sacrifice my life and everyone else's life for hers . . . except your life."

More treacherous tears slipped out. This time, I didn't swipe them away. I was too busy staring at Vlad as I bared the most vulnerable, selfish part of my soul.

"That's the real reason I wasn't going to tell you about the spell transfer until after we had safely retrieved Mircea. No matter how much I love Gretchen, I love you more, so if it somehow came down to your life or risking hers by giving Gretchen the hex, I'd choose you."

The tears fell faster now, until everything in the room seemed to waver from my looking at it through a liquid lens.

"And I know you'd choose me. That's why I didn't want you to know that I could transfer the spell to

Gretchen. I knew what you'd say. There's nothing either of us wouldn't do to save the other, but unless it *is* your life on the line, I'm not doing it. I can't, so be furious with me because I chose Gretchen over Samir, but please, don't ask me to transfer the spell again."

Vlad didn't say anything. He just folded me into his arms and held me hard enough to force the remaining air out of my lungs. When I felt something burning brush across on my forehead, I knew it was his lips.

"I'm not furious with you," he murmured against my skin. "I'm not even angry. You're fighting for those you love the most. How could I, out of all people, fail to understand that?"

"You might not have to choose between Vlad and your sister," a cool voice noted behind us. "I know a way to give Gretchen the spell without it endangering her."

Chapter 30

 My head jerked up and the arms around me tensed. I hadn't noticed Leotie coming down here, yet she now stood in the cell's open doorway.

"How?" Vlad asked before I could.

Leotie raised a graceful brow. "Legacy magic transforms into whatever the person needs most at the time of transfer. When I received it, I most needed to hide from my pursuers, so it gave me the gift of shape-shifting. When Leila received it, she most needed to survive a lethal dose of voltage, so it gave her the gift of making that electricity a functioning part of her body. Right now, Gretchen most needs blood, but in a few weeks . . ."

Leotie let the sentence dangle. I picked it up with an almost crushing sense of relief.

"She'll be over the worst of her cravings, so if I wait to transfer the legacy to her, then what she'll *most need* is to be protected from the lethal effects of my spell."

Leotie nodded, and I wanted to cry from sheer joy this time. Could the solution really be that simple? Was the break we'd so desperately needed finally within our grasp?

"But you'll have to wait until then," Leotie said,

looking at Vlad now instead of me. "Otherwise, Gretchen's uncontrollable craving for blood will trick the magic, making it believe that blood is what she needs most. Not only would you lose the chance to protect her from the spell, her gift could turn dark in order to provide ways for Gretchen to fulfill her insatiable hunger."

A catch. Of course there was a catch. "It can do that?"

Leotie's smile was grim with the kind of firsthand knowledge that I didn't want to have. "Oh yes. Magic this powerful can be as terrible as it is great."

"Okay, so we wait," I said, glancing up at Vlad. "Right?" When he said nothing, I said, "Right?" more emphatically.

"Right," he replied in a light tone. Then he flashed a smile at Leotie that caused all my muscles to tense. Why was he giving her his charming, death-will-soon-follow smile? "But you will still show Leila how to transfer the magic now."

Leotie's aura flared, sending ripples of power over the room. The accompanying scent of her anger was almost redundant by comparison. "You try to command me, Impaler?"

"No he doesn't," I said quickly, giving Vlad a don't-you-dare glare. "But after Gretchen's through her hunger craze, we might need to do the transfer right away. If you happen to be unavailable for instructions, we'd be in trouble."

Leotie smiled although her power continued to fill the air. "I despise most modern American colloquialisms, but 'Don't bullshit a bullshitter' is appropriate for this moment."

"So is 'Don't test me,'" Vlad replied, his aura bursting forth to bathe the room with dangerous levels of heat.

"Can you two stop?" I snapped, abandoning my attempt to smooth things over. "Vlad, I better not see so much as a spark out of you. Leotie is family, so the agreement you and I made long ago about you never harming any of my family applies to her, too." Then I rounded on Leotie. "Yes, you're eight hundred years old, and in additional to your obvious power, I'm also sure you still have some magical tricks up your sleeve. But you shook Vlad's hand when you met him, so that gave him the ability to toast you before you can say abracadabra. And now that we've confirmed everyone here is a scary badass but we agree that *no one's going to hurt anyone*, can we move on already?"

Leotie's smile changed into that weird form of annoyed pride as she looked at me. Then she looked at Vlad, who muttered something in Romanian I hoped she didn't understand. Still, his aura folded back in like a dragon tucking away its gigantic wings, and Leotie's aura dissipated until I no longer felt like I had tiny, spiked medieval flail balls rolling over my skin.

"Good, we're all being reasonable," I said, blowing out a sigh. Honestly, old vampires were the supernatural equivalent of human flashers sometimes. They just couldn't stop themselves from showing other people what they had and how capable they were of using it.

"Now, Leotie," I continued, "please show me how to transfer my magic legacy onto Gretchen, even though I won't do it until it's safe," I said, emphasizing those last few words.

As if she hadn't been in a dangerous standoff moments before, Leotie lifted her shoulder in something too careless to be a shrug. "You seal your mouth over hers and breathe the power into her while simultaneously willing it out of yourself."

"That's it?" I said, my surprise echoed in the dubious expressions on both Vlad's and Maximus's face.

Another casual shoulder tilt. "The mechanics aren't complicated. Only the matrilineal family requirement is."

That was for damn sure. If it wasn't, I could be transferring this legacy and its hitchhiking deadly hex to the first evil person I found. Then again, maybe we wouldn't be able to kill that person afterward. The magic would protect him or her, making us guilty of giving a monster superpowers. Guess that waiting for Gretchen to get over her blood craze was the best possible play for a variety of reasons.

"Okay, well, now we know how to do it," I said. It still sounded too easy, but then again, what had I expected it to entail? Sacrificing a unicorn? "So now I'm going to do what I came down here to do, which is get Gretchen cleaned up."

Leotie walked off without another word. Vlad's gaze followed her, but he said nothing. If he still had doubts that she'd told us the truth about the spell transfer, he was obviously willing to wait until later to confront her. Good. I wasn't ready to referee another pissing contest between them.

I picked Gretchen up, trying not to notice how my stomach clenched at the heavy scent of blood emanating from her. I glanced at one of the unused blood bags on the floor, then gave myself a mental slap. I couldn't take that. Gretchen needed all of them, and I could go out later to find my own meal. I was getting pretty good at feeding from the wrist without nicking the wrong artery, in fact. I'd graduate to the neck soon—

Twin points suddenly speared my bottom lip, and I

sucked the accompanying drops of blood away while hoping that no one else noticed. What kind of a vampire stabbed herself in the lip with her own fangs? Some days, I was still such a noob at this.

"Bring her back here when you're done. I'll use one of the other bathrooms to get myself cleaned up," Maximus said, thankfully not seeming to catch what I'd done. Neither had Vlad. He was still staring at the open doorway even though Leotie was now up the stairs and out of sight.

"She's hiding something," he said, his voice so low that it wouldn't carry beyond this room.

"Probably," I agreed, keeping my voice equally soft. At eight hundred years plus, Leotie had to have lots of secrets she hadn't revealed yet. "But I don't think it's the transfer details, and I also don't believe she wants to do us any harm."

The look Vlad gave me was jaded to the extreme. "Sometimes we harm the ones we love whether we want to or not."

I couldn't argue that point, so with a slight shake of my head to indicate that we'd discuss this later, I went back upstairs with Vlad and Maximus following me. When we arrived at the main level of the house, I saw that Leotie had already disappeared into her bedroom. That was just as well since Vlad's radar was clearly set to discover-and-destroy mode. Ian and Marty were now out of their rooms, and they hadn't been earlier.

They both sat on opposite couches in the family room, and they both looked tired. With it being barely an hour past dawn, I had been sure that they'd be asleep. Maybe our arguing below had woken them up. With how tense things had gotten, they might have thought they needed to stay awake in case they had to go downstairs to jump in and break things up. Or join in.

"Don't get up. I'm just taking Gretchen to my room to clean her up," I said to Marty, waving him off when he rose to help.

Ian stood up and gave a full-bodied, lazy stretch. "Not that I was eavesdropping, but now that you have your witch relative to assist you with any future magical muckety-mucks and you have a way out of your dastardly spell, it seems to me that I've fulfilled my oath and can take my leave. It's been grand fun—and by that, I mean more boring than an extended version of midnight Mass—but it had to end sometime—"

"You're not done yet," Vlad cut him off. "We're going after a group of necromancers tonight and we need your skills."

Ian's mouth curled downward. "Of course you do. Why would I want to survive the task Mencheres forced me into?"

Vlad gave a dismissive grunt. "Save your complaints for him. These necromancers are supposed to be magical Acolytes of Imhotep's, and Mencheres was a contemporary of his, so he might know more about them than he realizes. That why I texted him earlier and told him to call me."

I hoped Mencheres knew about Imhotep and his cult. I only recognized his name because Imhotep was the villain in the nineties remake of the movie *The Mummy*, yet I doubted that would help.

"Grand," Ian said in a tone that implied he felt the opposite. "Does anyone else feel the sudden need for a shag?"

I blinked. "What?"

He waved dismissively. "'Course you don't. You

and Tepesh already had yours. Thought the two of you would bang the bed right through the floor, and here I had to listen to that while forced into an unnatural state of celibacy."

Now I was openmouthed at his audacity, not to mention his questionable priorities if he really thought he was going to die tonight. Ian didn't pay any attention to that. His gaze lit up as Leotie came back into the family room.

"Ah, Leotie, my beauteous poppet, I take back everything I said about you being an uppity crone. Take me to your bed, I promise endless delights. I'll even limit myself to tongues only. Always happy to accommodate a preference."

"No," Leotie said, her tone turning withering. "And if you make me say no again, your blood will be on the floor."

Ian's mouth curled into a pout. "Wish you were talking about foreplay, but clearly you're not. Very well, I can take an honest refusal, so I shan't bother you again." Then his tone brightened. "But I will offer one last chance for any takers among the rest of you?"

When all he received back was glares, Ian sighed as if wounded. "Bunch of sexual hoarders, the lot of you. Have you no pity for the last request of a dying man? Blimey, if I do live through tonight, I won't be responsible for what I do to the next thing in my path that doesn't require consent. Take that chair over there. Mmmm, looks soft, doesn't it? Sturdy, too. Why, if that were a La-Z-Boy, I might be pounding the stuffing out of it right now—"

"Here, look at this," Leotie said in annoyance, holding a small object up. A mirror, I realized. Why would she—?

My surroundings vanished and I was suddenly bombarded by thousands of visions of my own reflection. It felt as if I'd somehow been transported inside the world's biggest magic mirrors funhouse. At once, I set Gretchen down and tried to find the way out, but with every move I made, our reflections only increased, until I could see nothing except endless versions of myself with Gretchen lying prone at my feet.

Chapter 31

 I couldn't find a way around the mirrors, so I began to beat on them with all my strength. Yet somehow, I was unable to break a single one. I tried lashing them with my whip next, with the same dismal results. Desperate, I began to will the electricity in me into higher and higher levels, until I was worried about becoming a danger to Gretchen, yet my whip still had absolutely no effect on the mirrors. A horrible realization filled me. None of my abilities could free me from this trap.

"Don't be frightened, Leila."

Leotie's voice echoed all around me, although I couldn't see her. All I could see was endless versions of myself in the mirrored walls of our prison. Then I screamed when Gretchen suddenly disappeared from those reflections.

"Don't be frightened," Leotie repeated. "The spell will dissipate after I've had time to get Gretchen safely away."

"Why are you doing this?" I spat, cursing myself for ever trusting her.

"I have a sense about people. It's never wrong, and it's telling me that your husband is hiding something."

My snort was bitter. "Vlad said the same thing about you."

"You might not believe me now, but I'm doing this to help," Leotie replied, those odd echoes fading a bit. "When Vlad said that he would wait to transfer the spell to Gretchen, I could tell he was lying. You confirmed that you would do anything for him, so I cannot trust you, either. That is why I'm taking Gretchen away until she is over her bloodlust."

I didn't say anything for a moment. I would never forgive her for tricking and trapping us this way, but I also understood why she did it down to my very soul.

"Vlad will come after you," I finally said. He wouldn't have any conflict of emotions over what Leotie had done. She had to have Vlad trapped, too, or he would have already burned her to death for doing this to me. When he eventually got out, he'd want vengeance for this betrayal.

Leotie's light laughter trickled through the infinity mirrors. "I would lose my respect for him if he didn't. But I was old long before he was born, Leila, and I've had centuries to relearn all the magic that was stripped from me. Your husband won't find me unless I want him to."

Her voice was so much closer during that last part, I expected her to appear in the countless reflections from the mirrors. She didn't, yet somehow, her next words sounded as if they were whispered right into my ear.

"I left you the secret of this spell beneath my mattress. Take it with you tonight. It's so ancient; the necromancers might not know it, and if you catch them in it, they'll be as helpless as you are now. I also overheard that the man you're seeking is in a cave. Black quartz absorbs magic, so that is the only kind of cave that necromancers would put a fellow sorcerer in. Farewell, Leila. I hope to see you again one day."

"Leotie, wait!" I shouted.

She didn't reply. I kept calling out to her, but only heard endless echoes of my own voice in response. Then, despite my previous failed attempts, I resumed my efforts to break the mirrors. Maybe Leotie had only been saying that we were all helpless so I wouldn't get out earlier than she wanted me to.

What felt like several hours later, I sat down in defeat. I also closed my eyes so I wouldn't have to keep seeing countless versions of my own reflection. If I'd still been human, I would have had a puking migraine from all the repeating, blinding flashes of light from my whip as I kept lashing the mirrors in a futile attempt to break them. It hadn't worked. I hadn't even scratched their surface. Leotie hadn't been lying about the effectiveness of this trap, that was for damn sure.

I was worked up from my efforts, but also so tired I thought I might pass out. It probably would be a good idea if I did try to sleep. That was at least something beneficial I could do while trapped in this unbreakable spell. But questions, fears, heightened electrical currents, and hunger wouldn't allow me to relax, let alone to sleep. Yes, Leotie had said that the spell would dissipate once she and Gretchen were safely away, but she hadn't said how long that would take.

What if the spell wouldn't deactivate for days? Worse, what if there was a magical malfunction and it didn't deactivate at all? Would that leave me, Vlad, Marty, and Maximus trapped in our mirrored prisons, until Gretchen was finally past her blood craze and Leotie returned her to us in a week or two?

I tried to push back my rising panic at the thought. Not only would I go insane with hunger by then, but if Mircea's captors gave Vlad a new demand, he wouldn't be able to carry it out even if it were something as simple as burning down a house. Then they'd kill me in retaliation, and none of us could do a thing to stop them. Even if they didn't send new demands, we weren't safe here. This was Cat and Bones's house, not one of Vlad's. At any time, someone else could come by. I wasn't worried if it would be Cat or Bones, but what if one of their other friends showed up? Maybe someone with a grudge against Vlad? He certainly had no shortage of enemies—

A loud crashing sound snapped my head up in time to see the mirrors shattering, countless pieces of glass disappearing as soon as they hit the floor. In the next moment, I was staring at Vlad, Ian, Maximus, and Marty. We were all still in the family room, standing exactly where we had before, and we all had similar degrees of shock in our expressions.

Then Vlad reached me in two long strides, his fingers digging in almost painfully as he gripped me by the shoulders. "Are you all right?"

"Yes," I said, blinking because seeing things in single form suddenly seemed strange.

"That filthy little witch," Ian breathed, looking around warily as if expecting mirrors to pop up and cage him in again. "Foxed us good and proper, didn't she?"

Maximus began storming around the house. I didn't know why until he yelled, "Gretchen's gone!" in a frantic tone.

Yeah, I already knew that. Then I met Vlad's gaze. One look into his simmering copper depths, and I knew that Leotie had told him why she'd done this, too. His emotions were locked down, but his smoky cinnamon scent sharpened with barely controlled rage, and if his hands got any hotter, my clothes would catch fire.

"Leotie said not to bother linking to either of them because she'd block your attempts," Vlad said, confirming my suspicions that she'd talked to him, too. "You still need to try. Needless to say, I don't trust her word on anything now."

Marty came over, and I felt the tremble he didn't show as he gave me a comforting pat and then slipped his hand into mine.

"Don't mean to be rude because Leotie's your family," he said in a laconic tone. "But if I see that witch again, I am kicking every inch of her spell-casting ass—"

He stopped speaking when something slammed down hard enough to make the whole house tremble. Whatever it was, it had landed right outside the cabin. Vlad let go of me, his hands bursting into flames. I tried to snap out a whip, then cursed when nothing happened. I had spent myself on those damn unbreakable mirrors and now who knew what danger had shown up outside!

"Knife!" I hissed. Marty still had those two long silver daggers on him. He tossed one to me and I grabbed it out of the air when the flames on Vlad's hands abruptly extinguished.

"It's all right," he said tersely.

At the same moment, the front door tore itself from the hinges as if yanked by huge, invisible hands. Then it was flung away and Mencheres swept into the room. His aura broke out with the intensity of multiple tidal waves, causing me to stagger back. I'd never felt anything that strong before. Mencheres must have always been masking his aura before, but he wasn't now, and those currents continued to grow until I expected to either fall over completely or start spontaneously combusting. Good God, he felt like the power line I'd touched back when I was thirteen!

Mencheres's dark, piercing gaze swept the room before touching each of us with quick, assessing glances. Then he visibly relaxed and that incalculable power whooshed back into him as if sucked by an invisible vortex. At last, his gaze settled onto Vlad and he arched a single, inquiring brow.

"So," Mencheres said in a casual tone. "What did I miss?"

Chapter 32

I caught the reason for his dramatic manner of entry when I went downstairs to see if Leotie had taken all the blood bags with her. Apparently, Mencheres had been calling Vlad over and over and had gotten worried when there was no response. That's why he'd opted for his sudden, explosive arrival instead of merely showing up by car or helicopter. Not that I could blame Mencheres for being worried. A few minutes ago, all of us had been caught in a witch's trap.

A glance at the clock showed that we'd been in our mirrored prisons for over six hours. It had felt much longer than that, and I was now so hungry that I didn't trust myself to feed from a human. Thankfully, I found a blood bag that Leotie had left behind by accident or because she knew how ravenous I'd be once I was finally out of her trap. I drained it, feeling oddly guilty even though Gretchen was long gone by now.

I tried not to worry about her as I listened to Vlad fill Mencheres in on everything that had happened since they'd last spoken. Leotie wouldn't hurt Gretchen, I reminded myself. She'd gone to rather extreme lengths to prove that, in fact, but I hated that my sister was still with a virtual stranger at the most emotionally vulnerable and turbulent point in her life.

And dear God, I didn't even want to *think* about what would happen when my father found out that Gretchen was now a vampire *and* I'd let someone snatch her away to parts unknown. To say he'd be angry was an understatement. He'd only recently started speaking to me again after my own transition from human to undead several months ago. Once my dad discovered that Gretchen had chosen to go all creature-of-the-night, too, he might pop a blood vessel.

Then again, my father might also go looking for a silver knife to stab me with. He'd consider Gretchen's change and her subsequent kidnapping to be my fault since I'm the one who exposed Gretchen to vampires in the first place. I doubted that telling him about our even-freakier witchy lineage would soothe my dad, either. Family. Why was nothing easy with them?

"Imhotep?" I heard Mencheres say, and my ears perked up. "But Imhotep has been dead for over a thousand years."

"It appears that his followers live on," Vlad replied in a brusque tone. "What do you know about them?"

I slipped back upstairs during Mencheres's pondering silence. When I reached the main room, he was looking out the window and Vlad was standing near the fireplace.

"Imhotep was unusual," Mencheres said. "History remembers him as one of the earliest known architects, physicians, and engineers. He was a vampire, of course, or we never would have met because he was born a full hundred years before me. He was also the person who taught me most of the magic I know."

Now we were getting to the meat of it. I moved

closer, not wanting to miss a word of this. Mencheres turned around, his dark gaze flicking between me and Vlad.

"But despite Imhotep knowing far more of the dark arts than he taught to anyone, even me, he didn't view magic as a weapon. Instead, he sought to use it for knowledge, for healing, and for securing Egypt against her enemies. He had many followers, yes, but he taught magic to very few of them because he was concerned about it being misused. If all practitioners of magic had been as principled as Imhotep, the Law Guardians might never have outlawed it in the first place."

"But they did, and if our information is correct, his followers strayed very far from Imhotep's example," Vlad said, sounding impatient now. "Do you know any who are still living?"

"None." Mencheres's expression darkened. "Aside from Patra, the only other one I knew of died in the fifteenth century."

"Who's Patra?" I'd never heard that name before.

"Mencheres's former wife," Vlad said shortly. "Thankfully dead, so the bitch has no part in this."

"Hey, harsh," I muttered.

Vlad gave me a jaded look. "Had you known Patra, you would have considered 'bitch' a charitable descriptor."

Mencheres looked understandably ill at ease over the topic, so I seized on the other pertinent point. "The other guy died in the fifteenth century, huh?" I cast a slanted look at Vlad. "That's the same time period that Szilagyi recruited Mircea and had *someone* teach him a whole bunch of super-powerful magic that even Mencheres doesn't know about. Coincidence?"

"Maybe not," Vlad replied, green starting to fill his eyes. "We've been tricked more than once by someone pretending to be dead who wasn't. Who was this person, Mencheres? More importantly, what kind of special magical abilities or powers did he have?"

"She," Mencheres said, his expression darkening again. "And she only had one, yet it was more than enough."

Tonight, we were going up against three members of Imhotep's secret cult of necromancers, one of whom might be the sorceress that Mencheres used to know. But first, we had to fly more than twelve hours to reach Belarus, the country in Eastern Europe where Mircea said the other necromancers were. I didn't mind the long flight, in truth. After several futile attempts to link to Leotie or Gretchen—Leotie hadn't been lying; I found myself blocked each time—I used the rest of our flight to grab a few hours' sleep. That's how tired I was. Even prebattle nerves and all my worries couldn't keep me awake the whole time.

Mencheres came with us. Vlad had argued over this, saying something about needing to fight his own battles, but Mencheres had insisted. Almost no one was able to get Vlad to change his mind once he'd made it up, so I could only guess that Vlad's love for Mencheres combined with his "honorary sire" status in Vlad's life had been the cause of his unusual relenting.

Whatever the reason, I was glad. Mencheres's telekinesis would come in very handy against the necromancers, if they were as tough as Mircea warned me about. Combine that with Vlad's firepower, Maximus's brute strength, Marty's bravery, my own electrical abilities, and whatever Ian could do, and I felt a lot more hopeful about our chances, even if one of the necromancers did turn out to be Mencheres's former acquaintance.

We landed in Minsk, Belarus, at a little after noon, their time. The bright sunlight was intensified by all the snow on the ground, and the instant blast of freezing air when we exited the plane had me molding my coat tighter around me. Winter was fully here in this part of Eastern Europe. Still, Belarus wasn't that far from Romania, and seeing the snow reminded me that it had also been winter when Vlad and I first met. How was that less than a year ago? Some days, it felt like several lifetimes ago.

We needed two cars to fit all of us and our luggage, which consisted mostly of weapons. Even with everyone's supernatural abilities, Vlad didn't want to take any chances, and I was all for the extra caution. Marty and I rode in the first car with Vlad while Ian and Maximus rode behind us with Mencheres. Vlad spoke Russian to the driver of our vehicle, which meant I didn't understand a word that he was saying.

I assumed we were going to a hotel or someone's residence since those places were Vlad's norm when we traveled. Instead, a little over an hour later, we pulled up to a ramshackle farm complete with a barn that looked like it would buckle from the weight of the icicles hanging off its roof.

"Is this where we're staying?" I asked, surprised. I could literally see through to the other side of the farmhouse, there were so many holes in the building's frame.

Vlad's lips curled. "I know, it's far beneath my usual standard, but that's the point. My expensive tastes are well-known, so few would expect to find me here, even if word of our arrival in Minsk did manage to make the rounds."

"Few indeed," I said, suppressing a smile. I'd lived on the street for a little while before I met Marty, so this didn't faze me, but Vlad was used to living in an actual *castle*. I couldn't wait to see his expression if we had to sit on piles of hay versus actual furniture.

"I have to get a picture of you next to that barn," I went on, stifling a laugh at the glower he gave me. "If you could find a pitchfork and hold it up, too—"

"Not in this lifetime," he cut me off.

"Princes," I said to Marty, with an exaggerated eye roll. He only grunted in reply, but the side of his mouth turned up. He might not be Vlad's biggest fan, but he wasn't immune to being amused by my playful needling of Vlad.

We could all use something to smile about right now. In a few hours, we'd be in a life-or-death fight, and we didn't know if our advantages would be enough since magic was the ultimate wild card. Some of us might not make it through tonight. I hoped we would, but in case these were the last hours of our lives, I didn't intend for them to pass under a cloud of worry or regret.

That's why, as soon as the car came to a stop, I got out and went right over to the nearest snowdrift. Then I bent down and began packing up the snow into roughly shaped spheres.

"What are you doing?" Vlad called out.

My reply was throwing a snowball that hit him square in the chest. He looked down at the white remains on his cashmere coat, and his brows almost disappeared into his hairline.

The disbelief on his face was priceless. My next snowball smacked him in the chest again. Then Marty laughed out loud as my third one went high and hit Vlad right in the nose.

"Nice one, kid!" Marty shouted, climbing out of the car. He ran over to me and began forming his own snowballs while eyeing Vlad with open intent.

"Don't you dare, Martin," Vlad growled, forming a ball of pure fire over his palm in warning. Then he looked at me with exasperation. "Come now, Leila, enough of this."

"I don't think so," I said, grinning at him. "How long has it been since you've been in a snowball fight?"

Now his brow arched with distinct haughtiness. "Never."

"Never?" I asked, and lobbed another fluffy white missile at him. He ducked, so it sailed over his head instead of hitting him. "You didn't even play in the snow when you were a kid?"

"I was in a dungeon by age ten, remember?"

I wouldn't let his curt tone or past memories ruin this. "That gave you nine years to do it. You're saying you didn't?"

"No." But there had been the slightest hesitation before that single word, and I pounced.

"Come on, Vlad, don't lie to me!"

He drew himself up to his full height. "As you noted, I am a prince. Thus, my father didn't allow me or my brothers to demean ourselves with foolish antics in the snow."

Allow. I snatched at the inference. "So you wanted to, but you couldn't."

"My brothers refused to disobey Father, and there was no point in playing outside alone," Vlad muttered.

For a split second, I could picture him as a child trying to incite his brothers into breaking the rules for a few minutes of illicit fun. My heart swelled, but Vlad wouldn't want me to be sad over all the ways his youth had been tainted. Instead, I deliberately began forming another handful of snow.

"Then I'm not letting you go another day without being in a snowball fight. Put out the fire, Vlad, and pick up some white stuff. I'm playing to win, so you'd better watch out!"

So saying, I flung my latest snowball at him. Marty joined in and threw his pile of hastily made snowballs at him, too, until Vlad had to spin and duck to avoid all of them. His scowl faded. With a wolfish grin that both warned and delighted me, Vlad finally bent down and began grabbing up handfuls of snow.

"Know what elevated body temperate is really useful for?" he asked in a conversational tone. "Melting things."

Then he threw five snowballs at us in rapid succession, beaning Marty and me. When they landed on us with far more weight and force than normal, I laughed.

"Cheater!"

He only grinned wider. "You're the one who said to play to win, Leila."

I laughed again, throwing snowballs as fast as I could make them. Vlad used the side of the car as a shield while he formed more special snowballs that had their exteriors melted by his hot hands until they had formed into icy shells. That made them faster as well as harder, and for someone who'd never done this before, Vlad was a natural at snowball fights. He managed to match the same number of snowballs that Marty and I threw at him, and when the second car finally pulled up, all three of us were covered in snow and ice.

Mencheres got out and looked around. Vlad was still crouched behind the other car, and Marty and I were behind our makeshift barrier of an overturned barrel.

"Are you doing what I think you are doing?" Mencheres asked, returning his gaze to Vlad with open disbelief.

Vlad stiffened and made a noise that, on anyone else, I would have called part defiant and part abashed. "Yes."

Vlad's real father had forbidden him to play in the snow on the pretext that it was demeaning. I hoped that Mencheres, Vlad's honorary sire and secondary father figure, wasn't about to be equally scornful now, even if Vlad was several centuries past when this activity would have been normal behavior.

At last, very formally, Mencheres stretched out his hands.

"It is on," he said in a surprisingly good impression of street talk. Then dozens of snowballs began forming on their own before rising to whirl like aimed, suspended missiles.

Ian bounded out of the car like a puppy that had finally been let off his leash. "At last, some fun!" he crowed, and began forming snowballs next to us.

I shrieked with laughter as the first round of snowballs that Mencheres had telekinetically created began to pelt me, Marty, Ian, and Vlad. Then we all made Mencheres the focus of our attacks as we began returning that snowy fire as fast as we could. Even with four-on-one odds, Mencheres's abilities made him easily able to keep up. Soon, so much snow was flying between us that it looked like a concentrated blizzard.

"Come on, Maximus, we need you, Mencheres is killing us!" I shouted.

After a final, disbelieving stare at Vlad, Maximus got out of the car and joined us. "This isn't the kind of fight I expected to be in today," he muttered as he began forming snowballs.

I just grinned at him. "Always expect the unexpected with vampires, right?"

Chapter 33

 When Mircea had told me where to find the necromancers, he hadn't said that we needed to show up at any particular time. Vlad picked midnight for us to make our appearance, and it didn't escape my notice that this was also known as the witching hour. Whether that was coincidence, strategy, or Vlad exercising his streak of dark humor was anyone's guess.

Ian glamoured us to disguise our appearances and everyone but me hid all but the weakest slivers of their auras. Now, the collective power of our group was lowered until it would feel like we were simply a bunch of new vampires looking for some after-hours fun, which was the façade we were going with.

Of course, Ian having his own sense of humor, we all looked like a bunch of sexy *female* vampires looking for some after-hours fun. Ian said it was because women were universally underestimated and thus would arouse the least amount of suspicion. That's why I now looked like a six-foot-tall Nubian goddess and Vlad was a five-foot-two, bouncy-haired blonde. Maximus now appeared to be a sultry Southern redhead, Marty a dusky-skinned, raven-haired beauty, and don't get me started on Mencheres. He now looked like a barely-legal-aged Asian girl, complete with a schoolgirl's uniform and knee-high socks.

"Real women don't do that," I hissed at Ian as he played with his new boobs.

"Then they should," Ian replied, giving his ample bust another two-palmed squeeze. "I could fondle these darlings for days. Should've thought to do this before tonight—"

"Enough," Mencheres said, the single word no more than a whisper, yet it thankfully stopped Ian in mid-train of thought.

I smirked at Ian for his instant, if somewhat sullen, compliance. Only Mencheres seemed able to command his respect that effectively. One day, I'd love to find out the story between the two of them, but now wasn't the time.

Ian caught my smirk, guessed the reason behind it, and flipped me off. I returned his one-fingered salute, but dropped my hand when Vlad said, "We're here."

After the grandeur of the element-themed hotel and the mystique of the underground speakeasy, I was surprised by the rather drab street of buildings in front of us. I even checked the address to see if Vlad had gotten it wrong. No, this was the place.

"Do you see something we don't?" I murmured to Ian.

He'd already dosed us with the same sparkly, eye-opening dust that had allowed us to see the hidden hotel in Savannah, but what if this place required more potent stuff? For all I knew, there could be an entire enchanted castle on top of this run-down line of warehouses.

"Don't see anything other than a dreary warehouse, poppet," Ian whispered. "Still, I feel vibrations, don't you?"

I did, though I'd thought they were from the cars on the nearby highway. It might be late, but we were hardly the only people out in this section of Minsk at this hour. Now I concentrated and realized that the vibrations came from both the highway behind me *and* this supposedly empty strip of warehouses.

"Let's go," Vlad said, the cold determination in his voice completely at odds with his glamoured, wispy feminine tones.

By increasing my concentration, I realized that the vibrations weren't random, but rhythmic. Someone was blasting music in the building ahead of us. We might not be able to hear it due to soundproofing or a muting spell, but it was there.

That was why, when we entered the building and saw two burly-looking men on either side of a door across the room, my first thought was *Bouncers*. As we approached them across the long, empty space, one of them spoke to us in Russian.

"Password?" Vlad repeated in English, with a feminine laugh I would never get used to. "Did you get a password, Sylvie?"

My fake name. I giggled as if it were a joke while thinking, *Damn you, Mircea! You could have mentioned this part!* "No, but I'm hammered, so I wasn't really paying attention when the guy mentioned this place earlier. Did anyone else catch it?"

Ian responded by fluffing his boobs until their bulk nearly escaped the too-small bra he'd stuffed them into. Marty twirled a lock of his silky raven hair and Maximus let out a strained giggle that was at odds with his sultry Southern belle disguise. Mencheres, however, sauntered over as if he'd been born to look like a hot, naughty schoolgirl.

"This is my password," he said, turning around in a slow, provocative circle.

The guards took in long, lustful glances. "Good enough for me," one said in heavily accented English, and opened the door.

I gave a slight nod of acknowledgment in response to Ian's arch look. Okay, so Ian *had* been right about his choice of the guys' disguises, his subsequent boob fondling notwithstanding.

"Hope to see you two later," Ian cooed as he passed the guards, fondling their meaty biceps with brief, teasing touches. I didn't know if Ian was acting or being serious. With him, either was a possibility.

Music hit us like a sonic boom the moment we crossed the threshold into the next room. This place didn't just have soundproofing, it had magic soundproofing. Otherwise, we would have heard the music as soon as the guards opened the door.

It didn't surprise me that supernatural soundproofing wasn't the only unusual thing about this place. I might not be an expert in dance clubs because I'd had to avoid them since I shocked anyone who came into close contact with me, but I didn't need vast experience to know that this one was unique.

For starters, the air was filled with tiny, floating lights that settled beneath people's skin when they were breathed in, making everyone appear as if they had stars inside of them. The interior lights were very low, emphasizing the occupants' inner glowing orbs, until it seemed as if the people were the ones lighting the room more than any artificial illumination.

Next was the music itself. It seemed to use the

smoke from the fog machine in visually dazzling ways. When the bass was booming, the fog formed into thunderclouds that hung heavy over the dancers and enveloped them inside the vibrations. When the higher-pitched treble segments came to crescendo, the fog thinned into cometlike streaks that darted between the gyrating patrons before striking certain dancers and sending them into blissful spasms. And within every manifestation of the fog, those tiny little orbs winked with their strange light.

"Don't breathe them in," Ian warned, his tone low yet urgent. "I know that sort of magic. It strips away glamour."

I clamped my lips shut to make sure that no lights inadvertently found their way into my mouth. Thank God we were all vampires and didn't need to breathe. Still, that took away our scent-deciphering advantage, and that was no small loss.

"How do we find these people?" Vlad murmured while leaning in and pretending to fix a hair clip on my head.

How indeed? When I'd asked Mircea what the necromancers looked like, he'd only responded with a cryptic "You'll know them when you see them." He hadn't mentioned the part where we'd have to pick them out of a crowd of hundreds at a magically enhanced dance club. I wanted to find the nearest corner and slice open my hand to link to Mircea and demand a more thorough description, yet if I did, I already knew what Mircea would say.

"Mircea is testing us," I whispered back, cursing Mircea once again. "We don't just have to be strong enough to defeat these people. We also have to be able to find them, too."

"They will be vampires," Mencheres said, giving a little wave to a group of guys who openly leered at him. "They cannot have amassed such great power otherwise. There aren't many of our kind here, so we will start with that."

"And they must be regulars, work here, or own the place," I added, trying to fill in more of the missing pieces. "Or else you-know-who would've told us to come on a specific night."

I wasn't saying Mircea's name out loud here. Like the fictional villain Voldemort, I was sure that bad things could happen if it reached the wrong ears.

"We split up," Vlad murmured, gesturing to Mencheres and Ian. "You two take this room. Leila and I will search the other sections. Maximus and Marty, see if there's a back room."

"What's the signal if we find something?" I asked low.

Ian snorted. "I expect the rest of us will simply follow the ensuing screams."

Vlad shrugged in concurrence. On that rather ominous note, we left in pairs to begin our search.

Chapter 34

 Ian's choice of our disguises had gotten us past the bouncers, but it didn't take long to discover their downside. I should have realized that looking like an African goddess while dancing with Vlad's buxom blonde disguise would result in a lot of turned heads, not to mention a ton of come-ons.

"No," I said to yet another offer to dance as Vlad and I continued to make our way toward the back of the club.

"Ah, American, yes?" the guy's pal asked, grinning down at a now-much-shorter Vlad. "I looove Americans. Especially blondes." Then the guy grabbed Vlad's hips and forcefully ground his pelvis against them. "Dance, baby, you like it with me!"

He might be wearing the face and body of a petite female blonde, but his smile was pure Vlad the Impaler as he turned around, grabbed the guy right in the crotch, and squeezed.

A high-pitched scream cut through even the piercing crescendo of an Adele remix song. Every head around us turned. The guy dropped to his knees while gasping, crying, and still screaming at the same time.

"Ruptured testicles can be serious," Vlad said, the

cold words at odds with his new, wispy voice. "Best seek medical attention."

His friend began yelling at us in Polish, which I didn't speak, but Vlad did. Whatever he said in reply shut the guy up. With a last, furious glance, he helped his still-sobbing buddy to his knees and began half supporting, half dragging him away.

"Is there a problem?" an accented voice asked behind us.

I turned. If I'd been my normal height, I would have needed to tilt my head to meet the gaze of our questioner. The woman had to be six feet tall in her bare feet. In her stiletto heels, she was almost Maximus's height, and she was beautiful in a way that defied convention. You would think her prominent nose and full, wide mouth would have had better symmetry with thick brows, but hers were pencil thin and her cheekbones were delicate compared to her strong jawline. Her almond-shaped eyes were a striking shade of burnt umber and her thick blond hair was styled in crisscrossing, elaborate braids.

More importantly, from the aura that wafted off her and added a sizzle to the air that hadn't been there before, she was an old vampire, no matter that her human appearance looked frozen at the south side of forty.

"No problem," I said at once. "Someone needed a new set of manners, and that happened to come with a pair of damaged balls."

She laughed in a husky, throaty way that denoted a blend of sophistication, amusement . . . and warning. "Perhaps, but you still overstepped yourselves. Our employees are supposed to manage the customers if they warrant managing. Not other customers."

Out of the corner of my eye, I saw Vlad shake his head and make a quick, dismissive motion. No doubt warning the rest of our group not to swarm after the guy's screams would have drawn their attention. Then he turned to the tall, striking vampire.

"*So* sorry," he said, widening his eyes to match his new, overly dramatic tone. "I don't mind being pawed at a little, but there's a *line*, you know?"

I tightened my lips to keep from smiling at his flaw-less American accent, not to mention his nasally, sulky manner. He was owning his blond bombshell disguise with this act.

The vampire cocked her head. "How old are you?"

"Twenty-two," Vlad replied in that haughty, sorry-not-sorry way that made me wonder if he were chan-neling Gretchen for motivation.

"In combined years?" the vampire all but purred.

Vlad huffed in a manner that would've done Gretchen proud. "Noooo, I'm twenty-five in combined years, but that's, like, not the same, is it?"

If the situation weren't so serious, I could've grabbed some popcorn and watched this act all night. Instead, I was trying not to show how I was tensing as I discreetly sized the woman up. *Old vampire. Sounded like she was a manager or supervisor here. Creamy, golden-brown skin.* It was possible that she was the Egyptian vampire sorceress that Mencheres had known before. Anyone could dye their hair blond, after all.

Then again, she could just be a vampire who hap-pened to work here and who had nothing to do with Mircea or the necromancers. Either way, we had to find out.

"Whose line do you belong to?" the vampire asked, narrowing those deeply colored eyes at us.

"Why, are we in trouble?" Vlad asked, actually managing to make his voice quaver this time.

"We'd rather not say," I interjected, glancing around as if worried about being overheard. "We don't want our sire to know. See, we met some guys earlier who told us about this place, and they said there were *special* ways a vampire could party here."

"Did they?" the woman drew out.

Vlad bobbed a nod. He was killing it. "Yeah, like, in magical ways?" he said, saying the last two words in an isn't-it-obvious manner.

Now her burnished umber gaze really narrowed. "Come with me," she said crisply.

We followed after her brisk strides, Vlad and I exchanging a glance that required no words. I drew in my electricity until no hints of it emitted from me. Now, in addition to being undetectable, it would also be more concentrated if I had to unleash it to strike. Either we were about to be shown a magical version of club drugs, or we were about to be interrogated so that management could find out who had been loose-lipped enough to tell a couple of strange vampires about this place.

Either way, we would find out who the higher-ups were, and if our suspicions were correct, at least one of them should turn out to be part of the necromancer group we were here for.

I expected to be ushered to a back room on the same floor. Instead, we were brought upstairs into a room where large glass panels overlooked the main dance floor. Must be a two-way mirror. From our old vantage point on the dance floor, this had been a black glass wall that dimly reflected all the glowing lights the people had absorbed, increasing the ethereal effect of the club's ambiance.

The room was empty, which was a disappointment, but Vlad made sure to brush his hand against the vampire when she curtly directed us to sit in one of the several chairs that faced the glass. We sat, and I pretended to twist my fingers in nervousness when in actuality, I was loosening my gloves.

"This place is only meant for humans, not vampires," she began without preamble. "If either of you want to see the sun rise again, you will tell me who told you about it."

"Why? We've done nothing wrong," Vlad said at once.

He'd touched her, so he could burn her now if he wanted to. He must be stalling so the female vampire would call for reinforcements to help with her interrogation.

"Yeah, this is bullshit," I chimed in to move that along. "You're a vampire and you're here, so why can't we be?"

She began to hum something as she rubbed her fingers together. At first, I thought she was mocking my complaint by doing a mime of the world's smallest violin. Then, as light began to form between her fingers, I realized she wasn't mocking me. She was forming a spell.

"I can make you talk," she all but purred at us. "But you will not like what happens if I do."

"There you are!" a feminine squeal suddenly said as the door opened and Mencheres bustled inside the room.

The vampire swung around so fast, her intricately

braided hair lifted off her back to snap around like a thick whip. "Get out unless you want to be in as much trouble as they are!"

I was surprised when Mencheres stopped in mid-step, his whole body freezing as he stared at the vampire. Despite wearing the face and body of a young girl, his ancient nature seemed to pour through the gaze he lasered onto the vampire's back.

"What an unusual tattoo you have. If I'm not mistaken, that is an Egyptian cartouche, yes?"

I stiffened. Mencheres wouldn't be mistaken. Not when one of the three most famous pyramids in Egypt was his. This was a message meant for us. Vlad met my gaze, and that single look said that the fight was about to begin. I pulled off my gloves.

The female vampire flipped her hair into place again, covering the series of shapes and images within two parallel lines that were inked onto the right side of her back.

"You're another vampire. Are you here with them?"

She suddenly sounded unnerved instead of angry. I didn't know the significance of the tattoo, but she obviously hadn't expected to reveal it, let alone have anyone comment on it.

"I have one as well," Mencheres said, ignoring her question. He opened his palms, revealing that he'd caught some of those strange floating orbs in his hands. Then he put them to his mouth and breathed them in, pulling up the back of his shirt at the same time. True to Ian's warning, as soon as he inhaled the lights, his glamour vanished and his well-muscled, very male physique burst through his former schoolgirl mirage.

He did have a tattoo on his back with another series of strange shapes contained within two parallel lines.

The vampire gasped more at that than she did at him suddenly morphing from an Asian teenage girl into an older, imposing Egyptian man.

"Mine is the mark of Menkaure, my birth name," Mencheres told her darkly. "And yours is the mark of Imhotep . . . necromancer."

Chapter 35

 What happened next happened very fast. Mencheres's power shot out, filling the room with the force of a dozen wrecking balls. That knocked me off my feet and even staggered Vlad, but the female necromancer was unfazed. She spun around and then shot forward as if she'd been fired from a gun, launching herself right at the glass wall behind us.

"Stop her!" Vlad shouted, his hands bursting into flames.

Incredibly, Mencheres didn't freeze her with his telekinetic abilities, and the fire that Vlad unleashed at the necromancer seemed to skip over her body instead of burning it. Shock over that combined with being knocked on my ass from the force of Mencheres's power cost me a precious second of inaction that the vampire used to dive through the glass wall.

Then I jumped through the glass wall after her. Shards slashed me in various places, but I ignored the pain. I also ignored the screams from the dancers as the female necromancer and I suddenly fell on top of them. She shoved people aside hard enough to fling them into the air as she ran away, and I hit more than a few of them by accident as I chased after her.

More screams sounded behind us. I didn't turn around as I fought to keep sight of her. She was headed for the door, and I didn't need Vlad's shout of "Stop her!" to know that I couldn't let her make it.

Fire erupted along the entire wall where the exit was, and the people inside naturally began to panic. The necromancer threw a fraught look over her shoulder, screaming something that could have been Russian or Polish. I remembered Elena's huge sinkhole spell and lunged toward her, now shoving aside people with the same disregard she'd shown. I could not let her activate a fail-safe spell.

Two forms whooshed over my head. Vlad and Mencheres flew over the crowd, their clear path causing them to reach the necromancer before she made it to the wall of flames blocking the door. They dropped out of sight as they tackled her, and that caused her to stop whatever she had been saying. Seconds later, I'd forced my way through the people to reach them.

Vlad had her in a choke hold, one arm locked around her throat, the other over her mouth to prevent her from completing whatever spell she'd been uttering. His hands were still lit up with flames, yet again, she didn't catch fire the way she should have. However, the walls of the club were burning just fine, and from the countless coughs and chaos, it was becoming dangerous.

"Do something; people can't breathe," I told Vlad.

The fire instantly vanished, although clouds of smoke remained. Vlad and Mencheres hauled the necromancer away from the door and Mencheres telekinetically flung it open. At once, a swarm of people headed for the exit.

"Your powers didn't work on her. Why?" I asked,

looking around for Ian, Marty, and Maximus in the crush of bodies.

"She must be infused with grave magic," Mencheres replied, referring to the most formidable form of magic because its power came from harnessing the darkest energies of the dead. "It's the only thing immune to my abilities as well as resistant to Vlad's."

Resistant. Not entirely immune. That's why the necromancer's body now smoked like a wet log thrown onto a fire beneath Vlad's hands. Still, we didn't have much time to get the answers we needed since our cover had been more than blown.

"Where are the other necromancers?" I demanded. "And if you utter one more word of a spell, you'll regret it."

Vlad removed his arm from her mouth so she could answer. "You lied to us, Impaler," she spat, only to be immediately silenced by Vlad before she could say anything else.

"Lied? I don't know what game you're playing, but you'd better stop," I told her tersely. "You might be throwing off *their* power, but my abilities aren't affected."

I wasn't bluffing. Vlad had once likened my seeming immunity to grave magic as my being "scorched earth" to those dark energies due to all the electrical currents in my body.

"So talk now, or talk after I cut you into ribbons with this," I finished, sending currents surging into my right hand. When she saw the whip that snapped out while sparks rained out of it, her eyes widened. Then a thunderous boom shook the club behind us. Alarmed, I spun around to see what had caused it.

Two unfamiliar vampires rose above the panicked throngs of people swarming toward what I assumed was an exit at the other side of the club. Their hands were held out, and what looked like a growing web of eerie light grew between them.

You'll know them when you see them, Mircea had said about the necromancers. This seemed proof enough, although Mircea's cryptic comment had probably been an allusion to the tattoos that marked the necromancers with Imhotep's name. I couldn't see if these two had them, but I wasn't going to wait until I did to assume that they were the other necromancers.

Then three forms barreled into them, causing the necromancers' web to break while they careened from the impact before smashing into the wall at the other end of the club. Ian, Maximus, and Marty had finally joined in the fight.

I turned around. "No need for you to tell us anything now—"

I stopped speaking when I saw that former faint glow in necromancer's fingers had turned a deep, brilliant blue and spread to her whole hand. Vlad couldn't see it from his view behind her, and Mencheres was focused on using his power to help people that had been trampled by the desperate escaping patrons. In a flash, I knew what that meant. She shouldn't have been able to finish her spell without the ability to speak, yet she had.

"Vlad, watch out!" I shouted, snapping my whip at her.

It severed her arm above the wrist, but not before she touched her indigo-infused hand to Vlad's arm. Then her severed hand held on despite the rest of her

falling away as Mencheres spun around and violently
yanked her back. Horrified, I watched as that blue
glow seemed to melt into Vlad's arm.

Vlad snatched her severed hand off and flung it
aside. Then Mencheres yanked her out of Vlad's arms
and shoved her away before she could touch either of
them with her other hand, which had turned bright
blue from magic, too.

"Don't touch her!" Mencheres said when Vlad
surged toward her to grab her again.

"That's right," she hissed. "Or you'll get another
dose of the curse of endless regret."

I wasn't sure if I was immune to this type of magic,
so I eyed the necromancer warily as I circled her. I
didn't need to touch her with my hands to take her
out. All I needed was to get close enough within a clear
space to strike.

Then a sudden, awful gasping came from Vlad. I
glanced at him in time to see him abruptly crumple to
the floor. That panicked me into rushing to him instead
of cornering the necromancer. Mencheres rushed over,
too, and the look on his face was almost as frightening as seeing Vlad gasp as if he were being choked by
something that had no form.

Mencheres looked helpless—and afraid. What kind
of spell was this "curse of endless regret"? "What do
we do?" I shouted.

"We can't help him." Mencheres's voice was harsh.
"This spell is designed to trap its victim inside their
worst memory, and if it takes Vlad to where I think
it will, we need to get everyone out of here or we'll
all die."

"Can't." Vlad managed to speak but his voice was

garbled, as if he was being strangled by the spell. "Can't let her . . . live."

"We'll get her later," I began.

"Now!" he roared, his voice agonized. "No . . . matter what!"

Then his eyes rolled back and he went completely limp. Before I could grab him, he suddenly stood as though yanked upward, and his eyes seemed sightless as he held out his hand. "Give it to me," he said in a visceral snarl.

I gaped at him. "Give you what?"

Mencheres hauled me away before I could reach him, and his rough shake almost rattled my teeth out of my head.

"You cannot help him now," he snapped. "But you are the only one who can stop the sorceress without being infected by her spell. Find her and kill her, Leila. Do it now."

Every part of me wanted to scream out a refusal. I couldn't leave Vlad like this, I couldn't! Yet maybe killing her would end this spell the way killing the earth mage sorcerer had ended the spell that had nearly finished Ian. That had to be it, and a vicious part of me needed revenge for what she'd done to Vlad.

I picked up her severed hand and took in a big breath. The floating lights I also inhaled caused my glamour to drop like a snake shedding its skin, but now I had her scent.

"Take care of Vlad," I said to Mencheres, then spun around and chased after the necromancer.

Chapter 36

 Mencheres's power didn't work to control the necromancer, but he used it to keep the doors of the club closed in an attempt to prevent her from leaving. Even amidst the smoke and scents from the dozens of people that hadn't evacuated yet, I managed to track her and found that she had made her own exit. The warehouse only had a few windows and they were so high up, none of the humans could reach them. That made it easy for me to find the smashed one that the necromancer had escaped through, and I vaulted after her with single-minded intent.

You're dead, bitch! You're dead.

Crowds of people were outside the warehouse, some crying, others huddled in shock. I paid them no mind as I chased down the necromancer's scent trail. It led me through the nearby traffic intersection, and the part of me that wasn't crazed with the need to kill was relieved that it was still only *her* scent, which meant she hadn't grabbed a hostage or two from among the patrons. I was also thanking my lucky stars that the necromancer must not have the ability to fly or she would have done so already, and I couldn't follow her scent if she flew away.

Yet a strong winter breeze scattered her scent when I rounded the next corner. I had a moment of panic until I heard tires screeching and the sounds of a crash in the highway up ahead. Something had caused a bunch of cars to suddenly slam on their brakes, and I was betting that it was her.

I increased my speed as I ran toward the sounds. When I got close, headlights momentarily blinded my vision as one of the cars abruptly spun the wrong way and faced me instead of the flow of traffic. I blamed the winter-slick, icy roads until the car suddenly elevated and came hurtling right at me.

Holy hell, the bitch was throwing a car at me!

I dove out of the way just in time. The car landed with a tremendous crash only a few feet away, followed instantly by an explosion that pelted me with flames and flying glass. I only paused to spare a single, pitying glance at the flaming wreckage before I got up and started after the necromancer again. No human could survive that explosion, but I could save Vlad, if I didn't let her horrifying defensive tactic work by wasting time trying to help people who were already dead.

By the time I was close enough to see her, she was already hefting up another car to chuck at me. This time, I wasn't blindsided by shock, so instead of ducking, I ran toward it, aiming for the terrified, screaming driver. I smashed through the windshield right when the car went airborne. In the mere seconds before it hit the ground, I used a spinning maneuver I'd learned from my Olympics tryouts to twist in midair in order to yank the driver out of his seat belt. Our continued backward velocity combined with the car's forward momentum sent both of us barreling through the back windshield. I twisted around again so my body took the brunt of the impact, yet the driver was still bleeding and hurt when we came out the other side.

I dropped him as soon as we cleared the wreckage. He might have serious injuries, but he'd live, which was more than I could say for the other poor driver. Now I had to stop this bitch from flinging any more cars with innocent people in them.

I jumped up and grabbed the nearest streetlight, shoving my right hand into it. That shot electricity into me with a dizzying rush, yet I didn't pause to savor the sensation. I used the pole as a springboard to launch myself at the necromancer, and torpedoed into her right as she was reaching for a new car to hurl my way.

We tumbled in a mass of flailing limbs down the embankment next to the highway, and I shot all that excess electricity into her as we rolled. Her other hand had grown back, and she tore into me with agonizing ferocity. Her age meant that she was far stronger than me, too. I couldn't win this fight with fangs or fists and we were too close for me to use my whip, so I took the punishment while gripping her with my right hand and forcing more electricity into her. After a few more painful moments, she stopped attacking me and began to fight to get away instead.

I didn't let her go, even when I saw her hands turn blue. She grabbed me, trying to send that awful spell into me while she hissed out curses. I held on, hoping the same electricity-fueled immunity that had previously protected me from Remnants—another manifestation of the dark energies of grave magic—would protect me now. Even if it didn't, killing her would negate any spell she hexed me with, so all I had to do was *not* succumb to it before I could finish her.

Soon, the words of her spell turned into screams as

her flesh began to split and blacken, unable to heal fast enough to counter the devastating effects of the unceasing electricity I kept forcing into her. Her grip on me loosened and her eyes grew impossibly wide, then burst open as if they were smashed eggs.

In another mood, I would have found that disgusting. Instead, I was filled with ruthless exultation as I kept shoving more currents into her. Her face blackened and split, exposing tendons and bone. Then her limbs started bursting open while parts of her caught fire. My hands and clothes also ignited from the contact, yet I still didn't let go. I kept filling her with currents, vaguely aware that I was smiling with a savageness I hadn't known I was capable of. *You tried to kill Vlad! Die screaming for it, bitch, die!*

With a *pop* that was sweet, gruesome music to my ears, her whole body burst apart from the overload of currents. I fell forward onto what was left of her torso, watching with dark satisfaction as her skull began rolling down the embankment.

I wanted to take a second to savor my victory as well as metaphorically catch my breath, but the guys might need help with the other two necromancers. I wasn't trapped in an awful memory, so I had proved to be immune to the blue-handed spell this necromancer had tried to take me down with. If the other necromancers' first instinct was to use grave magic, too, then I had the best chance out of everyone of not being affected by it.

I jumped up, brushing away the charred pieces of the dead necromancer's body as I began to run back toward the warehouse. When I passed the highway, a quick glance showed that other drivers had stopped to help the injured man from the second wreck, and I noted with a mixture of relief and concern that I heard sirens coming this way. Someone had also called the police. That was good for the driver who needed medical attention, yet it wouldn't take long for the former patrons of the dance club to hear those sirens and run toward them to tell the authorities about the chaos at the nearby warehouse.

We really didn't need police interfering while we tried to take on the other two necromancers. Yet with luck, Vlad was already coming out of the spell now that I'd killed the female necromancer. Hopefully, the other two's magic wasn't as potent as hers and the guys had already subdued them. In case they hadn't, I ran back toward the warehouse as fast as I'd left it.

As I rounded a corner, I could see a telltale orange glow in the sky over where the warehouse was supposed to be. Why would it be on fire again? Vlad had doused the flames so that none of the people still trapped inside would get hurt—

My bound around the next corner brought the warehouse into view. The previous crowd of frightened patrons had scattered, leaving only a handful of people that were actively running away. The reason why was obvious. Huge groups of flames shot from the top of the warehouse in vertical streaks, as if fire tornados were dancing along the roof.

"What's going on?" I shouted when I saw Mencheres, Ian, Maximus, and Marty about a block away from the warehouse. They had all shed their glamour, so they were easy to pick out.

"Stay back," Mencheres called out in reply.

His hands were outstretched, and as I watched, a metal Dumpster flew down the next street and landed on the side of the warehouse, joining the other various pieces of urban debris that were stuck to the side of it as if welded there by a giant. Then screams and repeated pounding noises reached me even though I was still a street length away.

"What are you doing? Where's Vlad?" I said, running over and ignoring Mencheres's demand to stay back.

"Inside," Maximus said, his expression very grim.

I was aghast. "You left him alone in there with the two necromancers?" The fire couldn't hurt him, but they could—

"All of you, leave now," Mencheres said, stunning me. "I will ensure that the necromancers do not escape."

So that's who was screaming inside. Guess it also explained why Mencheres kept telekinetically transporting more and more heavy objects onto the exterior of the building. He might not be able to use his powers on the necromancers directly, but Mencheres could use it to keep them from tearing a path to freedom through the building's walls and windows.

Now this scene made sense. Being semi-fire-resistant due to grave magic was one thing. Surviving a blazing inferno was another. "So when Vlad's spell broke, he stayed inside to burn one of them to death while you're making sure that the other doesn't get out until Vlad nabs him?"

No one said anything for a loaded moment. Then Marty came over and put his arm around my waist.

"Kid," he said, his voice cracking. "I don't know how to tell you this, but . . ."

"The spell didn't break," Ian supplied bluntly. "And

he's so barmy from being trapped inside his worst memory that he's burning everything and everyone near him, including us."

I was so shocked, I began to argue. "That can't be. I killed the necromancer who hexed him, so he should be fine now!"

"He's not," Mencheres said with such pity that I felt the cold touch of despair despite the heat pouring off the nearby warehouse. "This necromancer knew the curse of endless regret. It is steeped in grave magic, and grave magic curses do not end with the death of the caster like regular magic or even necromancy. They only end with the destruction of the cursed object."

"But the cursed object is Vlad!" I all but shouted.

Mencheres's features twisted with grief. "Yes."

Chapter 37

 Mencheres could not mean what he seemed to mean. He just couldn't. And even if he did, I refused to accept it.

"This is all wrong," I snapped. "I know Vlad's worst memory because I saw it the first time I touched him. It's of him screaming by a river while holding his dead first wife, *not* of him burning everything down around him!"

"That might have been his worst memory back when you two met," Mencheres said in a painfully gentle tone, "but since then, it has been superseded. Before things became too dangerous to stay near him, I watched Vlad repeatedly hold out his hand and say, 'Give it to me' before mimicking the appearance of putting an object into a slot. He stares silently for several minutes, then erupts into rage and manifests ever-more-powerful bursts of fire."

Why did that sound familiar? When Maximus looked away, his face crumpling, I understood.

"He's reliving the memory of when he received Szilagyi's video of my supposed rape," I said, anguish gripping me.

I wanted to kill that bitch a thousand times more for trapping Vlad inside this spell, and I also wanted to weep. I knew the agony Vlad had felt centuries ago when he'd found his wife's broken body because I'd relieved it when I first touched him with my right hand. To know that his soul had been scarred even deeper by the brutal videos Szilagyi had sent him . . .

Mencheres let out a sigh that sounded as if it were a choked sob. "The memory keeps repeating, stalling Vlad from accessing his full strength, yet eventually, he will do more than burn down this warehouse. He will destroy this entire block by morning, and left unchecked, the destruction will continue."

"He'll tire out eventually," I said, grasping at straws. "He has to. He can't flame everything down forever!"

Mencheres gave me another pitying look. "Yes, but with his strength, by then it will be too late. Such a public display of superhuman power will draw the attention of every Law Guardian. Whether Vlad was magically compelled or not, he will surely be executed for endangering the secrecy of our entire race."

"Then you have to stop him!" Rage and grief made my demand a scream. "*He's* not coated in grave magic, so do something!"

"I can't," Mencheres said with such fervent frustration; his power flared and the words hit me like a literal slap. "Fire is a natural element. It does not obey my telekinesis any more than air or water do. His powers have also grown to where I cannot smother his flames with exterior objects, either. He would merely melt them down in the same way that he melted his castle the day he received that video."

"There must be something else," I snarled. "Ian," I said, abruptly turning to him. "What about that reality spell you hit me with the other day? Wouldn't that work to snap him out of this memory?"

He didn't give me a pitying look, which was good because I couldn't stand one more of those. Yet from his expression, he obviously didn't think I was very smart.

"Pitting a mid-level spell against this form of advanced grave magic? A Chihuahua would have better luck surviving a death match against a werewolf."

That was a firm no, but damned if I'd give up. I spun back around to Mencheres.

"Come on, you don't know any magic that can break this? You're over four and a half thousand years old, you have to know *some*thing that can help!"

He drew in a breath to reply, and my cry of "Wait!" stopped him. The answer was suddenly so clear, I should have thought of it first thing. "Let me in the warehouse. *I* can break this."

"How?" four voices asked in unison.

I was already heading over to the warehouse, wincing at the heat that poured off the building. This could work, if I didn't burn to death before I reached Vlad.

"The necromancer tried to cast the same spell on me, blue-handed grip and all, but it didn't take for the same reason that the Remnant attack didn't do anything to me months ago. Regular magic and necromancy-infused magic might stick to me, but for some reason, the natural energy of my voltage makes me immune to the dark energies of grave magic. That means all I have to do is fill Vlad with enough of my voltage to make *him* immune to it, and break the spell!"

Mencheres's expression went from compassionately grim to cautiously hopeful, then back to compassionately grim.

"Even if your theory is correct, you might not survive to do this. The fire grows in intensity with every new memory cycle. Moreover, I have a barricade around Vlad to protect him against the necromancers trapped inside the building, but I will not be able to do the same for you, and they will surely try to kill you if you enter."

"Tell me something I don't know," I muttered. "I've got a plan for that, too, but we can't waste any more time by me explaining it. Just trust me, Mencheres, and let me in there so I can break this spell before it gets Vlad killed."

"Leila." Marty caught up to me and grabbed my hand. "Don't go in there, please." His gaze started to shine with pink tears. "I already lost one daughter. I can't bear to lose you, too."

Maximus said nothing, yet he looked equally pessimistic about my survival chances, and Ian's expression said that he was downgrading his opinion of me from stupid to outright deranged.

"I'm not going to die," I said, and hoped that was true. "But this is the only solution that doesn't end with Vlad's guaranteed death. Yes, it's dangerous, but I couldn't live with myself if I didn't try, so"—I flashed a lopsided grin at Ian—"Chihuahua-versus-werewolf odds or no, I'm doing this."

"You know it's madness," he said in response.

"And Vlad wouldn't want you to sacrifice your life for his," Maximus added, finally breaking his silence.

I was done debating with them. Every second spent out here downgraded my chances to worse than what they already were.

"Enough. This is my decision, and I've made it. Mencheres, either open a door for me or I'll cut out an opening myself."

He met my gaze. For a tense moment, I braced to hit him with all the voltage I had if he tried to restrain me. Then he said, "Let me know when you have dealt with the necromancers and I will drop the barricade around Vlad," and an opening appeared in the side of the warehouse as if the metal had become curtains that someone drew back. Despite the instant blast of heat, I ran through it without a backward glance.

"That's love for you," I heard Ian say. "Glad I'm too corrupt to fall victim to *that* form of intelligence lobotomy."

"I hope you fall head over heels for someone who insists on monogamy!" I called out right before Mencheres closed the metal slit behind me. Then a roar of fire claimed all my attention as a huge swath of flames poured out of the door across the room and headed right toward me.

Chapter 38

I hit the floor, keeping low enough that the fire passed over me instead of hitting me. Even though the flames didn't directly touch me, their heat was so intense that my skin started to blister. After a few minutes, I had to fight an instinctual urge to crawl back to the same wall I'd entered through and bang on it until Mencheres let me out.

Yet I didn't. The large fire swath dissipated after another minute, which meant that Vlad's memory must now be on the "staring silently" side of the endless loop. That gave me a few minutes before he would start burning things again. I got up and headed farther inside the long, empty room that led to the door marking the club's official entrance.

The two bouncers who'd previously guarded it were long gone, but a few charred bodies remained near the entrance. These couldn't be the necromancers; they had been pounding on the walls a mere few minutes ago, so they were still alive. They must be some poor patrons who'd either gotten trampled in the stampede to escape, or caught by one of those fire-hose sprays of flames that, moments ago, had been jetting out from the open door. The fire would only get worse, as

Mencheres had said, but I took consolation in the fact that there were sections of this room that were still untouched by flames.

Maybe it wasn't just the constant resets as Vlad's memory rewound to the beginning of that awful moment and interrupted his power from reaching its full potential. Maybe, just maybe, a thread of Vlad's consciousness remained, and he was fighting back against the spell.

I fervently hoped so. Otherwise, Mencheres was right and soon, there wouldn't be a single inch of this place that wasn't covered in flames. Then the whole warehouse would be a melted-down pile of rubble by morning, and things would only get worse from there.

But Vlad hadn't fully unleashed his powers yet, so there was still a chance that I could interrupt the spell before that happened. Before I could reach him and attempt to short-circuit the spell's hold by giving him an overload of electricity, I had to get past two trapped, desperate necromancers first.

I pulled a small, square object out of my bra and ran my fingers over it, careful not to look at it. No feel of cracks, good. The only reason it hadn't broken was because of the Kevlar vest that Vlad had insisted I wear beneath my top. He'd done so out of concern over silver knives or silver bullets. Instead, the vest had ended up protecting Leotie's mirror.

Now, I only hoped I hadn't screwed up the spell Leotie had left for me, because this was my best chance to get past the necromancers without their killing me (worst case scenario) or my wasting a lot of time (second worst.)

"I know a way out," I called to them as loudly as I could. With luck, they'd assume that I was an innocent survivor trying to help instead of their enemy baiting them into a trap. "If anyone else is still alive in here, follow me!"

Nothing but the creaking noises of overheated, overstressed metal for a few moments, then I heard another rushing noise. At first, I thought I'd misjudged the amount of time between Vlad's fiery eruptions. Then I heard crashing noises and that rushing sound increased. It was headed right this way, yet there was no intense blast of heat preceding it.

This wasn't more fire from Vlad. It was the necromancers blasting their way out of whatever debris had been in their path to fly toward the sound of my voice.

I couldn't wait to act until I saw them. By then, it might be too late. I held up the mirror that Leotie had used to trap all of us earlier and once again called out in a loud voice. "I know a way out. Come with me if you want to live!"

Two large forms suddenly tore through the narrow door, flying so fast that it took a few moments to register that they were completely naked except for the soot covering them. Their speed made me gasp, as did their murderous expressions when they saw me and clearly pegged me to be foe, not friend.

Maybe they recognized me for who I was, now that my appearance was no longer disguised by glamour. Maybe it was enough that I was a vampire and they figured I was with the group of vamps that had done all this damage tonight. Either way, they bared their fangs and arced toward me as if they intended to tear me apart with the impact of their bodies. I couldn't snap out my whip to defend myself. If I did, then they'd look at that instead of what I needed them to look at. Yet the mirror was hard to see with all the smoke and its small size. *Come on, look at it*, I silently urged them.

They didn't. Instead, in the moments right before they were about to hit, they snarled something in a guttural-sounding language that was probably the start of a spell. I braced, trying to power up my hand without releasing any incriminating sparks, and waved the mirror so it would catch any tiny flashes of light that were still left.

Look at it, dammit, look! I silently screamed.

A few feet from hitting me, they suddenly dropped out of the air as if they'd been shot down by missiles. Their bodies thudded onto the floor, and I jumped back just in time to avoid one of them hitting me as he slid from his velocity. When they came to a stop, they were completely limp yet still stretched out in that arcing, torpedoing form they'd used when they'd been about to slam themselves into me.

I snapped out my whip at last. They didn't move and their eyes stared sightlessly ahead in the eerie way that Vlad's had when the spell first took hold of him. I wasn't sure if this was an act, so I lashed the nearest one of them in the leg. My electric cord cut all the way through and severed his limb at the knee, yet he didn't so much as twitch.

If you catch them in it, they'll be as helpless as you are now, Leotie had promised me when I was trapped in the mirror spell. Good Lord, she hadn't been kidding. The two of them looked more than helpless; it's as if they were catatonic. Was that what had happened to me? Had I only *thought* that I was banging on the mirrors and hitting them with my whip when all the while, I was as immobile as these two?

Had to be. Otherwise, I might have accidentally

slashed the people near me while thinking that I was lashing the mirrors. Come to think about it, Vlad would also have probably burned the whole house down because his first reaction to being trapped would no doubt have been to try and melt the mirrors. We all must have been as immobile and unaware as these two. The power of the mirror trap was truly stunning, yet I didn't have time to stand here and keep admiring it. I also didn't have time to abide by "fair" rules of fighting.

It takes a special coldness to kill when your life isn't in danger and you're not driven by anger or revenge, Vlad had said. Turns out, I had that same coldness, because I snapped my whip and one of the necromancer's heads severed from his shoulders while his body began to wither from the effects of true death. The other I kept alive. We'd need to interrogate Mircea's location out of him later, if we were still alive later.

"The necromancers have been dealt with," I called out loudly to Mencheres. "Now, drop whatever barricade you've got around Vlad so that I can get to him!"

Chapter 39

 Another warning blast of heat caused me to drop to the floor. This time, the flames that followed were so intense that despite my staying low, pain and a horrible stink let me know that I'd just lost my hair. I covered my head with my arms and felt the scorch of flames. The fire tore a path down my back, turned the metal clasps on my shoes into brands, and caused me to press against the floor as if trying to tunnel into it.

It was only a couple minutes, but agony made it feel like hours before the fire stopped. As soon as it did, I tried to get up and immediately cried out as the charred flesh all along the back of me split from the sudden movement. The pain was almost as awful as being burned, and I gritted my teeth to keep from screaming as I waited for my body to heal.

What the fuck? an enraged voice suddenly howled in my mind.

Mircea. I hadn't linked to him, but the boomerang response from my burns must have alarmed him into contacting me. I gritted my teeth again, trying to ignore him as I raced into the room beyond. I only had a few minutes before the next fire blasts. Barely enough time to find Vlad, let alone to break the spell on him.

Why are we on fire? Mircea continued to demand as I stumbled into the room, tripping over a body that I hadn't seen due to the thick smoke. I ran into several more that the choking haze concealed as I rapidly made my way deeper into the room. The smoke was almost blinding, yet I thought I had glimpsed a flash of green between those heavy, noxious-smelling layers. Could that be the glow from Vlad's eyes?

Answer me! Mircea roared loud enough to make my brain ache.

We're on fire because of you! I snarled back, still doing that run-stumble-run-again thing as I made my way to what I hoped was Vlad and not some random remaining lights. *We killed the necromancers you sent us after, but not before one of them slapped a memory spell on Vlad that's NOT agreeing with him.*

A memory spell? You meant the curse of endless regret? Mircea asked, sounding surprised.

Winner, winner, chicken dinner, I replied sarcastically.

I was now close enough to be positive that I'd found Vlad. I couldn't see much of him except for his gaze, yet it cut through the smoke like tiny green lasers. When a shift in the air briefly cleared the smoke surrounding him, I saw there were piles of large, burnt objects in a circle around him, as if every piece of heavy equipment, furniture, nonstructural beams, and pieces of sheet metal had huddled close in a mute plea for him to make the fire stop.

I have a barricade around Vlad to protect him against the necromancers, Mencheres said. Looked like he'd telekinetically stripped this club bare to form it. It also explained the necromancers' odd nakedness. Unable to get out, they must have turned their attention toward trying to kill the cursed object to stop the spell and its fiery consequences. They had to have attacked that barricade over and over to get all their clothes burned off in those fire-blast loops. Without Mencheres's power holding these objects together as a makeshift fortress around Vlad, they would have succeeded in killing him, too.

Ah, cursed with an endless repeat of horrible memories, Mircea went on with vicious satisfaction. *It couldn't have happened to a more deserving person.*

A vicious satisfaction of my own coursed through me as a telltale blast of heat began to fill up the air. *Before you continue to gloat, you might want to brace. We're probably about to get fried again.*

So saying, I dove to the floor, grabbing every large object I could get my hands on and piling them on top of me. From the stench, some were bodies, yet some were pieces of furniture and parts from Mencheres's former barrier. Either way, they were all protection against the flames that now lit up the smoke with terrifying shades of orange right before another blast of fire roared out with the sound of an oncoming freight train.

My tactics covered most of my body, yet my feet were left exposed. Mircea's scream echoed in my mind as those became engulfed by the flames that rushed over the room. I screamed, too, and fought against curling into the fetal position because I didn't want it to shift more of my protective barrier off me.

Get out of there, get out, get out, get out, get out! Mircea howled, the words a frantic, mindless repeat.

I wanted to. Oh, so badly! Aside from the pain that

shamed every previous torture I'd experienced, every survival instinct I had was howling as loud as Mircea now was, urging me to run for the nearest exit as soon as the flames stopped. Yet I wouldn't. My need to reach Vlad was greater than even the awful pain and my fear of knowing that it would only get worse.

That need drove me to shove the now-charred bodies and debris off me as soon as the fire stopped. I hadn't waited until after I healed, so every movement I made felt like it was splitting my feet open to the bone. But I didn't stop. I had to save him. That's why I ran toward Vlad instead of toward the greater safety of the other room, and ignored Mircea's continued curses and screams as he felt all the same pain that I did.

Vlad had just straightened from his mime of putting the DVD into the player. He must have breathed in some of those glowing orbs since I last saw him because his glamour had vanished. The flames on his hands were now out, too, but that would only last a few minutes. I seized my chance, grabbing him by the shoulders and shooting electricity into him while I tried to make him see me instead of that awful memory on endless replay.

"Vlad, listen to me, none of this is real!" I said, shaking him as I continued to send more electricity into him.

Nothing. His ramrod-straight posture didn't change and his emerald gaze seemed to stare straight through me. I increased the voltage, grateful that he was fire-proof and the currents couldn't harm him the way they did the necromancer that I had blasted apart earlier.

What are you doing? You need to get away from him, not get closer to him! Mircea screeched across my mind.

Shut up! I thought back at him. To Vlad, I said, "I'm right here; you need to stop this. Look at me, Vlad! I'm right here!"

He can't see you, imbecile! Mircea shouted. *Now leave, before he fries us both to ashes!*

"I'm not leaving," I shouted back, out loud this time. Then I increased the voltage that I was sending into Vlad. "Come on! You don't want to burn me to death."

Yes he does, look around you! Mircea's voice was too loud to ignore despite how much I tried. *He obviously wants to burn EVERYthing, and you're part of everything, Leila!*

Shut up so I can concentrate! I thought back savagely. *This will work. My currents make me immune to grave magic, so they can make him immune, too, if I can get enough into him.*

You're immune to grave magic? Mircea sounded shocked, but a sudden blast of heat from Vlad had me dropping my hands, spinning around, and looking for the nearest pile of debris.

I covered myself just in time. The new barrage of flames crashed over me with even more ferocity than before. They melted the less fire-resistant part of my makeshift barrier until it was no more than a dripping hunk of metal on top of quickly charring wood. I screamed with unspeakable anguish as several parts of my body were exposed to the brutal flames. Then I scooted forward to bury myself beneath another section of my barricade even though it was dangerous to move.

When the fire finally stopped, I forced myself to shove away what was left of my barricade. Every movement was the worst form of agony and pieces of my skin remained fused to parts of the molten remains, meaning I had to tear them off to get free.

Don't do that again, Leila. This time, Mircea wasn't yelling and he didn't sound angry. Instead, he sounded afraid. *We'll die if you do. You must know that.*

He was probably right. I still couldn't see much with the smoke, but it didn't take a genius to figure out that the pieces of the barricade Mencheres had formed around Vlad were being burned to the ground as Vlad's fire grew in size and intensity. I'd have to hide beneath piles of stuff in the other room to survive the next onslaught of flames. After that, I'd have to move farther away, until eventually, I wouldn't have enough time between the cycles of fiery bursts to reach Vlad at all.

The smoke shifted again, blown back due to the hole above him where his fire had burned away that entire section of the roof. I stared at Vlad, filled with the heartbreaking realization that I would probably never see him again. Either I would die if I stayed, or he would eventually be killed if I left.

After all we'd been through, how could it have come down to this?

Chapter 40

After another aching moment, I blinked in shock as a new gust of wind cleared away the smoke around his feet. Could that be real? It looked like there was a narrow, half-foot radius encircling Vlad that wasn't even sooty, let alone burned. How?

A second later, I answered my own question. With all the power he was unleashing, Vlad's aura would have flared out, too, rendering that narrow radius as fireproof as he was. I looked at the circle with new hope. It would be tight, but it might be wide enough for me to be protected from the flames.

It was my only chance, and I ran over as fast as my still-healing limbs could take me. *If you believe in God,* I told Mircea as I pressed as close to Vlad as I could, *then you'd better start praying.*

Great, we're all going to die now, my hated inner voice commented, popping up to join the mental party. *Looks like you've finally succeeded in killing yourself, Leila.*

Fuck off, all of you! I snapped back while shooting pain-and-desperation-fueled voltage into Vlad. *We're not dead yet!*

We will be if you don't stop this and run, Mircea retorted.

I ignored him as I kept shooting currents into Vlad while telling him over and over that I was there and none of this was real. All the while, he stared through me with those empty eyes, seeing what the magic compelled him to see instead of what was right in front of him.

When his power flared and I felt that deadly eruption of heat again, I wrapped my whole body around him, tears streaming from my eyes. It hadn't worked. How could my voltage save me from that spell, yet not be enough to save him?

Leila, run, this our last chance! Mircea shouted with almost crazed desperation.

I'm not running! I shouted back, steeling myself. *If I can't save him, at least I'll know I died trying.*

The truth of that gave me comfort even amidst the clawing, awful pain that started along the entire back of me. I was as close to Vlad as I could get, yet it must not be enough, and he'd just started with this new wave of flames. By the end of this, I'd be finished, and even if I changed my mind, which I hadn't, it was now too late to run.

At least I also had the satisfaction of knowing that I was taking Mircea down with me. In fact, I was almost sorry that Mircea couldn't see my pained grin because my face was buried in Vlad's chest as I hugged him for the last time.

Bet you're regretting casting that spell on me now, aren't you? I thought with the dark amusement of the condemned.

Fine. You insist on staying? Then I refuse to let Vlad kill me through secondhand means, Mircea snarled, his former frightened tone gone. *If I am to die by his hand, he will damn well show me the respect I am due by killing me in person! Now listen to me, you ignorant amateur. Magic this powerful can't be broken, but it CAN be tricked into ceasing on its own. If your voltage makes you immune to grave magic, what you need to do is disrupt the grave magic in Vlad with your electricity while you reach his mind to tell him that what he's seeing isn't real.*

You think I haven't tried that? I shot back because answering him was better than focusing on the appalling pain. Those flames were increasing, engulfing my legs, back, and head.

Don't try, do, Mircea stressed, the word ending on a scream as that pain ripped through him, too. *The voltage won't make Vlad immune as it does with you, but it should give you a brief window. Use that window to reach his mind and make him see you.*

Another scream caused Mircea to stop speaking, then he went on in a rush.

Once Vlad's mind sees you *instead of the memory from his curse, the curse will consider itself completed and stop. If you didn't doubt yourself so much, you could have already finished this because you are more than powerful enough to reach him!*

If I wouldn't have been in agony, I would have laughed. *Now you suddenly believe in me?*

Another burst of fire claimed both our attention. I tried to push my way through it by talking to Vlad and focusing on the voltage that I kept pushing into him, but it kept growing, until it was all I could do not to run out of sheer, mindless panic.

Your abilities have saved you more times than I ever believed they could, Mircea said, pain making his voice a ragged roar. *You linked to me through this spell despite that requiring the skill level of a powerful sorceress, not a second-rate psychic. I don't know how you have such power, but you DO*—

Our combined screams cut him off as the flames kept eating through my skin faster than I could heal. The pain was horrific, all-consuming, and relentless, until I was convulsing against Vlad and barely able to think. Yet Mircea's voice still reached me because it was a roar of defiance.

You do HAVE the power, Leila! Now, for the sake of both our miserable lives, stop doubting yourself and fucking use it!

I latched on to Mircea's confidence because my repeated failures had drained away all of mine. Then I tried to push past the crippling, madness-inducing agony to try one last time since I *had* done all those other things and it might not be too late to do this, too!

With the last bit of strength and coherence I had, I slapped my burning hands onto Vlad's face and forced back the screams that continued to rip from my throat. Instead, I used my mind to release the agony that caused everything in my body to viciously contort as my muscles began what I knew to be death contractions.

I'm here, I'm here, I shouted with my thoughts instead of my voice. *None of what you're seeing is real! It's the spell, and you need to stop burning everything. You're burning me, too, so put out the fire, Vlad! Put it out, out, out, out, OUT!*

My thoughts lost cohesion at the next flash of fire. It burned me right through to my bones, and I fell back, my charred legs snapping beneath me. For a torturous moment that seemed to stretch into forever, all I knew was pain, and I could no longer see the fire because my vision had gone black.

Then, as if coming out of a nightmare, I heard my name and felt the unbelievable relief of something warm, not agonizing, running over my body.

"Come on, Leila, you need to heal. Heal, my darling, heal, please!" an anguished voice bellowed.

I opened my eyes. Vlad's face was a blur from either the soot in my gaze or my eyes still healing, yet when that haze finally cleared after I kept blinking, I realized that he was staring at me and *seeing* me, not just looking through me. That, plus not being on fire anymore, let me know that the spell's grip on him had finally ceased.

"You said please," I whispered, smiling when his relief flooded my emotions with the force of a thousand dams breaking. "I'm never going to let you live that down."

Chapter 41

 Vlad wouldn't let go of my hand. Not when he stripped off his shirt to cover me because my clothes had burned off, and not when Marty, Maximus, and Mencheres all enveloped me in hugs after they ran into the room, knowing from the sudden lack of fire that my efforts had succeeded.

"You are remarkable," Mencheres said, brushing my other hand with a formal kiss after he released me from his embrace.

"I had help," I replied, still feeling stunned by it all.

Mircea, who had been the reason behind the countless awful things that had plagued both Vlad and me this past year, had also been instrumental in saving us. Yes, he'd done it because it had saved his own skin, too, but the fact remained that I owed my life and Vlad's life to him. I wasn't sure how I felt about that, so for now, I didn't want to dwell on it.

Ian was the only one who didn't give me a celebratory hug. Instead, he stared at me, a smile ghosting across his lips. "Seems that next time, I'll know to bet on the Chihuahua instead of the werewolf."

"Yeah? Well, 'though she be but little, she is fierce,'" I quoted with an answering, if much wearier, smile.

Ian laughed, but the look he gave me was appraising, as if he were mentally ranking me into a whole new category.

"More authorities have arrived," Mencheres unnecessarily noted as a new wail of sirens joined the other noises outside the warehouse. "You should all leave. The necromancer needs to be secured before the mirror spell wears off. I will stay behind to reinforce the story that a performing band's faulty pyrotechnic display caused this blaze."

I was all too happy to get out of here, so he didn't need to tell me twice. When we reached the other room, Maximus scooped up the necromancer and hoisted him over his shoulder as if he were a sack of potatoes. As soon as we stepped outside, a blast of freezing wind cut through the thin shirt I was wearing and felt like it formed ice crystals on my newly bald head. I shivered even as the irony struck me. How strange to be cold now when mere minutes ago, I'd been burning to death.

Vlad felt my shiver and stopped the police officer nearest us, green-eyeing him into removing his coat.

"Don't, he needs that," I protested.

"He'll get another one," Vlad said shortly.

From his intractable stare, he wasn't going to take no for an answer. After an apologetic glance at the cop, I put the coat on. It might be frigid out, but this place was now crawling with authorities, ambulances, and fire trucks, so there were plenty of blankets and additional coats for him. Most of the rescue workers spoke Russian or Polish, but from the few snatches of English I caught, they were dumbfounded that the huge warehouse fire had been extinguished without a drop of water being used.

Mencheres had his work cut out for him explaining *that* one.

We piled into both cars since there was no way all of us could fit into one. We were leaving Mencheres without a ride, but he could either mesmerize someone to drive him back or he could simply fly, which would probably be quicker. Maximus rode with Vlad and me, taking the driver's seat out of habit, no doubt. Vlad pulled me tight against him when we settled into the backseat. The necromancer was unceremoniously dumped into the trunk of Ian and Marty's car, and we drove behind them to monitor the trunk in the very unlikely event that the spell broke early and he tried to escape.

The first twenty minutes of the drive passed in absolute silence. I caught a glimpse of myself in the rearview mirror, then made sure not to look again. Every single strand of hair on my head had been burned off, and I was so covered in soot; I looked as if I'd dived into a pool of it on purpose.

Mencheres knows a hair-growing spell, I reminded myself. This was the second time this year that I'd need to use one. Between the tortures, the gas line explosion, the skinning, getting shot, and now this, if my body could talk, it would probably tell me it wanted a divorce.

Oddly, I wasn't devastated over this loss the way I had been after Szilagyi's henchman had cut all my skin off. Maybe it's because this had been my choice versus someone's cruel whim. In fact, Vlad was probably more upset over it than I was. Not that I could tell from his emotions. He'd concealed them behind the wall he'd dropped into place as soon as the rest of the guys had come into the warehouse.

I didn't press him to talk. For one, we had an audience, and for another, it might be too soon. I could only imagine how traumatizing it must have been to come out of the horrible memory loop only to find me nearly burned to death at his feet by his own fire.

And it only would have taken a few more moments of my being exposed to that fire before I would have been all the way burned to death. If Mircea hadn't told me to trick the spell into thinking that it was completed by psychically invading Vlad's mind and interrupting the loop—

"Mircea," I said out loud, suddenly sitting straight up instead of leaning against Vlad. "He hasn't contacted me since we came out of this."

Vlad gave me an inscrutable look. "Why would he?"

To *rub it in that he had helped to save us, to insult me for not thinking up the secret of disrupting the spell earlier, to complain about getting repeatedly torched* . . . "To make sure that we'd succeeded in keeping one of the necromancers alive," I said, going with the most pertinent reason.

Another unreadable look. "Why would he know we'd attacked them tonight?"

"Come on, you think he wouldn't reach out to me to find out why he was being burned within an inch of his life?" His expression clouded, and I was instantly sorry I'd reminded him of that. "I mean, um—"

"Leila." Now the look Vlad gave me was jaded, even though his feelings briefly burst their walls to scald me with a geyser of regret. "There's no glossing over what I did."

"What the spell did," I instantly corrected.

His mouth tightened as another, darker emotion shadowed his face, yet when he spoke, his tone was deceptively light. "Of course. Now tell me, did the necromancer who cast it escape?"

A swell of deep satisfaction filled me at the memory of her head rolling down the embankment. "No. I killed her."

His shields slipped again and I was puzzled by the relief that flowed through our connection before his walls went back up. Gladness I could understand. Hell, if I were Vlad, I'd want to dance on her bones for trapping me in that nightmarish spell. But why would he be *relieved* by her death? He had to know that killing her hadn't worked to stop the spell.

Or maybe, he didn't know that. All he knew since he came out of the spell was that at some point, he'd almost burned me to death. Maybe he didn't remember how it had been broken, or more accurately, how it had been tricked into stopping itself.

I'd tell him all that later. Right now, we had more important things to focus on.

"I'm going to link to Mircea and make sure he's still where he was before. It would suck if we went through all this, only to find out that he'd been moved to a new location that our captive doesn't know."

I raked my palm across my fangs, cutting a deep line into my skin. As the blood welled, I focused on thoughts of Mircea, summoning his face in my mind and blocking out thoughts of everything else.

Nothing. I frowned, cutting myself again after that wound healed. No telltale haze indicated my surroundings falling away, no thread appeared in my mind so I could pull on it and find him on the other end . . . there was absolutely nothing. It was if my psychic abilities suddenly had an "Out to Lunch" sign on them.

Vlad stopped me by catching my hand when I was about to cut my palm to try again. "What's wrong?"

"I must be tired," I muttered. "Or maybe, I maxed out my abilities before because I can't seem to reach him—hey!"

I tried to snatch my hand back as his suddenly caught fire. He held on, his mouth tightening when a fear-driven current surged into him in response. I hadn't thought I'd been affected by what had happened, but apparently, I was now afraid of fire. How ironic, considering who I was married to—

"I'm not burning," I said in surprise, feeling no pain as the flames caressed my skin instead of scorching it. "Why?"

"I must have coated you in my aura when I was dousing the flames on you. I didn't intend to do it, but it's not as if I were thinking clearly at the time."

"Fuck," I said with feeling.

Now I wasn't only rendered fireproof; I was also rendered psychically impotent! "You mean we're stuck with *hoping* nothing's changed with Mircea's location?"

Then I felt instantly guilty for being so vehement over my dismay. "I mean, it's not your fault, of course—"

"Stop worrying about me," he cut me off, and his eyes flashed green. "I will carry pain over tonight whether you wish me to or not. Yet it will not break me, Leila, so you need not walk on eggshells around the topic. I am stronger than what I feel, and more than that, it is *my* pain. Don't try to protect me from it."

"I can't do that," I said with naked frustration. "I understand what you're saying. I do, and you're right.

You're not some fragile little thing that needs coddling, but just like you couldn't stop yourself from overreacting and coating me in your aura before, I can't see you in pain and *not* try to ease it. It doesn't mean that I think you're less of a badass vampire or even less of a man. It means that I love you."

He let out a rough sound even as he kissed me. "Even if I hadn't known that before," he said against my lips, "I would certainly know it after tonight."

When his mouth finally left mine, he pulled away so he could stare into my eyes. He didn't speak, but he dropped his shields, and his naked, unguarded emotions flooded into me. At once, I felt drowned by his love, scalded by his regret, humbled by his pride, and overwhelmed by his determination to keep me safe at any cost. Those emotions grew until tears began to trickle down my cheeks, and I held his face while I tried to find the right words to tell him that I loved him in the same recklessly fierce way.

"I wish you could feel me like I feel you," I whispered, finally giving up because words would never be adequate to convey what he meant to me. "Then you'd know I would go through tonight all over again, a thousand times if I had to, if it meant being in your arms like this."

The faintest smile curled his mouth and deeper, richer swaths of emotions began sliding through mine. "I don't need to feel you to know it, Leila," he murmured, leaning forward until his forehead touched mine. "Every day, I see the truth of it in your eyes."

Chapter 42

I should have guessed that there was more to the ramshackle farmhouse than appearances first suggested. Yes, the exterior frame looked held together by frozen termites and I wouldn't dare walk on the second floor for fear of falling through the ceiling. But, as I had found out earlier, it had a fully furnished, two-bedroom, very stocked basement. Even better, the frozen ground all around it acted as a natural, reinforced barrier.

Before they began dealing with the still-unconscious necromancer, all the guys took off the feminine clubbing outfits they were wearing and put on clothes that protected against the frozen atmosphere. I was waiting to change until I took a shower, but first, I wanted to make sure I didn't need to whip out the mirror to re-up on the spell. I wasn't sure if the instructions Leotie had left me were set with the same six-hour time frame that she'd used to keep all of us trapped in the mirror spell.

After changing, Vlad spent about five minutes texting who I assumed was Mencheres since who else would he urgently need to talk with right now? Finally, we carried the necromancer down into the basement's cellar since that room was surrounded on all sides with the hard, packed earth.

I expected the chains that Vlad and Maximus began to restrain the necromancer with, but I was surprised when Vlad began to melt some silver knives he'd also brought down here with him.

"Why are you doing that?"

"So I can do this," he replied, and wedged the necromancer's mouth open. Then he poured the now-liquidized silver down the vampire's throat.

I couldn't stop my wince as I imagined how much it would hurt to have a belly full of slowly-hardening silver. If the spell wasn't still rendering the vampire into a comatose state, he'd be going nuts right now. As it was, he shuddered, his body registering the pain even if his mind was numbed to it.

Then Vlad heated up another handful of silver knives. He didn't melt them into liquid this time, but left their pointy tips intact while molding their handles and over half their blades into something that looked like a grisly version of one of the snowballs he'd made today. Once the spherelike mass had hardened, he shoved it into the necromancer's mouth, where the whole brutal bundle now doubled as a spiked silver ball gag.

"Now we won't have to concern ourselves with him attempting any spells once he wakes up," Vlad said.

I was actually starting to feel a little sorry for the necromancer. Sure, he'd tried to kill us and we intended to kill him as soon as we found out what he knew, but I wasn't comfortable with torture.

Ian, however, regarded Vlad's handiwork with his usual twisted mentality. "Blimey, if his pipes still worked, he'd be shitting silver for a week."

"Now bleed him," Vlad told Maximus, ignoring that.

Maximus took a spare silver knife and then sliced open every artery the vampire had and kept reopening them after they healed. If he'd had anything resembling a normal heartbeat, blood would have been gushing out from the necromancer. Instead, slow red drips began to pool onto the floor. This was to further weaken him once the mirror spell broke, and that might make the difference between him escaping or not. Still, I'd seen enough.

"I'm going upstairs to get some fresh air," I muttered.

Vlad gave me a look I couldn't read, then said, "I'll be finished here soon. Ian, stay with her."

I didn't remind him that Marty was also here, or that "here" was in the middle of snowy nowhere. Or mention the fact that earlier, Vlad himself had set up cameras all around the perimeter to make sure that no one snuck up on us. We'd all had a stressful night and all our nerves were stretched. If it made Vlad feel better to have two vampires tasked with keeping me safe in addition to all the above, so be it.

However, some things I was going to do alone. When we left the cellar and entered the main room of the basement, I turned to Ian and said, "I'm taking a shower to wash this soot off, so you can stand down until I'm done."

He didn't smirk, wink, or offer to help, which I would have expected. Instead, he shrugged. "I'll stay outside the door."

I snorted. "You don't have to take Vlad's instructions that literally. Besides, Marty's watching the perimeter and our only interior hostile is still spellbound."

"If he wakes up early, you're the one who trapped him, so you're the one he'll most want to kill," Ian pointed out. "Besides, I'm not doing it for Tepesh," he added, an eye roll indicating Vlad back in the cellar. "You surprised me tonight. Very few people do that, so I tend to respect the ones who do, and what I respect, I also willingly protect."

He seemed to be sincere, but that was something I hadn't seen from Ian before. "You respect me, but not Vlad?"

Now it was his turn to snort. "I said I respect people who *surprise* me. Your husband's brutality, ruthlessness, and cunning are not surprising. They're what I expect from him."

"There's more to Vlad than that," I said quietly.

He met my gaze with a frankness that continued to throw me because it was so unusual coming from him. "There's more to all of us. Yet most times, we still only see what we expect to see."

Then his tone brightened and his expression changed into that arch, part-mocking, part-lecherous one I was used to.

"Now, if you insist that I treat you like the luscious little morsel you are, I'm all too happy to oblige—"

"I'll stick with respect," I interrupted.

He winked. *There* was the Ian I knew. "Your loss, poppet."

I took my time in the shower, telling myself that I kept the water cold because there were six of us and I shouldn't be greedy by taking all the hot water.

Right, that's why you're doing it, my inner voice mocked. *It's totally not because you're more affected by nearly burning to death than you're letting on, to the point where you don't want to feel anything hot touching you.*

I hated that bitch, but the few times that she was right, she was really right.

Okay, so I might be dealing with some mild post-traumatic stress after what had happened tonight. Admitting that didn't mean I was weak; it meant that I was strong enough to own my true feelings, even my traumatized ones. This new issue might end up causing me to stumble or fall a few times, but it wouldn't break me. And even if it did, I wouldn't stay broken forever. I'd heal.

Until then, I didn't need to indulge in an imaginary argument with my hated inner voice. I needed a real conversation with the necromancer who still hadn't popped up in my mind to either take a bow or tell me that he was okay.

Mircea had to have survived. I wouldn't be here if he hadn't. So why was he suddenly being so silent?

"Someone's coming," I heard Marty shout through the video feed that fed in from the exterior cameras.

I threw a sweater and jogging pants on and left the bathroom. Ian was already on his way up the stairs, a silver knife in each hand. I grabbed one from our weapons cache in the main room and called out toward the cellar, "Vlad, company!"

"I heard," he replied, saying, "You know what to do," to Maximus before they both swept out of the cellar.

"You want me to stay and watch him?" I asked, surprised that they were leaving the necromancer unattended.

Vlad grabbed my hand. "He's fine. Come with me."

Now I was really surprised. I'd expected him to insist that I stay below in the basement, not half drag me up the stairs with him to meet whoever this new threat might be. Once we reached the main level, the holes in the house's frame revealed that a car was headed toward the farmhouse.

No one would accidentally stumble across this place. Vlad had chosen it for its remoteness. I started willing electricity into my hand. My psychic powers might be smothered by Vlad's aura, but my voltage worked just fine.

"I can see the driver . . . it's Mencheres!" Marty called out.

I relaxed and stop charging my hand. Ian tucked his knives into his back pocket. "That was fast," he commented.

True, but with his mind-manipulation skills, I supposed it wouldn't take long for Mencheres to mesmerize a bunch of cops and fireman into believing his story. Besides, a pyrotechnic display gone wrong was pretty close to the truth, anyway.

Mencheres pulled up to the front of the house and got out. In addition to compelling someone to give him a car, he also must have green-eyed someone into giving him a change of clothes. Now, instead of his former female club gear, he wore black pants, a dark green sweater, and a long black coat.

"Mencheres," Vlad said, walking up to him. Then, he began to stroke his face in a public display of tenderness that he usually reserved for me. "I need you to know that I am sorry."

"For what?" Mencheres said, clasping Vlad's hand and squeezing it with equal affection.

"For this," Vlad said softly.

A loud *pop* sounded, like what you'd hear if a balloon was burst by force instead of by a pinprick. But there was no balloon. Instead, I watched with stunned disbelief as Mencheres's head exploded right off his shoulders.

Chapter 43

"*NO!*"

Ian's agonized shout coincided with Maximus grabbing him from behind. I hadn't noticed him coming up on Ian, but he must have, and now he bear-hugged Ian with brute force.

My mouth opened and closed, but no words came. I could only stare in mind-numbing shock as Vlad's now-flaming hands slowly lowered to his sides at the same pace that Mencheres's headless body crumpled to the ground. Then Vlad knelt in the snow, the flames on his hands extinguishing as he picked up the largest, smoldering piece of what used to be Mencheres's head and gently placed it next to his slowly withering body.

"What the fuck?" Marty got out, his gaze swinging back and forth between them as if he couldn't believe what he was seeing.

That made two of us. My eyes registered that I'd just watched Vlad kill Mencheres, but my mind refused to accept it.

"How could you?" Ian howled, struggling fiercely against Maximus. "He loved you!"

"And I loved him." Vlad's voice rang out like a

sword smashing against a shield. "Yet it wasn't Samir's name that Mircea's captors burned into Leila's flesh when they made their demand. It was Mencheres's, and if I didn't kill him, they were going to kill her."

But that . . . that's . . . that . . . My mind sputtered like a car engine that wouldn't turn over. Then, as if to make up for it, a slew of images and memories began to bombard me.

The look on Vlad's face when he first read that message. How he'd paused before saying that Samir was the target. The hurricane of rage and regret I'd felt from him before he shut me out. Mircea's warning that we were both dead because Vlad would never agree to his captors' demands. The female necromancer's shock when Mencheres revealed who he was, and her strange accusation of "You lied to us, Impaler" afterward. Vlad's insistence that we kill her no matter what, and his strange, fervent relief when I told him she was dead . . .

That's why he'd been so emphatic about our killing the female necromancer. She'd seen Vlad with Mencheres and reasoned that Vlad was partnering with Mencheres instead of carrying out their demands to kill him. If she'd lived, she would have no doubt repeated that revelation to Mircea's captors.

And my death would have probably followed.

I sank into the snow because my legs refused to keep me upright anymore. "You loved him like a father."

"Yes." One word that vibrated with the pain of six hundred years' worth of memories. "But I love you more."

Maximus suddenly flew backward with such force that he smashed through the entirety of the house behind him and kept on going. I didn't know how Ian managed to do that, and I became even more alarmed when Ian snatched one of his silver knives from his back pocket.

"Don't," Vlad said in a deadly tone.

"Oh, I'm not going to kill you," Ian hissed, then to my disbelief, began stripping off his pants. "I'm going to let Mencheres do that."

Then Ian grabbed the side of his crotch and hacked something off.

"What the fuck?" I gasped out at the same time that Ian roared, "Dagon, I summon you!"

Vlad lifted his hands, fire breaking out over them—

And everything froze. Not in the normal way where time felt relative because shock or fear caused everything to *seemingly* slow down. It froze as if this moment had been transformed into a living picture that I was somehow still a part of.

Vlad stood statuelike about a dozen yards from me. His arms were still in mid-lift, and the fire that had been erupting from his hands didn't even flicker. Instead, it now resembled pale orange and blue ribbons around his fingers. Marty was facing me, one foot off the ground as if he'd been in the process of leaping to my aid. Ian still had the knife in his hand and his pants down around his ankles. A gaping wound between his groin and the crease in his thigh showed where he had hacked off a large piece of flesh. Incredibly, some of the blood from the wound still hung in the air instead of splattering to the ground. Even the snowflakes that had been swirling moments ago were now in the same eerie state of suspended animation.

I was the only one who seemed to be unaffected. I took a few steps forward to prove that I could still move of my own free will. Yep, it worked. This had to be the result of a spell, but why was I not frozen in place, too?

A twig snapped, breaking the new, complete silence. I whirled, expecting to see Leotie since she was the only one who had been powerful enough to render all of us simultaneously helpless before. Instead, a tall, square-jawed man with champagne-blond hair cocked his head at me, his smile turning crooked as he looked me up and down.

"And who are you, my pretty one?"

"Who are you?" I countered, putting my right hand behind me while I filled it with as much electricity as I could.

He laughed, tossing that light gold hair. "I'm Dagon, of course."

That's right, Ian had shouted, *Dagon, I summon you!* right before everything had frozen. The word *summon* along with everything getting really weird and a guy showing up out of nowhere told me who the blond stranger was. I gave his Icelandic blue eyes a wary look. They weren't red now, but I'd bet my electrified right arm that he was a demon.

"You did this," I said, a sharp nod indicating the artificially suspended world around us.

He hopped forward with the kind of gaiety usually reserved for children. "Isn't it beautiful? I bet you've often wished that you could hit a pause button on life. Behold"—he spun around in a blissful circle, his smile beaming—"paused."

Just as abruptly, that smile and his childlike glee vanished, and he became as menacing as a nightmare.

"Yet as much as I enjoy this, it's time to start the killing now," he said, striding past me as he headed toward Vlad and the others.

I snapped out the whip I'd been hiding, lashing it at him. Fear focused my aim and it followed my intended path, cutting right through the demon's neck and coming out the other end.

"Yes!" I shouted with an overwhelming sense of relief.

But the stranger's head didn't fall off. Unbelievably, it stayed on. Then, to my complete and utter shock, Dagon turned around and gave me a chiding look.

"Never celebrate unless your opponent is truly dead, and you must not know much about demons if you thought *that* could kill me. Decapitation doesn't work on my kind."

"I—I can see that," I managed, stunned into stuttering.

He gave me a cheery grin. "I'll overlook your rudeness this time, but here is your second lesson about demons: Don't piss us off. Ian didn't learn that lesson, which is why I'm going to kill him now. Don't interrupt, or you'll make me angry, and as I just taught you, you don't want to do that."

So saying, he snapped his fingers, and Ian suddenly came to life. After a brief shiver as his eyes met the demon's, he glanced down, then pulled up his pants in a nonchalant manner as he gave Dagon a one-handed wave.

"I expected you to be prompt, and you didn't disappoint."

"Oh, I've been waiting a long time for your warding tattoo to be damaged enough for me to find you." Dagon's easy tone was at odds with his truly murderous expression. "I don't know why it appears as if you cut it off yourself, let alone why you summoned me, but no matter. I'm going to enjoy killing you."

"Killing is always fun, but I have an even more enjoyable offer," Ian said, leaping back as Dagon swiped at him with a hand that had somehow morphed into a monsterish paw.

"Nothing could be more enjoyable than your death," Dagon growled in a voice that suddenly sounded more animalistic than human.

Ian continued to leap out of the way while wagging his finger at Dagon. "Haste makes waste. Why kill me only once when you can do it countless times over the course of eternity?"

Dagon stopped in the middle of his latest cat-playing-with-a-mouse charge. His hand changed back to normal, and he jerked it upward. At once, Ian was propelled forward as if hauled by a tractor beam.

"You're offering me your soul?" Dagon asked, sounding both surprised and intrigued.

"Not offering, bargaining," Ian corrected, with a rakish smile that was completely out of place for the topic. "Nothing this corrupt should be given away for free."

"Ian, *don't*," I said with a gasp.

"Shut her up, will you?" Ian said in a casual tone. "Don't know why you animated her in the first place."

The demon shrugged. "I didn't. This power doesn't work on one of our own, however far removed the connection."

"One of your own? I'm not a demon," I said, aghast.

Ian let out an impatient snort. "You did catch the part about all magic originating from demons and your being a trueborn witch, right? 'Trueborn' means exactly that: born of the originating line. What's the originating line? Demons."

When put like that, it sounded obvious. However,

I'd thought that demons had only taught magic to the first witches and warlocks, and the magic had somehow infused in them, similar to the legacy transfer. Yeah, it had infused, all right, just not the way I'd first realized.

"Now that we've cleared *that* up, kindly stay out of this, Leila." To Dagon, Ian said, "Her piece of shite husband killed my friend, but you have the power to undo that. Therefore, in exchange for making Mencheres alive again, I will give you my soul . . . after the usual waiting period, of course."

Dagon glanced at the crumpled body in the snow, then began to laugh with such heartiness that he bent over, holding out his hand as if he couldn't stand to hear anything else this funny.

"The price you want for your soul is for Mencheres to be alive?" he got out in between guffaws.

"Ian, please, don't do this! Mencheres would never want this for you," I tried again.

He shot a glare at me that actually made me back up a step. "Not another word, Leila. I like you, but I *will* kill you if you ruin this for Mencheres. Now, Dagon, I agree that this is foolishly, hilariously sentimental of me. However, if you're quite finished with your giggles, do we have a deal?"

Dagon straightened, his mirth gone. Now a predatory, bone-chillingly anticipatory look took over his face. "You don't get the usual waiting period before I collect. That is for people who have never crossed me. *You* made a laughingstock out of me, so you only get one year before I come for your soul."

"One?" Ian blanched, then recovered quickly. "Yes, you have a right to be pissed, so let's make it an even twenty, and that's a mere tick of the clock for a vampire."

"One," Dagon repeated.

I wanted to do something to stop this, especially considering the smile that Dagon flashed at Ian. If evil could form into flesh, it would look just like that. But what could I do? I'd already cut the demon's head off, and it had done nothing except make him scold me. Furthermore, Ian threatened to kill me himself if I interfered again.

Ian made an exasperated noise. "All right, you drive a hard bargain. Ten years, not a moment less, and that's a deal you can brag to Hell itself about."

Dagon shoved Ian forward until their mouths were close enough to kiss. "My best offer is two years. Take it, or I kill you now with no deal."

"Don't do it!" I shouted despite Ian's threat.

"Done," Ian replied in a shockingly calm tone.

I sucked in a breath out of horror. As soon as Ian said that single word, something shimmered around Dagon, as if his aura had become visible and its color was pure black. Then it fell to his feet and began streaming toward Ian as if it were tiny, incandescent snakes. They curled around Ian's feet until they stretched out and rose in the same darkly gleaming mass, shimmering around Ian in the way they had haloed Dagon.

The whole mass wavered for a moment, as if fighting against something unseen, then it began to swirl together until it formed one long, continuous swath. That swath suddenly rose high and then plunged itself into the right side of Ian's crotch. Ian shuddered, his lips flattening as if he were trying very hard not to scream.

"Hurts, doesn't it?" Dagon's voice was back to that deadly, caressing purr. "That pain is only a taste of what's to come when I return for you in two years. Until then, I will smile every time I think of my brand being where the warding tattoo used to be."

The last of that dark stream disappeared into Ian's body. He shuddered violently before sagging forward, as if all his strength had left him. Then, he forced himself upright and flashed his teeth in something that wasn't a smile.

"Your turn," Ian said, gesturing to Mencheres's body.

Dagon began to laugh. Not those hearty guffaws that had bent him double or even those childlike giggles. No, these were low, satisfied chuckles that oozed with malevolence. My skin began to crawl and I found that I'd started backing away again.

"My part in this bargain was for Mencheres to be alive," Dagon said with luxuriant hatred. "Already done, because the dead man over there isn't Mencheres."

"What?" I exclaimed.

Ian's jaw dropped with disbelief. The demon gave him a friendly chuck under the chin. "See you in two years."

With that, Dagon disappeared.

Chapter 44

 Everything was a blur of motion in the next moment. Marty lunged in my direction, fire flashed out of Vlad's hands, and through the large hole in both sides of the farmhouse, I saw Maximus running flat-out toward us, his blond head bloody.

But what registered the most was Ian's face. It was filled with all of the shock I felt, not to mention a growing sense of dread that I couldn't even begin to understand because I had nothing to relate it to. After all, what could possibly compare with finding out that you'd bartered your soul away for nothing?

"Put your fire out, Vlad," I hoarsely told him. "And while you're at it, tell me who the hell you just killed, because it sure wasn't Mencheres."

Vlad swung an amazed look my way. Marty skidded to a stop right before reaching me. Maximus was so stunned, he tripped and did a barrel roll in order to avoid faceplanting in the snow.

"How did you figure it out?" Vlad asked in a flint-like voice. "His glamour hasn't begun to fade."

Glamour. *That's* how he'd tricked us into believing that the man who'd arrived was Mencheres! But why?

"How did we figure it out?" Ian snarled, striding over to Vlad and hauling him up by the shirt collar. "At the cost of my soul, that's how!"

"Don't!" I shouted when Vlad smiled in a dangerously genial way. "He has a *really* good reason for being upset, trust me!"

Vlad looked at me, then back at Ian. "Explain," he bit out.

Ian let him go in disgust. "Why? You didn't explain anything to us. No, you had a whole bloody plan worked out in order to fox Mircea's captors into believing you'd done their bidding when you had no intention of complying. And I should have known! This isn't the first time I've witnessed a doctored execution. That's where you got the idea from, isn't it? Is that Denise over there? Damn you, Denise, is that you?"

I didn't know who Ian was talking about, but Vlad must have because he said, "No. Denise has a heartbeat and the tape might have picked up on that. That's one of the reasons why I needed a vampire instead of a shape-shifter."

"And you didn't bother sharing your plan with any of us first." Then Ian's gaze landed on me. "Or did he?"

"I didn't know," I said, feeling sick. "I swear, I would have *never* let you barter your soul to that demon if I had!"

"You did what?" Vlad's gaze narrowed and he looked around warily, as if expecting a demon to pop up. "When?"

Ian muttered a string of profanity and didn't answer. Instead, he walked toward the farmhouse, kicking the snow as he went as if he were furious with it, too. I didn't try to stop him. After everything that had happened, I'd be in an incurably foul mood, too.

"Apparently, some demon named Dagon has been after Ian, but Ian kept him away with a groin tattoo," I filled Vlad in. "Don't ask me how—I'm not clear on that. Anyway, when Ian cut it off, Dagon appeared and somehow froze time in this spot except I—I wasn't affected." I'd go into why later. "That's why none of you were aware of what was taking place, but Ian offered Dagon his soul in exchange for Mencheres's life. The demon agreed, and after he sealed the deal, he told Ian that Mencheres was already alive because the body over there wasn't his. Then he disappeared and time unfroze, or whatever."

Vlad's brow had kept rising as I spoke until, at last, it nearly melded with his hairline. Finally, he said, "If anyone else had told me this, I would swear they were lying or insane."

"I'm not lying, but you did," I said, my hurt showing in my voice as I remembered trying to comfort Vlad after believing that he was torn up over killing Samir. "You lied every moment since Mircea's captors carved that message into me. Why?"

Vlad gave me an unreadable look. "For one, I needed the recording I just made to look authentic. You have a terrible poker face. So does Martin. And Mircea's captors needed to believe that I had killed Mencheres as they ordered me to, especially when they hear that three of their members are missing and one of their nightclubs burned down. Worse, if they saw Mircea being burned at the same time that the warehouse fire took place, they'll know it was me, so only my supposed obedience with Mencheres's death will save your life."

I hadn't thought of that. Mircea *had* been screaming his head off when he'd gotten burned through me.

His captors were vampires; our only chance that they hadn't heard him was if they hadn't been anywhere near him at the time.

Yet if they had been, then they'd have to be stupid not to put together Mircea being burned through his connection to me with the club fire. Maybe this was why I hadn't heard from him since. He hadn't wanted them to know that we had a mental link as well through our flesh. If they were watching him like a hawk now, he wouldn't be able to risk hurting himself to link to me.

"Fine, I'm a bad liar, Marty is, too, and you needed our reactions to look real on the tape." And boy, would they ever! "But Ian isn't a bad liar," I went on. "In fact, he probably lies for a living. Why didn't you tell him what you were doing?"

"Exactly for that reason," Vlad said softly, glancing at the house that Ian had disappeared into. "I didn't trust him."

I closed my eyes. Did I blame Vlad for that? No. Was I so, so sorry for the consequence of that lack of trust? *Yes.* "Then why did you go to Romania, if not to kill Samir? Or was that whole trip a lie, too?" I asked, opening my eyes.

Vlad glanced at the body, which was still only a few feet away from the car.

"It wasn't a lie." Sadness that wasn't mine flitted across my emotions. "I went to Romania to ask for a volunteer from among my people for this very purpose." Now pride and regret wrapped around my feelings. "They all volunteered, yet I chose Henri because he wasn't part of my fighting force. You might remember Henri; he worked with Isa in the kitchens."

I started to rake a hand through my hair before remembering that I didn't have any. I was so relieved to know that Samir was still alive, but I *didn't* remember Henri, and I felt terrible about that. He'd voluntarily given his life in a ruse designed to save mine. I should never forget someone as loyal, brave, and self-sacrificing as that.

"How were you able to do the glamour spell to begin with?" Ian hadn't helped him with it. That much was obvious.

Vlad gave me a jaded look. "I learned it on my flight over to Romania and practiced it on my flight back. Yet appearance-altering glamour alone wouldn't be enough. I also had to show a body withering or Mircea's captors would know that it wasn't Mencheres. That's why I couldn't use the shape-shifter Ian mentioned earlier. It's also why I couldn't use a human. Furthermore, I had my people procure bones as old as Mencheres, if Mircea's captors demand additional proof of his death."

He'd been thorough in his scheming, and I'd had no idea. From the lack of surprise on Maximus's face, he had.

"You told him, didn't you?" I said accusingly.

Vlad didn't say anything and a spike of his irritation pricked my emotions. I jumped all over it.

"Don't you dare start with the whole 'I've been outwitting my enemies for several hundred years, and I don't need someone second-guessing my decisions now.' I'm your wife, not one of your minions, so since you didn't see fit to tell me all this before, you're damn sure going to tell me now."

"I was going to tell you," Vlad said, a hint of defensiveness coloring his tone. "I was going to tell everyone. All I needed was a few minutes of footage with authentic reactions first. I only told Maximus in advance because I knew Ian would react violently, and I didn't want to stop him by lethal means. I didn't, however, expect him to do *that*."

None of us had. If I hadn't seen Ian barter his soul for Mencheres's life with my own eyes, I might not even believe it.

"I also didn't intend to do this today, even though I mounted cameras around the exterior earlier just in case," Vlad went on, sounding frustrated now. "When Mircea's captors gave me their demand, I wrote back, 'Ten days' because I intended to find them and slaughter them by then. Henri's death and this ruse was only to be a last resort, but the club fire forced my hand. Now this video should buy us a few more days to search for them—"

"They're in Pleystein, Bavaria, beneath a church that's built on a quartz-filled mountain."

All of us turned. Ian was in front of the farmhouse, a satchel slung over his shoulder and blood coating him from the waist up. I was shocked at his statement, not to mention all the blood on him, but Vlad gave him a coldly appraising look.

"How do you suddenly know that?"

Ian smiled. Or at least, that was the closest thing I could call the cold tug of his lips.

"Until you have to pay up with eternal damnation, a demon soul-bartering brand has its power perks. Add those perks to a century of learning all the dark magic I could memorize, plus slicing up our captive enough to get his attention despite the mirror spell, and I was able to yank Mircea's location right out of the bastard's brain. Where he is, his captors will be, too. And now, since I've more than fulfilled my oath, I'm leaving. I only have two more years left, and I'm damn well not going to spend another minute of it with your lot."

I was momentarily speechless. We'd gone through so much to get Mircea's location, to now have Ian give it to us when there was still time enough to save more lives . . . well, saying thank you would be insultingly trivial. Yet how could I not say it?

"Ian, thank you so much. Really."

He waved as if it were nothing. "I truly hope that you survive taking on these necromancers, Leila. Tepesh"—now his voice hardened—"don't you dare tell Mencheres what I've done. He doesn't need to grieve my decision when there's nothing he can do to change it. Maximus"—a nod in his direction—"hope your loyalty doesn't get you killed, and Marty"—another wave—"you seem a good lad, so stay out of trouble unless it's fun."

With that, Ian walked over Henri's headless body, took the car keys from the dead man's pockets, and got into Henri's car.

"Wait!" I called out, running over to him.

He gave me an irritated look but stopped in the middle of backing up. "What is it?"

"It's just that . . . I'm so sorry." Once again, words were beyond inadequate in these circumstances, but no one had said that yet and someone needed to. "Isn't there anything we can do to get you out of this?"

His mouth twisted. "If Dagon were dead, I'd be free, but that's impossible. I could kill him myself if he were only a regular demon, yet he can pause time. He'd piss himself laughing while I stood frozen in mid-attempt to stab his eyes out."

I seized on the chance. "I wasn't affected by his pausing time, so *I* could kill him."

He laughed, then stopped when he saw that I was serious. "Time freezing isn't Dagon's only trick, poppet. He would rip you into pieces before you even got close enough to kill him. Thanks for the offer, but no need to throw your life away for nothing."

A flash of rage flooded with immeasurable degrees of *oh HELL no!* also told me that Vlad would never go for this, either. Fine, I wouldn't do it, but maybe there was someone both strong enough and immune to Dagon's time-pausing thing who could.

"A few hours ago, I told you that people see only what they expect to see," Ian said, his tone musing now. "Yet I didn't credit Vlad with caring about Mencheres enough to be incapable of killing him. Instead, I saw what I expected to see—someone so ruthless that he'd murder Mencheres despite their long history together."

"That's what I thought I saw, too," I said softly, my heart breaking both for him and for my own lack of faith in Vlad.

He snorted. "Yes, but if I hadn't made up my mind that Tepesh was a coldhearted murdering bastard, I would've sensed magic's presence from that other fellow's glamour. I didn't, and that's on me. It's why I'm not killing your husband for what his trick ended up costing me," he added in an almost offhand way.

I bristled even though I still felt horrible for him. "You mean, why you didn't *try* to kill him," I said, my tone making it clear that he wouldn't have succeeded.

Ian snorted again. "Among too many other things to list, I managed to avoid one of the underworld's most powerful demons for over five decades. Think a normal vampire can do that? No, luv. You of all people should know that sometimes, what looks like an ordinary Chihuahua is really a werewolf in disguise."

Then, with a distinctly wolflike smile, Ian began backing the car up again. This time, I didn't try to stop him.

Moments later, another car appeared, this one heading toward us. Ian honked twice when he passed it, but he didn't slow down. When the other vehicle got close enough, I saw that it was Mencheres. The real one. When he finally parked and got out, he looked at the headless body on the ground with more exasperation than concern.

"*Now* what did I miss?"

Vlad's emotions breached his walls, and the flashes I felt made me realize another shocking truth: Ian, Marty, and I hadn't been the only ones he'd kept in the dark.

"Why didn't you tell him?" I whispered.

A flash of ice-cold ruthlessness brushed my emotions, as quick as a bolt of lightning and as grim as the grave. That, combined with Vlad choosing to answer me this way instead of out loud, told me another shocking truth. He hadn't told Mencheres in case he had to kill him for real in order to save my life.

And he didn't want anyone to know that, especially Mencheres.

"No time to fill you in now," Vlad replied, his emotions closing off again. "I'll tell you while we're on our way to Bavaria."

Chapter 45

Winds tossed the falling snowflakes back up in the air, making the church they swirled around look like a snow globe someone had shaken up. The lone white building sat on top of a rocky outcrop of the quartz-rich mountain, making it tower over the surrounding landscape and town. A blanket of white bathed the flatter terrain below it before dappling the bare trees and landing in heavier dollops on the evergreens.

If we weren't here for a fight to the death, I would have been charmed by the lovely winter scenery. It reminded me that Christmas was only a week away, if we survived to see it.

As it was, I surveyed the church and its surrounding landscape with only tactical appreciation. The late hour and freezing temperatures, combined with Pleystein being a sparsely populated town, meant that we didn't have to worry about a lot of bystanders. That was good because the necromancers wouldn't care about collateral damage, and while we might care, Vlad still wouldn't be pulling any of his punches.

Neither would I. This was our one chance to end

this before anyone else we cared about got hurt or worse. Vlad had uploaded his truncated video to the Internet before we left Minsk, telling his people to spread it among all their allies so it would eventually reach Mircea's captors. I didn't think that would take long. Shockwaves would go through the undead world at the supposed sight of Vlad blowing the head off one of the most powerful vampires in existence.

Wait until Mencheres sees it! my inner voice taunted. *Then you'll* really *be in for it.*

I'd wanted Vlad to tell Mencheres what he'd done on the flight over to Pleystein, yet he hadn't. He'd brushed off explaining who the dead man was with a muttered "later" and also glossed over exactly how Ian had had the power to get Mircea's location from our now-dead hostage.

I, however, snuck a text to Ian that I hoped he bothered to read. I couldn't let Mencheres's wife think that he'd been killed. That would be too cruel.

Besides, Mencheres would doubtless be more inclined to get over Vlad's ruse and the reasons behind it if he knew that Kira hadn't been harmed by it. Vlad had said himself that he wouldn't forgive someone for hurting his wife even if he were the forgiving sort. Mencheres was probably the same.

Of course, once these necromancers realized who was attacking them, the jig would be up. They'd probably kill Mircea first thing in retaliation, which would be curtains for me, too. That's why we couldn't attack with a large force. No, we had to be stealthy above all, so Vlad had only called in one additional person, and I'd been stunned when he said it was a Law Guardian.

"Haven't we been avoiding Law Guardians because

we've been breaking magical laws left and right?" I'd argued. "We just used *more* magic an hour ago to get my hair to grow back!"

"That is trivial compared to the prize of uncovering an old, illegal nest of powerful necromancers," Vlad had countered. "It's also the point. We deliver these necromancers to the Law Guardian with the understanding that her judgment will be immediate execution. She gets a feather in her cap for ending such flagrant abuse of vampire law, and in exchange, we get immunity for any minor infractions we committed to do this."

Like a video showing you using glamour to dupe the world into thinking that you murdered Mencheres, I had realized. Vlad was covering *all* his bases with the same brutality, ruthlessness, and cunning that he was famous for.

That's how we ended up crouched below a rocky ledge about a mile from the church we were going to attack. This was where we were meeting our Law Guardian backup. I didn't hear any noise and nothing disturbed the air around us, yet Mencheres suddenly said, "Veritas" in a low voice.

I looked behind us, surprised to see a slender form clothed in white ski wear no more than twenty yards away from us.

"Imagine," Mencheres went on, an undercurrent of humor now in his voice. "The last time you, me, and Vlad met under clandestine circumstances, you were threatening to arrest me."

Huh? Then I got a closer look at the person who was moving in a crouch so she wouldn't stand out against the background beyond her. Wait a minute. This sunny-haired, caramel-skinned, lithe young beauty could *not* be our only backup.

"The Law Guardian's a frigging teenager?" I blurted out.

Ocean-colored eyes met mine, and I instantly realized my mistake. Her gaze had a strange weight to it that I'd only seen before from really old vampires, and the undetectable aura she'd given off suddenly flared. Instead of filling the space around us, hers somehow managed to direct itself into a thin, laserlike line that drilled me right in the midsection.

It didn't just knock me on my ass like Mencheres's unleashed aura had done. *This* one plowed me several feet into the dirt as if I'd been dropped from a plane.

"What I meant to say was, nice to meet you," I panted, stunned. Damn! Pretty baby was *fierce*.

She moved in a blur of speed to beat Vlad into offering me a hand up, coolly returning the glowering look that he gave her.

"No one calls you Dracula without regretting it, and no one disrespects me without remembering it."

"Oh, I'll remember it," I agreed, accepting her hand up.

In addition to regretting my words for obvious reasons, I also felt bad that my rude comment had hit her in what must be a sore spot. The vampire world could be a very sexist place at times, much like the human one. It must be hard in general for a woman to attain the exalted position of Law Guardian. Doing so while also looking as if you were better suited to be a high school prom queen had to have been even harder.

"Sorry," I said as stood up. "I didn't mean to—"

That's all I got out before her ridiculously pretty features hardened and she yanked me close, sniffing deeply.

"Dagon," she hissed. "You've been with *Dagon*."

At once, Vlad yanked me out of her grip. Veritas yanked back. Soon, I was being pulled back and forth between them as if I were a toy and they were two dogs playing tug-of-war.

"Stop!" I snapped, with a worried glance toward the church. We could *not* be caught arguing near the place we intended to attack in a few minutes! "Yes, I was with Dagon, but—"

"Where?" Veritas interrupted again, her sea-blue gaze glittering with a thousand emerald lights. "I need to find him."

Why? "You know he's a demon, right?"

"Oh, I do," she said with a malevolent purr that sounded uncomfortably like his had.

Why would anyone *want* to see a demon? "You're not trying to deal your soul away for something, are you?"

"No, I'm going to kill him," she snapped, then looked unsettled, as if she hadn't meant to reveal that.

I gave Veritas a sharp look. Ian had said that Dagon was too powerful to kill, even for someone who wasn't affected by his pausing-time trick. Veritas knew the demon well enough to recognize his scent, so she had to know what he was capable of, too. She was either suicidal for going after him, or . . .

"Pause time like Dagon can, and I'll tell you what you want to know," I said, taking a huge leap of faith.

Her eyes widened. Then, before I had a chance to feel stupid about my misassumption, the snowflakes halted in midair, all sound vanished, and everyone around us stilled as if doing the world's best impressions of living statues. And Veritas narrowed her eyes when she saw that I was unaffected by it.

"Demon kin," she said after a surprised moment of silence.

No point in denying it, even if the ruling body of vampires had been responsible for wiping out most trueborn witches, aka demon descendants. "I prefer Leila, thanks."

"How did you know that I could do this?" Her wave indicated the supernaturally paused world around us. "No one knows, not even Mencheres, and he is my oldest contemporary."

I gave her a jaded look. "Mencheres doesn't know that pausing time is one of Dagon's many tricks. You do, and you're too old and powerful to be an idiot, so to me, that left only one explanation: you can pause time, too. I don't know how and I don't care. What I do care about is that Dagon tricked a friend of mine into signing away his soul. If you kill Dagon, he's free, and since they have some bad blood between them, I'm betting that he knows how to find Dagon."

Veritas leaned forward, then caught herself, as if she didn't want to reveal how eager she was. "Who is this friend?"

"His name is Ian, and if we live through tonight, I'll tell you where he is." Banging his way through every whorehouse between Minsk and wherever he was headed was my guess, but I'm sure I could narrow it down more than that.

Veritas gave me a measured look. "I have waited millennia to find Dagon. This little fight will not stop me."

That's what she called a death match against an unknown number of necromancers? She'd better be as good as she was cocky. "Then let's get to it, and feel free to use your time-pausing trick. That'll make things a lot easier."

She frowned. "It requires too much power. It will take me days before I can do this again."

I gaped at her. "Then why did you do it *before* the fight?"

"Because you insisted that I do it now," she countered.

"If I'd known that you could only do it once—" I began, then stopped. "Whatever, it's too late now. Hit the start button again; we have a battle to fight."

Her gaze became so hard, her eyes resembled ice-encrusted sapphires. "You will not reveal to anyone that I can do this."

"Fine," I said, fighting a sudden shiver.

She smiled, revealing that she had a dimple next to her mouth. She couldn't have been older than eighteen or nineteen when she was changed, and here I thought Gretchen had been too young at twenty-three. "Good," she said. "I would have disliked killing you."

With that dubiously comforting statement, our surroundings abruptly returned to normal.

"No need for impossible tests, Leila," Vlad said, unaware that Veritas had already passed with flying colors. "Veritas, after this is over, you can ask Leila everything you want about Dagon, but until then"—he gave a predatory look at the church across the valley divide—"we have work to do."

Chapter 46

We crouched beneath the covering boughs of evergreens at the base of the mountain that the church was perched upon. Despite the many fights I'd been in, this was my first big ambush. There was so much riding on it; I was glad I didn't have a pulse anymore. If I did, it would have been pounding.

"You know your priorities," Vlad whispered to Mencheres.

He nodded, his charcoal gaze hard. Then his eyes closed and he stretched out his hands. The faintest hum reverberated through the mountain and I tensed. If the necromancers inside happened to figure out what the cause of that slight noise was, I was about to die.

"I can feel the people inside," Mencheres said, his voice no louder than the sound that the snow made as it slipped onto the ground. "Most of them are soaked in grave magic."

Vlad exchanged a grim look with me. We'd expected that, but it still sucked. Now neither of their powers would be effective against Mircea's captors, either to fight them or keep them from killing Mircea. We'd have to rely on quickness and luck alone.

I glanced at the mountain beneath the church. It

had both milky and smoky quartz inside it; I knew that from a quick Google search. But what Google didn't know was that there was also a large pocket containing huge pillars of pure morion, or black quartz, and Mircea was smack dab in the middle of it.

Maybe there *was* another way.

"Black quartz absorbs and negates all magic," I whispered. "It's why it's the only prison that can hold a sorcerer or necromancer. If you can find a way to protect Mircea, the rest of us can force them inside the area containing all that black quartz. Once they're there, their magic won't work anymore."

Vlad's smile was a savage slash. "Do it," he told Mencheres.

Mencheres closed his eyes again. After several minutes that sliced across my nerves as if someone were ice skating on them, Vlad turned to Maximus and Marty. "Be ready as soon as he finds it."

They nodded, their expressions both calm and deadly. I wished I felt the way they looked.

"Leila, you stay in the back."

I pursed my lips but nodded. If not for my needed immunity to grave magic, Vlad would have refused to let me here at all.

Vlad's stare lingered on me, and though his feelings were locked down tighter than Fort Knox, his gaze told me everything that our circumstances couldn't allow him to say.

I love you, too, I wordlessly replied. If my psychic powers hadn't been smothered by his aura, the words would have resounded through his mind from how much I meant them.

The faintest smile touched his lips, then it vanished when he turned to Veritas. "You're with me. And remember—no matter what, I need the black-haired boy alive."

"For the thousandth time, yes," she muttered.

I stifled a laugh. He caught my muffled snicker, and his brow arched as if to say, *You'll pay later for mocking my concern over you.*

Mencheres opened his eyes and said, "I have him." Then his hands met together in a firm, silent clap. "If I am correct, I have now pulled a protective barrier around Mircea."

A breath exploded out of me as if I'd been hit in the chest. Before I could process the relief, a set of ominous vibrations came from deep inside the mountain. Then the bell on top of the church began to ring.

"They've either felt or spotted us," Vlad said darkly.

Without another word, he and Veritas exploded into the air. They crashed into the church before my next thought. At once, a shower of flaming plaster, wood, and stone rained down. From the way the church crumpled beneath their assault, Vlad wasn't just setting things on fire; he and Veritas were also using their bodies as living wrecking balls.

Maximus grabbed Marty and flew him up there. I waited impatiently for Mencheres to do the same with me, but he only stood there, his hands still clasped together.

"Any time now," I said.

"Not unless Vlad gives the signal," Mencheres replied. "Keeping Mircea safe and keeping you here with me are my top priorities."

Fury raced through me. I'd agreed to stay in the back, not stay behind entirely. "Oh, Vlad is *not* pulling this shit again!"

Something like a snort came out of Mencheres. "If

you expected anything else, you have only yourself to blame."

Then an invisible lasso felt like it wrapped around my waist, stopping me before I got two steps into my angry ascent up the mountain. I swung around, sparks shooting from my hands.

"Let's forget the fact that if they get hit with a spell, they're all dead because they're not immune to grave magic like I am," I gritted out. "If they're deep inside a mountain, how will you even *see* the signal that Vlad's supposed to give you?"

Mencheres arched a brow. "Like this."

A hole suddenly tore out of the mountain as if a bomb had gone off. Huge pieces of rock headed right for us. I threw up my arms, but then they defied gravity to swing to our left and right instead. The ground shuddered over and over as enormous slabs of stone continued to fall, until Mencheres and I were surrounded by the hulking pieces.

"Vlad's enemies destroyed part of the mountain beneath his home a few months ago," Mencheres said, a cold smile wreathing his lips. "He wanted me to return the favor tonight."

I was speechless as I stared at the destruction he'd wrought without once moving from his spot. Yes, I knew Mencheres was powerful, and I'd seen him move things through his telekinesis before. But I hadn't known that he could do *this*. I hadn't known that any vampire in the world could.

Yeah, we'd see Vlad's signal now, I thought, staring at the multiple tunnels that were now revealed from the hundred-yard hole that Mencheres had torn into the mountain. Soon, we'd probably see a lot of things. The color of the quartz veining the mountain seemed to grow darker the farther down it went, so Vlad would be forcing the necromancers deeper into the mountain.

My guess was proved right moments later when an unfamiliar man ran through one of the tunnels that Mencheres's power had exposed. He spun around in disbelief when he saw the gaping hole where the side of the mountain used to be. Then he ran right for that instead of going deeper into the mountain. I watched with frustration. How could Vlad force anyone into Mircea's prison if there was now a huge exit they could escape through?

"Incoming!" I yelled at Mencheres, snapping out my whip.

The man was airborne long enough for me to see that he had light brown hair and tattoos snaking up the sides of his face. Then two huge chunks of rock shot up and smashed him between them. The impact was so incredible, it turned the rocks into gravel and him into nothing more than a boneless, gooey pulp.

"You double-swatted him with boulders," I said, both admiring and disgusted as red glops started to splatter me.

Mencheres noticed and flicked them away before more hit me. "I might not be able to use my abilities directly on the necromancers, but I can use them on everything else."

"Talk about making the best of what you're working with," I muttered.

I don't know why I had my whip ready to shoot out over the next several minutes as we waited to see if anyone else would try to run out of the hole. Mencheres could more than handle them on his own, as he'd proved with his smashing-boulders trick. Still,

I was too keyed up to stop the currents from building up in my right hand, so I stayed tense, ready to spring into action if anyone else tried to run for it.

All of a sudden, fire roared along the lip of the hole in the mountain. Instead of growing to curtain the open space with enough flames to prevent anyone else from using the huge hole as an exit, the flames abruptly extinguished.

Mencheres's face darkened. "That is Vlad's signal," he said, going over and clasping me to him. "They need help."

Before I could speak, he vaulted us into the air. As we flew, the fallen pieces of the mountain began to fly, too. I had a second to see them sealing over the enormous hole as if they were huge puzzle pieces being put back into place, then that view was cut off as Mencheres dropped us onto the smashed remains of the church.

To my shock, Mencheres backed away as soon as he set me on the ground. "Vlad ordered me not to go in. If I am stricken by magic, I will lose my hold on the barrier protecting Mircea. Whatever powers you have, Leila, you need to unleash them. Vlad would not have sent that signal unless the situation was dire."

My alarm turned into barely controlled panic. They had only gone in there less than ten minutes ago! How powerful were these necromancers if things had gotten that bad, that fast?

I ran into the crumpled church, Mencheres using his power to pull aside the flaming piles of debris in front of me. With those cleared away, it didn't take long to find the trapdoor leading to the tunnel entrance below the church, and I jumped into it while sending more currents surging to my right hand.

Chapter 47

 Bodies littered the tunnel. Some had had their heads ripped off, but a few were in charred heaps, so Mencheres had been right and not everyone here was covered in grave magic. I assumed the ones that hadn't been were average guards instead of the necromancers, not that that made me feel any better. Vlad's fiery SOS hasn't been sent because the fight was too easy. Something was going very, very wrong.

I kept charging my whip as I ran deeper into the tunnels, careful not to lose my footing when they sloped steeply downward. They forked once or twice, too, but it was frighteningly easy to know which way to go. I only had to follow the sounds of strange chanting and intermittent screams.

An orange glow lit the next section after I rounded a sharp corner, and my pace quickened. Fire meant Vlad. This long stretch of tunnel didn't have any bodies, and from how the echoes grew louder, the source of the screams and the chants was at the end of it.

I sent so much voltage into my whip it was raining sparks and coiling like an angry snake when I reached the door-shaped opening at the end of the tunnel. I wanted to charge right through, especially when I realized that the screams came from Marty, but I forced myself to slow down. I might not be a pro, but I wasn't amateur enough to run in and get ambushed on my blind sides by whatever was making Marty scream.

The last ten feet, I slid and sent my whip out in front of me. My little push for momentum plus the downward slope caused me to rocket forward and I leaned back, making myself as low as possible.

I'd been right to worry. Something big smashed through the air instead of my head as a guard hiding on the right side of the door struck. I slid right past him, snapping my whip at his legs. It cut through them and he dropped like a felled tree. I snapped my whip again when he hit the ground, aiming for his neck. It ripped his head off and sent it flying through the air, yet my first clear look into the large antechamber had me not even noticing when his head bounced like a ball as it landed.

Vlad, Maximus, Veritas, and Marty were all in the room, yet none of them seemed to notice me. Veritas was kneeling on the floor, scratching something into the stone, and the rest of them were staring at the huge, pale thing that rose up from what looked like a fire pit in the center of the room.

At first glance, I'd thought it was some kind of weird smoke. It reached all the way to the twenty-foot ceiling, yet it didn't spread out like normal smoke. Instead, it was almost man-shaped, if giants existed. Even stranger, it appeared as if individual, separate smoke trails were slowly coming out of Vlad, Maximus, and Marty. Those trails fed into the manlike smoke mass, and although Marty was the only one screaming, Vlad and Maximus also looked as if they were in a lot of pain.

"What's going on?" I said, running over to Vlad.

He didn't move even when I shook his arm roughly, but Veritas's head whipped up.

"Leila," she said with relief. "You are demon kin, so the soul spell won't work on you. I've tried to counter the magic, but even with the added supernatural benefit of the convergence of ley lines in this place, I do not have what I need to do it. I have to kill the necromancers who cast it to stop it. Until then, your electricity should buy us time."

Veritas leapt up, but I yelled "Wait!" before she disappeared through the door at the other end of the room. "How am I supposed to electrocute all of them at once?"

"Not them," she said, with a swipe at the huge, smoky thing. "*That.* Every time a life is taken by force, a trace of dark energy from the murdered person remains on their killer. This spell pulls that energy out and magnifies it into the creature you see before you. Yet you are filled with natural, electrical energy, so it should counter the creature's strength. You must hurry, Leila. Once the last of the dark energy remains are pulled from your friends, their own souls will follow."

I looked at the wispy trails leaving Vlad, Marty, and Maximus with new, horrified understanding. Those weren't thin, scarflike puffs of smoke. Those were dark energy fragments from all the people that Vlad, Marty, and Maximus had killed during their very long lifetimes.

I lashed my whip at the creature. It turned its faceless body toward me and let out a roar that blasted out my eardrums and made me clutch my head. If every voice silenced by the grave could suddenly scream, it would sound like that.

Then I forced myself to lower my arms and to strike the creature again. Another roar had blood coming out of my ears, but I didn't stop to grip my head this time. Instead, I continued to lash it, noticing with fearful hope that every time I did, it seemed to slow the progression of dark essences that were trailing out of Vlad, Marty, and Maximus. For once, I was glad that Vlad's past had been an almost nonstop array of brutal battles. He had plenty of slain dark energy remains in him, and Maximus was a thousand-year-old former Templar knight, so he did, too.

But Marty didn't. Aside from when he'd been mindless from hunger as a new vampire, he'd only killed in self-defense, and he'd hardly led a violent life on the carnival circuit. His screams intensified, and fear for him made me lash the creature harder. My whip couldn't cut him down, however. It sailed right through the thing, and those writhing, dark energy essences immediately re-formed back to their manlike shape.

This wasn't working. I needed more electricity. I cast a quick look around the antechamber. It must have been the site of a lot of dark magic rituals because its walls were covered in symbols, and now that the creature had moved away from the pit, I saw that it was filled with various bones and other strange, menacing-looking objects. But it didn't appear to have any light sockets or electrical wiring that I could pull more voltage from. Whatever rituals the necromancers had held here, they must have only used torchlight for illumination.

Marty's scream grew anguished and he fell to his knees. "Hold on!" I shouted, lashing the creature so madly that it swung at me. I was slammed back against the stone walls. Pain exploded in my head and I heard the sickening crunch of bones as my skull fractured.

Blood filled my vision and the pain was so intense, I wanted to throw up. Yet I pushed myself to my feet, using the wall for balance since everything seemed to be swaying. Then I stumbled back toward the creature, my whip recharging as my body began to heal. I raised it, bringing it down once again.

Marty's screams abruptly stopped. He fell forward, something shimmering rising from his body. Then it tore free and flew toward the creature. The worst kind of horror filled me when I saw that what had flown out of Marty was a mirror image of him, except in filmy, diaphanous form.

"No!"

The scream tore out of me with more force than what the creature had used to yank Marty's soul from his body. Rage and grief slammed into me, filling me until my skin felt like it would burst. At the same time, ferocious determination sent a surge of power to my voltage that I didn't know I had in me.

I wouldn't just kill the thing that had killed Marty and was still trying to kill Vlad. I would fucking *destroy* it.

My vision blurred from the tremendous surges of electricity building in me. This time, I didn't hold any of them back. I let them come, using my seething emotions to feed them, until I was shaking from the overload of electricity that had sparks flying from every part of my body.

The creature swung that couch-sized fist at me again. This time, I ran toward it, flinging myself into the air with such force that my leap caused me to clear it. I landed on the creature's torso instead.

At once, I blasted out all that raging voltage, howling like a banshee surrounded by death on a battlefield. The sharp scent of ozone filled the air as bolt after bolt of pure electricity shot from me, as fast and deadly as lightning. The creature screamed, exploding my eardrums, but I loved the pain. It fueled my voltage, joining all my other raging emotions and making more electricity shoot from me. I had never let myself fully embrace my power before, yet I did now, and it was viciously glorious. Soon, I was mindless from giving myself over to it, and the electricity kept shooting out of me to slam into the horrible, magic-made monster that had dared to hurt and kill the ones I loved.

A *boom* penetrated the haze of my grief-soaked battle lust, and my vision cleared enough to see the dark energies from the creature began to crumble. They took me down with them before spilling onto the ground as if whatever inner structure that had allowed them to stand upright had shattered. I tumbled onto the ground along with them, landing only a few feet from Marty, and something broke inside me when I saw that his body had already started to wither.

Then I forced that pain back and ran over to Vlad when he, too, crumpled to the ground. Terror paralyzed me and a ball of pure agony rocketed up into my throat. No, no, NO!

But he didn't start to wither. He shook his head as if clearing it and his coppery gaze immediately searched the room.

"Where are the necromancers? There were six of them; three chanting in a circle and three fighting us."

"They were gone when I got here," I said, throwing my arms around him. "God, Vlad, I thought you were dead!"

He hugged me back for only a second before pulling away. "Not yet, and I intend to—" He stopped talking and a harsh sound escaped him.

I followed his gaze to where Marty lay, his body shrinking as it rapidly decomposed to match his true age of a hundred and thirty-nine years. Another painful ball clawed its way into my throat and I almost choked swallowing it back.

"I know." Then I forced myself to look away from him. He would want me to finish this and avenge his death. Not stare at his body while his murderers had the chance to get away.

"Veritas went after them," I said, gesturing toward the door. "She must have killed the three who cast the spell that made the creature, but that means there are three more that could still be alive."

Vlad didn't run; he flew through the door that she had disappeared through. Maximus walked over, giving Marty's body a quick yet sympathetic glance, then he held out his hand to me.

I took it, fighting back the tears that threatened to blur my vision for a different reason this time. Instead, I fed the rage that had allowed me to weaken the creature enough to buy Veritas the time she'd needed to kill its spell-casting creators. To be honest, I wasn't even sure if she'd done it as quickly as it seemed, or if I'd been lost to the rage, grief, and power for longer than I realized.

"Stay behind me," Maximus said, running toward the door after picking up two silver knives he must have dropped at some point.

"Who just saved who?" I muttered, but followed him.

The door opened to a fork, but it was easy to see which way to go. Vlad had left a thin trail of fire behind, and we followed it, careful not to step on the flames and burn ourselves. Maximus could have flown, so he must be running to stay close enough to me to protect me.

A scream up ahead made him grab me and fly us both the rest of the way. The tunnel was narrow and he was big, so both of us hit the sides a few times, yet seconds later, we had descended into the darkest-veined section of the mountain. A huge stone that appeared to be pure morion quartz was leaning against the side of an open doorway, and the screams were coming from inside it.

Chapter 48

The first thing I saw was the body parts. They were strewn around the black quartz cavern we entered as if the people they'd belonged to had been killed by a tornado. Then I saw Veritas circling a tall, black-haired man who kept trying to dart past her. Vlad was beyond her, and though I couldn't see all of him around the solid black hunk of rock that interrupted this section of the cavern from the next, judging by the screams and the sudden stench of burnt flesh, he was burning someone.

"Don't try it," Veritas warned the black-haired man when he feinted to her right again.

I stared at him with a morbid sort of fascination. He was part of the group of necromancers that had made the most horrifying thing I'd ever seen, yet stripped of his spell-casting power by the black quartz cell they'd used to imprison Mircea in, he seemed so helplessly *normal*.

But he was here, so he'd helped to kill Marty. Fury crashed through me as I thought of my best friend's body slowly withering in the room beyond this tunnel, and I pushed past Veritas while cracking my whip.

"No," I said in a growl. "*Do* try it."

He charged me at the same time that Veritas yanked me back. Even though she was blindingly fast, my whip wrapped around the black-haired vampire as if they'd been lovers long separated. Then I ripped it backward, and everything from his shoulders up flung forward while his lower body did a short, mad circle that spurted blood everywhere before it crumpled to the floor.

"Stop burning him! I need the other one alive!" Veritas shouted to Vlad.

I didn't pay attention. I kept lashing the man, not satisfied when he was in more pieces than he could ever heal from. Marty was dead. Gone forever. He wasn't only my best friend; for years, he'd been my only friend after he'd taken me in when no one else had wanted me. And he'd died screaming because I hadn't been able to save him the way he'd saved me all those years ago.

"Leila!"

Mencheres's voice caused me to pause in my near-frantic lashing and turn around. I hadn't heard him come in. Then again, I'd been pretty focused on turning the necromancer into bloody, tiny little pieces.

"Stop now," Mencheres said in a gentle tone. "He can't feel it anymore."

No, he couldn't, and yet I could still feel all the grief that had led to me to julienne a person.

Then, as if moving in a daze, I pulled my whip back inside me with more speed and control than I'd ever been able to use before and walked past the black quartz boulder that had cut off the other part of the cavern from view.

Vlad stood in front of a raven-haired woman who was on her knees, fire circling her in ever-growing waves. If she moved at all, she'd get burned, and from the charred state of her hair and clothes, it wouldn't be the first time.

Then I saw something else that made me keep walking, until the farthest corner of the cave was revealed. One look at Mircea and I understood why he hadn't been able to contact me. He was now entirely encased in glass, preventing him from even twitching, let alone forging a connection through our flesh by cutting himself. The tight cluster of black quartz that had previously surrounded him now surrounded the glass, and while I wasn't about to touch that since it negated Mircea's abilities, I did punch the glass around his head hard enough to cause it to shatter and fall.

"You found me," were his first words.

"A friend helped," I said, thinking about what it had cost Ian to get the power he'd used to yank Mircea's location out of the other necromancer's mind.

Mircea shot a half-defiant, half-wary look over my shoulder, where I felt Vlad come up behind me. "Well, well, stepfather dearest. It's been a long time, hasn't it?"

"Both too long and not long enough," Vlad said, his eyes turning green as he stared at Mircea.

A scrambling sound followed by a scream had both of us spinning back around, then Vlad let out a dangerously charming laugh as he saw the female necromancer dousing the new flames on her arms and legs.

"Did you really think you could escape those if I merely turned my back?"

She hissed something rapidly at him in a different language. It might have been a spell, because her face crumpled a second later when we didn't drop dead or turn into frogs or something equally awful.

"Your magic doesn't work here, Neryre," Mencheres said, coming into this section of the cavern.

Her dark gaze snapped up to him. "Menkaure," she said in a venomous tone, calling him by his Egyptian birth name.

"Is she the sorceress you knew way back when?" I asked.

"Yes," Mencheres said, shaking his head almost sadly. "Why did you align yourself with this group, Neryre? They are not true Imhotep acolytes. They twist everything he stood for."

"They fight for what he gave up on," she snapped. "What you gave up on. Your powers could have been great, Menkaure."

"They are," he replied without sounding arrogant. "But not in magic. They are great in what I have honed myself. Now tell me, Neryre, why did your coven try to force Vlad to murder me?"

Vlad's head swung around, although the fire prison around the necromancer didn't waver. "You knew?"

Mencheres glanced at me and a smile ghosted across his lips. "My wife just texted to reassure me that she would tell no one that the video going viral in the vampire world was fake."

Vlad looked at me in disbelief next. "You *told* her?"

"Kinda. I didn't have her cell number, so I told Ian to tell her." Guess he'd checked his text messages after all.

"You didn't merely hide this from me, Vlad. You lied to me. Why?" The words, softly spoken, still fell with the weight of a thousand bricks.

Vlad met Mencheres's gaze, and though his shields cracked and a poignant sadness flitted through our connection, his stare was unflinching.

"You know why."

Mencheres stared back and his incredible aura began to flare. Alarm flashed through me, covering even my overwhelming grief over Marty. Vlad's meaning couldn't have been clearer. Was Mencheres about to retaliate for Vlad admitting that he would have killed him if his glamour ruse hadn't worked? Good Lord, could we even fight him off if he *did* retaliate?

"You would have widowed Kira." Mencheres's words were a harsh rasp. "You would have brought war between our two lines, forcing Bones into a fight against your people that would have resulted in many deaths. Our allies would have been forced to choose sides, too, bringing more death, until you could have shattered the peace we've had since Appollyon failed to incite a war between vampires and ghouls—"

He stopped speaking, and I saw understanding dawn on his and Vlad's face at the same time that I figured it out, too.

"Sonofabitch," I whispered, turning to the necromancer.

Neryre's expression was as stony as our surroundings, but her eyes flicked a little too quickly between Vlad and Mencheres. Her scent changed, too. Now I knew what "busted" smelled like.

"You sought to destabilize the vampire world by pitting two of the most powerful undead lines against each other," Veritas stated, coming into this section as well. "Why?"

"My people would have restored order." Neryre's gaze manifested pure hatred as she stared at Veritas. "We would have been the only ones powerful enough to bring peace between all these warring sides, then the rule outlawing magic would have had enough support to finally be overturned."

I was stunned by how callously she admitted to plotting so many deaths. Yet deep down, the part of me that was growing harder by the day also admired the simplicity of their plan. All they had needed to get that disastrous ball rolling was the death of one powerful vampire due to the betrayal of another.

Then Neryre stabbed a finger in Mircea's direction. "He had committed himself to freeing our people, yet he left our order to pursue petty vengeance. That is why we hunted him down, and why we were going to kill him until we discovered his tie to her and the Impaler. Without intending to, Mircea handed us the easiest means to enact our chaos."

"How many more are in your order?" Veritas asked, ignoring that last part.

Neryre smiled in an oddly dreamy way. "I don't know, and if you torture me for a hundred years, you will still get the same answer. Long ago, our leaders determined that we would not know anything about each other, so that if one coven was caught, it would not endanger the others. Our cause *will* triumph. If not today, then another day."

"Oh, I'm all for people being free from oppression," I said, "but you can't build any real freedom on top of piles of bones. Vampires were wrong to hunt and murder witches, yet you admitted that your order would be just as brutal, if given the chance."

"They deserved it," she snapped.

"You're wrong," I said softly. "Yet you're not going to live long enough to see that, because the good man you helped murder in the other room *will* be avenged."

Then my whip shot out, but before I could snap it, Neryre exploded as if she'd swallowed a nuclear warhead. Vlad stared at the flaming remains a moment before his gaze met mine.

"Now you have your vengeance, Leila, and if there are consequences for her death, they will fall on me."

Veritas gave Vlad a truly exasperated look, as if she didn't know whether to yell at him or start punching him. "No matter what Neryre claimed, I could have gleaned more information out of her."

"It's nothing you can't learn for yourself with a little due diligence," Vlad countered. "We agreed that there would be no survivors except one, and he is coming with me."

"He hasn't said if he's going to let you leave," Veritas said, with a meaningful glance at Mencheres.

I stiffened. She was right; Mencheres hadn't said what he was going to do about Vlad's potentially lethal intentions toward him.

"Well?" Vlad asked Mencheres.

His emotions snapped closed, giving me no idea if he was preparing to fight for his life, or if he loved Mencheres enough to be willing to face whatever was about to happen without fighting back.

I wasn't willing, and despite knowing that Mencheres could rip my head off with a mere thought, I started to send electricity into my whip. No matter what, I would never stand by while someone tried to hurt Vlad.

Maximus moved closer, his body relaxed, but I knew he hadn't picked that exact moment to merely stretch his legs. He wasn't about to stand by and let anyone hurt Vlad, either.

Mencheres said nothing for so long, my nerves were screaming from the tension. Then, at last, his mouth stretched into a thin smile.

"I will not fulfill the necromancers' plans by striking you down and causing the same chaos that they sought to cause when they used Leila's tie to Mircea against you."

I almost sagged in relief, yet Vlad's shields dropped and sadness poured through our connection despite his gaze remaining steady.

"I will not ask for your forgiveness. My intentions were unforgivable, but I hope you know that if it had been any other life except hers that they had held over me, I never would have even considered harming you."

The faintest smile curled Mencheres's lips. "I do know that, because if I were ever forced to choose between Kira's life and anyone else's, she would live and they would die. Besides"—here his voice turned husky—"I might be angry with you, but a father always forgives his children, even if those children are not of his own blood."

A choked sound came from the other side of the room, and tears pricked my eyes as I got the subtext. Vlad did, too, and shock flashed through his emotions. Then he looked back and forth between Mircea's prison and Mencheres's face.

"You want me to forgive *him*? He'd still love to kill me!"

Mencheres moved closer. "Centuries ago, I decided to take a bitter, violent young man under my wing even though I knew at the time, he would kill me if he could. If you are grateful for my choice then, you will honor my wishes with Mircea now."

"Don't do me any favors, you fucking poor excuse for a father and a man!" Mircea shouted.

Mencheres's mouth quirked. "Children. They say the sweetest things, do they not?"

Annoyance, anger, and admiration threaded through my connection to Vlad. "If this is your punishment for my former actions, then I commend you on your cruelty."

Mencheres patted the side of Vlad's face. "I knew that you out of all people would appreciate it."

Then Vlad looked at me. "Mircea won't stay in our house. After all he's done, you need not have him near you."

"It's okay," I said. Yes, Mircea had done a lot to me, but he'd been acting out of his own awful pain, and he'd also saved us, too. "We'll just rename the dungeon the time-out room."

"I am not going with you!" Mircea continued to rage. "As soon as I am free from this quartz, I will disappear!"

"Excellent point," Vlad said dryly. "You'll need to keep him encased in that black quartz all the way back to my castle, or he'll use his dematerializing trick to escape."

Mencheres smiled. "That can be arranged."

Chapter 49

 I found myself walking very slowly back through the tunnels. I'd been able to restrain the worst of my grief out of revenge-lust and fear for everyone's safety, but now I didn't have that. When we reached the antechamber and I saw Marty's lifeless form again, it would ruin me.

"I'm not leaving with you," Veritas announced, giving a critical look around the tunnel. "I might not have any prisoners for the council, but other Law Guardians will want to see this nest. It could hold clues to the others in this cult. The tokens in the pit that were used to manifest the creature hold enough magic to warrant further investigation in and of themselves."

Vlad stopped in mid-step, almost causing me to walk into his back. "Yes, the creature that almost killed us. Tell me, how were you not caught in that spell along with the rest of us?"

My gaze swung over to Veritas. I'd been so wrapped up in everything else, I hadn't had time to wonder that, but it was a really good question.

She arched a brow. "I ducked behind the door when I saw them beginning to cast the spell. Didn't you see all the warding symbols painted on the walls? They were there to contain any magic into that antechamber alone."

Her explanation was plausible, but somehow, I wasn't buying it. Sure, that would explain how she'd been unaffected by *this* spell, but it didn't explain how she'd been able to corral five necromancers into Mircea's prison without getting affected by any more spells, and they had to have been casting them. It also didn't explain how she could pause time the same way that a super-powerful demon could. No, Veritas had secrets. Big ones.

But I had no interest in finding them out. She could keep them, especially since I wanted her to keep my secrets, too. I didn't need her sharing my trueborn witch, demon-kin status with the rest of the Law Guardians. They had proved to be far less than receptive to my kind in the past.

We entered the antechamber, and I braced for the pain that was about to deal me a knockout blow. Yet when I saw Marty's body, I blinked in shock, wondering why I was seeing two of him.

One Marty was still sprawled on the ground, his head lolled back and his body now withered enough to resemble an ancient mummy. The other Marty floated next to the body, taking turns staring at it in a bemused way while also staring at his hand as if admiring how he could see the floor through it.

"Marty!" I shouted, and ran over to him. Yet when I tried to hug him, I ran right through him, my arms still outstretched. Then I spun around to find him shaking his head at me.

"You can't hug a ghost, Leila, and unless this is the really low-rent version of heaven, that's what I am now."

I knew he was right. His being see-through while his dead body was lying in front of us made that abundantly clear, yet I still found myself fighting to process it.

"But you're—you're still *you*," I sputtered.

He grunted. "Yep, seems so. Most ghosts I've come across aren't, but there are some who keep their marbles."

I was torn between being overjoyed to see him and being concerned for him, well, still being here. "Didn't you, ah, see a light or a tunnel or anything?"

Even transparent, he managed to pull off a very jaded look. "You think I'd still be here if I had?"

"Some ghosts stay on to do one last thing," Vlad said, slowly coming forward. "Some remain a while longer to make sure that their loved ones are safe. Some never leave. I've met a few of those. They form new lives out of their afterlife."

Marty gave him a faint smirk. "New life, huh? Guess if I can go through walls, you can't threaten to keep me away from Leila if I return to the carnival circuit during season."

"No," Vlad said quietly. "I can't keep you from doing anything now."

Marty glanced back at me. "There's even a bright side to being dead. Who knew?"

I couldn't believe that he was taking this with such a blasé attitude. I could hardly keep it together, and I wasn't the one who'd just been murdered and come back as a ghost.

"Marty, I . . ." I tried to get the words out without crying, and I failed miserably. "I'm so sorry I failed. I wish I could have saved you."

"Oh kid." He started to put his arms around me, then stopped when they went through my waist.

"Let's try this," I said, sniffing back my tears as I got on my knees so we were eye level. Then I held my hands up. He smiled crookedly, putting his up, too, and I felt a slight tingle as his palms merged into mine.

"You didn't fail me," he said in a gruff voice. "You fought hard. That's all any of us can do, and sometimes, things don't turn out the way we want them to. That doesn't mean you have anything to feel bad about. It's just life."

"I know," I said, trying to smile. "You don't have to worry about me." Maybe his "one last thing" was making sure that I'd be okay. That was so like him. "I'll be all right, Marty."

"I know you will, kid," he said, chucking my chin without touching it. "You're tough. Always have been."

"So are you, and I love you so much," I said, choking back the tears.

He smiled. "Love you, too." Then he looked up toward the ceiling. I did, too, but I didn't see anything except more warding symbols, so I was surprised when he patted my cheek as best he could and said, "I, uh, think my ride is here, kid."

Wait, no! I thought, but I forced another smile. *Don't cry. Don't you dare let the last memory he has be of you breaking down in tears!*

"Then you'd better go. Say hi to your daughter for me, and tell her she has the best father ever, okay?"

He started to float up, and with every foot he ascended, he started to fade even more. "I will," I heard him say, his voice growing fainter. "And I'll tell her that one day, she'll meet her other sister, too . . ."

That's all I heard before he disappeared. I waited for several minutes, staring so hard that my eyes burned. Then, at last, I felt Vlad's hand on my shoulder.

"He's gone, Leila."

"I know," I said, my tears breaking free because saying it made it real.

He turned me around and pulled me into his arms, dropping his shields so that the warmth of his feelings matched the comforting cocoon of his arms.

"I'm here," he murmured. "And I always will be."

I gripped him back, glad when his arms tightened even more. "I'm going to hold you to that for the rest of our lives."

Epilogue

 "The house is beautiful," I said, looking at the countless strands of garland that hung along the walls and the mistletoe sprigs that dangled from every crystal chandelier, not to mention the gigantic tree in the great hall. I had never seen Vlad's castle decorated for the holidays before, but he did it the way he did everything else: impressively.

"It still seems hard to believe that this is our first Christmas together," I went on, a pang hitting me as I realized it would also be the first Christmas in many years that I would spend without Marty. At least Leotie had called, promising to drop Gretchen off at our house tomorrow morning. Either she was over her hunger, or Leotie knew the danger of my transferring the legacy to her before Gretchen was ready had passed. Not that I intended to transfer it to her now. I hadn't wanted this power, but somewhere along the way, it had become a part of me.

Just like Marty would always be a part of me, no matter that he was gone. At my request, Vlad had cremated his bones into a fine powder, and I'd split up the remains into little urns that I sent to some of Marty's old friends on the carnival circuit. They'd promised to take him with them when they traveled next season. It was the closest I could get him back to the job he had loved so much.

Vlad's brows drew together. "That seems impossible."

I let out a dry chuckle. "Well, time flies when someone's constantly trying to kill us, right?"

"That's not what I meant," he replied, drawing me in his arms. Then a warm, rich swath of emotions brushed mine, growing in intensity, until it felt like I was sinking into a pool of heated silk. "I can't have only loved you for less than a year. Every day, I am more and more convinced that you have always been a part of my soul."

I slid my arms around him, staring into his deep, coppery-colored eyes. "No," I whispered. "You've always been a part of mine, even before we met."

He kissed me, his mouth, lips, and tongue causing a lot more heat to build in me, then he drew back with a slow smile.

"Since it's Christmas Eve, I'm going to give you one of your presents. You should like this one. It's a secret I haven't told you before."

"Let me guess; you're the inspiration behind the Frankenstein novel, too," I teased.

He arched a brow with familiar arrogance. "The drivel I inspired is at least much more successful than that." After my laugh, he got serious. "You know that I resisted telling you that I loved you to the point of letting you walk out on me, but deep down, I think I knew it from almost the first."

I couldn't stifle my slight snort, remembering what he'd told me before the first time we'd slept together. *I can give you honesty, monogamy, and more passion than you can stand, but not love* . . . "Then you sure had a strange way of showing it."

"You remember my summoning Mencheres almost immediately after I brought you to my castle?"

I frowned. "Yeah, to help you find some artifacts for me to pull essence imprints from so I could track down who'd kidnapped me and tried to make me find you for them."

"And to ask Mencheres a question," Vlad replied, his tone deepening. "You don't remember that part?"

I thought back, once again amazed that eleven or so months felt like years ago. "I vaguely remember something about a question you didn't want Bones over-hearing . . ."

He snorted. "Indeed I did not." Then his expression changed, and the feelings that brushed mine were tinged with the painful sting of loss. "After my wife and my son died, I was consumed with rage and the need for vengeance. Yet after I killed everyone I believed to be responsible, I felt no better. Instead, the worst kind of emptiness filled me. It kept growing, invading the deepest parts of me, until eventually, anything seemed better than the bottomless nothingness that had taken residence in my soul. Anything."

I knew what he meant. Oh, how I knew. I didn't have the physical scars on my wrists anymore, but the memory of the pain that had led me to such an act was a scar that would never fade. "I understand," I said, tears pricking my eyes.

He gave me a jaded look even while his fingers brushed my wrists in a gentle caress. "I know you do. Mencheres sensed it in me, and he told me something that I immediately dismissed as a meaningless, compassionate lie."

"What did he tell you?" I asked softly.

His hands slid from my wrists, one rising to grip my newly grown hair, the other splaying possessively on my back and pressing me closer to him.

"He told me that one day, I'd meet someone who would fill all that emptiness." His mouth twisted. "As I said, I didn't believe him, and so I threw all my efforts into solidifying myself and my people into a kingdom that could never be overrun by the greedy or the corrupt, as my country and my family had been. In fact, I had long forgotten about Mencheres's delusional, well-intentioned lie . . . until I met you."

Another rush of his feelings filled me, causing me to close my eyes. Yes, we'd still face struggles, grief, and even fights with each other in the future, but this unbreakable, unspeakably beautiful bond between us made everything worth it.

"I can't say it was love at first sight," Vlad went on, his mouth curling sardonically when I opened my eyes. "Especially since you were only a voice in my head on our initial encounter and you electrocuted me within five minutes of our first meeting in person."

"Hey, a girl's gotta play hard to get," I said, my laughter shaky as my own emotions swelled inside me.

His teeth flashed in a grin that was both seductive and a touch feral. "If that was your intention, you failed because you were in my bed within a week."

My arms tightened around him. "Yeah, well, that was my best effort. You were a crazy scary bastard with an ego even bigger than your medieval castle, but despite all that, I was drawn to you in a way I'd never felt before."

"As was I," he whispered. "That was why I called Mencheres, because after centuries of feeling nothing for any of my former lovers, suddenly I was consumed by thoughts of a woman that I barely knew. Nothing was enough when it came to you. Not being near you, having one of our infuriating conversations, reading your mind, having you drink my blood, and when I touched you"—his voice turned into a growl, and a hot swell of lust poured through our connection—"I didn't only want to fuck you. I wanted to make you scream until my name was the only word you were capable of remembering."

If he kept sending those waves of lust into me while his hot, hard body molded to mine and his stare promised endless nights of screaming ecstasy, I wouldn't be able to finish my thought, let alone this conversation, before demanding that he make good on those promises.

"And then?" I managed, my voice breathy from barely restrained passion. "Mencheres told you that I was the one he'd predicted would end your emptiness?"

Vlad's head lowered until his mouth hovered over mine. "No, he didn't."

At my stunned gasp, his laughter teased my lips.

"Like the mythical Yoda, Mencheres rarely gives a straight answer when it comes to the most important questions. Instead, he asked me why I would suddenly demand to know if the prediction he'd made so long ago was truly a glimpse of the future, or if it had been nothing more than a kind lie."

Nothing Mencheres believed—or didn't believe—about our relationship would change what Vlad and I meant to each other, yet I had to admit that I was curious. "And what did you say?"

Vlad closed his eyes as if remembering his exact words.

"I told him I felt drawn to you in a way that concerned me because I knew so little about you. I told him that I should want to kill you for experiencing my deepest sin through your abilities, yet somehow, I felt connected to you instead. I told him I wanted you with an irrational lust because I normally waited months before choosing someone as my lover, yet I could scarcely keep my hands off you. And I told him"—he smiled here—"that you irritated me almost as much as you intrigued me, so I knew that it would be a terrible decision to take you as a lover."

I poked him in a teasing way even as my heart constricted from absorbing all this. He opened his eyes, green rolling over his gaze as he stared at me.

"Then I asked, 'Does this mean that your prediction was real? Is she the one?' and he said, 'Do you know the words you just used over and over? You said, "I feel."'"

His stare grew brighter, until I blinked from the overwhelming emotions that were filling me and from the blazing intensity of his gaze.

"I didn't need to hear anything more," he finished softly. "It didn't matter to me if he had predicted you or not. I did feel again, for the first time in centuries, and in a way that I never had before."

I kissed him with all of the love, passion, and fierce devotion I had in me. He returned it with everything I gave him and more, until my mind was spinning and it took me several moments to realize that during our kiss, he'd carried me up four flights of stairs and we were now in our bedroom instead of the castle's great hall.

"I have a present for you tonight, too," I whispered.

His smile promised a thousand different things, all of them decadently sensual and some of them downright wicked.

"Later."

Don't miss the next
exciting installment
in Jeaniene Frost's paranormal world.
The Night Rebel series,
featuring Ian and Veritas,
will be coming soon!

Now take a peek into the
Night Huntress world and discover
why #1 *New York Times*
bestselling author
Charlaine Harris raves:
"Cat and Bones are
combustible together."

Halfway to the Grave

*Half-vampire Catherine Crawfield is going after
the undead with a vengeance . . . until she's cap-
tured by Bones, a vampire bounty hunter, and is
forced into an unholy partnership. She's amazed
she doesn't end up as his dinner—are there actually good vampires? And Bones is turning out to
be as tempting as any man with a heartbeat.*

"*Halfway to the Grave* has breathless
action, a roller-coaster plot . . . and a love
story that will leave you screaming for
more. I devoured it in a single sitting."

Ilona Andrews

"Beautiful ladies should never drink alone," a voice said next to me.

Turning to give a rebuff, I stopped short when I saw my admirer was as dead as Elvis. Blond hair about four shades darker than the other one's, with turquoise-colored eyes. Hell's bells, it was my lucky night.

"I hate to drink alone, in fact."

He smiled, showing lovely squared teeth. *All the better to bite you with, my dear.*

"Are you here by yourself?"

"Do you want me to be?" Coyly, I fluttered my lashes at him. This one wasn't going to get away, by God.

"I very much want you to be." His voice was lower now, his smile deeper. God, but they had great intonation. Most of them could double as phone-sex operators.

"Well, then I was. Except now I'm with you."

I let my head tilt to the side in a flirtatious manner that also bared my neck. His eyes followed the movement, and he licked his lips. *Oh good, a hungry one.*

"What's your name, lovely lady?"

"Cat Raven." An abbreviation of Catherine, and

the hair color of the first man who tried to kill me. See? Sentimental.

His smile broadened. "Such an unusual name."

His name was Kevin. He was twenty-eight and an architect, or so he claimed. Kevin was recently engaged, but his fiancée had dumped him and now he just wanted to find a nice girl and settle down. Listening to this, I managed not to choke on my drink in amusement. What a load of crap. Next he'd be pulling out pictures of a house with a white picket fence. Of course, he couldn't let me call a cab, and how inconsiderate that my fictitious friends left without me. How kind of him to drive me home, and oh, by the way, he had something to show me. Well, that made two of us.

Experience had taught me it was much easier to dispose of a car that hadn't been the scene of a killing. Therefore, I managed to open the passenger door of his Volkswagen and run screaming out of it with feigned horror when he made his move. He'd picked a deserted area, most of them did, so I didn't worry about a Good Samaritan hearing my cries.

He followed me with measured steps, delighted with my sloppy staggering. Pretending to trip, I whimpered for effect as he loomed over me. His face had transformed to reflect his true nature. A sinister smile revealed upper fangs where none had been before, and his previously blue eyes now glowed with a terrible green light.

I scrabbled around, concealing my hand slipping into my pocket. "Don't hurt me!"

He knelt, grasping the back of my neck.

"It will only hurt for a moment."

Just then, I struck. My hand whipped out in a practiced movement and the weapon it held pierced his heart. I twisted repeatedly until his mouth went slack and the light faded from his eyes. With a last wrenching shove, I pushed him off and wiped my bloody hands on my pants.

"You were right." I was out of breath from my exertions. "It only hurt for a moment."

ONE FOOT IN THE GRAVE

Cat Crawfield is now a special agent, working for the government to rid the world of the rogue undead. But when she's targeted for assassination she turns to her ex, the sexy and dangerous vampire Bones to help her.

"Witty dialogue, a strong heroine,
a delicious hero, and enough action
to make a reader forget to sleep."

MELISSA MARR

"Hallo, Kitten."

I was so preoccupied with my breakdown that I didn't hear Bones come in. His voice was as smooth as I'd remembered, that English accent just as enticing. I snapped my head up, and in the midst of my carefully constructed life crashing around me, found the most absurd thing to worry about.

"God, Bones, this is the ladies' room! What if someone sees?"

He laughed, a low, seductive ripple of the air. Noah had kissed me with less effect.

"Still a prude? Don't fret—I locked the door behind me."

If that was supposed to ease my tension, it had the opposite result. I sprang to my feet, but there was nowhere to run. He blocked the only exit.

"Look at you, luv. Can't say I prefer the brown hair, but as for the rest of you . . . you're luscious."

Bones traced the inside of his lower lip with his tongue as his eyes slid all over me. Their heat seemed to rub my skin. When he took a step closer, I flattened back against the wall.

"Stay where you are."

He leaned nonchalantly against the countertop. "What are you all lathered about? Think I'm here to kill you?"

"No. If you were going to kill me, you wouldn't have bothered with the altar ambush. You obviously know what name I'm going under, so you would have just gone for me one night when I came home."

He whistled appreciatively. "That's right, pet. You haven't forgotten how I work. Do you know I was offered a contract on the mysterious Red Reaper at least three times before? One bloke had half-a-million bounty for your dead body."

Well, not a surprise. After all, Lazarus had tried to cash a check on my ass for the same reason. "What did you say, since you've just confirmed you're not here for that?"

Bones straightened, and the bantering went out of him. "Oh, I said yes, of course. Then I hunted the sods down and played ball with their heads. The calls quit coming after that."

I swallowed at the image he described. Knowing him, it was exactly what he'd done.

"So, then, why *are* you here?"

He smiled and came nearer, ignoring my previous order.

At Grave's End

Caught in the crosshairs of a vengeful vampire, Cat is about to learn the true meaning of bad blood—just as she and Bones need to stop a lethal magic from being unleashed. Will Cat be able to fully embrace her vampire instincts to save them all from a fate worse than the grave?

"A can't-put-down masterpiece that's sexy-hot and a thrill-ride on every page. I'm officially addicted to the series. Marry me, Bones!"

GENA SHOWALTER

I was sitting at my desk, staring off into space, when my cell phone rang. A glance at it showed my mother's number, and I hesitated. I so wasn't in the mood to deal with her. But it was unusual for her to be up this late, so I answered.

"Hi Mom."

"Catherine." She paused. I waited, tapping my finger on my desk. Then she spoke words that had me almost falling out of my chair. "I've decided to come to your wedding."

I actually glanced at my phone again to see if I'd been mistaken and it was someone else who'd called me.

"Are you drunk?" I got out when I could speak.

She sighed. "I wish you wouldn't marry that vampire, but I'm tired of him coming between us."

Aliens replaced her with a pod person, I found myself thinking. *That's the only explanation.*

"So . . . you're coming to my wedding?" I couldn't help but repeat.

"That's what I said, isn't it?" she replied with some of her usual annoyance.

"Um. Great." Hell if I knew what to say. I was floored.

"I don't suppose you'd want any of my help planning it?" my mother asked, sounding both defiant and uncertain.

If my jaw hung any lower, it would fall off. "I'd love some," I managed.

"Good. Can you make it for dinner later?"

I was about to say, *Sorry, there was no way*, when I paused. Tate didn't even want me watching the video of him dealing with his bloodlust. Bones was leaving this afternoon to pick Annette up from the airport. I could swing by my mom's when he went to get Annette, and then meet him back here afterward.

"How about a late lunch instead of dinner? Say, around four o'clock?"

"That's fine, Catherine." She paused again, seeming to want to say something more. I half expected her to yell, *April Fool's!* but it was November, so that would be way early. "I'll see you at four."

When Bones came into my office at dawn, since Dave was taking the next twelve-hour shift with Tate, I was still dumbfounded. First Tate turning into a vampire, then my mother softening over my marrying one. Today really was a day to remember.

Bones offered to drop me off on his way to the airport, then pick me up on his way back to the compound, but I declined. I didn't want to be without a car if my mother's mood turned foul—always a possibility—or risk ruining our first decent mother-daughter chat by Bones showing up with a strange vampire. There were only so many sets of fangs I thought my mother could handle at the same time, and Annette got on my nerves even on the best of days.

Besides, I could just see me explaining who Annette was to my mother. *Mom, this is Annette. Back
in the seventeen hundreds when Bones was a gigolo,
she used to pay him to fuck her, but after more than
two hundred years of banging him, now they're just
good friends.*

Yeah, I'd introduce Annette to my mother—right
after I performed a lobotomy on myself.

"I still can't believe she wants to talk about the wedding," I marveled to Bones as I climbed into my car.

He gave me a serious look. "She'll never abandon
her relationship with you. You could marry Satan himself and that still wouldn't get rid of her. She loves you,
Kitten, though she does a right poor job of showing it
most days." Then he gave me a wicked grin. "Shall I
ring your cell in an hour, so you can pretend there's an
emergency if she gets natty with you?"

"What if there *is* an emergency with Tate?" I wondered. "Maybe I shouldn't leave."

"Your bloke's fine. Nothing can harm him now
short of a silver stake through the heart. Go see your
mum. Ring me if you need me to come bite her."

There really was nothing for me to do at the compound. Tate would be a few more days at least in
lockdown, and we didn't have any jobs scheduled, for
obvious reasons. This was as good a time as any to see
if my mom meant what she said about wanting to end
our estrangement.

"Keep your cell handy," I joked to Bones. Then I
pulled away.

My mother lived thirty minutes from the compound. She was still in Richmond, but in a more rural
area. Her quaint neighborhood was reminiscent of
where we grew up in Ohio, without being too far away

from Don if things got hairy. I pulled up to her house, parked, and noticed that her shutters needed a fresh coat of paint. Did they look like that the last time I was here? God, how long *had* it been since I'd come to see her?

As soon as I got out of the car, however, I froze. Shock crept up my spine, and it had nothing to do with the realization that I hadn't been here since Bones came back into my life months ago.

From the feel of the energy leaking off the house, my mother wasn't alone inside, but whoever was with her didn't have a heartbeat. I started to slide my hand toward my purse, where I always had some silver knives tucked away, when a cold laugh made me stop.

"I wouldn't do that if I were you, little girl," a voice I hated said from behind me.

My mother's front door opened. She was framed in it, with a dark-haired vampire who looked vaguely familiar cradling her neck almost lovingly in his hands.

And I didn't need to turn around to know the vampire at my back was my father.

DESTINED FOR AN EARLY GRAVE

They've fought against the rogue undead, battled a vengeful Master vampire and pledged their devotion with a blood bond. Now it's time for Cat and Bones to go on a vacation. But Cat is having terrifying dreams of a vampire named Gregor who's more powerful than Bones . . . and has ties to her past that even Cat herself doesn't know about.

"Frost's dazzling blend of urban fantasy action and passionate relationships make her a true phenomenon."

Romantic Times BOOKreviews

"Who is Gregor, why am I dreaming about him, and why is he called the Dreamsnatcher?"

"More importantly, why has he surfaced now to seek *her* out?" Bones's voice was cold as ice. "Gregor hasn't been seen or heard from in over a decade. I thought he might be dead."

"He's not dead," Mencheres said a trifle grimly. "Like me, Gregor has visions of the future. He intended to alter the future based on one of these visions. When I found out about it, I imprisoned him as punishment."

"And what does he want with *my wife?*"

Bones emphasized the words while arching a brow at me, as if daring me to argue. I didn't.

"He saw Cat in one of his visions and decided he had to have her," Mencheres stated in a flat tone. "Then he discovered she'd be blood-bound to you. Around the time of Cat's sixteenth birthday, Gregor intended to find her and take her away. His plan was very simple—if Cat had never met you, then she'd be his, not yours."

"Bloody sneaking bastard," Bones ground out, even as my jaw dropped. "I'll congratulate him on his cleverness—while I'm ripping silver through his heart."

"Don't underestimate Gregor," Mencheres said. "He managed to escape my prison a month ago, and I still don't know how. Gregor seems to be more interested in Cat than in getting revenge against me. She's the only person I know whom Gregor's contacted through dreams since he's been out."

Why do these crazy vampires keep trying to collect me? My being one of the only known half-breeds had been more of a pain than it was worth. Gregor wasn't the first vampire who thought it would be neat to keep me as some sort of exotic toy, but he did win points for cooking up the most original plan to do it.

"And you locked Gregor up for a dozen years just to keep him from altering my future with Bones?" I asked, my skepticism plain. "Why? You didn't do much to stop Bones's sire, Ian, when he tried the same thing."

Mencheres's steel-colored eyes flicked from me to Bones. "There was more at stake," he said at last. "If you'd never met Bones, he might have stayed under Ian's rule longer, not taking Mastership of his own line, and then not being co-Master of mine when I needed him. I couldn't risk that."

So it hadn't been about preserving true love at all. Figures. Vampires seldom did anything with purely altruistic motives.

"What happens if Gregor touches me in my dreams?" I asked, moving on. "What then?"

Bones answered me, and the burning intensity in his gaze could have seared my face.

"If Gregor takes ahold of you in your dreams, when you wake, you'll be wherever he is. That's why he's called the Dreamsnatcher. He can steal people away in their dreams."

THIS SIDE OF THE GRAVE

Cat and Bones have fought for their lives as well as their relationship. Just as they've triumphed over the latest battle, Cat's new and unexpected abilities are making them a target. And help from a dangerous "ally" may prove more treacherous than they've ever imagined.

"Cat and Bones are combustible together."

CHARLAINE HARRIS

The vampire pulled on the chains restraining him to the cave wall. His eyes were bright green, their glow illuminating the darkness surrounding us.

"Do you really think these will hold me?" he asked, an English accent caressing the challenge.

"Sure do," I replied. Those manacles were installed and tested by a Master vampire, so they were strong enough. I should know. I'd once been stuck in them myself.

The vampire's smile revealed fangs in his white upper teeth. They hadn't been there several minutes ago, when he'd still looked human to the untrained eye.

"Right, then. What do you want, now that you have me helpless?"

He didn't sound like he felt helpless in the least. I pursed my lips and considered the question, letting my gaze sweep over him. Nothing interrupted my view, either, since he was naked. I'd long ago learned that weapons could be stored in various clothing items, but bare skin hid nothing.

Except now, it was also very distracting. The vampire's body was a pale, beautiful expanse of muscle, bone, and lean, elegant lines, all topped off by a gorgeous face with cheekbones so finely chiseled they could cut butter. Clothed or unclothed, the vampire was stunning, something he was obviously aware of. Those glowing green eyes looked into mine with a knowing stare.

"Need me to repeat the question?" he asked with a hint of wickedness.

I strove for nonchalance. "Who do you work for?"

His grin widened, letting me know my aloof act wasn't as convincing as I'd meant it to be. He even stretched as much as the chains allowed, his muscles rippling like waves on a pond.

"No one."

"Liar." I pulled out a silver knife and traced its tip lightly down his chest, not breaking his skin, just leaving a faint pink line that faded in seconds. Vampires might be able to heal with lightning quickness, but silver through the heart was lethal. Only a few inches of bone and muscle stood between this vampire's heart and my blade.

He glanced at the path my knife had traced. "Is that supposed to frighten me?"

I pretended to consider the question. "Well, I've cut a bloody swath through the undead world ever since I was sixteen. Even earned myself the nickname of the Red Reaper, so if I've got a knife next to your heart, then yes, you should be afraid."

His expression was still amused. "Right nasty wench you sound like, but I wager I could get free and have you on your back before you could stop me."

Cocky bastard. "Talk is cheap. Prove it."

His legs flashed out, knocking me off-balance. I sprang forward at once, but a hard, cool body flattened me to the cave floor in the next instant. An iron grip closed around my wrist, preventing me from raising the knife.

"Always pride before a fall," he murmured in satisfaction.

One Grave at a Time

Cat's "gift" from New Orleans's voodoo queen
just keeps on giving, and now a personal favor
has led to doing battle against a villainous spirit.
But how do you send a killer to the grave when
he's already dead?

"Every time I think I know all there is to
know about Cat and Bones, Ms. Frost creates
new layers of depth. . . . Prepare yourself
for blood and gore galore, interspersed
with tons of dark, witty humor, fierce
fighting, and one-of-a-kind romance."

Joyfully Reviewed

"We summon you into our presence. Heed our call, Heinrich Kramer. Come to us now. We summon through the veil the spirit of Heinrich Kramer—"

Dexter let out a sharp noise that was part whine, part bark. Tyler quit speaking. I tensed, feeling the grate of invisible icicles across my skin again. Bones's gaze narrowed at a point over my right shoulder. Slowly, I turned my head in that direction.

All I saw was a swirl of darkness before the Ouija board flew across the room—and the point of the little wooden planchette buried in Tyler's throat.

I sprang up and tried to grab Tyler, only to be knocked backward like I'd been hit with a sledgehammer. Stunned, it took me a second to register that I was pinned to the wall by *the desk*, that dark cloud on the other side of it.

The ghost had successfully managed to use the desk as a weapon against me. If it hadn't been still jabbed in my stomach, I wouldn't even have believed it.

Bones threw the desk aside before I could, flinging it so hard that it split down the center when it hit the other wall. Dexter barked and jumped around, trying to bite the charcoal-colored cloud that was forming into the shape of a tall man. Tyler made a horrible gurgling noise, clutching his throat. Blood leaked out between his fingers.

"Bones, fix him. I'll deal with this asshole."

Dexter's barks drowned out the sounds Tyler made as Bones slashed his palm with his fangs, then slapped it over Tyler's mouth, ripping out the planchette at the same time.

Pieces of the desk suddenly became missiles that pelted the three of us. Bones spun around to take their brunt, shielding Tyler, while I jumped to cover the dog. A pained yelp let me know at least one had nailed Dexter before I got to him. Tyler's gurgles became wrenching coughs.

"Boy, did you make a colossal fucking mistake," I snarled, grabbing a piece of the ruined desk. Then I stood up, still blocking the dog from any more objects the ghost could lob at him. He'd materialized enough for me to see white hair swirling around a craggy, wrinkled face. The ghost hadn't been young when he died, but the shoulders underneath his dark tunic weren't bowed from age. They were squared in arrogance, and the green eyes boring into mine held nothing but contempt.

"*Hure*," the ghost muttered before thrusting his hand into my neck and squeezing like he was about to choke me. I felt a stronger than normal pins-and-needles sensation but didn't flinch. If this schmuck thought to terrify me with a cheap parlor trick like that, wait until he saw my first abracadabra.

"Heinrich Kramer?" I asked almost as an afterthought. Didn't matter if it wasn't him, he would regret what he did, but I wanted to know whose ass I was about to kick.

UP FROM THE GRAVE

Cat and Bones should have known better than to relax their guard. A rogue CIA agent is involved in horrifying secret activities that threaten to cause an all-out war between humans and the undead. As Cat and Bones race against time to save their friends from a fate worse than death, their lives—and those of everyone they hold dear—will be hovering on the edge of the grave.

"Featuring superior writing as well as a thoughtfully structured plot, Cat and Bones's final adventure is appropriately splendid and satisfying."

Publishers Weekly (★Starred Review★)

"I want their bodies."

Madigan showed more surprise than he had when I lunged at him. "What?"

"Their bodies," Bones repeated, his tone hardening. "Now."

"Why? You didn't even like Tate," Madigan muttered.

My murderous haze cleared. He was stalling, which meant in all likelihood, he was lying about their deaths. I tapped Bones's arm. He released me, but one hand remained on my waist.

"My feelings are irrelevant," Bones answered. "I sired them so they're mine, and if they're dead, then you have no further use for them."

"What possible use would *you* have?" Madigan demanded.

A dark brow rose. "Not your concern. I'm waiting."

"Then it's a good thing you don't age," Madigan snapped as he rose from his chair. "Their bodies were cremated and their ashes disposed of, so there's nothing left to give you."

If Madigan wanted us to believe they were dead,

then they must be in serious trouble. Even if Madigan wasn't behind it, he clearly intended to leave them to their fates.

I wasn't about to.

Something in my stare must have alarmed him because he glanced left and right before flinging a hand in Bones's direction.

"If you're not intending to let her complete her term of service, then both of you can get out. Before I have her jailed for dereliction of duty, desertion, and trying to attack me."

I expected Bones to tell him where to go, which was why I was stunned when he merely nodded.

"Until next time."

"What?" I burst out. "We're not leaving without more answers!"

His hand tightened on my waist.

"We are, Kitten. There's nothing for us here."

I glared at Bones before turning my attention to the thin, older man. Madigan's face had paled, but underneath the heavy scent of cologne, he didn't smell like fear. Instead, his blue gaze was defiant. Almost . . . daring.

Once more, Bones's grip tightened. Something else was going on. I didn't know what, but I trusted Bones enough not to grab Madigan and start biting the truth out of him like I wanted to. Instead, I smiled enough to bare my fangs.

"Sorry, but I don't think you and I would have a healthy working relationship, so I'll have to decline the job offer."

Multiple footsteps sounded in the hall. Moments later, heavily armed, helmeted guards appeared in the doorway. At some point, Madigan must have pushed a silent alarm—an upgrade he'd installed since my previous visit to his office.

"Get out," Madigan repeated.

I didn't bother with any threats, but the single look I gave him said that this wasn't over.

35674056232847

G ive in to your Impulses!

These unforgettable stories only take a second to buy and give you hours of reading pleasure!

Go to *www.AvonImpulse.com* and see what we have to offer.

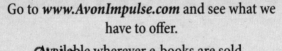

Available wherever e-books are sold.

AVONIMPULSE

IMP 0811